Servant of the Crown

Melissa McShane

Night Harbor Publishing
Salt Lake City, UT

The Eidestal

Northern Wastes

☆Ranstjad

Ruskald

Wasteland

Kepa River

Snow River

Daxtry

Marandis

Highcop

Steepridge

Avory

Tremontane

Silverfield

☆Aurilien

Olontor

Cullinan

Veribold

Harroden

Waxwold

Kingsport

☆Haizea

Ravensholc

Huddersfield

Eskandel

Umberan ☆

Tremontane
and Environs

For Jacob,
because it's your favorite

PART ONE

Chapter One

Alison alighted from the carriage, accepting the coachman's hand with a smile and a nod. It was a tradition dating to an era when all women of rank wore huge skirts, never trousers, but the man seemed to take pleasure in doing this small service for his Countess, and she was pleased to let him. She entered Quinn Press with another smile for the receptionist, who waved her over. "Mister Quinn left this for you this morning," Molly said, handing Alison a sheet of paper.

Alison scanned the page and scowled a bit. "Coward," she muttered. "He didn't want to tell me this to my face, Molly."

"I thought he was trying to maintain a professional relationship with you," Molly said.

"He is. I'm just not sure why he thought this would be better than telling me in person. He's totally wrong—it's going to make a terrific book. Thanks, Molly."

She bounded up the stairs, dancing from side to side to make them creak musically. She was having a wonderful day, this message aside. The weather was clear, the first hunt of the season was coming up, and she wasn't even dreading the Harvest Ball that accompanied it. Quinn Press was going to almost double its publications this year, from 250 to 480, making it the biggest publisher in Kingsport thanks to adopting the new printing Devices that were so much faster than engravings. This little message was nothing by comparison.

She passed her own office and went all the way to the end of the hall. The sign on the scuffed, unvarnished door read MARTIN QUINN, EDITOR. Not "editor in chief" or "publisher," just "editor," as if he alone hadn't built this business from nothing. She wondered again why he'd never moved the offices to a nicer part of the city, one where the sounds and smells of horses pulling wagons to and from the port

1

didn't remind you forcibly of how modern Kingsport wasn't. Someone should invent a Device to clean the streets.

Alison pushed the door open without knocking. The office beyond was painfully tidy, the walls lined with portraits of men and women whose faces the amateur artist Martin Quinn had found interesting, the drapes pulled back from the single window to let in the autumn sunlight as well as the noise from the street below. She waved the sheet of paper in her father's face. "You're not even giving it a chance," she said.

Father took his feet off the desk and kicked an inkwell that Alison, moving quickly, caught before it could splash more than a few drops onto her hand and the floor. "Sorry," he said.

"Not even a chance," Alison repeated. She flipped the cap closed and set the inkwell precisely in the middle of the worn oak desk that was older than she was. "I'm telling you, a history of the Consorts of the Kings and Queens of Tremontane will do very well now Zara North is on the verge of marriage again."

"The key word being 'again,'" Father said, pushing his thick gray hair back from his face with both hands. "This is, what, the third time since she came to the throne? I think it's just rumor. Queen Zara is a canny woman. I don't see her as someone who will share power easily."

"Choosing a Consort isn't sharing power. You didn't become a Count when you married Mother, did you? And you're changing the subject."

Father spread his hands in acquiescence. "Convince me."

She reached back to shut the door. "Thurford's a new — oh, excuse me!" She'd managed to nearly shut the door on the post boy, who let out a grunt of pain and staggered a little. Alison caught the parcels and the black scroll case that slid off the sack of mail, revealing the boy's face; he was the only person on Quinn Press's staff shorter than she was. "Sorry about that," she said, and set the parcels and case on her father's desk. The post boy blushed and rather hurriedly and forcefully dropped the sack beside them, then muttered an apology and rushed out the door.

"I think he's in love with you," Father remarked. He opened the mail sack and began taking out letters.

"I think I just intimidate him," Alison said. "Let me have your knife." She began cutting the strings of the first package. "I think these are the new self-inking pen Devices you ordered from Aurilien. I can't wait to try them out. Their motive forces are supposed to be the size of a pea and last for over a year."

"Trust you to get excited about pen Devices," Father said, picking up the scroll case and twirling it absently like a baton in his thick fingers. "I only have bills. There are always too many of those." He took the address tag of the case in one hand and went very still. "Alison," he said.

"What?"

He held the scroll case out toward her. "Read it."

Puzzled at his odd reaction, she took the tag rather than the case. Her full name and title were printed on it in block lettering: ALISON QUINN, COUNTESS OF WAXWOLD. She looked at her father, then took the case from him and examined it closely. It was sealed at both ends in dark blue wax with an imprint she knew well, that everyone in Tremontane knew well: the rampant panther sign and shield of the royal house of North.

Alison looked at her father. Her fingers had begun to tingle in apprehension. "You'd better open it," he said.

She used her father's knife to pry the seal off one end, then tipped the case on end and shook it to make the roll of buff parchment—actual parchment, no one used parchment now that clean white paper was readily available—fall out onto the desk top. Parchment meant serious business. Setting the case aside, she picked up the parchment and unrolled it, holding it open, and began to read. The first few lines were her full name and title, and then—

"What under heaven is she *thinking!*" she exclaimed. She tossed the parchment with some force onto the desk, where it curled up on itself and rolled a few inches. "It's ridiculous," she said. "I can't possibly be expected to comply." She prodded the scroll with her fingertip, making it roll further. "I've been summoned to Aurilien," she said. "To serve the Dowager Consort. As a lady-in-waiting. For six months. How do they expect me to give up my life for *six months* to sit around in an uncomfortable dress and keep the former Consort company? I tell you, it's unbelievable!"

Father picked up the scroll and furrowed his bushy eyebrows at it, as if its contents might somehow have changed since Alison threw it down. "Dear heaven," he said. "Why would they pick you?"

"If I weren't so furious, I'd take issue with that statement."

"You know what I mean. Do you suppose the Norths have a list somewhere of all the gently-born unmarried women in Tremontane from which they pick Rowenna North's companions?"

"I neither know nor care. How can I get out of it, Father?"

He shook his head. "Did you see anything in that language that suggested this was something you could decline?"

"I was hoping you'd noticed something I hadn't."

Father glanced over it again. "I can't think of anything Zara North wouldn't see through. And I don't want to insult the Queen. And neither, I think, do you."

Alison covered her face with her hands. She could feel a headache coming on, one of those skull-throbbing monsters she only ever got when a deadline was thundering down upon her. "I don't." She pushed a curly lock of her pale blond hair behind her ear. "I have to hold court in two days, and there's the Harvest Hunt, and I've already put Patrick off for a week about the land grants. That's before I even get to my Quinn Press responsibilities. I'm a Countess, for heaven's sake!" She couldn't quite bring herself to say *The Queen is out of her mind*, but she could certainly think it.

"You'd have the same problem if this were a summons to serve your turn on the Queen's Council," her father pointed out.

"Council duties don't demand every waking hour of your life, and you can at least travel to and from your county when you have to."

"I'm sure the Queen knows that. And it's not as if your cousin Patrick isn't capable of taking over for a few months. He's your heir; he ought to gain some experience."

Alison rubbed her temples. "It's only six months, right? I can endure anything for six months?" she pleaded.

His blue eyes softened with compassion, and he put his hand over hers. "Of course." He paused, shifted a few letters with the fingers of his left hand. "You will behave yourself, won't you?"

"What is that supposed to mean?"

"You don't like society, and you're not shy about showing it. That's all very well here in Kingsport, in your county seat. In the capital, you will—I'm not saying this well."

"You don't appear to be saying it at all."

He sighed and picked up a stack of letters, tapped them on the desktop to square them. "I'm saying you've grown prickly, these last few years. Heaven forbid a man should try to approach you—"

"We've had this conversation before," said Alison irritably. "I don't see the point in dealing with someone who's only interested in my money, or my title, or how beautiful I'd look hanging on his arm."

"You know not all men are like that—"

"No, only the ones who want to single me out for their attention. And those are the only ones I meet."

"That's not true either. You just never take the time to learn what kind of men they are."

"Because when I do take the time, they turn out to be fortune-hunters or never raise their eyes higher than my chest. Better just to skip the whole process."

Father sighed again. "Let's not argue, all right? I just want you to show the world the face I see, not that prickly protective shell you've developed. Will you promise me to at least pretend to be civil?"

"I know how to behave myself," Alison said, but inside, the reproach burned. Was she really so...so detached? (She refused to describe herself as *prickly*.) It wasn't her fault the only men who wanted to befriend her turned out to have ulterior motives, or that she'd learned to defend herself against them. *Only six months*, she reminded herself, *and you can come back to your own life.*

"It won't be as bad as you think," Father said. "From what I've heard, the Dowager doesn't require much of her ladies. You should have plenty of time to pursue your own interests. And—" he wagged his index finger in her direction—"think of the Library."

"The Library," breathed Alison. "I'll be able to visit the Royal Library. Think of all those books. You know they have first editions of everything Landrik Howes ever wrote?"

"So it will be all right," her father said cheerfully. "And I'll hold your job for you until you return."

"As if you could replace me," she scoffed, smiling fondly to take away the sting.

Ten days later Alison sat with her feet up on the opposite seat of her carriage and watched Aurilien grow up around her. Outlying farms became tiny settlements that turned into villages and then to extensions of the capital itself, as if the city's golden walls could not contain its people and let them spill out like water slopping over the side of an overfull glass. Past those walls, hundred-year-old buildings, their wooden frames softened by time, sat beside construction sites; neighborhoods of wattle-and-daub gave way to stores and houses made of the same golden stone as the city wall. Unlike Kingsport, which treasured its status as the oldest city in Tremontane and maintained its construction accordingly, Aurilien seemed determined to embrace change, and as rapidly as possible.

Alison wiped her palms on her trousers, then pushed her hair back from her face. It was almost certainly frizzy in this heat. Frizzy, sweaty, exhausted, and on edge: she would make a grand impression on her new...employer? Mistress? Liege lady? There didn't seem to be a good word to describe what Rowenna North would be to her, but Alison had already made up her mind to be polite and demure to the woman.

She knew very little about the royal family. The popular Rowenna North was King Sylvester's widow and mother of his children, Zara and Anthony. Queen Zara was twenty-six and had been Queen for six years. Her brother and heir Anthony was three years younger, nearly Alison's age, and had a reputation for being a man about town, including having had a number of affairs. Alison was a little appalled by that; the bonds that joined Tremontanan families together were severely strained by sex outside marriage, and a Prince ought to respect his family bond better than that. That was the extent of Alison's knowledge. She cracked open a window and breathed in fresh air that only smelled a little of the manure of hundreds, possibly thousands of horses. She would probably learn a great deal more about them in the coming six months.

The carriage turned to make its way up the curving palace drive, and Alison caught glimpses of the palace, glinting in the sunlight. It had grown up with the city and had a patchwork appearance, like a quilt of stone and metal and glass. Left of center stood the oldest tower, a skinny black stone finger pointing at ungoverned heaven as if issuing a challenge. If you looked at it the right way, the gesture was a rude one. Domes and shorter towers and ells spread out from that tower in defiance of any known theories of architecture. It might be a metaphor for Tremontane itself, patched together centuries ago from tribes who came together for mutual protection and stayed together because of the lines of power that crisscrossed the land and bound its people to ungoverned heaven and to each other. But it was more likely just the end result of generations of rulers who didn't know how to stop building once they'd started.

The carriage came to a halt at the foot of the black marble steps, and a man liveried in navy blue and silver, North colors, opened the door and offered Alison his hand. "Welcome to Aurilien, milady Countess," he said.

"Thank you," Alison replied. "I don't suppose you know where I should go?"

"The Dowager is expecting you in her apartment," he said. "I'll have someone escort you there, and your luggage will be sent on after you." He turned and gave some kind of imperceptible signal, because a woman in the same livery trotted down the steps and bowed to Alison.

Calling the palace a maze was a little like calling the ocean a collection of water drops. After they passed through the entry and made a few dozen turns, Alison lost track of where she was and hoped she wouldn't be expected to find her own way back to the front door. Eventually the woman led Alison down a short corridor to a small white door outside which stood another pair of armed guards, knocked, and waited. The guards ignored them both. After a minute, a woman wearing something Alison would have called a uniform if it hadn't been a soft pink opened the door. "The Countess of Waxwold," Alison's escort said, and the pink woman opened the door more fully and bowed Alison in.

Alison took two steps and was afraid to take any more, for fear of leaving smudges on the brilliantly white plush carpet. This room contained only a pair of sofas facing one another, upholstered in white velvet with gilded legs, and a long, low table painted white and gilt that bore a floral arrangement taller than Alison was. Gilt-framed paintings of fanciful landscapes lined the white walls between white doors with brass knobs and gilt trim. There were seven doors—eight, if you included the one Alison had entered by—and between the doors, the pictures, the sofas, and the table, the room contained more gilding than Alison had ever thought to see in one place. It was a style that had been old-fashioned fifty years earlier. Alison began to form a picture of the Dowager in her head: lots of white, lots of lace, lots of ribbons on her gown and on the lace cap she wore on her iron-gray hair, pulled back into a severe bun. She probably liked sentimental poetry, too. This might turn out to be a very long six months.

The door at the opposite end of the room opened, admitting a lovely young woman with sleek black hair coiled at the back of her head and shining ringlets hanging down the sides of her face. Alison resisted the urge to touch her own hair, which felt even frizzier now by comparison and was almost certainly free of her hairband on one side. The woman was dressed in an elegant day gown and her feet made no noise on the white carpet as she approached. "Good afternoon," she said, her voice surprisingly deep. "I am Elisabeth Vandenhout." She paused as if expecting Alison to react to this. Alison had never heard of the Vandenhouts, so she merely smiled and nodded. "Milady has asked me to see you settled in before joining her and her ladies. You have no luggage?"

"They're bringing it in," Alison said.

"I see," Elisabeth said, in a tone of voice that suggested she thought Alison low-class enough to have arrived only in the clothes she was standing up in. "Well, your maid can help you freshen up a little. I'm sure Milady will understand your...condition. Where is your maid?"

Alison mentally kicked herself. How had she expected to get into a corset by herself? "I, ah, had to let my last maid go before I left Kingsport," she said. "I intend to hire someone here."

"I see," Elisabeth said again. "Well, that's unfortunate. I suppose you'll just have to do your best." She indicated a door and added, "That will be your suite while you're with us. Feel free to...well, refresh yourself." There was a sneer lurking somewhere behind her words. Alison smiled again and reminded herself, *Polite. Demure. But wouldn't it be nice to smack her across the face?*

There was a tiny sitting room just inside the door, less ornate than the antechamber, but drenched in the scent of fresh flowers on the table on the far side of the room. Another door led to a dressing room with two wardrobes stained dark walnut and a matching marble-topped vanity table. Alison looked in the mirror and shuddered. Her hair *was* falling down on one side, and somehow she'd acquired a smudge high on her left cheek. She scrubbed at it with her sleeve and quickly turned away. Beyond the windowless dressing room was a small bedroom, its four-poster bed dominating the space with its white and gold quilt and pillows. Two tall, narrow windows flanked a fireplace with a mantel of ivory marble, on which was another display of fresh flowers. Under each of the windows were brass boxes about the size of a shoebox that contained some complicated Devices, gears and wires that hummed with energy and, with the push of a button, would generate heat. The fireplace was either an artifact of an earlier time, or for added comfort when the snows fell. Alison felt her resentment turn into guilt. The Dowager had clearly made an effort to welcome her, and she could at least add "gracious" to "polite and demure."

The bathing chamber was completely modern and had a very large tub of white porcelain, whiter even than the carpet, with shining brass fittings. She took a few minutes to admire the self-cleaning toilet—some of the facilities at Waxwold Manor still had chamber pots—and to wash her hands and face. Her skin was still clear and unblemished despite the journey—she'd never needed cosmetics, not like Elisabeth, whose careful use of them hadn't entirely been able to hide a few blotches on her nose and forehead. Alison patted her face dry and went back to the dressing room, which thankfully had been furnished with a full set of brushes and combs. Alison tidied her hair, tied it back again at the nape of her neck, and pinched her cheeks to give herself some color, then returned to the antechamber, where Elisabeth wasn't bothering to conceal her impatience. "Don't you look nicer," she said. "Considering what you had to work with, that is."

"Why, thank you, Elisabeth," Alison said with her brightest smile. "I would like to meet…Milady…now, if you don't mind?"

Elisabeth smiled that almost-sneer again. "This way," she said.

The room beyond that farthest door was a smaller, rounder version of the antechamber. Seven or eight chairs, gilded and upholstered in white, stood in a loose circle around the room, their cushions heavily embroidered with fanciful floral wreaths in dark purples and golds. The afternoon light filtering through gauzy curtains cast a soft glow over the furnishings, and Alison had a sudden powerful memory of herself as a child reading at her mother's feet, leaning against the rich velvet of her skirt and rubbing it against her cheek while the light from her mother's study window flowed over them both.

Five women looked up at Alison's entrance, one of them lowering a book to her lap. Four of them were young, the oldest possibly in her late twenties. The fifth was an attractive older woman, her graying chestnut hair cut short and framing her face like a cap. She wore a matron's dark gown, much plainer than what the other women were wearing, and several rings adorned the fingers of her right hand, including her wedding band on her middle finger. "You must be Alison Quinn," she said in a lovely fluting voice, and stood, shifting her embroidery frame to one side and coming forward to kiss Alison gently on both cheeks. "I am so glad to meet you. Will you join us? I know you have no work to do, but reading time is almost over and perhaps you will enjoy listening."

Alison took a seat, horribly conscious of her travel-worn state and her probably filthy trousers that would leave a mark on the white velvet. She perched on the edge of the chair, leaned forward so as to bring as little of herself into contact with it as possible, and listened with half her attention to the monotone of the young woman reading a volume of poetry by Shereen Wilson that Alison herself had edited. She felt a little ashamed of the assumptions she'd made about the Dowager, and watched the woman covertly through her downcast lashes.

Rowenna North's needle flew in and out of the cloth, deftly sketching out shapes Alison could only barely see; she seemed to be monogramming a napkin set, something prosaic Alison would not have expected the widow of a king to be engaged in. The other women pretended to be engaged in their own needlework, but she could feel their eyes on her. Alison was uncomfortable around other women of her social class, most of whom were so conscious of her rank they were stiff and overly formal. She hadn't had a close friend since she left the Scholia, four years earlier, when her best friend Tessa and her husband Henry Catherton had moved east to Barony Daxtry. Henry had been one of Alison's professors, not Tessa's, but he had lost his position at the Scholia anyway when it came out he and Tessa were involved. It had been completely unjust, and the memory made Alison burn a little inside with remembered anger. She didn't regret her time at that institution, had learned so much there, but Henry's ouster was just another example of how rotten the Scholia was in far too many ways. Perhaps one or more of these young women might become her friends—well, probably not Elisabeth—but Alison wasn't here to make friends; she was here to do her service to the Crown and then return to her real life.

"Thank you, ladies, that will be all. Supper will be served in one hour, and then you are free to amuse yourselves as I have no engagements this evening. Alison, dear, if you wouldn't mind staying?" The Dowager gestured to Alison to take the chair just vacated by the reader, and Alison again perched on its edge while the young women carried their embroidery frames to concealed cabinets in the walls and then left the room, all but Elisabeth Vandenhout casting curious glances in Alison's direction.

"I hope your journey wasn't too taxing," the Dowager said. "It's two days from here to Kingsport, isn't it? I should have allowed you to rest immediately on arrival, but I was so eager to meet you I simply couldn't help myself."

"Eager, your—I mean, Milady?"

"Because of your work, dear. I do love reading, and I'm eager to hear what it's like to be an editor." The Dowager clasped Alison's left hand in both of hers, her eyes shining. "I am *so* happy you accepted Zara's invitation," she said. "I look forward to hearing your insights into the books we read, particularly if any of them are books you've worked on! And you have such a lovely voice, dear, it will be a genuine pleasure to hear you read to us."

Zara's invitation? More like a royal command. "I…it's an honor to serve you, Milady," Alison stammered. "I hope I'll be satisfactory." The Dowager clearly had no idea the Queen was strong-arming the young noblewomen of the country to entertain her mother, and Alison guessed it would break Milady's heart to learn the truth. From her greeting, Alison felt the Dowager really was as sweet and guileless as she appeared. Telling her how much Alison had had to give up to be her companion would simply hurt her, and Alison had no intention of doing that.

"Oh, my dear, I don't think of it as service," the Dowager said, releasing Alison's hand. "I simply enjoy the company of young people. It invigorates me. And I hope it will not be entirely unrewarding for you. Now, let me tell you what I expect of my ladies. We breakfast at eight-thirty every morning, which I realize is early, but I no longer keep court hours with such exactness as I used to. Then three days a week I pay calls from ten until noon, and two of my ladies join me for those; you'll be told when your turn is. I nap after dinner and then for two hours in the afternoon we do needlework while one of us reads aloud. I trust you do sew?"

"I do, Milady, but I rarely have time for it these days."

"Well, you won't be able to say that anymore!" The Dowager trilled a laugh. "You'll be expected to take your turn as reader, but I suppose that will pose *you* no challenge. Then most evenings we will attend some sort of public event, dances or concerts or the opera. The rest of the time is yours to fill as you please."

"That's very generous of you, Milady."

"Not at all. This is meant to be an honor, not a constraint. I simply expect you to behave like a lady in public. Your behavior reflects on me, naturally."

"Of course, Milady," Alison said. "Thank you for making me feel so welcome." No, she certainly would not give this woman any indication she resented being there. *Polite, demure, gracious, and enthusiastic,* she thought. *I think I can manage three out of four of those at once.*

Chapter Two

The vaulted hallway looked as if it had been carved out of living rock rather than built. Even in her soft-soled shoes, Alison's footsteps echoed. Dark gray walls absorbed the light from the glass and bronze Devices that hung at ten-foot intervals from the ceiling, some twenty feet above. The dim lighting and the cavernous interior of the passage made Alison feel as if she were creeping along to some secret rendezvous, or traveling through enemy territory to bring critical information to the Queen. It was exactly the sort of hallway she would expect to lead to the Royal Library. She'd been walking for nearly fifteen minutes and hoped she would be able to find her way back to the Dowager's apartment later. Well, the palace might be a maze, but so far Alison had found it impossible to lose herself in it, because there was always someone around the next corner to tell her how to find her destination, or at least where to go next.

She passed a small door and had to back up because she glimpsed, as she went by, a bronze plaque the size of her two palms spread wide that said ROYAL LIBRARY on it in archaic script. It didn't look like the door to Tremontane's oldest repository of written knowledge. It looked like the door to a storage closet. It had a simple latch and no lock, and the bottom quarter of the door looked as if it had been kicked a hundred thousand times before. Alison pressed the latch down and pushed the door open gently without resorting to kicking it. It swung inward silently, which was another disappointment; it ought to groan on ancient hinges and need a hefty push to move it. On the other hand, groaning was probably counter-indicated, in a library, so the silence was just as well.

The room beyond was as cavernous as she'd hoped, and smelled deliciously of old paper and fresh ink, but there were no bookshelves and almost no books anywhere. The ceiling was so high shadows gathered like cobwebs in its furthest corners—at least, Alison hoped they were shadows and not actual cobwebs; she would hate to meet the arachnid that could produce webs of that size. Grimy windows high in the stony walls let very little light into the room; it was mostly illuminated by light Devices attached to the thirty or forty unadorned and very modern-looking desks lined up in three rows in the center of the room. So, not the Library; a scriptorium. At the far end of the chamber, a much longer desk with a modesty panel ran nearly the length of a foot-tall platform, seven or eight feet long. Cabinets painted a dull mustard yellow covered the wall behind the desk. There were two men behind the long desk, dressed in the robes of Scholia Masters, and half a dozen men and women sat at desks in the center of the room and read or took notes on the books spread out in front of them. One woman was standing at a lectern, flipping the pages of a large volume that was chained to it. A couple of young men in apprentices' tunics wandered between the desks, checking the inkwells. No one paid any attention to her arrival.

To her left was a door, iron-bound and enormous, probably ten feet wide and several more than that tall. It looked as if it had stood there since before Aurilien had been founded, as if it had waited for a city to grow up around it so it could fulfil its purpose as guardian of Tremontane's greatest literary treasure. It looked exactly the way she'd imagined it. She crossed quickly to it and turned the knob at the center of the right-hand door and pulled. It didn't open. She pulled once more before realizing the door was locked. Yes, they would need security, but surely they wouldn't lock the Library during the day, when everyone was here?

"Is there something I can help you with?" A skeletal old man put his hand on hers and removed it from the knob. His eyes were a strange green that reflected the light as if they were made of glass and his slight smile had no good humor in it. He smelled strongly of a musky cologne and, more faintly, of the sour reek of an unwashed body. He spoke in a low voice, not quite a whisper.

"I came to see the Library," Alison replied at the same volume.

"I'm afraid that's impossible. No one sees the Library." He said it in the way someone might say the sun rises in the east.

"I wouldn't disturb anything. I just want to see it. I've come from Kingsport—my father is a publisher—"

The smile slipped away. "Being related to a merchant is nothing to recommend you." He thrust her hand from him as if she were contagious.

"I've also had four years at the Scholia, if that matters to you," Alison said, stung.

"It might, if you'd achieved the robe while you were there." The man put his hand on her elbow and steered her away from the door. "Feel free to use the catalog to request books," he added. He indicated the book on the lectern. "The Library is open to all."

Alison wrenched away from his grasp and went to the lectern, her face burning. Open to all indeed. She'd only wanted to see it. The Masters at the Scholia, most of them anyway, tended toward arrogance and territorialism, but she'd thought the Royal Library would be different, because…what had she expected? That they'd open their doors to her because she really, truly wanted them to? Putting her hand on the catalog's cover, worn from years of other hands touching it, she had to laugh at herself. Apparently Alison Quinn wasn't as important as she believed herself to be. Well, she was here, closer to the Library than she ever imagined she'd be, and she would take as much advantage of her six months' stay as she could.

She lifted the cover of the catalog and paged through the first section, breathing deeply to inhale the scents of paper and old leather, the smells of her childhood. She flipped back a few pages. By heaven, this was a stupid way to keep a catalog. It seemed they only wrote in the entries as they received books and didn't bother with indexing or grouping by subject. How anyone might find anything in this mess—

but then, she knew from her years of study that Scholia-trained librarians developed their own organizational systems they wouldn't share with others. They claimed it was to teach reasoning and independence of thought, but Alison was certain they did it to make themselves the gatekeepers of knowledge; a library was worthless if you couldn't find what you needed to know. She turned a few more pages. They'd cut the spine and wedged in new pages at the back so the book was nearly five inches thick. She turned all the way to the back. They dated the new entries—how strange, the final entry was nearly two years old. Surely the Royal Library hadn't stopped acquiring books?

"Excuse me," she said to the skeletal man, who was still hovering near the Library door as if he were afraid she might try to break it down, "I notice it's been a few years since the Library bought anything new. Why is that?"

He fixed her with his eerie green-glass eyes. "We only accept the highest quality literature," he said. "Much of what is being printed today is worthless, of no interest to the ages. We see no reason to clutter our shelves with such."

"But—"

"Your father is a…publisher, yes? You must know better than most the truth of what I say. Now excuse me. I have work to do." He didn't move, just stood there and stared her down until, a little unsettled, she turned and left the scriptorium, pretending she wasn't running away.

In the hallway, she stood for a moment and stared at the door. A dozen cutting remarks suddenly came to mind, now that it was too late to use them. It wouldn't have made a difference even if she had thought of them in time. She dug in her pocket for her watch Device; it was nearly time for afternoon reading, anyway. She'd come back, and perhaps next time the skeletal man wouldn't be there, or would be in a better mood, but at any rate she wasn't going to give up on her dream when she was close enough to touch it.

No gown was worth this amount of pain, but there was no help for it, so Alison braced herself against the footboard of her bed and tried not to breathe. Her maid Belle drew the strings of Alison's corset tighter another half inch. "Happen that's enough, milady," she said in her melodious northeastern accent, like the accompaniment to an invisible orchestra.

"I hope it's enough. One more pull and you would have cracked my ribs," Alison said. She released her grip on the footboard and stood erect—well, it was the only way she *could* stand, strapped into this cage of metal and bone and fabric, her breasts pushed up high and her waist almost small enough for her to circle it with her two hands. She let Belle dress her like a life-sized doll in the bodice of yellow satin the color of fallen linden leaves, sewn with tiny pearls along the neck and hem, and the matching skirt Belle tied tightly around her impossibly narrow waist. Alison kicked at the layers of the skirt, making it bell out around her, then slid her feet into golden dancing shoes and waited for Belle to fasten them. Pearl ear-drops and a double strand of larger pearls that hung to her navel completed her Equinox Ball costume.

She sat gingerly on the bench in front of her vanity table, lit softly by a dozen Devices the size of her pearls, while Belle arranged her long, tight curls into something elegant that would probably be frizzy before the night was over. It would be a long night. She knew no one in the capital except the Dowager and her ladies, none of whom could dance with her, and she felt herself begin to freeze up when she thought about dancing with strangers. *All those men who only think about one thing*, her inner voice said, and she tried to tell herself it wasn't true. It was possible the Dowager would allow her to leave after only an hour or possibly two, and she could escape the ball and her corset and spend the rest of the evening reading.

"That's all, milady, and you look so beautiful," Belle sighed. She was young, sixteen or seventeen and fresh from some frontier town in Barony Steepridge Alison had never heard of, but she had come highly recommended and after two days of her service Alison could see why; she was bright, quick to anticipate Alison's needs, and had a cheerful disposition. Tonight she wore her brown hair parted in the middle and coiled in two knots at the base of her neck, and she'd done something to her pink uniform that made it look fashionable. Alison wasn't sure that was permitted, but Belle's initiative in doing so had impressed her so much she didn't want to chastise her.

"Thank you, Belle. Though most of my appearance is due to your care, so I think you're complimenting yourself," Alison teased, and the girl's cheeks went pink. "I'll wake you when I come in. I certainly can't get out of this getup on my own."

"Very well, milady. You're sure you don't mind if I borrow your books?"

"They're here to be read, and I'm so pleased you want to. Now, please check to see that my hem is straight, and then I suppose I'll have to join the others."

The other ladies were waiting in the antechamber for the Dowager, all of them as erect as Alison was. Elisabeth caught her eye, gave her a slow once-over, then smiled a nasty smile and turned away. Alison suppressed her laughter. She'd learned, finally, that the Vandenhouts were an old Tremontanan family, wealthy but not titled, and that Elisabeth was terribly proud of her lineage. She seemed to think, because of the state Alison had arrived in and despite her extensive wardrobe, that Alison was an impoverished noblewoman from the rough frontier, and Alison hadn't bothered to correct her. Only ignorance could prevent anyone from recognizing the name of one of Tremontane's eleven governing districts, let alone paint County Waxwold uncivilized, and Alison Quinn's personal fortune could no doubt buy the Vandenhouts several times over.

"Oh, Alison, you look incredible," Simone said, hurrying over to embrace her. The tall, dark-skinned woman wore shades of cream just barely acceptable as autumn colors; white made her skin glow. "Those pearls are just the perfect touch. I've never seen any so well matched."

"Yes, and I have to admit I'd never have guessed yellow would suit you so well, with that hair," Philippa said.

"Neither did I, but my couturier insisted, and she's always right," Alison said.

"Well, I'd try to steal her from you, but I doubt she'd be willing to move all the way to Barony Daxtry for me," Philippa said. She shook out her copper skirts, perfectly coordinated with her red hair, and added, "We all do look stunning, don't we?"

"Oh, my dears, that you do," said the Dowager. She entered the room and saluted each of her ladies with a light kiss on the cheek. She smelled of lilacs and powder and her lips brushed Alison's cheek like the softest rose petals imaginable. "Now, I hope you will all enjoy yourselves tonight. I will be returning at midnight, but you need not feel obligated to attend me. I simply want to remind you we will all rise for our normal breakfast hours, and I expect you to exercise the good sense each of you has. Now, our carriage is ready, so if you don't mind?"

They left the Dowager's apartment and went, not to the ballroom, but to a door where two carriages waited to drive them the three hundred yards or so to the palace entrance. Alison wasn't sure whether that was to gratify the Dowager's fancy or to give her ladies a proper entrance, but the oversized white and gilt carriages certainly drew the attention of the other waiting guests. The palace glowed with thousands of fairy lights, making its patchwork construction look like the set of a play, something out of scale and not quite real. It made her feel a little disoriented, like an actor waiting for her cue, costumed and not quite sure what her lines were.

She followed the Dowager up the black granite steps that shone gold with reflected light and across the threshold, trying not to bump up against the other guests. There were so many people pressing forward across the marble entry Alison couldn't imagine the size of the ballroom that could hold them all. She passed through a gallery, half-paneled in dark walnut and painted an eggshell blue above, that was lined with pedestals bearing busts of famous dead Tremontanans, their blank eyes staring past her as if looking at something far more important than any of the people passing now. She glimpsed the bust of Landrik Howes, one of her favorite playwrights, and wished she could stop to ask what play she'd walked into and what her role was this evening. She would have welcomed a script and a director.

They came out of the gallery into the rotunda, four stories tall and capped with a dome depicting the great deeds of King Edmund Valant, last king before the North dynasty took the Crown. Willow North must have had a robust sense of humor to leave those paintings intact—or possibly she just knew most of King Edmund's deeds had been exaggerated or fabricated and therefore were no threat to her. The real power in those days had been the Ascendants, men and women with inborn magical abilities who used their magic to dominate Tremontane's government and society, and Willow had been the cause of their downfall. Alison had trouble picturing anyone capable of bringing an entire magical caste to its knees being afraid of anything. She realized she was lagging behind and hurried to catch up to the Dowager, who'd swept her party past the rotunda, down a sloping hall covered in a dark green woven carpet, and past a pair of golden grilles, currently open, to the top of a landing overlooking the ballroom.

Alison's imagination had fallen short of the reality; the room was easily one hundred feet wide and twice that in length. She blinked and turned her head to avoid being blinded by the chandelier of brass and crystal, lit by thousands of tiny Devices, that hung from the center of the ceiling and was level with the top of the stairs. Looking up and away from it, she saw the midnight blue ceiling was painted with constellations that resembled those of Midsummer Day, probably the exact configuration of stars that hung over Aurilien on that most important of holidays, when the lines of power drew heaven and earth closest together and family bonds were at their strongest. Music beckoned Alison to enter, and she turned her head, trying to discover where the music was coming from; it seemed to emerge from the air itself.

"The Countess of Waxwold," the herald at the top of the stairs said, and Alison jumped a little and stepped forward to descend to the ballroom floor. *This would be a perfect time for me to trip over my shoes and go tumbling down all these stairs,* she thought, and held her head high and stepped very carefully. A forest of trees had been sacrificed to make the shining surface where men and women danced. The highly waxed, almost black floorboards were parallel to the stairs and became paler the further they went from the staircase until they were almost white, then gradually darkened until at the far edge of the room they were nearly black again. It gave Alison the illusion that the couples dancing at the center of the room were turning and dipping in a valley, or possibly atop a ridge, and she had to look at the walls to keep from getting dizzy. Doors painted pale rose to match the walls stood at long intervals around the room; from her reading, Alison knew they opened on smaller rooms where business had once been conducted, long ago when this had been the throne room. She suspected they were now used for lovers' trysts, though how anyone could bear to conduct a courtship with so many people moving around just outside was difficult for her to understand.

She took a final step and was safely on the varnished floor that only looked like it was sloping away from her. She was the last of the Dowager's ladies to descend, and none of them had waited for her; she could see the Dowager moving away in the company of several other ladies her own age. Alison took a few more steps so as not to be in the way of whoever was coming down behind her. Then she stopped and clasped her hands in front of her, pretending she was enjoying the view of all those bright autumn colors darting about as if tossed like leaves, all those dark suits like trees doing the tossing. She felt a familiar iciness begin to spread across her body and descend over her face. She had not been introduced to any of these men and saw no way to gain an introduction, so how on earth was she to spend the evening dancing? Perhaps she should follow the Dowager and her knot of women...but how embarrassing, to go begging like that when she didn't much enjoy dancing anyway. She should sit down, accept a glass of wine and pretend it was what she wanted to do—

"Excuse me, milady Countess, but would you care to dance?"

Alison turned, startled, to look at the middle-aged man who'd spoken to her. He had a kind smile and his hand was outstretched to her. "I—we haven't been introduced, sir—that is, milord—"

"Just sir," he said, a friendly twinkle coming to his eye. "So many people come and go through Aurilien that we've dispensed with the need to be introduced to someone before you dance with him. Or her." He took her unresisting hand and bowed over it. "But if it makes you more comfortable, my name is Jackson Albright."

"I—yes, Mister Albright, I would be happy to dance with you," Alison said, still a little off guard, and allowed him to lead her to where the dancers were gathering. He'd looked at her with admiration, true, but he hadn't leered at her or made suggestive comments, and as they started into the first steps of the dance, he smiled at her with such friendliness that she smiled in return.

She hadn't realized until that evening that she really did enjoy dancing, when she had the right partners. Was it luck, or was it just Aurilien, that she never had to freeze up to protect herself from unwanted compliments or men trying to see down the front of her gown tonight, never had to turn down an invitation to dance with an unwanted partner? She stumbled once, was caught by her partner, and rather than feeling mortified she was able to laugh with him at her mistake. She felt for the first time in years as if she were not defined by those externalities of title and fortune that had nothing to do with who she really was. Part of her warned *Don't be so incautious,* and she found it easy to ignore that little voice.

Finally, her feet beginning to ache and her throat dry, she politely waved away more invitations to dance and went in search of a glass of wine. Small tables and chairs stood scattered near the walls, occupied by dancers in need of a rest or people carrying on boisterous conversations loudly enough to be heard over the music. Alison tried to sit, but her corset dug into her hips and thighs, so she stood well out of the way of the dancers and sipped her wine, which was a little fruitier than she liked but soothed her dry throat. She had no idea what time it was. Perhaps she wouldn't return with the Dowager at midnight, after all. She took a somewhat longer swallow and patted her lips with her fingers. She'd purchased several dozen pairs of gloves only to learn they were unfashionable in the capital for evening wear, and now her hands felt naked, as if the absence of gloves meant something more sensual than mere bare skin. It had felt a little scandalous to dance hand in hand, skin to skin, with her partners, scandalous and a little thrilling. She needed to get out in society more often if something that prosaic thrilled her.

"Alison, dear! Do join us!"

Alison turned and saw the Dowager waving at her from a nearby table. She was seated with a number of other women about her age and a dark-haired man who half-turned to see whom the Dowager was waving at. He was astonishingly good-looking, with a strong, smooth jawline, firm lips, shapely cheekbones, and a pair of vivid blue eyes that set off his fair skin. Alison approached and made her curtsey to the Dowager, then glanced back at the young man, who had those blue eyes fixed on her with an expression that was far too familiar. Alison felt herself begin to freeze up for the second time that evening. *So much for my good luck.* She ignored the man and gave all her attention to the Dowager, praying to ungoverned heaven she could extricate herself from the conversation quickly.

"Ladies, this is Alison Quinn, the Countess of Waxwold. She's my newest companion and I do so enjoy her company!" The Dowager reached up and laid a soft hand on Alison's wrist. "Alison, dear, I want you to meet my son, Anthony. Anthony, Alison Quinn."

The young man rose, a little unsteadily. "Milady Countess," he said, and his voice was a rich baritone every bit as handsome as the rest of him. Alison tried not to flinch at the smell of alcohol that came off his breath. She let him take his hand and kiss it, his lips lingering much longer than was socially acceptable, and kept herself from yanking it back when he was finished. She bowed her head and curtseyed politely, murmuring, "Your Highness."

"Anthony's just returned from the country and I'm so glad he was able to attend this ball," the Dowager said. "Anthony, I wish you would dance with Alison. She seems quite without a partner. Alison, you'd like to dance with Anthony, wouldn't you?"

Alison was certain the Dowager didn't realize her son was drunk. She looked up at the Prince—he had to be almost a foot taller than she was—and froze a little more at his lazy smile and the light in his eyes that said he knew exactly how handsome he was and that his looks could get him anything he wanted, including, naturally, the Countess of Waxwold. He surveyed her body once again and said, "I'd *love* to dance with you, milady Countess," and offered her his hand.

For half a second Alison considered rejecting him. But the Dowager was sitting right there, smiling with innocent pleasure at having arranged things so neatly, and it would offend her so much if Alison refused. So she took the Prince's hand, smiled a frozen smile, said, "Thank you, your Highness," and allowed him to lead her to the center of the floor.

Alison was conscious of being stared at for the first time all evening; she hoped it was actually her partner they were staring at, though she had a momentary wild thought of what a beautiful couple they must make despite the difference in their heights, her blond curls, his dark hair. Half the room was no doubt envying her right now; the other half was probably envying him. Alison caught a whiff of stale brandy again and breathed through her mouth until it passed. How fortunate the corset wouldn't allow her to breathe any more deeply than that.

North stopped under the largest of the crystal chandeliers and rather abruptly took Alison in his arms. "No need to be tense," he said, "this is a very simple dance."

"I realize that, your Highness," Alison replied. It was a familiar and popular dance, and it was also a very intimate one, requiring partners to dance close together, his arms around her waist, her arms around his shoulders. An old, painful memory of dancing like this with another man, one who'd said he loved her, flashed through her mind, and she focused on the shoulder of North's frock coat to dispel it. He'd said so much more when she'd turned down his advances: *frigid, tease, haughty. Probably a terrible lay.* As if her current situation weren't painful enough without reminders of her equally painful past.

She stumbled a little through the first steps, disliking the feeling of North's strong arms drawing her close. North was a good dancer, despite being drunk, and Alison tried to focus on the steps and reminded herself it was only one dance, because two would mean they were interested in one another and two in a row would be a declaration of courtship. North would certainly not return later for another dance no matter how much he admired her body.

"How long have you been in Aurilien? Milady countess," North said as they circled each other and then drew close again, clasping right hands.

"Nearly a week, your Highness."

"Are you enjoying my mother's company?"

"I am, your Highness."

North leaned in until his mouth was even with her ear. "You can

27

just call me Anthony, you know. Milady."

"I'd prefer not to be so informal when we've only just been introduced, your Highness."

North laughed. "Very well." He slid his hand from the base of her spine up to caress her back and the bare skin at the base of her neck, a swift stroke that probably no one noticed. Alison's cheeks went blotchy with anger and embarrassment. And to think she'd been having such a nice time. This always happened, always, she would let her guard down and some man would take advantage of that, as if she were nothing more than firm breasts and a well-rounded bottom. They were in the middle of the ballroom, spotlighted by a hundred thousand sparkling rainbows. She had nowhere to go. She felt ice fill her from deep within her chest, radiating out to the rest of her body. Frozen, where this arrogant Prince couldn't touch her.

They separated again, briefly, and North held her at a distance for several steps longer than he should have, his eyes caressing her as his hand had done. "You are *incredibly* beautiful," he said, his words a little slurred. "Do you realize how beautiful you are?"

A mask of ice descended over her face, her lips. "Modesty requires I not answer that, your Highness."

He laughed and drew her close again, finally, breaking the rhythm of the dance. "Oh, you're beautiful," he said, his breath hot on her ear. "But I'll wager you're even more beautiful with that dress off. I would *love* to see you without—"

Without thinking, Alison whipped her hand out of his grasp and brought it around hard to slap the Prince's face. The sound of her bare palm striking his cheek carried unnaturally far in the crowded, overfull ballroom. The dancers nearest them stopped to stare, and their stillness spread outward until half the floor was occupied by unmoving figures. The music went ragged and then stumbled to a halt. The Prince stood with his hand pressed to his cheek, his eyes wide and unblinking in surprise. Alison felt her breath coming in short, quick pants that left her dizzy. Her hand throbbed. "How *dare* you, sir," she snarled, and pushed past him at a near-run, shoving her way through the forest of observers without caring whom she bumped into. She lifted her skirts and fled up the stairs, feeling propelled by the attention of everyone in the ballroom as if their combined gazes were goading her to greater speed. By the time she reached the top of the steps, she was running as fast as her dancing shoes would allow.

With the help of a few liveried servants and a lieutenant on her way to a shift change at the east wing door, she eventually found the Dowager's apartment, flung the door open without knocking, to the surprise of the guards, and ran to her suite, where she began tearing at the knots securing the tapes of her skirt. They were too tight, Belle had tied them too well, there was a knife somewhere in the vanity table and she would cut the damn thing off.

"Milady, what's wrong? Let me do that for you," Belle said. Her eyes looked sleepy; Alison still didn't know what time it was, but if she'd left the ball an hour ago, none of this would have happened. She let Belle remove her bodice and corset and sucked in a great deep breath of flower-scented air. She was never wearing a corset again, if only because the Dowager would probably send her home after this. Alison stripped out of her chemise and drawers and yanked her nightdress over her head, then realized her hair was still elaborately arranged on the top of her head. Blotchy again with fury, she yanked pins out while Belle watched, her eyes wide with astonishment. Good for Belle not to interfere. Alison needed something to destroy right now. She flung the last pin away as if throwing a spear at Anthony North's lecherous heart and dragged a comb roughly through her curls, not caring how it tugged.

Someone pounded on her suite door. "Alison Quinn!" the Dowager shouted. "How dare you enact such a scene? I have never been so humiliated in my entire life!"

She was humiliated? Alison flung the comb so hard at the vanity table that two of its teeth snapped off and went flying wherever the pins had gone. She stormed through the dressing room and the tiny sitting room, but in the sliver of time between throwing the comb and putting her hand on the doorknob, rationality reasserted itself. The Dowager was not at fault here. As guileless as she was, she might have no idea what her son was like. So Alison drew in another wonderfully deep breath and opened the door quietly. The Dowager was alone. She had her hand raised to knock again and looked a little surprised at Alison's appearance.

"Milady, I apologize," Alison said before the Dowager could do more than open her mouth. "My behavior was shameful and I deeply regret how it reflected so poorly on you, because you've been so kind to me. The Prince offered me such an insult that I reacted without thinking. I'll pack my things and leave in the morning."

The Dowager's eyes narrowed. "What insult?" she said.

"I'd rather not repeat it—"

"What insult?"

Alison dropped her gaze to look at the Dowager's right hand, with all its rings, that was now twisting the folds of her orange-gold gown. "He said he would like to see me with my clothes off, Milady."

The hand clenched. "My dear, I am so sorry," the Dowager said, her voice quiet and subdued. "Was he terribly drunk? I'm afraid I never notice, anymore."

"He was moderately drunk, I believe." Alison risked looking at the Dowager's face and saw only sadness there.

"Not that it's an excuse," the Dowager said. She moved past Alison and lowered herself into the sitting room's only chair. "You were completely right to take offense, much as I might wish it hadn't been so very public, for your sake."

"I'm leaving in the morning, so it won't matter what people think." The idea of going home, of being free from this sentence—not that it was all that onerous a requirement—made the ice in her chest melt away. No more corsets, no more Elisabeth Vandenhout, no more skeletal librarians…she could have her life back, and none too soon.

"Oh, no, please don't leave!" the Dowager exclaimed. "I would miss you terribly if you left."

"But, Milady, you can't have a companion who's known to be quick-tempered and violent!"

"Don't worry about that, dear. True, it will be embarrassing for a time, but eventually it will be forgotten. And you were sorely provoked; I can hardly blame you for reacting as you did, even if Anthony is my son."

Alison saw her untrammeled future begin to vanish into the distance and she made a last grasp at it. "But all anyone will know is that I slapped the Crown Prince in public! I really can't allow your reputation to be so tarnished."

The Dowager waved her ringed hand as if shooing a fly. "My reputation is more robust than that. Please, Alison, don't leave. I know none of the other ladies would want you to either."

I bet Elisabeth would pack my trunk for me, Alison thought, but said, "All right, Milady. I just hope neither of us regrets this."

The Dowager rose and kissed Alison lightly on the cheek. "I'm sure it will all work out very well in the end. I'll see you at breakfast, won't I, dear?"

Alison shut the door behind her and leaned against it. Staying was a bad idea, but she'd agreed to it, and she would just have to weather the gossip until it died away or was supplanted by someone else's scandal. She went to wash her face and then climbed into bed and pulled the white and gold counterpane over her ears. The memory of the Prince's stunned face rose before her, and to her surprise she giggled at it. The throb and stinging pain in her palm had been worth it. Probably dozens of other women who'd been the objects of his lascivious attention were cheering her right now. She fell asleep cheerfully grasping that memory.

She woke a little late and hurried through her toilette, dressing in a white muslin day gown and asking Belle to arrange her hair in a simple style. The other ladies would no doubt want to know the details of her very public assault on the Crown Prince, and Alison wanted to be as comfortable as possible when they pressed her on the subject.

Someone knocked quietly on the suite door, and Belle left Alison with her hair pinned only on one side to answer it. She returned with a folded and sealed piece of paper which she handed to Alison. "It was someone in North blue," she said, "and he didn't say anything, just gave me that for you."

The wax seal bore no imprint, just the mark of a thumb pressing into the hot wax. Alison broke the seal and unfolded the paper. She felt her fingers go numb with horror. "It's from the Queen," she said. "She wants me in her office in half an hour."

Chapter Three

Alison had never given any thought to what Queen Zara's office might look like, but if she'd been forced to make a guess, she would have pictured old stone, vaulted ceilings, narrow stained glass windows that curved to a point at the top, heavy three-hundred-year-old furniture that should be in a museum, and possibly statues carved of worn granite so old it had a soapy patina. She wouldn't have imagined a tall, narrow room hung with faded tapestries picturing extinct or imaginary animals, or a single bookshelf crammed with bound ledgers that had papers sticking out of them. She wouldn't have guessed Zara would have a sleek, modern desk of ash illuminated by brass light Devices, or an armchair with no cushion that had two owls carved into the knobs tipping its back. The chair Alison sat in looked like it might have come from a kitchen somewhere. There was an identical one next to her, unoccupied.

Queen Zara sat at her desk, leaning back a little, her fingers interlaced and resting on the surface in front of her. The Queen had the same dark hair and blue eyes as her brother, but her face had a sharpness to it that gave her a direct, intense look, as if to say whomever she was speaking to had better not be wasting her time. Alison opened her mouth to say something and the Queen raised a finger to her lips, shushing her. Alison subsided. What could the Queen possibly have to say to her, aside from "thank you for humiliating my family, leave now and never return"?

The door behind Alison opened. The Queen raised the same finger and crooked it, beckoning forward whoever had just entered. Alison tilted her head just enough to see Anthony North take his seat beside her. Turning her head fully to look at him was unthinkable. She could tell he was dressed haphazardly, as if he'd only just risen from bed, and she could again smell stale brandy on him. He rested his hands palm-down on his knees and turned his head just a little to look at her. Alison quickly faced forward, trying not to meet the Queen's blue-eyed gaze, a glare that could have cut diamond.

The Queen still said nothing. She tapped her finger on her lips and looked from Alison to North to Alison again. Alison was sure the Queen could hear her heart hammering away like a fleeing rabbit inside her chest. *Say something*, she pleaded inwardly, *anything, just get it over with.*

"Well," the Queen said, lowering her hand. "You disrupted the ball rather spectacularly, didn't you, Countess?"

Alison nodded, feeling her cheeks go blotchy with remembered humiliation. Why hadn't she had more control? Heaven only knew what stories were being told about her today.

"Your lack of self-control embarrassed my mother and, I might add, made you appear quick-tempered and haughty. Not a good impression for your first public appearance as my mother's lady-in-waiting." Alison nodded again.

"But," the Queen continued, "I understand you were provoked." She turned her stare on her brother. It was North's turn to look away. "And I feel I must apologize to you for my brother's crass behavior."

"I—if you must, your Majesty," Alison said. The idea that the Queen of Tremontane might apologize to her for anything struck her as ludicrous.

"Unfortunately, you appear to be the villain in this melodrama, and I see no way of spreading the truth of the matter without exposing you to further humiliation." The Queen paused, then added, "And I would prefer the name of North not be dragged any more through the mud than it already has been." Again she glared at her brother. His gaze fell to his lap.

"After some reflection, I have come up with a solution I'm sure neither of you will like, but has the advantage of redeeming your supposedly stained reputation, Countess." Queen Zara put her elbows on the desk, leaning forward on them. "I'm going to require the two of you to appear in public together, once a week, until I judge the situation has passed. Anthony, you will be on better than your best behavior and make it clear you hold no grudge against the Countess. Your ladyship, you will endure my brother's company with a smile and demonstrate that you do, in fact, have self-control. I don't care if you like each other or not so long as you act as if you do."

"Zara, you can't seriously expect me to—"

"You listen to me, Anthony," the Queen said in a low, intense voice. "I grow tired of cleaning up your messes. You have insulted this woman in a way that gives her no recourse to defend herself. You will do as I say or by heaven I will make your life more miserable than it already is."

Alison's cheeks heated again. She wished she hadn't heard what should have been a private reprimand. She wondered that the Queen, who had a reputation for intelligence and cunning, should be so careless as to humiliate her brother in the presence of someone who'd humiliated him already. She still couldn't bear to look at the Prince, who must surely resent her now.

North said, "Very well, Zara." She heard him turn in his chair, so she finally looked in his direction. He didn't look nearly so handsome as he had the night before. His eyes were bleary and he hadn't shaved yet. She felt a moment's satisfaction that she'd now seen him without the glamour he'd worn the night before. She felt as if it restored some kind of balance between them. "Countess," he said, "I will call on you later today, if I may."

"Thank you, your Highness," she replied. No *I look forward to your visit* or *I will be happy to receive you*. She felt the sting of Queen Zara's punishment, and she had no doubt it was a punishment, and a weary dread fell over her. Endure her brother's company indeed.

"But *why* did you slap the Prince?" Marianne said, needle in one hand and thread in the other. "He's so handsome, I wish he'd danced with *me*."

I wish he'd danced with you, too, Alison thought. "I'd rather not discuss it." She turned her attention to her embroidery frame, hoping her skin had not gone too blotchy with embarrassment.

"I suppose it's the sort of reaction Kingsport manners demand," Elisabeth said, "for even the smallest slight, isn't that true, Alison?"

"Now, ladies," the Dowager said, causing the women to curtsey as she entered the room and took her place at the center of their circle, "dear Alison was simply overwrought and took issue with my son's behavior. Please don't tease her anymore about it. It's simply not worth discussing. Now, I believe it is Philippa's turn to read to us."

As Philippa's dull voice droned its way through the classic *Eironos*, Alison tried and failed to focus on her needlework. North had said he would call, but surely he meant he would send an invitation? If he showed up on his mother's doorstep, she wasn't prepared to face him yet. *Once a week, only once a week,* she told herself. *Only five months and three weeks left.* She'd begun to think of it as a prison sentence. Philippa's voice set her nerves on edge. Surely this sewing time wasn't meant to be a penance? Alison picked up her needle and stitched the outline of a pansy, willing it to calm her. The Prince would not appear. She had nothing to worry about.

When the two hours of reading were nearly up, one of the Dowager's servants entered and said, "Miss Alison has a caller."

Alison froze. She looked at the Dowager, who was clearly prepared for this. "Alison dear, you may be excused early," she said.

The Prince stood in the entry hall, once again groomed and handsome. He had the nerve to smile at her as she approached. "Good afternoon, Countess," he said, and if his eyes didn't exactly caress her body as they had the night before, they were certainly appreciative. She swallowed a sigh. "I wish to apologize for my behavior last night. I should not have appeared in public in that condition and I certainly should not have said anything so crass to you. I hope you will be able to forgive me. It will make things so much easier if we can be friends." He extended his hand to her.

After a moment's thought, she accepted his hand, which he shook rather than conveying it to his lips as she'd feared. "I accept your apology," she lied. "I hope I can be better behaved toward you than I was last night." She would not let her temper get the better of her again, no matter what provocation he offered. He would not see more of her than the frozen mask.

"I've taken the liberty of reserving us a table at Francel's," he said. "It has the advantage of being very public as well as being an excellent dining establishment. If you don't mind, I'll call for you just before seven o'clock. A trifle early, but despite my sister's instructions I'd rather we not be stared at by too many people, this first week." He smiled again. "And I admit I'm looking forward to sharing your company, now I'm sober enough to appreciate it."

She gave him a smile that barely tugged at the corners of her frozen mask. "Thank you for arranging matters. I'm sure I will enjoy it." *The way I would enjoy a broken leg.*

He bowed politely and left the room. Alison closed her eyes and her fists and willed herself composed, then returned to the sitting room. Philippa paused in her reading, and all eyes except those of the Dowager turned to her. Alison took her seat and again picked up her needlework without saying anything. As soon as she sat, the Dowager stirred and said, "My goodness, is that the time? I'm afraid I was so interested in the story I didn't realize how late it was. Girls, you're excused for the evening as I have no other plans. Alison, a word with you, dear?"

The other women put away their needlework and left, alternating glances at Alison with glances between themselves. When the door was shut behind them, the Dowager patted the seat where Philippa and her book had been just moments before. "Zara explained the situation to me," she said. "I know this must be hard for you, but you have to admit we cannot allow you, as one of my ladies, to seem uncontrolled and quick-tempered."

"I'm so sorry I've made you look bad," Alison said.

"Not to worry, dear. Zara is clever and I believe she's right that your appearing to be friends with Anthony will help both of you. I simply wanted to assure you that you have my support. Please don't hesitate to tell me if I can do anything to help, perhaps extend my son an invitation, or if you need to be excused from attending me? Within reason, of course."

"Milady, you are too good to me," Alison said.

"Nonsense. I simply—" The Dowager cleared her throat. "I do love my son, you know," she said, and it seemed she was controlling her tears. "I know he isn't always…the man I might have wished him to be, but he has a good heart. I hope you might become real friends, if you are willing to overlook the wrong he's done you."

Alison felt the Dowager's love for her son had overridden her good sense, but she said, "I have already forgiven him, Milady, and I will try to see his good qualities." The chances of her befriending the swaggering, shallow Prince were about the same as the chances of her running off to join an Eskandelic harem, but she liked the Dowager enough to pretend to generosity of spirit.

It seemed as if every evening gown she owned had a neckline that revealed every inch of her bosom. Alison finally settled on a rose-red gown that made her feel slightly less exposed and, to her relief, did not require a corset. Belle arranged her hair in a severe knot at the base of her neck, no loose tendrils falling free, and with that and a simple gold chain Alison felt equipped to cope with whatever the Prince might bring to bear on her that night.

The other ladies were waiting in the entry hall when she emerged from her suite. "Do tell us who your mystery caller was," Simone said.

"That dress looks divine on you, by the way."

"Thank you," Alison said.

"I think it was that Veriboldan noble, the one who wore all that silver," Carola said. "You did dance awfully close with him."

"Oooh, was it Stefan Argyll? He's *so* handsome!" Philippa said.

Alison could feel her cheeks begin to go blotchy. "It was the Prince, if you must know," she said.

The other women fell silent. Philippa's jaw dropped. Elisabeth laughed. "After that display, the Prince comes here to speak to you? You must be joking, Alison."

As if on cue, someone knocked at the door. Alison took half a step toward the door, but hesitated when one of Milady's servants sailed in and opened it. The Prince entered and gave a polite nod to the servant. "Your ladyship," he said to Alison. "If you're ready, my carriage is waiting for us."

Where the silence before had been one of astonishment, it now became a silence of five women bursting with questions and exclamations they had to stifle with physical exertion. Alison couldn't help smiling demurely at Elisabeth. "Have a pleasant evening, everyone," she said. She took the arm North offered her and allowed him to lead her outside and help her into his carriage.

They rode in silence. Alison couldn't think of anything to say to her companion, who contrary to her fears did not ogle her body, but sat gazing out the window. She twisted her skirt around her finger, then forced herself to smooth the fabric and sit quietly with her hands clasped in her lap.

"Have you been to Francel's before, your ladyship?" North asked, still gazing out the window.

"No, your Highness, I rarely come to Aurilien," she replied.

Silence fell again. Alison felt it was her turn to speak, and cast about for a subject. "Have you been to Kingsport, your Highness?"

"That's your county seat, isn't it? I come for the races, sometimes."

"I've never been to a race. I understand they can be very exciting."

"Very, especially when your horse wins."

"Do you have many horses, then?"

North turned to look at her. "If this is the kind of conversation we're to have this evening, we might be better off staying silent," he said with a smile.

Against her will, Alison found herself smiling back. "It is rather awkward," she admitted. "I'm sorry. I don't really have a gift for conversation."

"I imagine you don't need it often." His smile turned into something with a different meaning. Alison stiffened. *And so it begins.*

"I'm sure I don't know what you mean," she said.

The smile vanished. "I've offended you," he said. "And we haven't even reached the restaurant."

"I don't care for compliments like that, your Highness."

"And yet—forgive me—you must hear them often."

"Unfortunately, yes."

"I'm not sure I understand. At the risk of feeling the flat of your hand again, I'm compelled to point out you are quite beautiful and I think it's unreasonable to expect people not to notice that."

Alison felt her face begin to freeze over. "I'd prefer to talk about something else, your Highness, if you don't mind."

North spread his hands wide to indicate he would acquiesce to her wishes. At that moment, the carriage came to a stop in front of a low-roofed building of red brick. A striped canvas awning sheltered the nondescript door, next to which was a small silver plaque that read FRANCEL'S in scrollwork lettering. North smiled wryly as the footman opened the carriage door. "You should probably smile," he said, helping her down. "It will be so much more believable if you do."

His expression was so comical that Alison gave him a genuine smile, and he responded by smiling back at her, a natural, uncomplicated smile. That wasn't what she'd expected. Perhaps it wouldn't be so bad.

It took less than five minutes for her to realize she was completely wrong. It was very bad. Not the restaurant; it was lovely, understated but elegant, the china and silver and crystal of a quality even the Dowager's very well appointed table could not match, the food exceptional, and the wine better than Alison's own cellars, product of her mother's passion for oenology, could produce. Alison made a mental note to return someday. With a different dining partner.

Being stared at by all the other diners was bad enough, but either the romantically dim lighting or the intimate atmosphere inspired North to do his best to win her heart. *He probably can't help himself,* she told herself as she smiled rigidly at yet another meaningless compliment, *he's just so used to seducing women he keeps smoldering at me like that out of habit.* His heavy-lidded smile, his incessant comments on her beauty, his accidentally-on-purpose brushing of his hand against hers when they both reached for the salt cellar at once, were all so studied she would have laughed if she hadn't been so miserable. Perhaps there was some book, somewhere, with instructions on how to charm a woman. Well. A woman who wasn't Alison Quinn, to whom those insincere compliments meant only that the giver was more interested in her body than herself. It had taken her far too long to recognize the difference between false and genuine. She couldn't afford to freeze up here, in public, when she was supposed to be enjoying herself and proving to all that she and Anthony North were good friends. So she smiled and deflected his compliments — she had years of experience in doing *that* — and tried to steer the conversation in a direction even North couldn't turn into innuendo.

"I realize our first conversation was rather rocky," she said, "but I *am* curious about what you said, about your horses winning the race. Do you own many horses, your Highness?"

There was that natural, non-seductive smile again. "I do," he said. "I have an excellent stable, if I say it myself, and several of them are prize-winners. Do you ride?"

"Not in any races," she said with a laugh. "But yes, I enjoy riding. I rarely have the chance to do it, what with my work, so I'm afraid my riding these days is confined to the city. But every year I lead the Harvest Hunt, the first hunt of the season."

"You work? I'm surprised you need to."

Inwardly, she sighed. He'd gone nearly a full minute without taking that seductive tone. He was so much nicer when he wasn't staring at her breasts. She should have worn a different dress. One with a neckline that went to her chin.

"I *choose* to work because I enjoy it," she said patiently. "I love books. Always have. There's never been a time when I didn't love running around the publishing house, getting in the way of the printers and restacking the piles of books I'd knocked down." She smiled at the memory. "I even enjoy working with the authors, though they're a strange bunch and some of them need their egos coddled more than they need an editor."

North sat back in his chair and frowned. "I never thought about books being produced. You see them in a library, or a bookstore, and they're just...books."

"The publishing process is quite complicated, I assure you."

"I believe it." He threw his napkin down on his plate and checked his watch, a large gold disc on a gold chain. He swore, and apologized. "I thought dinner might go on longer. I'd take you home, but I think Zara would say we'd cheated." He showed her the time. Her heart sank. He was right.

"I'm sorry, your ladyship, but I'm afraid I didn't plan for anything else tonight." He paused, and she waited for him to make some kind of suggestive remark as to what they might do to occupy another hour and a half, or however long might satisfy the Queen. But he only looked at her as if waiting for her to make a suggestion. Amazingly, an idea suggested itself. It was something she'd like to do, anyway, and she'd be damned if she'd let this royal annoyance ruin her evening.

"Show me your watch again," she said, and made a quick calculation. Just enough time. "I have something I'd like to do, and you may join me if you wish. But we have to hurry." She put her own napkin down and waited for North to pull out her chair, then hurried out of the restaurant, forcing him to move quickly to keep up with her. At the carriage, she told the driver, "Waxwold Theater."

Chapter Four

North gave her a confused look. "You want to go to a theater?" He lowered his voice. "Your ladyship, I don't know what things are like in Kingsport, but here in the capital, theaters aren't the sort of places a lady should visit."

"I know," she said. "You'll have to trust me." She gave him a half-smile and said nothing more. They shouldn't miss more than the first couple of minutes, even if the driver was slow. Her *companion* was certainly slow, if he couldn't put the name of the theater together with the name of her county. Theater in Aurilien might be nothing more than slapstick farce or an excuse for making sexual jokes, but she and her partner Doyle intended to change that. She leaned against the windowsill and looked out eagerly, waiting for her first glimpse of her theater. She wished she dared jump out of the carriage and run ahead of it, dodging pedestrians and animal waste until she came to the theater door.

And there it was. Oh, it was more beautiful than she'd imagined. It had been nothing but a skeleton four months ago, the last time she'd been able to visit. Now the gray brick, solid edifice extended back behind its gleaming white façade, delicate and dreamlike, which rose a full story higher than the surrounding buildings. Night had fallen while Alison and the Prince were in the restaurant, and in the darkness the light Devices picking out the edges of the marquee were visible as soon as the carriage turned the corner. They sparkled and cast interesting shadows on the ground in front of the theater and across the few passersby, all of whom looked up at the marquee as they passed. The silver-lit letters proclaiming the play was *Two Came to Kingsport* were even more vivid than she'd imagined. It was beautiful and it was *hers* and she felt a rush of satisfaction like nothing she'd experienced in the two weeks since Zara North's summons had interrupted her life.

The carriage pulled up to the curb in front of the brass double doors. Alison hustled the Prince out of the carriage, conscious of the passing time. "Come along, your Highness," she said, then had to take North's hand and draw him along after her when he stood gazing up at the marquee.

Alison waved at Francesca, managing the ticket booth, and Francesca grinned when she recognized Alison. "Milady! You're just in time. It's almost a full house, but of course your box is empty. If you hurry, you'll make the curtain." She gave North an appreciative glance that said she didn't know who he was, but was happy to take a second look if he'd hold still long enough. North was bewildered enough he didn't notice. Alison tugged on his hand and led him through the shining brass doors. Oh, it was a beautiful place, her theater.

She led her unwanted companion through the foyer, with its blue carpet and softly upholstered walls—those were Doyle's idea, and she was grateful now that he'd stood up to her objections—up the shallow winding stairs and down the dimly-lit hall that curved along the back wall of the theater to box 3, her private box and one Doyle was never, ever to sell, on pain of her displeasure. She'd certainly sunk enough of her money into the place that she thought that wasn't unreasonable. The curtain was rising as they entered, so the box's light Devices were dimmed to nothing and the six chairs were little more than shadows in the secondhand light from the stage. North took a few steps inside when Alison did and stood still, gaping a little. His confusion had been funny at first, but Alison was tired of it. She pushed him into a chair and whispered, "This is a play. You know what a play is? I'm going to watch and you can, I don't know, take a nap or something. But don't talk or I'll kick you out, whatever the Queen says."

She'd seen it performed before, back in Kingsport, but this was her theater, her players—Doyle hired them, but she paid the bills—and it was one of her favorite comedies. She forgot all about North until the donkey appeared in scene five and, to her surprise, her laughter harmonized with a man's deeper chuckle. She glanced over and saw North leaning forward, avidly intent on the stage. He laughed again, harder, with no trace of the studied sensuality he'd displayed at supper, no sign of self-awareness, and for a moment Alison felt a completely unexpected sense of companionship with him. *It won't last,* she told herself, and went back to watching the play.

At intermission she stood and stretched, forgetting for the moment that she was elegantly gowned and standing where anyone could see her. Now that the house lights were up, she realized people *did* see her, and saw her royal companion as well. Zara certainly couldn't complain about this.

"Is it over?" North asked. She looked down at him and saw an uncharacteristic eagerness in his face.

"This is the intermission. It's so the audience and the performers can rest for a bit. Use the facilities, get a drink, things like that."

"I didn't know theater was like this. I thought it was all people hitting each other with sticks or hopping in and out of other people's beds." North did a little stretching of his own. "I think I will use the facilities myself, if you'll show me where they are. You seem very familiar with—oh, of course. The *Waxwold* Theater. Are you the owner?"

"Part owner. Davis Doyle and I are partners. He's the manager— does almost everything around here. But you'll have to hurry if you don't want to miss the second act. It's considered rude to enter after the curtain's gone up."

She showed him where to go and decided to refresh herself as long as she was there. North was back in the box when she returned, looking out over the crowd, occasionally nodding to people he recognized. "Why is it I've never heard of this place? So many courtiers, so many nobles...it seems very popular."

"The theater only just opened last month. I wanted to come before the final performance."

North looked at her in astonishment. "Won't people want to see it anymore?"

Alison smiled. His unmannered enthusiasm was refreshing. "Yes, but more people will want to see a new play after a while. I can't remember what they're doing next. *Horatia Virga*, I think. No, it's *After the Spring Rains Fall*. It's a tragedy. Doyle said—never mind, the curtain's going up."

The second act of *Two Came to Kingsport* was even funnier than the first, and North laughed until tears ran down his face. *He's a totally different person,* Alison thought. *I almost like him, if I didn't know he would revert to type once we're out of here.*

North applauded loudly as the cast took their bows. "This was a wonderful idea," he said. "I'm actually grateful supper took so little time."

An idea struck her. "Would you like to meet them? The cast, and the director?"

"We can do that?"

"It's my theater," she reminded him with a laugh.

They waited for the crowds to exit, then Alison led him down the back stairs to the rear of the stage. "That was almost a disaster," she heard Doyle saying in his gruff voice. "If they can't—Allie!" He turned his back on the stage manager and approached her with his arms outstretched.

She embraced him. "I told you not to call me that."

"Which is why I do it whenever I can. Hello, who's this? Friend of yours, or a *friend* of yours?" He waggled his eyebrows suggestively.

Alison laughed and shook her head. "Just a friend, Doyle, and you're embarrassing him. This is, um, Tony…Sutherland," she said. At the last minute it occurred to her she probably should have consulted North before inventing an identity for him, but her instinct told her he'd enjoy himself more if no one knew his royal identity.

North glanced at her in surprise, but played along. "I loved the show, Mister Doyle," he said, shaking the man's hand. "I have to confess I'd never seen a play before, but her ladyship insisted."

"Glad you came, are you? Always enjoy creating a new theater aficionado. Allie, I've got to see to things, but Jerald is here and if you wouldn't mind…?"

Alison groaned. "Doyle, you owe me a favor."

"You can subtract it from the two you owe me. Seriously, you're saving my life."

Alison sighed and turned to North. "I suppose you get to meet the playwright. Try not to be too overwhelmed by him."

Before North could ask her to explain herself, she again took his arm and led him around to a short hallway that terminated in a largish room with brick walls painted thickly with white paint, noisy with people talking and laughing. A pair of ratty sofas whose brocade was threadbare in places were occupied by several actors still in costume, including the rear half of the donkey. Two women tossed three lopsided balls back and forth in a complicated pattern. "This is the green room," Alison told North.

"It's not green," he pointed out.

"I know. It's just where the actors gather offstage. I don't know why it's called that. Eve, that was a lovely performance," she told a woman with a shapely bust and a pert nose, who nodded at Alison but reserved most of her attention for North. North returned her look with a slow once-over of appreciation that annoyed Alison until she realized his interest in Eve meant he wasn't leering at *her*.

"QUINN!"

The man who approached her was a giant, tall and muscular with the beginnings of a pot belly and a balding head that rose from the circle of his remaining hair, which was long and shaggy as if in compensation. Alison took a deep breath and reminded herself that she did not want to antagonize this man, that he was a major reason for the

Waxwold Theater's success, and it didn't matter if he yelled at her or made outrageously false accusations—

"You have let me down for the last time! Where are the proofs for my book? I specifically told your father I expected to see those proofs three weeks ago! This is an outrage! I demand my money back!" The peculiar green carpet slippers he wore flapped off his heels, and as he approached Alison could see more clearly that his hair and scalp were greasy. He always claimed genius could not be chained by worldly expectations of physical appearance. Too bad for everyone around him that he was every bit the genius he thought he was.

Alison took another deep breath. "Mister Flanagan, *we* are the ones who pay *you*. And you know the proofs were delayed because you refused to let us have the final draft." Alison realized her jaw was clenched and tried to relax it. She had no idea what North, standing beside her, made of this scene. "As I recall, you insisted on 'one last change' that turned into fifteen last changes. I assure you—"

"I don't want your assurances, Quinn, I want to see my book. I want to hold it in my hands and caress its leather-bound cover and watch it sell a thousand copies and retire to bed at night knowing my reputation is secure. If you can't handle this, I'll take it to Knoxbury instead."

"Mister Flanagan, Knoxbury refused to work with you anymore," Alison said, hearing her voice rise an octave. "So did Struthers & Fine. Quinn Press is the only one—"

"Don't try to threaten me, Quinn, I swear—"

"Excuse me," said North loudly. "Did you write the play we just saw?"

Flanagan halted in mid-rant. "Who are you?"

"Uh...Tony Sutherland. I'm a friend of the Countess's."

"Which Countess? You mean Quinn? Am I supposed to care?"

"I just wanted to shake your hand, Mister Flanagan." North grabbed the large man's hand and pumped it enthusiastically. "Your play was simply astonishing. I don't know when I've laughed so hard. You have a tremendous gift. Is...Quinn...publishing a book of your plays? I know I'd buy it. I'd have to buy several copies so I could share your gift with everyone I know. Really amazing, sir."

Alison stood dumbfounded. It would have been too much, coming from anyone else. But it seemed the Prince's ability to stroke someone's ego actually worked on some people. Flanagan preened and soaked up the compliments as if he were a sponge. A dirty, scabby sponge.

"Young man, I always enjoy meeting an admirer. Did you know I wrote act two, scene two on a tablecloth at a tiny restaurant on Belafleur Street? It's true. I have to write where and when the mood strikes me." He put his arm around North's shoulders and steered him away from Alison. Alison watched them in bemusement. Had North done that on purpose? No, surely not. But either way, Alison was free of Flanagan's tirades for a while.

She greeted the actors and congratulated them on their performance, asked about rehearsals for *After the Spring Rains Fall*, then covertly observed North and Flanagan. Flanagan was holding forth about something; by the gestures, he was talking about *Horatia Virga* and how cruel Alison was for forcing him to use light Devices to mimic flames instead of simply lighting a fire on the set, which would be more realistic. She ought to rescue North from Flanagan's grimy clutches soon, but it was satisfying—a guilty satisfaction, but still—to see him trapped into listening to Flanagan's ranting, like balancing the scales from the unpleasant supper she'd endured.

"Sicced him on the Prince, did you?" Doyle said into her ear, his breath tickling her cheek and making her jump.

"The—no, of course he's not the Prince."

"Of course not. He's only got the most well-known face in Aurilien. Please, Allie, give me a little credit."

"Sorry, Doyle. I just thought he'd be more comfortable if he could be anonymous for a while." She turned to look at Doyle, who was watching the interplay between North and Flanagan. North was nodding enthusiastically and saying something, and Flanagan was nodding along with him. "Have you ever known Jerald to shut up long enough to listen to anyone but himself?"

"Your Prince certainly seems to have made himself at home. And what are you doing with him, anyway? Don't take this wrong, but you're not really his type."

"It's a long story." Flanagan had apparently told a joke, because the Prince was roaring with unrestrained, clearly unfeigned laughter. It was...unexpected. Completely out of character for the man she'd sat through supper with. North glanced around, caught her eye, and smiled, a natural, engaging smile that had nothing sensual about it. Caught off guard, she smiled back. *Not even a leer,* she thought. *Who knew there was someone nice under that swaggering exterior?*

"Well, I'd like to hear that story someday, but for now I'm just going to be grateful Jerald's not ranting at me," Doyle said, clapping Alison on the shoulder. "Come down here sometime, we've got business to discuss. I still want you to look at those investor proposals."

"It's too soon for more growth."

"Don't say that until you've seen the paperwork, all right? Are you planning to bring your friend 'Tony' back again?"

Alison looked back at North, who was shaking Flanagan's hand again with no apparent distaste for its unwashed state. "I...don't know. Maybe. Is everyone going to know who he really is?"

Doyle shrugged. "I'll keep it quiet if I can. Most of these people don't move in the sort of circles your Prince does. And sometimes it does these royal types good to get away from the foofaraw for a bit. If he can keep Jerald occupied like that, he can come any time he likes."

North approached Alison, nodded to Doyle, and said, "It's rather later than I planned, Countess, so if you wouldn't mind...?" He offered her his arm. After a moment's consideration, Alison took it.

"My proofs, Quinn!" Flanagan shouted, but it was a half-hearted shout and he'd turned away to accost someone else before she'd even responded.

"Later, Allie. Nice to meet you...Tony." Doyle saluted them both with a casual wave, then North drew Alison along, through the lobby and out to their waiting carriage. Alison was a little surprised to see it still drawn up a short distance from the theater. Probably when one was royalty, one could demand that sort of service. North assisted her into the carriage and then sat opposite her. He grinned at her, his eyes bright.

"That was exhilarating," he said. "Meeting someone as brilliant as Mister Flanagan—I had no idea writing plays could be so exciting."

"We are talking about the same Jerald Flanagan, aren't we?" said Alison. "The man who's so convinced of his own genius that he signs his autograph on random pieces of paper and forces them on people?"

"Is that true?"

"I wish it weren't."

"All right, I can see what you mean. He *is* arrogant. But I really do think he's brilliant. Once you parse out the egotism—"

"Which is one in every three sentences."

"—yes, that's right, but after that it's astonishing how much he knows about the theater. At least...well, it's not as if I know very much, but he certainly seems knowledgeable."

"I have to admit he is," Alison said with a yawn. It must be nearly midnight. What would the Dowager think? "Do you remember what I said about working with authors who need their egos coddled? He's three of them."

North laughed. It was such a genuine sound that Alison smiled. "Your ladyship," he said, more formally, "I thoroughly enjoyed this evening. Quite a surprise, actually."

"I agree on both counts." Alison looked out the window because she could feel his eyes on her. He sounded sincere, but if he was back to leering, she didn't want to know about it. "I'm pleased you enjoyed the theater so much. I love the place. When I come to Aurilien, I spend most of my time there."

"I can see why." He paused, then said, "May I pay you the compliment of saying I enjoy your company?"

There was a note in his voice she hadn't heard before, and it surprised her into looking at him. He wasn't watching her at all. He was looking out the window. "Thank you," she said, remembering that genuine smile. "I...I believe I enjoy yours as well."

Chapter Five

Alison only needed directions once this time, and she was fairly certain she would be able to find her own way back to the Dowager's apartment from the Library. The scriptorium was as empty as before, with only a handful of people reading at the desks and one very small apprentice mopping up an ink spill. The skeletal librarian wasn't there. A librarian Alison hadn't seen on her first visit, young and too thin with a prematurely receding hairline, stood behind the long desk; he looked up when the door opened, glanced at her, then did a comical double-take and stared at her, his mouth slightly open as if he were starring in a slapstick farce and had just seen the leading actress simper her way on stage. Alison kept her eyes averted and went immediately to the catalog. Attention from someone as innocuous as this young man seemed to be was less objectionable than, for example, Anthony North undressing her with his eyes, but she hated knowing that nothing she said or did was ever going to be more important to some people than the way she filled out a dress.

She paged slowly through the catalog, conscious enough of the librarian's gaze on her that she had trouble focusing on the listings. A title caught her eye in passing, and she turned back to read it again. *Heaven Unbounded*, the first novel ever printed, two hundred and seven years old—and this was the first edition. She kept herself from skipping to the desk; she was a sedate and proper woman who deserved to be entrusted with something so valuable. "I would like to borrow one of your books," she told the librarian, who had begun reddening as soon as he realized she was approaching him and was now the color of a ripe tomato all the way to his distant hairline. Not only farce, but bad farce. Alison felt a little sorry for him.

"We...I'm so sorry...we don't lend out the books," the young man whispered, a little more quietly than the Library warranted. He glanced around the room as if afraid someone might hear him.

"You don't?" Alison tempered her surprise. Of course they wouldn't risk loaning books to people, who might do heaven knew what to them even by accident. The fact that Alison Quinn had never in her life damaged a book, accidentally or on purpose, wouldn't matter. And shouldn't. It was a good, if frustrating, policy. "Yes, of course. I'm sorry. Can I look at one of them, in here?"

He nodded and fumbled around for a pencil and a scrap of paper. "Write the title and the author, if there is one, and I'll bring it to you if I can."

Mulling over that "if I can," Alison wrote down the information and handed it to him. He bobbed his head a few times, opened his mouth as if to say something, then hurried away to unlock the Library door. That lock still annoyed Alison. What did they think was going to happen to the books, with all the librarians watching the door like foxes skulking around a rabbit hole?

Time passed. The young man didn't return. Alison tapped her fingers on the desk. She reached beyond its top and found some more paper and began doodling. More time passed. It was probably close to twenty minutes before the librarian returned, empty-handed. "We don't have it," he whispered.

"You don't have it?" Alison exclaimed, a trifle too loudly for the room, and the librarian cringed. "How — what's your name?"

"...Edwin?"

Are you sure? "Edwin, explain to me how you don't have a book that's listed in your catalog."

"I...we...." Edwin went to the catalog and ran his finger down the page. "Sometimes books get old and too damaged to fix, and we have to destroy them." Alison shuddered. "But it's too hard to find them in the catalog, so we just wait until...." He drew through the entry carefully with his pencil.

"But to just destroy —" Alison began.

"Is there a problem?" the skeletal librarian said, his unique scent warning her of his presence half a second before he spoke. It was surprising he didn't rattle when he walked. He looked down his bony nose at Alison. "I remember you," he said. It didn't look like it was a pleasant memory.

"I'm just...this lady wanted a book we don't have anymore, and I was just fixing the catalog. Like you told us to," Edwin said. He'd gone from red to pale and wasn't meeting anyone's eyes now.

"Very good, Edwin. You may return to your duties now," the skeletal man said. He turned to Alison. "My apologies—"

"Alison Quinn, Countess of Waxwold," she said, "and I'm sorry, I didn't catch your name."

"I am Master Charles Bancroft, Scholar and Royal Librarian," he said, and Alison heard every one of those capital letters. "We do try to keep our catalog up to date, but with all the books we handle...." His voice trailed off as if what he hadn't said was so obvious he hadn't needed to say it.

"I'm a little surprised you only have one copy of *Heaven Unbounded*. It's such an important part of literary history—"

"As I believe I told you on our first meeting, our space is limited and we must restrict the titles we acquire. I'm sorry you were disappointed. Perhaps you might come another day."

It was such an unequivocal dismissal Alison was halfway down the hall before she realized what had happened. She stood there in the dim light of the hall and fumed. *Can't find the books I want, can't borrow the books they don't have,* she thought, and continued onward at a furious pace. Bancroft was enough to sour a lesser person on reading entirely. But Alison Quinn didn't give up so easily. He might think he was lord and master of his tiny domain, but it was still the *Royal* Library and she had a perfect right to be there.

She arrived at the Dowager's apartment out of breath, with her hair falling down a little in the back. The guards looked at her only long enough to identify her, though she was certain they were both amused at her condition. Let them laugh, if in fact their humorless faces could make that expression. In her suite, she threw herself into the sitting room chair and kicked her feet out in front of her. She still had an hour before dinner and nothing to do. Reading seemed like too much work, and she was still frustrated at not having seen *Heaven Unbounded*.

"This came for you, milady," Belle said, emerging from the dressing room with a folded and sealed note in her hand. Alison accepted it and turned it over. The word "Countess" was scrawled across the front, no name, and it was sealed with a blob of dark blue wax into which was pressed the seal of the royal house of North. Alison groaned. Of course he would choose today of all days to impose on her. She counted backward—one week to the day. She groaned again and broke the seal with some force, and read,

Your ladyship,

Might I request the pleasure of your company at one o'clock this afternoon for a ride in the Park? My apologies for the short notice, but I have been in the country these last five days and I think Zara will be upset if we fail to meet her conditions. I hope you will enjoy the mount I have chosen for you.

Anthony North

She groaned a third time, but weakly. A ride in the Park wouldn't be so bad. He'd have fewer opportunities to shower her with flowery compliments, and it *had* been a while since she'd ridden. And it would be extremely public, enough that the Queen might decide to end her penance early. "Belle," she said, crumpling the paper, "would you ready my riding habit? It seems I'll have need of it today."

At one o'clock exactly she arrived at the palace stables, located to the west of the palace complex and easy to find by the rich stink of manure and the musk of dozens of horses in a relatively small space. There were several rows of stalls, most of them occupied by horses of every imaginable color who observed her as she passed, some tossing their heads as if in welcome. Her shining boots kicked up straw and dust, but not much of it, and she sidled past a young woman sweeping the packed earth between the stalls who stopped to bow to her. "Can you tell me where the Prince is?" Alison asked.

"In the yard, milady," the woman said, pointing. "Past the carriage houses."

The carriage houses were brown and black buildings the size of barns, with peaked roofs shingled in short wooden planks. One of them had its door flung wide open and several men were trundling out the Dowager's white coach, its white canvas top folded back, glossy except where its sides were spattered with mud. Alison gave them a wide berth and found, beyond the carriage, the Prince and a couple of stable hands who held the reins of two elegant horses.

"Milady Countess! You're as beautiful as ever," North exclaimed. "I must say that riding habit suits you *very* well." His eyes were surveying her body, lingering on her hips where the habit fit most closely.

"I don't believe you *must* say it, but I thank you for the compliment, your Highness," Alison replied with a frozen smile. She had hoped their visit to the theater had changed him, but it appeared she wasn't going to see that man again. That disappointed her. He'd been so much nicer, so enthusiastic about the play and even about Flanagan—it hadn't been awful, spending time with him. Instead she was going to endure an hour with the Prince and his unwanted attentions.

"This is Pacer," North said, indicating a chestnut gelding with a somewhat longer than average face. "Pacer, say hello to her ladyship."

To her surprise, Pacer bobbed his head up and down, exactly as if he'd understood North's words. "He's very intelligent," North said, smiling at her surprise. "I think he's not happy with being confined to the streets and the Park, so I take him out every so often for a ride in the countryside. I'd suggest we do that, but there wouldn't be anyone around to witness. So I hope you don't mind the Park."

Alison eyed him warily. The suggestive look had left his eyes and his voice had that same enthusiasm she'd heard that night a week ago, coming home from the play. The rapid transformation confused her. "That will be fine, your Highness," she said, and resisted the urge to add *I wish we could ride outside the city too.* Suggesting that she wanted more of his company would be disastrous, even if the idea of running wild across the fields surrounding Aurilien was compelling.

"And this is Ebon Night," North said, indicating the second horse, a beautiful black mare with glossy sides and a mane that had been brushed until it shone. "She should be the right height for someone as petite as you—though I don't mean to suggest there's anything wrong with your height; you're quite perfect as you are."

And there it is again. "Thank you, your Highness," she said, offering Ebon Night the back of her hand to sniff, then stroking the mare's neck so she wouldn't have to see that look in North's eyes. She mounted without assistance and turned Ebon Night in a tight circle. "Shall we ride?"

North led the way out of the stable yard and around to the palace drive, the horses' hooves clopping along the stones to the accompaniment of unseen birds singing in the trees. It was so peaceful that Alison almost regretted it when they came out onto Queen's Way Road, where the rhythmic noise of their passing was drowned out by the sound of carriages rattling by and more horses ambling along. It was another beautiful autumn day, the air just chilly enough to be welcome against the rays of the sun, the linden trees now golden, with half their leaves piled around their roots like treasure waiting to be picked up.

"Tony! What about tonight at Averill's? You promised you'd be there," a young man shouted from his perch high atop a passing carriage, pulling up just enough that his horses protested.

"I'll be there, Dev, don't worry, and you'd better bring a fat purse!" North replied. "Have you met the Countess of Waxwold? Countess, my friend Terence Deveraux."

"How do you do, sir," Alison said. It was a good idea, drawing this man's attention to how friendly they were, but the surprise of it made her freeze up inside.

Deveraux's expression went from admiring to surprised. "And the two of you so friendly? Maybe I should find a beautiful woman to slap *me*, not that you probably didn't deserve it, Tony!"

"It was a misunderstanding. We're good friends, aren't we, Countess?"

Alison made herself nod, though she was certain she was blotchy with humiliation. So no one had forgotten yet. How much longer would she have to endure this?

North was accosted half a dozen more times before they reached the Park, and Alison remembered what Doyle had said about the Prince having the most well-known face in Aurilien. He was certainly more natural in greeting his friends—but then, none of them were women, and she didn't think he was the type to leer at men. Only about half of his friends realized who she was, and none of them were so crass as Deveraux had been to refer to the scandal, but she was still tense as they entered the Park.

Alison had never visited the Park before, so she had no idea whether the steady stream of pedestrians and riders that went in and out through the wide-open iron gates was usual, or if the clear weather had brought more people out to enjoy it. Neatly trimmed box hedges lined the walk for about fifty feet, where the path opened up in three directions, two of them passing on either side of a flowerbed shaped like a many-pointed star. Zinnias filling the bed echoed the star motif, their waxy petals of red or yellow or magenta giving off a faint scent that reminded Alison of her first governess, who'd loved the flowers; Alison thought them stuffy and pretentious. The noise of traffic was already muted, even this short distance from the street, and the people walking or riding past spoke with hushed voices, as if appreciating the quiet.

"This way, Countess," North said, indicating the third path, that veered off in a direction paralleling the Park's outer wall. "It's unofficially the horse trail. Have you ever visited the Park before?"

Alison shook her head. "I never have time for sightseeing."

"Well, it's a sight worth seeing. Much like yourself, your ladyship." He smiled at her, and Alison successfully kept from rolling her eyes. Really, did he not realize how ridiculous his compliments were?

She managed to trail behind him enough that conversation was impractical. He was right, the Park was beautiful. Their route took them through a series of low rises covered in fine, short-cropped grass that was still emerald-green despite the lateness of the season. The rises gave way to a forest of oak trees, their branches half-bare, though no leaves cluttered the ground surrounding their roots. "Where are all the leaves?" she said, then remembered too late she didn't want to give the Prince more opportunities to "compliment" her.

"The grounds crew rakes them up every night," North said, reining in a little to walk next to her. "Rakes the leaves, mows the grass, gets rid of the dead flowers, all the other little maintenance tasks to keep this the most well-groomed patch of earth in Tremontane. Even the palace gardens aren't so thoroughly cared for."

"You sound as if you disapprove, your Highness." She kept her attention on a tree just over his shoulder, where a bird was darting in and out of a hole in the trunk. She felt certain if her eyes met his, he would think of something suggestive to say to her.

"I don't like the artifice of the place. Landon North scooped it out of Aurilien proper over a century ago because he was too lazy to hunt outside the city walls, but the citizens and the Council threw a fit at how much land he wanted for a hunting preserve. So he compromised on this and made it a gift to the city. Everything you see here was brought in from somewhere else. Even the waterfall—"

"There's a *waterfall*?"

North laughed. "A small one. It feeds into the lake. It's all such a...so contrived, actually. Recreating the beauties of nature so no one has to visit the real ones. There's a very nice place just outside the city walls, in fact—it's a park, true, but it was built around a lake that's older than Aurilien and it looks more natural. I greatly prefer it."

"I agree with you," Alison said. "Though I can see how this one serves its purpose. I imagine there are many people in Aurilien who never have the time to travel to see the real thing."

"The next time we go riding, we'll have to go there. And have a bit of a run," North said. Alison, startled, looked to see if he was joking and was surprised to discover he wasn't even looking at her; he was gazing off down the trail, craning to see beyond the next rise. "I think we might have a bit of a run now, if you're game, Countess," he said, turning his attention on her. His grin was completely unselfconscious and free of any hidden meanings, and, again caught by surprise, she smiled back at him. "I think the trail is clear. Shall we?"

Without waiting for her to agree, he shouted to Pacer and was off down the trail. Ebon Night took a few steps after her stablemate, and Alison could feel her quiver with the desire to run. "Let's catch them, shall we?" Alison told her, and urged her through a walk into a canter that brought them back within sight of North, who was leaning well forward in his seat and taking the gentle curves of the path with an ease that said he'd done this before. The speed of the horse and the sunlight shining through the branches made Alison laugh with joy. It had been a long time since she'd done anything so spontaneous. She looked ahead at North, who made a fine figure despite his character flaws, his broad shoulders, the fine muscles of his back and his...*Alison Quinn, you're no better than he is.* At least she had the decency to keep her ogling to herself. If only he weren't so hell-bent on leering at her all the time, his company might be enjoyable. It occurred to her that most of her thoughts about the Prince began with *If only*. If only he weren't so self-absorbed...if only he'd stop handing her meaningless compliments...if only he'd be the person she'd glimpsed a few minutes ago, the man who'd gone to the theater with her.... Alison thought the Dowager might be right; there was a good man in there somewhere, *if only*....

"Whoa!" North shouted, reining in abruptly, and Alison took Ebon Night off the path to avoid running into Pacer's broad flank. "I beg — Alex!"

"What a surprise, Tony," said the man just guiding his dappled gray horse around the next curve toward them. "I didn't know you rode in the afternoons." He was quite a bit older than North, possibly in his mid-thirties, with a long, brooding face and curly dark hair. His crooked eyebrows, and the deep lines beside his nose, made him look as if he were permanently sneering at something, but his smile was pleasant enough and he seemed happy to see North.

"I didn't know you rode at all," North said. "But it's good to see you, of course."

The man looked past North's shoulder at Alison. "And who is your charming companion?" he said.

"Oh, of course." North glanced once at Alison, and for the briefest moment Alison thought she saw uncertainty in his expression. "This is the Countess of Waxwold. Your ladyship, my very dear friend Alexander Bishop."

"Of course. Tony's mentioned you," Bishop said, bowing slightly. "A pleasure to make your acquaintance, milady Countess."

"I am pleased to meet you as well," Alison said, though she hadn't liked the way he'd said *Tony's mentioned you* as if he knew very well how she and "Tony" had been introduced. It was just the way his eyebrows crooked; they made him look like a villain in a melodrama, and he was probably perfectly nice. Not that it mattered, since she was unlikely to see him again and it certainly didn't matter to Bishop what she thought of him.

"So you've taken up running down innocent bystanders, have you?" Bishop said, raising one of those crooked eyebrows with a smile. It made him look even more like a villain, and Alison half expected to see him pull out a silver-headed ebony walking stick and begin holding forth on how he planned to destroy her and North both. "Really, Tony, what if I'd been a nursemaid with a pair of babies?"

"I've never run anyone over, and you're giving the Countess a very bad impression of me," North said, laughing, and this time Alison saw him glare at his friend, the briefest flash of an expression. *He's warning Bishop off,* she realized, *he thinks Bishop is trying to ruin his chances with me,* and the urge to laugh was so strong she had to lean forward and bury her face in Ebon Night's mane, breathing in the woody scent of the oil the groom had used on her. The Prince was truly self-absorbed if he thought his seduction was working.

"Don't worry, milady Countess, Tony's an excellent rider," Bishop said. "I'd ask to join your party, but I have an engagement I'm going to miss if I don't move along. I quite enjoyed meeting you, milady Countess, and I hope you'll have a pleasant ride."

"Thank you, Mister Bishop," Alison said, and bit her lip to keep from laughing again, because North's relief at his friend's words was so obvious it was hard for her to pretend she hadn't seen it.

"I'll see you at Averill's tonight, Alex?" North said. Bishop waved a hand in assent and disappeared around the nearest rise. North watched that direction for a few seconds, then turned back to Alison and said, "I'm afraid our mad dash has wreaked havoc on your coiffure, milady."

Alison put her hand up to feel her curls slipping down in back. "One moment, your Highness," she said, and plucked pins out until she could twist her hair back up tightly and secure it, probably not as well as Belle might have done, but at least it wasn't hanging loose around her face. She could feel North's eyes on her and gritted her teeth, waiting for an innuendo-filled comment on her masses of curls, but he said nothing, merely turned Pacer and set him at a sedate walk down the trail. "We should be moving on," he said. "I promised my mother I'd have you back before her reading time."

"Thank you for your consideration, your Highness."

North made an exasperated sound and wheeled around to face her. "Would you stop calling me that all the time? I know what I am. I would prefer you call me Anthony."

His abruptness startled her into stammering, "I…your Highness, I don't believe we know each other well enough to make free of our given names like that."

"Aurilien society is not so formal as Kingsport, then."

She didn't want to explain it was her own preference. "Apparently not. Will 'milord' do as a compromise?"

"If you must." He clicked his tongue at his horse and they rode on in silence for a while. They came out of the miniature hills to a lake, perfectly round, with a waterfall no more than seven feet tall pouring into it. Alison watched a pair of swans glide past, serene and unworried about the approaching winter. "I don't suppose you'll tell me how long we must know each other, according to polite Kingsport society, before we may make free of one another's given names?" North said.

He sounded annoyed, which amused Alison, and she said, with a perfectly straight face, "I believe after six months it is acceptable for friends to call one another 'sir' and 'madam.' After another six months they may call each other by their given names so long as they also use their surnames."

North looked back at her, more annoyed than before. "Begging your pardon, but that's a ridiculous—" His eyes narrowed. "That was a joke, wasn't it?"

"I'm afraid I couldn't help myself, milord."

He burst out laughing. "Countess, you astonish me. I had begun to believe you as humorless as a block of wood. Though, come to think of it, you did laugh at the play."

"True. So did you."

He came back to ride beside her. "I can't remember the last time I laughed so much." He glanced over at her, then added, "It made you seem a very different person."

This startled Alison. She had felt like a different person, more like herself, at the play, but she hadn't realized he'd come out of his self-absorbed state to notice. "I might say the same of you, milord."

"Well, theater-going is a new experience for me. Will there be a new play soon?"

"In two or three weeks, milord."

"I'd like to go again, if you wouldn't mind accompanying me."

"I—" There he was again, assuming she would want to voluntarily spend time with him. Was he so certain his seduction was working, that he believed she would be eager for his company? But…he didn't have that look in his eye that said he was thinking about what she might look like naked; he sounded as if he were making a genuine offer. "If my schedule permits, milord," she said.

"I'm sure I can arrange it with my mother. It's the sort of thing she approves of, evening artistic performances. Isn't she taking you and the rest of her chattering ladies to a violoncello concert this evening?"

Alison nodded. "I don't know if I'm looking forward to it. I don't really enjoy musical performances."

North's eyes widened in mock horror. "Don't ever let her know that. You might as well be a Kirkellan savage as admit to not liking music, as far as she's concerned."

"The Kirkellan aren't savages, and their music is as complex as anyone's. But I thank you for the warning."

"How do you know the Kirkellan play music at all?"

"I read about it. Hana Bullen wrote three excellent memoirs of her time among the Kirkellan tribes, and then there's the book by

Fortunato."

He raised his eyebrows at her. "You enjoy reading, then? Not just publishing?"

"I don't think there's a single person involved in publishing who doesn't love reading. Imagine a barman who didn't enjoy beer."

"Interesting. I'm afraid I'm not very literate. Not much time for it, really."

"Well, I forgive you, milord. You're brave to admit such a failing."

He laughed again. "Two jokes in one afternoon. Be careful, countess, you'll use up your supply."

"I think humor is a thing that replenishes itself," she said with a smile. He was so much nicer to talk to when he forgot to stare at her body. If he could go on forgetting....

They came around a final corner and were back in a more obviously groomed part of the Park, with rosebushes of varying colors planted at intervals so the last flowers of autumn made a rainbow sweep from white through yellow and peach to deepest red and then blue-black. It would be beautiful in the height of summer. North said, "Well, I'm sorry you have to sit through the concert tonight, countess. Though I'm certain no one will be watching the performers so long as you're in the room."

Alison looked at him just in time to see his heavy-lidded, sensual gaze slide over her back and hips again. She felt herself freeze right to her core. A tiny voice inside her head wailed, *But I actually liked him!* The frozen mask descended over her face, covering her cheeks and her mouth, and distantly she heard herself say, "I believe we should make haste, your Highness. It's later than I thought."

North made an exasperated sound. "You've gone all stiff again."

"Have I, milord?"

"Yes, *milady*, you have. I thought you'd finally broken through that reserve. Or is that Kingsport manners again? You certainly seem to use them as an excuse to keep me at a distance."

That's exactly the point. Alison considered half a dozen possible responses and went with, "I believe I've told you I'm uncomfortable with such compliments, and yet you persist in giving them to me."

"Because you're beautiful, and I've told you it's unreasonable for me to pretend not to notice that."

"Then I can hardly fail to be aware of how I look, and I don't need to be reminded of it constantly." She could hear the bitter edge to her voice, and cursed herself for being drawn into the conversation with someone she had no interest in sharing confidences with, even so small as one as this.

North said nothing. They came to the entrance of the Park and proceeded along Queen's Way Road in silence. Alison wondered what he thought of her directness and refused to feel guilty about her words. He was the one at fault, not her. A couple in a passing carriage hailed the Prince, who waved at them perfunctorily and did not stop to chat. They continued to the stable yard in silence, and Alison dismounted and handed Ebon Night's reins off to a groom, giving the horse one last pat. "Thank you for the ride, milord," she said.

"Do my compliments really offend you so much?" North said, looking down at her from Pacer's back. His face was expressionless, but his eyes were narrowed, and she had the feeling he'd been thinking hard about her words all the way back from the Park. If he was finally taking her seriously—she cast about for something to say that would make him understand, if that was what he truly wanted.

"What offends me," she said, "is not just what you say, but the fact that you continue to say it after I've asked you not to. We may not be friends, but I think even acquaintances such as we are should respect each other's wishes."

He regarded her silently for a moment, then swung down from the horse and extended his hand to her. "I apologize," he said, "and you're entirely right." He smiled, and it was the natural, non-seductive smile that made him look so much nicer. "Will you forgive my presumption?"

The unexpected appearance of the man from the theater startled a smile out of Alison. She clasped his hand and said, "I forgive you, milord."

"Thank you." He released her hand, began to turn away, then said, "One of my horses is racing in three days; would you care to see it? I realize it's sooner than one week, but this is the last race of the season, and you did seem interested."

Alison hesitated. The agreement had been for the two of them to appear in public here, where anyone who'd witnessed Alison's loss of control might see them. But surely the nobles of Tremontane went to the races? And, she admitted to herself, she'd always wanted to see a horse race. "Thank you, milord, I would enjoy that very much," she said.

He smiled again, still that natural, cheerful smile, and said, "I look forward to it, then. But I warn you, now I know you actually have a sense of humor, I intend to find ways to make you laugh."

"That sounds like a challenge, milord," Alison said.

"Ah, but if I make you laugh, I think we both win." He winked at her, a friendly gesture and not a lascivious one, then led Pacer away in the direction of the stables, leaving Alison to stare after him. That had been unexpected. *It won't last*, she told herself, *he'll be back to his old self when I see him next.* She hoped she was wrong.

Chapter Six

The Prince was a good driver, but even he couldn't do anything about the condition of the road on the way to Hartsgate, where the race would be held. He kept the horses to a sedate pace, but the carriage still jolted and bounced down the rutted road. "I'm sorry this is such a rough ride," the Prince said, interrupting the silence in which they'd ridden for the last two miles. His eyes were bleary and there were dark circles under his eyes. Alison suspected he was hung over.

"I don't—oof—mind," she lied. "How much farther?"

"Only another half an hour. I should have brought my other carriage, which is better sprung, but it was such a nice day I wanted to ride in the open." His words were a little abrupt, terse, and Alison wondered if his condition would make him less inclined to ogle her out loud.

It *was* a lovely day for early autumn. A light breeze came and went through the trees, bringing with it the smell of earth, warmed by the sun that shone in a cloudless blue sky and made Alison a little uncomfortable inside her heavy garments. She wished she'd dared wear trousers, but this was a public event if not a formal one, and she'd opted for a dark blue ankle-length coat over a lighter blue gown with a fitted bodice and a high neckline. The trees lining the road held on to some of their vividly colored leaves while the rest made piles like brown and gold confetti on the dark earth around them.

A deep jolt nearly sent Alison off her seat. She grabbed hold of its edge and gripped it tightly, and laughed a little to cover her discomfort.

"You might take my arm, instead of that slippery seat," North said.

"No, thank you, milord, I am well enough as I am," she said.

They rode in silence a little while longer, then North said, "I won't eat you, you know."

She looked at him and saw his face had gone a little wooden and he wouldn't meet her eyes. *By heaven, I've hurt his feelings,* she realized, and felt red blotches rise across her face. "I'm sorry. That was uncivil of me." She hooked her right arm through his left and clasped her left hand over her right hand. "Thank you."

He glanced down at her. "You don't blush well, do you?" he remarked with a smile.

She gave him an outraged look, then had to laugh. "No, milord, I do not," she said. "Nor do I cry well. It's my curse."

"I suppose everyone needs a flaw or two." He seemed about to say more, but then subsided back into silence. *He had the perfect opportunity to say something suggestive, just there,* Alison realized. It boded well for the rest of the day.

"Tell me more about the race," she said. "I don't know what to expect."

"There are several races," North said. "My horse, Sandy Dan, is running in the third. It's only his fifth race and he came second the last two times, so I have high hopes for his prospects. The purse in this case—"

"The purse?"

"The prize money. It's not very big, but as this is the last day of the season, everyone will be looking to see what to expect next year. So it's a fairly important race. And my rider gets the money anyway; I have no need of it."

"You don't ride in the race yourself, then."

He laughed, but not mockingly. "I'm far too big for the horse. Jackley is an excellent rider and I'd trust him with any of my animals."

"What about...I hear people bet on horse races."

He stiffened. "Sometimes."

"Do you?"

"Sometimes." Once again he wouldn't meet her eyes. Alison let it pass.

"You'll notice many people come to see and be seen rather than to watch the races," he continued. "I admit I enjoy that part myself, when it's not my race."

"I think the horse would appreciate your attention."

He looked down at her as if wondering if she was mocking him, decided she wasn't, and laughed. "I think of my horses as a little like people. They all have their own personalities, their own likes and dislikes. Some owners keep a stable, it seems, because everyone else is doing it, delegating its care to employees. I don't see the point of that."

"You sound as if it matters to you very much." The carriage hit another deep rut, and she squeezed his arm more tightly.

"It does. I try to get out to my estate every other week, see how things stand, take some of the horses out for exercise. I love the city, but it's good to get away sometimes."

Alison almost said *I'd like to see your estate* and stopped herself just in time. *Don't forget this Anthony North never stays for long,* she reminded herself. *Do you want to be trapped in the country with the other one?* She couldn't think of anything else to say, so she clung to North's arm and watched the scenery slide by.

A few carriages passed them, going the other way, and North swung wide each time to let them pass. "During the summer this road is thronged with racing enthusiasts," he said. "I would have thought, the weather being this nice, we'd see more travelers, even if it is the end of the season. Here, we're coming up on Hartsgate. The road to the race track isn't very good."

"I shudder to imagine what that might be like, if it's worse than this one."

He chuckled. "Just hold on. It's not much farther." He turned right off the main road into another that was closer to being a path than a road, muddy and showing signs of many carriages and horses having passed by frequently. Alison clung to North's arm and hoped her hat wouldn't fall off. If it did, and landed in this muck, she probably wouldn't bother retrieving it; the thick soup looked like it was made of more than just wet dirt.

After a few more minutes of painful bouncing, they came out from beneath the trees into a wide field, or whatever an expanse of mud was called. Beyond this expanse lay a grassy oval, its green somewhat dull with mud, two fences made from ropes tied between upright posts defining a track running the outside edge of the oval. Tiered wooden structures, gray and a little uneven, stood facing each other across the long sides of the oval, their risers lined with white wooden chairs. Men and women dressed in colorful riding habits led horses onto the grass toward a pair of white posts that marked off an invisible line.

"That's the first race," North said, steering his carriage wide of the spectator stand to an area where several other carriages were parked. Alison released his arm so he could step down from the carriage. "Muddy," he remarked with distaste, and reached up with both hands to help her down. Alison hesitated for a moment, then gritted her teeth and let him grasp her around the waist and lift her out of the carriage as easily as if she'd been an infant. His hands were firm and, surprisingly, showed no inclination to stray. North himself behaved as if nothing were out of the ordinary, only set her down lightly and then offered her his arm again. After another hesitation, she took it. *Perhaps he has changed,* she thought, *but we'll see how long it lasts.* North looked down at her, and smiled, no hint of a leer in those attractive blue eyes. He really was too handsome for his own good. Alison resolved to be friendly. If he could behave himself, so could she.

Alison was grateful for North's arm as they picked their way carefully across the uneven ground. Falling here would be far worse than losing her hat. Despite the muck, a number of men and women milled about the area, talking intensely, some of them receiving money pressed upon them and making notes in tiny books. "I don't understand what they're saying," Alison said. "What does 'four to one against' mean?"

She felt his arm go tense. "Those are bookmakers," he said. "They take wagers on different races and pay out to the winners. Four to one against means the bookmaker wagers against the horse winning and is willing to risk paying out four times the amount of your stake—the money you wager—if it does."

"But you get nothing if your horse loses."

"Naturally. Let's go to the stands—" He steered her heavily around the group of bookmakers, but someone called out, "Milord Prince!"

North stopped, then turned around with a smile, bringing Alison with him. "Arthur," he said. "I'm not wagering today."

Arthur flicked his gaze at Alison and back again. "Thought you might be interested in Muddy Waters in the third at two to one against. He's a favorite."

"You know I never bet against my own horses. Next time, Arthur." North turned and resumed his relentless march toward the stands.

"Would you mind slowing down? I feel as if I'm being dragged," Alison said.

North glanced at her, then slowed his pace. "I'd rather not be stopped again. I want to see this first race." A shout went up, and they could hear horses running all out somewhere beyond the stand. "Or, apparently, the second race," he said with better humor. Shouting and cheering poured out of the stands, individual words lost in the noise. Alison felt as if it might sweep her away if she let it.

On a whim, she said, "I wonder you're not wagering today. That man seemed to know you well, so you must place wagers often."

"I'm not betting today because you're going to tell my mother every detail of our excursion, and she hates it when I wager on the horses."

"Why? Do you often lose?"

North looked at her incredulously, then began to laugh. "Countess, you have the strangest sense of humor. Yes, sometimes I lose. Sometimes I win. But my mother knows it's a low-class habit and she gives me the most disappointed look whenever she hears of it. I would rather not give her any opportunity to do so."

The cheering went from ecstatic to frenzied. Spectators began leaping from the stands and rushing past them to speak to the bookmakers, waving bits of paper. Alison, without thinking, pressed closer to North and felt him put his arm around her shoulders, drawing her close. "Come this way," he said, and Alison, a little flustered, stumbled along with him and accepted his hand to step into the stand filled with white folding chairs. "This will give us an excellent view, I think."

He led her up a few steps and then across to a place near the central aisle, then held her seat for her. "It will take some time for them to ready the track for the next race. Now's the time for us to see and be seen, Countess." He grinned at her, then sat back in his seat and stretched out his long legs. Alison settled herself and looked around at the spectators. She hadn't expected such a cross-section of Aurilien society. Women in trousers sat next to men in full morning dress. Young women in dresses far too sheer for the chilly air huddled together, gossiping and giggling. Young men in fashionable coats stood around for the young women to gossip about. Some of them caught sight of her and North and paused in their conversations, elbowing their friends and covertly pointing in their direction. Alison pretended not to see them. Being noticed was the point of this outing, after all. Well, that and the races.

Alison looked at her companion; he'd gone from sitting back to leaning forward with his elbows on his knees and his chin resting on his clasped hands, his attention focused on the track. He had an exquisite profile and, with his dark hair falling forward over his forehead, he looked younger, like a boy waiting for something exciting to happen.

"Should I be worried that you're staring at me?" he said, not looking away from the track.

Alison felt a blush beginning. "I was trying to think of something to talk about, since nothing's happening yet. I'm surprised everything seems so...unfinished, if racing is so popular."

"This style of racing is the newest thing. It's why the construction here is so raw," he said. "Racing carriages is actually more common, men and women driving ten or twenty miles across country. But those long races are only of interest to spectators at the end, and there are so many factors beyond the quality of your horses, like the kind of carriage and how well you handle it. Eliminating the carriages, and shortening the track, makes things more evenly matched and I think makes it more exciting."

"Have you raced carriages, then?" Alison said.

"Of course. I usually race my grays, though I've gone four-in-hand once or twice. It's a pity, really, that this new form of racing means most of us who are accustomed to racing carriages aren't able to ride our own horses, but I think it's a fair trade-off." There was that light in his eyes again, the light she'd seen the night they'd gone to the theater. He'd forgotten to be seductive in his passion for racing—*but,* Alison thought, *he hasn't paid me one extravagant compliment or given me a single suggestive glance all morning. Maybe he's changed, after all.*

"There, see that woman down there? She has the signal flag to tell the riders when to start," North said. "Should be—"

The black and red striped flag swooped down and the horses took off across the earth surrounding the grass, angling to get to the inside of the track as quickly as possible. The crowd surged to its feet, taking Alison with it, and her cry of protest was cut off by the beauty of eight horses pounding around the track, their flanks heaving, their necks stretched out. She didn't realize she was shouting until the first horse crossed the finish line, reaching out with its neck and head as if that would give it that much more speed. She turned to say something to North and was caught by the excitement in his blue eyes, an excitement that so matched her own that she grinned at him in pleasure and found him grinning back at her. She almost wished they were friends at that moment; if he could be like this all the time, what a pleasant companion he would be.

"Wait until you have a stake in one of the runners," North said. "It's ten times as exciting. It's the next best thing to running the track yourself."

"I don't think I could bring myself to wager on a race. I'm not fond of risk."

"No, you seem a fairly conservative person. But you might choose a horse and *pretend* you've placed a fortune on it." He winked at her in such a comical way that she laughed.

"Then you will pretend to be a bookmaker, and…is it give good odds on my wager?"

"Indeed, your ladyship. I—Alex!" At the bottom of the stand, Alexander Bishop saluted North with a casual wave. He'd looked as surprised to see North as North had been to see him, but Alison had been looking toward the track, had seen him begin to raise his head before the Prince had said anything, and was certain Bishop had known perfectly well North was there. Why he was pretending surprise, Alison didn't know, but she glanced at North and saw his smile was a little too fixed for genuine pleasure. The Prince hadn't expected Bishop to be there, and Bishop knew it; Bishop's presence made North nervous. If North really did think Bishop was trying to ruin his chances with the Countess of Waxwold, did that mean Bishop was interested in having her for himself? She studied his long, sneering countenance as he climbed up the steps to greet them. He didn't look at her the way a man looks at a woman he's interested in—something she had years of experience in recognizing—he looked at her the way a man looks at a one-year-old filly he's planning to buy. Whatever his interest in her, it wasn't courtship.

"Alex, you remember the Countess of Waxwold," North said, having regained his composure.

Bishop bowed, very correctly, over her hand. "Countess, it's a pleasure," he said. "Tony, interested in taking a flutter? I've heard Daisychain is eight to one against in the next race."

"Sandy Dan is running the next race. You know I don't bet against my own horses, Alex—"

"Be sensible, Tony. You know I love Sandy Dan like he was my own, but word is Daisychain underperformed on purpose at the trials and I think it's a sure bet. Come on, what do you say?"

North glanced at Alison. "I…think not."

Bishop seemed surprised. "Don't tell me you're not up for a little wager? I was sure you'd be eager to act on this tip. You wouldn't want the lady to think you afraid to take a chance, would you?" He smiled at Alison, but his eyes were unexpectedly cold, and she felt herself freeze up a little from the strange expression in them.

North looked at Alison again, then back at Bishop. "Well…you've never steered me wrong before. Let's hurry before the book closes. Your ladyship, please excuse us." He and Bishop loped down the stairs, leaving Alison with an unvoiced protest on her lips. She watched their retreating forms and fumed. Bishop had just used her to manipulate the Prince. She felt her good mood evaporate. North had said he wasn't going to bet against his own horse. Then Bishop came out of nowhere and suddenly North was off placing a wager. For all his faults, she'd never seen him easily led. Who was this Alexander Bishop, and why did the Prince care so much for his good opinion, enough to compromise his principles?

The horses were coming onto the track before North and Bishop returned. North again sat beside Alison, while Bishop, to Alison's dismay, sat on her other side, bookending her like a folio on a shelf. "That's the horse," North said, pointing at a chestnut mare in the middle of the pack.

"I didn't realize a horse named Sandy Dan might be female," Alison said.

"No, that's Daisychain. Sandy Dan is on the far side." The horse's light yellow coloring made it clear why he was named Sandy Dan. Alison determined to cheer for him, and Daisychain be damned.

"Eight to one odds means we will win eight times as much as we wagered," Bishop explained. "You can see Daisychain is a high-stepper, can't you? I feel certain you have an instinct for horses."

"You flatter me, Mister Bishop," Alison said, trying to remain polite and wishing she dared tip him out of his seat, not that she was nearly strong enough; he wasn't as tall and broad-shouldered as North, but he was still a good deal taller than she was. "I believe I would have chosen Sandy Dan."

"Ah, but there's more to racing than just the horse," Bishop said. "There's the rider's experience, and the horse's knowledge of the track, and even the weather can change the outcome of a race. You'll see."

"I believe I begin to see already, thank you, Mister Bishop," Alison said coldly. "But I'll stand by my choice, if you don't mind."

The flag dropped, and the shouting began, North and Bishop roaring out Daisychain's name, Alison screaming for Sandy Dan in a way she didn't think she had in her. She felt as if she were running the race herself, flying across the rough ground, passing the others contemptuously because they were no match for her. Daisychain didn't even deserve to run the same track as her. She—Sandy Dan passed the finish line well ahead of his nearest rival, and Alison jumped and cheered before realizing how ridiculous she looked. She sat down again. North and Bishop looked glum. "Too bad about the track," Bishop said. "Daisychain can't have been familiar with it. Next time for sure."

"Next time for sure," North echoed. "I should congratulate Jackley. Countess, would you care to join me?"

"Thank you, milord, I would enjoy that."

"Alex? Or are you off to place another bet?"

"I was actually on my way home when you saw me," Bishop said. "Thank you, Countess, for allowing me to join you, but I think I'll take my leave."

North shook his hand. "I'll see you tonight?"

"At the club, certainly." Bishop took Alison's hand. This time, he brushed his lips against the back of it. "Countess, your servant."

"Good afternoon, Mister Bishop," Alison said, retrieving her hand with a little more force than necessary. Far from being offended, Bishop smiled, a surprisingly smug expression that made Alison wonder what he thought he'd accomplished by "accidentally" meeting North here today. He had no interest in courting her himself, she was certain of that, but for whatever reason, he didn't want North courting her either. The Prince must not have told him the reason he was escorting her so frequently. How petty of Bishop! Suppose North were genuinely interested in her, which he was not? What kind of person wanted to ruin his friend's happiness? An ache began behind her temples, which she rubbed surreptitiously as they left the stands to find Jackley and Sandy Dan.

Jackley was a pleasant-featured young man only an inch or two taller than Alison, and he seemed not at all overwhelmed by his royal employer. Alison managed a few questions about his job and petted Sandy Dan, but mostly listened to the technical conversation between North and Jackley. North treated Jackley without condescension and listened closely to his suggestions. He didn't mention betting against Sandy Dan and Alison didn't give him away.

They didn't speak much, the next few races, which satisfied Alison because her headache was worsening and she felt increasingly inclined to snap at North. By the end of the sixth race, her head was pounding as if something were trying to emerge from it. She was also hungry, which made her even more irritated at North that he hadn't thought to provide food for this long excursion. "Milord, I hate to cut short our outing, but I feel a little unwell," she said. "Do you suppose we might return now?"

"Of course," North said. He sounded genuinely concerned, which irritated her further. As if he really cared about her needs. She rubbed her temples again. That was unjust of her. He'd been such a pleasant companion, hadn't once ogled her body or said something suggestive, and during their shared excitement over the racing she'd felt for a brief time that they were friends. It surprised her to discover she wanted to be his friend—not the swaggering man-about-town, but the enthusiastic, genuine man who existed somewhere beneath that façade. *When was the last time you called a man 'friend'? When has any man been interested in something you cared about instead of your body?* Then Bishop had appeared and the Prince had changed again, behaving like a puppy wanting a treat—no, that was unfair, there was nothing puppyish about the Prince. But he'd certainly wanted Bishop's approval.

North helped her into the carriage, and they drove away from the race grounds. "Is there anything I can do to ease your discomfort, your ladyship?"

"Thank you for your concern, milord, but I simply need to rest."

"What's wrong, Countess?"

"Nothing, milord." She knew she sounded frozen. She was too tired to keep the mask from falling.

"That's not true. You only sound like that when you're upset. Are you angry with me?"

"Why should I be angry with you, milord?"

"That's not an answer." Now *he* sounded angry.

"I would rather not talk about it, milord."

"And now you're using a title every time you speak to me."

"Am I, milord?"

North swore and reined in the horses so he could give her his full attention. "I have behaved with perfect propriety toward you all day. I haven't paid you any of the attentions you've made it clear you don't welcome. And yet you're behaving as woodenly as if I've somehow disappointed you. Tell me, Countess, which of your impossibly high standards have I failed to meet this time?"

Stung, she retorted, "You weren't going to place a bet."

"And? It's not as if I killed someone. I enjoy wagering on races. And I think I'm free to change my mind if I wish."

"Is that what you call it? Freedom?"

"What is that supposed to mean?"

"I mean you had no intention of wagering, let alone against your own horse, until your friend Mister Bishop appeared."

North's lips were set in a hard line. "I don't recall asking you to approve my choice of friends, Countess."

"Not at all. You're free to choose whomever you wish to associate with."

"Countess," North said, "Alex Bishop has been my friend for many years. He supported me after my father's death. I owe him a great deal. Yes, I choose to be guided by his opinion, but that is because time has shown me it is an opinion worth heeding. I don't need a lecture from you on the appropriateness of his company."

"As you say. It's not for me to approve your choice of friends. I apologize for the insult." She didn't have the energy or the inclination to sound penitent.

North turned away and flicked the reins. As the team began to move, he said, "I would prefer you keep your opinions about my lifestyle to yourself, Countess."

"I will certainly do so in the future, your Highness."

They rode in angry silence back to the palace. Alison didn't wait for North to help her down. He didn't offer.

Chapter Seven

Alison's irritation with the Prince persisted for several days. He'd been arrogant. He'd been proud. He'd dared imply *she* was the one in the wrong. Well, it didn't matter to her if he wanted to be led by that awful Alexander Bishop. He was shallow and selfish and she didn't even like him. When, after five days, a sealed note with her title scrawled across it in his careless hand arrived, Alison snatched it up. Finally, an apology. But it merely requested the pleasure of her company at a concert featuring two of Aurilien's most popular opera singers. Alison crumpled the note into a ball and tossed it into the fire, then flung herself onto her bed. He knew she disliked concerts; this was a petty continuation of their battle. Typical. She went into the sitting room and penned a cold, formal acceptance. She didn't have to sink to his level. She would behave with propriety, not childishness.

The Prince arrived precisely on time that evening and offered Alison his arm with nothing more than a chilly, "Shall we go, your ladyship?" Alison responded with a curt nod. So he still thought himself wronged, after he'd spoken so rudely to her. Well, they didn't have to speak at all tonight.

They sat together near the edge of the concert hall, Alison clasping her hands tight before her to keep from drumming them on her knees with impatience. She did like music; she just liked it in company with something else, like a play or an opera. Watching two people sing about something that in isolation had no meaning bored her nearly to the point of leaping out of her seat and fleeing.

She covertly observed the Prince. North sat perfectly erect, giving no indication he was enjoying himself but not appearing bored, either. He really was handsome, not that it mattered to her at all, with those cheekbones and the strong curve of his jaw, the way his eyebrows swooped just the tiniest bit at the inner corners to draw attention to his absurdly blue eyes. He shifted minutely, and Alison whipped her gaze back to the performers, certain he knew she'd been watching him. It didn't matter how attractive he was, he was still shallow and incapable of thinking of her as anything but a potential conquest. What a fool she'd been to think they might ever be friends.

The lights came up, and Alison belatedly added her applause to that of the crowd. "Shall we take a turn about the room during intermission, your ladyship?" North said, his voice still cold. "Might as well make certain everyone sees how very friendly we are."

Alison stood and accepted his arm. "Even if we are not?" she said in a low voice.

"If we are not friendly, that's hardly due to me. You're the one who so high-handedly criticized me and my friend." He spoke so quietly his lips barely moved, then smiled at an elderly lady dripping with diamonds who bowed to him as they passed.

"Drawing attention to your poor-spirited behavior is hardly criticism." They'd reached the back of the room, which echoed with dozens of conversations so theirs was lost in the confusion, but she kept her voice low regardless.

North stopped and turned to face her, his face not showing any sign of the anger evident in his voice. Damn him. "I, poor-spirited? Because I failed to meet your expectations? I wonder that any man could ever do so, you seem so hell-bent on crushing the fun out of every experience."

"I beg your pardon?" Alison glanced around to see if anyone had heard that. "I am not the one who thinks women exist solely for his viewing pleasure!"

"I haven't made a single admiring comment all evening, much as I'd like to compliment you on that gown, and I've apologized for making you uncomfortable. You don't seem to be interested in giving me any credit for that. I'm beginning to think you had that sense of humor on loan."

"I—!"

A few chords rang out, indicating that the concert was about to begin. North glanced around and cursed. "I don't feel I need to excuse my behavior to anyone as judgmental as you."

"Better judgmental than completely incapable of making my own decisions!"

"You have the nerve—"

"You have the nerve—" she said exactly as he spoke.

They both went silent. North was finally glaring at her. She replayed their argument in her head, heard how shrewish she'd sounded, then began to laugh. "Your Highness, I apologize. My pride was so injured I made myself believe you were entirely in the wrong. I had no right to criticize your behavior and certainly none to speak ill of your friend, whom I barely know."

His eyes widened. "Countess, you don't have to apologize to me."

"Actually, milord, I think I do."

A smile spread across his face. "You're right. You were presumptuous."

"And *you* were arrogant."

They were almost the last ones still standing. The performers had again come to the front of the room, to general applause. "You're not enjoying yourself, are you," North said. Alison shook her head. North took her by the arm and drew her swiftly out of the room. "I see no reason for us to stay any longer, then," he said. They left the building and North led her to his waiting carriage, once again pulled up near the front doors. When the coach had set off along the street, North said, "We were both behaving like a couple of infants, I think."

"We were. How embarrassing. I thought I had better manners."

"So did I. You're the most correct and proper person I've ever met."

"I don't believe that's true."

"It is! You even sit like a correct and proper person. Do you even know how to slouch?"

"Do *you* even know what a corset is, milord?"

"Oh." North laughed. "All right, I hadn't considered that. We can't go home yet, you know."

"We can't? Why not?" The idea of returning to her suite, getting out of the detested corset and into a comfortable nightgown with a book and a glass of wine, had danced before her eyes, and the Prince's words had made it dissolve like chalk in rain.

"It's too early. Zara won't believe we've fulfilled her instructions." North sat back and gave her a steady look that had nothing of seduction in it. "Do you trust me? Or, I should say, *will* you trust me?"

Alison regarded him, his relaxed pose and those intent eyes. He hadn't behaved objectionably at all tonight, either. Perhaps she could give him the benefit of the doubt. "Yes," she said.

"Harvey," North called out to the driver, "take us up to Old Fort. I think you'll like this," he said to Alison. "It's—no, I think I'll let you see for yourself."

"Should I be filled with dread?"

"You said you'd trust me, right? I promise I have no ulterior motives." He turned to look out the window, where the tall, narrow mansions of brick and stone slipped by, their dark façades lit only by the street lamps' warm orange glow. Alison could smell snow on the air, and wondered how Kingsport looked now, where the first snows had fallen a week ago, blanketing the city with white. The small boats would all be locked up for the winter now, the larger fishing boats still going in and out of the harbor regardless of the weather. Waxwold Manor—had her father remembered to tell the gardeners to set out the bird feeders? Her mother had started the tradition, and although Alison suspected doing so was interfering with the natural order, she didn't have the heart to cancel it. He probably wouldn't order the Wintersmeet light Devices put up, with her not there. Martin Quinn was indifferent to every holiday except Alison's birthday, though the celebration was always the same: supper at an expensive restaurant and the gift of a rare book for her library at the manor. She would be returning from Aurilien just in time for it. The thought made her heart ache with homesickness as it hadn't yet since she arrived, and she turned her head further to keep North from seeing her eyes.

"So you won't tell me where we're going," she said to cover her emotional lapse. The last thing she needed was to cry in front of the Prince.

"It's the highest point in the city, and that's all I'll say," North said. Alison realized the coach had been ascending a gentle slope for several minutes. They were passing more mansions, more sprawling than those near the palace and more opulent. What was it about hills and wealth that the two so often went together? The lights were more widely spaced now, and shed a clearer, whiter light that flashed across the carriage windows, painting it first bright, then dark again. Beyond the mansions and the lights she could see the summit of the low hill Aurilien had been built around. She had read there had once been a fortress on that hill, but it had no source of water, and in the days before Devices that could burrow down hundreds of feet to reach hidden aquifers, it was ultimately indefensible and had been abandoned. Not that the current palace was any more defensible, with its sprawling wings and half a dozen entry points and the gate that was probably rusted open.

The coach came to a creaking stop. "This is it," North said, and helped her out of the carriage. Alison looked around. She saw nothing but the continued curve of the hill rising to the long-destroyed fortress and the patiently standing horses, the one on the left ducking his head as if he hoped to find a nosebag somewhere nearby.

North took her by the shoulders and turned her around. "*That*," he said, and Alison gasped, because laid out before her like a garment beaded with light lay all of Aurilien, girdled with walls of golden stone that glowed richly in the light of the Devices that burned all night long.

The lights made patterns: long lines marking out the grid of the business districts, curves where the homes of the wealthy circled the palace, sprinklings of glittering dust nearer the walls where the less wealthy lived, still bright thanks to millions of inexpensive Devices keeping the darkness, and the crime, at bay. To the right, a moving blotch lighter than the surrounding area showed where the lake North had mentioned lay, just outside the city walls, and to the left, a break in the clouds let the moon shine on fields dull and stubbly after the harvest.

"Over there," North said, pointing, and Alison looked at the palace, which seemed to burn white and gold from all the Devices lighting its roof and courtyards. "Can you see the front door? Look up and to the left."

Alison looked as instructed and saw a tiny spot of light that was an actual flame, not a Device, glowing high above the palace. "What is it?"

"Willow North's tower. They light the fire every night at sunset and it burns all night long. I don't know why. Something she wanted, I suppose. That's over two hundred years' worth of fires."

"Amazing," Alison breathed. "This really is astonishing. So beautiful."

"I hoped you'd like it," North said. He was standing close beside her, and for the first time she felt no awkwardness in his company. "My father brought me here when I was…ten, maybe? Just the two of us. I've never forgotten it."

Now she felt awkward. It was the most honesty she'd ever heard from him, and she shivered at it. "You're cold," North said, and put a hand on her arm. "I'm sorry, it didn't occur to me—my formal wear has a few more layers than yours—here." He removed his coat and put it around her shoulders, over her thin wrap, and now she felt *incredibly* awkward, because it was such an intimate gesture and he'd done it with no sly comments or suggestions. "Thank you," she said, and was certain her inner turmoil was evident in her voice. But he only said, "I think we can risk going back now," and helped her into the carriage.

They rode in silence back down the hill, and North said, "I think I should be honest with you."

Alison huddled further into his coat. "Yes?"

"That viewpoint...it's usually where lovers go. I didn't mean anything of the sort by it," he went on hurriedly, "but I thought I should warn you, before you tell people what we did this evening."

"I...thank you, milord," Alison said, grateful that he couldn't see how blotchy she'd gone. Of course it was a romantic rendezvous. But he hadn't said or done anything romantic, or made any suggestive comments, or told her how beautiful her breasts were in the light of the city. She'd felt comfortable with him for the first time, and that made her uncomfortable. *Don't let him fool you*, she told herself, *he's going to revert to form by tomorrow, and just think what would happen if you let him believe you really trust him when he doesn't deserve it.* But it was getting harder to believe the things she was telling herself, when all the evidence was pointing to a different conclusion.

"Still not Anthony?" he teased her.

"I don't think so, milord. After all, we still have five months and two weeks to go before we can be so familiar."

"Then I await that day with anticipation," he said with a smile and a wink, and she smiled back at him before she could remember to be cautious. *Not much longer, and you won't have to spend time with him,* that inner voice told her, *so what's the point?* Her inner voice appeared to be grasping for excuses now. If he stopped flirting with her, and went on being as open and natural as he'd been even when they were arguing...maybe he wasn't as lecherous as he'd seemed. Maybe they could be friends, after all.

"Thank you again for the view, milord, and for accepting my apology," she said when the carriage returned to the palace and North had helped her out of it. She hesitated, then extended her hand to him.

He looked a little surprised, but accepted it and bowed.

"And I'm sorry, for my part, that I took offense so deeply," he said. "May I have my coat back, milady Countess?"

Alison blushed again. "I'm terribly sorry, I forgot," she said, handing it to him. He draped it over his arm.

"Not at all," he said. "I imagine you regret ladies' fashion doesn't include oversized men's jackets. So much less restrictive than a corset."

"I intend to remove mine as soon as possible," she said, then heard her own words and wished the ground would open up and swallow her. Or him. North looked completely startled, then laughed and laughed until Alison had to either laugh with him or storm off in a fury. She chose embarrassed laughter.

"I want to point out, milady Countess," he said between snorts of laughter, "that I said nothing in response to what I'm sure you realize now was a completely inappropriate remark."

"I do realize that, milord, and I'm so grateful," Alison said, and dipped a graceful curtsey.

"Just so you're perfectly clear I mean to stand by my promise to respect your wishes," he said. "I would like us to be friends, your ladyship."

He was still smiling, but there was something about him that told Alison he was serious, and it startled her so much that she said, "I...think I would like that also, milord."

Back in her suite and free of the corset—she blushed with memory as Belle loosened its laces—she sat in front of the fire with her arms wrapped around her knees and watched the flames dance. Could he have changed so much in not quite three weeks? She could never be friends with a self-absorbed flirt who couldn't keep his eyes off her breasts, and now...it was just too big a change to be real. But was it changing, really, when he was simply revealing the person he was behind the swagger? *You don't know that's true,* her inner voice said, but she ignored it. *You're just lonely,* it taunted her, and she ignored it again. If North really was something more than the shallow Prince, her refusing to acknowledge it was just petty and fearful. And Alison Quinn would never let fear rule her.

Chapter Eight

"Alison, can I borrow your green satin shoes?" Philippa said, bursting into Alison's dressing room. She was wearing nothing but her corset and drawers and had a firm grip on her filmy stockings. "I changed my mind about what I'm wearing to the Berrises' ball and now my shoes don't match!"

"Go ahead," Alison said, and went back to combing her hair while Philippa rooted around in her wardrobe. Her own gown, violet silk with diamonds winking along the neckline, hung nearby. Philippa exclaimed in triumph and waved the dancing slippers in the air. "Aren't you glad our feet are the same size?" Alison said with a laugh at Philippa's expression of glee.

"Eternally so. I only wish the rest of me were your size, because I positively covet that cloth-of-gold dress of yours," Philippa said. "Don't you think it would suit my hair?"

"You know it would." Philippa's red hair stood out in all directions now, an effect only possible for someone who had tried on a dozen gowns and been satisfied with none of them. "Probably better than it does mine."

"Oh, bah, you're far prettier than I am, and with that hair you can wear anything," Philippa said placidly. "Thanks again for the shoes." She darted out the door and bumped into Belle, who squeaked. "Oh, I'm sorry, Belle!" she exclaimed. "Trust me not to look where I'm going."

"It's all right, milady," Belle said, but Philippa hadn't waited for her apology to be accepted. She advanced toward Alison and took the comb from her hand. "Let me do that for you, milady. Oh, I almost forgot." She dipped into a pocket in her pink uniform and pulled out a note. "The messenger just delivered it."

Alison turned it over and saw the North seal. How strange to realize just over two weeks ago she'd felt dread whenever she saw it. But it had only been two days since the concert, so why was he writing to her now? She broke the seal and unfolded the paper.

Countess,

You have behaved admirably toward my brother. Please consider your obligation fulfilled.

Zara North

Alison folded it again, slowly. So. No more forced outings. She never had to see North again if she didn't want to; any social events they both attended, such as the Berrises' ball, no doubt, were large enough they could easily avoid each other. No point in becoming friends now that they had no reason to spend time together; it was unlikely North would want to carry on the relationship now that it was unnecessary. He was a playboy and an accomplished flirt; she was an editor and a reader; they might share an interest in the theater, but that was all, and that wasn't really enough to build a friendship on. Her pleased feeling vanished. *I didn't really like him, anyway*, she thought, and despised herself for the ignoble thought.

The Berrises' mansion was one of those sprawling ones she'd seen when she and North drove up the hill, a memory that left her feeling a little empty now. She managed to smile and contribute a little to the conversation Simone and Carola were having about some minor nobleman they each thought was interested in the other one, but the idea of more than that wearied her. How unfortunate that she had to depend on the Dowager's carriage to take her home, or she would stand up for a few dances and make her escape. She closed her eyes briefly and told herself she was glad her penance was over.

When they arrived at the Berrises' front door, the Dowager took Alison's hand before she could exit the carriage and said, "Do cheer up, Alison dear. I know these social events are difficult for you, but you have made more friends than you realize."

"I have, Milady?" Had the Dowager been watching her that

closely?

"You always smile and have a kind word for anyone who has your attention," the Dowager said, "and I have never seen you refuse a request for a dance or for conversation. Other people notice these things too. And...." She bit her lower lip, hesitating. "And you have been so kind to my son when he had no reason to expect it. Thank you."

"I have not always been so kind, Milady," Alison stammered, "and I do not deserve such praise."

"I think you do, dear. Now, shall we go in? I predict you will have no shortage of partners, many of whom will ask you to dance not because of your beauty but because of your generosity of spirit. Don't blush, dear, you really don't do it well."

She felt uncomfortably blotchy, standing in the bright lights of the Berrises' ballroom, but before she could take more than a few steps, someone said, "Milady Countess! How good to see you!" and swept her away into the dance before she could do more than assent to it. She'd danced with the man before, but it astonished her that he was so genuinely happy to see her. The Dowager's last words to her echoed in memory as one partner after another approached her, men who looked at her eyes and not her bust line, and for the first time in...no, for the first time ever she was enjoying herself at a public event, no reservations, no qualifications.

After half a dozen dances she was hot and exhausted and cheerful and more than ready for a rest. She accepted a glass of punch from her last partner and chatted with him, trying to conceal the fact that she'd forgotten his name in the mad whirl of introductions and dancing, until a look of dismay swiftly crossed his face and was as quickly extinguished. "I beg your pardon," North said from behind her, "but I was hoping to ask the Countess for the pleasure of this dance. But I seem to have interrupted your conversation."

"Not at all, your Highness," the young man said with a bow, and accepted Alison's glass with no sign of resentment. "Wouldn't want to monopolize the Countess's time, yes? Your ladyship, it was a pleasure."

"Thank you for the dance, um...it was most enjoyable," Alison said, trying to make up for her lapse with a brilliant smile. She put her hand on North's arm and followed him to where the couples were forming a line. "I think you intimidated him," she said.

"Not on purpose," North said. He bowed to her as the music began, and she curtseyed low, conscious of how the neckline of her gown exposed her cleavage, but North's eyes never left her face. "You received a note from my sister?" he said as they took their first steps toward each other.

"I did, milord. It seems we no longer need share each other's company." Just saying the words gave her a pang she quashed before she could entertain it fully.

"It seems so." They separated to go down the line, bowing to the other dancers in turn, then joined hands once again. "Is it an unwelcome compliment to say I've enjoyed our time together?" he said.

"Not at all, milord, it has been most pleasant."

"It became pleasant, anyway. I'm not sure you enjoyed yourself very much that first time."

"I liked attending the play with you, milord."

"I had no idea how much fun that would be. I believe I owe you thanks for that." They separated again, went down the line, and came back together. "You know," he said off-handedly, "I saw *After the Spring Rains Fall* just started at the theater. I think I'd like to see it."

"I understand it's excellent. It's Flanagan's newest work and I've never seen it before, but Doyle says it's a tragedy and devastatingly sad."

"Why would anyone want to see something that made them sad?"

"I don't know what it is about tragedy that's so appealing.

95

Possibly it's because it draws out emotions we usually keep hidden and lets us express them without necessarily giving anything of ourselves away."

"That makes sense. You understand theater very well."

"Thank you, milord."

Silence fell again. "I was thinking," North said, "if you're not doing anything the night after tomorrow, you might like to come with me to see the play. If it's going to make me devastatingly sad, I'd like someone to share that with."

It was as if someone had lit a fire in that place where she normally only felt ice. "I would like that very much," she said, smiling at him, and then added, "Anthony."

His eyes widened, and then he smiled back at her, broadly. "I had no idea five months and—it's almost one week now, yes?—could pass so quickly. Alison."

The fire burned just a little brighter. "Well, I get very blotchy when I cry, so it's something I only do in front of friends," she said.

"There's going to be crying?"

Alison chuckled. "It's a Flanagan play. We might not be able to stop ourselves."

⚭

Alison clutched her handkerchief, which was sodden with tears, and closed her eyes as the house lights came up and applause filled the theater with a sound so loud she felt she was being swept by the tide. She swiped at her eyes one last time and clapped until her palms felt sore and the cast had taken their bows and left the stage. "That was incredible," she said. "I told you there would be crying."

"I didn't really believe you," Anthony said, wiping his own eyes, "and now my reputation as a carefree man about town is in jeopardy. I see now why you put up with Flanagan. He really is a genius."

"I wish he weren't so aware of it. He'd be less obnoxious." She drew a deep breath. "Am I presentable yet?"

"Still blotchy. How do they do the hanging scene? I don't suppose there are thirty Maximiliens waiting in the wings for their turn to dangle and choke."

"Why don't you ask the director? I think it's done with wires, but I'm not sure. From this distance, it's hard to tell if it *isn't* a different Maximilien every night. If Flanagan were director rather than playwright, he'd probably insist on it."

Anthony rose and gave her his arm. "If Flanagan were director, I imagine the cast would have lynched him before now."

Doyle pulled Alison aside the moment they both stepped backstage. "Allie, theater business," he said.

Alison said, "Just a moment. An—Tony, why don't you go ahead and I'll join you presently."

"I feel abandoned," he said with a smile, and continued down the hall to the green room.

"It's unbelievable," Doyle said. "It's only been four nights and we've already decided to extend the run to six weeks instead of four. I'd be thrilled if Jerald weren't so unbearably smug. This is going to make our reputation, Allie, not to mention our fortunes."

"That's wonderful," she said, grinning at him. "How's our director and her artistic temperament holding up?"

"Genevieve's flying high. She keeps trying to explain to anyone who'll listen how she came up with the hanging mechanism. Never mind that the stage manager actually engineered it."

"Well, she'll find a willing audience in Tony."

Doyle arched an eyebrow at her. "So it's *Tony* now, is it?"

"Shut up. He's a friend. Don't embarrass us both with your innuendo."

"I'm just saying you don't make friends easily, and you're the most reserved woman I've ever met. You remember when we were introduced? It took me weeks even to get you to call me Mister Doyle instead of 'sir'."

Alison laughed at the memory. "I just don't believe in casual intimacy. It encourages people to presume on a relationship."

"And by 'people' you mean men."

Alison stopped laughing. "Doyle, this sounds like it's shaping up to be a lecture."

"I'm sorry, Alison. No, I don't intend to lecture you. All I'm saying is I'm glad to see you relaxed enough to make new friends." He hooked his arm through hers and they strolled toward the green room. "Hear that?" Laughter rolled down the hallway toward them. "That must mean Jerald's not here tonight. They're never that uninhibited when he's around." He quickened his step.

"—without his pants!" shouted Larrick, tonight's Maximilien, clearly not dead. The actors, and Anthony, roared at whatever joke he'd just told, which, knowing Larrick, had almost certainly been graphically sexual. "Countess!" he exclaimed, and bounded over to kiss her on the cheek. "Was I or was I not magnificent tonight?"

"You were outstanding, Larrick," she said. "I half expected to find you draped over the sofa with your eyes and tongue bulging out." He might be standing upright, but Eve Kenford, the leading lady, had her arm draped over Anthony's shoulders and her considerable bosom pressed to his side. Irrationally, she felt depressed and angry all at once. It was none of her business whether he wanted to involve himself with a cheap tart like Eve, but she had begun to think better of his judgment.

"You were right, Alison, they do it with wires," Anthony said. He removed Eve's arm from around his neck without looking at her and came to join them. "It goes through the noose down the back of his coat and attaches to his belt. It really is most realistic," he told Larrick, who preened.

"It is. And congratulations to you all. I anticipate this will be more popular than the last, and I'm sure you know *Two Came to Kingsport* often played to a sold out house. I loved tonight's performance so much. Thank you." They cheered her, though she was sure most of them were really cheering themselves.

Anthony slipped his arm through hers. "I promised Mother I'd bring you back before midnight," he whispered in her ear. "Much as I'm enjoying the company, I'd rather not face her displeasure."

"Neither would I," she murmured back, though privately she had trouble imagining what the sweet-tempered Dowager's displeasure might look like.

They emerged from the theater into a thin but persistent drizzle that forced them to dash for the carriage door and fall, laughing, into their respective seats. Alison put down the hood of her cloak and wiped a few raindrops from her cheeks. "That first snow was deceptive. I didn't realize autumn in Aurilien was so rainy," she said. "It's not at all like Kingsport."

"We get more snow in the winter, now and then, but mostly it just gets dreary," Anthony said. "You'll be tired of it long before winter's over."

"I expect to be gone before winter's over. My six months are up before the Spring Equinox."

"True. I'd forgotten." Anthony stretched out his long legs. "You should visit the Zedechen Bethel just before Wintersmeet. They set up Devices in the old sanctuary, around the statues of the lost gods, and whatever it is they're made of glows in reaction. And you might like to see the permanent exhibit of artifacts from before the founding of Tremontane."

"What I *want* is to see the Royal Library just once before I leave."

"Why don't you go, then? My mother can't possibly occupy that much of your time."

"It's not the time. It's the Royal Librarian. I'm apparently not good enough to be allowed past the scriptorium because I don't have the robe." She sighed. "At least I can look at the books, if they can find them. I saw one of Landrik Howes's plays the other day, the first folio.

It was beautiful."

"Not as beautiful as the performance, I'd think."

"No, but beautiful in a different way. I wonder if Flanagan's book of plays is going to be as revered hundreds of years from now. I almost envy him. It must be so exciting to feel a play coming together."

"I think it would be exciting to be an actor. If the play is exciting to us as spectators, I can't imagine how invigorating it must be to actually be on the stage."

"I know Larrick, for one, is happiest when he's playing a role," Alison said, covering her mouth to yawn. She was going to be useless in the morning. "I've seen him the day after a play closes and he's always deep in a bottle or talking about how he'll never amount to anything again. Then he gets a new script and he's back to being the same old foulmouthed genius."

Anthony chuckled. "I don't think I've ever heard dirtier jokes."

"You've never heard Eve tell the one about the pickle."

Now he laughed out loud. "Which one is Eve?"

"Corinna. She was standing next to you when I came in." *Trying to mold herself to fit your body.*

"Oh, yes. I suppose I was too caught up in the story to notice."

Alison felt strangely comforted by this. She looked out the window and watched the rain fall, making the street shine in the places where the lamplight spread over the cobbles. Across from her, Anthony fell silent as well. She assumed he too was watching the street pass until she glanced over and saw him watching her, his elbow propped on the window's edge. "What is it?" she asked.

He shook his head. "I was just—nothing." He turned to look out the window.

"That was an awfully intent stare for 'nothing'."

"It was a line of thought I'm sure you wouldn't want me to pursue."

She went cold inside. "Something about my profile, no doubt?"

She knew her voice had an edge to it and didn't care.

"I was wondering," he said, not taking offense at her tone, "why you hold people at a distance. Why formality is so important to you."

The cold feeling turned to ice. "It appears to be the evening for people asking me about that. Doyle said much the same thing," she said lightly.

"I'm sorry to have brought it up, then," he said, never taking his eyes off the road.

They rode in silence for some while. "It just seems to me," he went on, "that it's a lonely way to live."

"Better lonely than miserable," she said, then wondered why she'd let him draw her out. Something about the dark, and the warm confines of the carriage against the cold and rainy night, seemed to have lowered her reserve.

"I think happiness is worth the possibility of being miserable."

"Then that is where we disagree, your Highness." She knew her mistake as the words left her lips. "Anthony, I'm sorry. That was rude of me."

"It's clearly an unpleasant topic for you. I apologize for bringing it up." Now he sounded offended. Alison bit her lip and continued to stare out the window.

After another long moment, she said, not looking at him, "I was sixteen, just barely an adult, when men started paying attention to me. It took me far too long to understand there were only three things they were interested in, and none of those three things was me. My father did his best, but…I'd lost my mother, newly come into the title, and I was…looking for reassurance, I think."

"What three things?"

"My fortune. My title. My body, obviously." She knew she sounded bitter. *You would think, after all these years, it wouldn't still bother me so much.* "There's only so much disillusionment you can bear before you begin to assume the worst of people before you've even met them.

Easier not to let them get close at all." She traced a line in the light fog where her breath struck the glass, a straight mark that paralleled the passing street lamps. Anthony said nothing. *All those men, all those times I thought they loved me when they never even saw me. What a fool I was.* She closed her eyes and cursed herself. She should never have told him anything this personal. Yes, she enjoyed his company, yes, she thought of him as a friend, but this went beyond friendship into an intimacy she didn't want to share with anyone, even her father.

Anthony shifted a little in his seat. "I'm sorry," he said, with a depth of emotion that startled her.

"What are you sorry for?"

"I'm sorry I gave you so much pain, when we first met," he said. "I was thoughtless. Alison, I should never have—" He broke off, and Alison saw he was looking down at his hands, closed loosely into fists on his knees. "I mean, it never occurred to me that my compliments might be offensive to anyone. All the other women seemed to enjoy them," he added, almost plaintively, and despite herself she smiled.

"You say what women want to hear," she said, "but you do it with a kind of possessiveness, as if a woman's beauty belongs to you and it's your right to say anything you like about it. It was never about me. It was always about you."

He raised his head quickly, as if startled. "That—" he began, paused, and said, "You have a gift for speaking truth, Countess."

"I'm sorry if I offended you."

"Of course you didn't. You're entirely right. I wish someone had told me sooner, that's all."

Impulsively, she leaned across and took his hand. "You are a good man," she said. "Your mother told me that once, back at the beginning. She was right."

His eyes were colorless in the lamplight. "She said that?" he said. He chuckled again. "My mother has always had a good opinion of me despite the evidence."

Something about the way he looked at her made her uncomfortable. She withdrew her hand and leaned back. "This is not the conversation I imagined us having on the ride home," she said.

"What did you imagine?"

"Oh…we'd talk about the play, and the actors, and I would tell you stories of how Genevieve gets so tense three nights before a performance that she hides backstage with a bottle of gin and then starts singing Veriboldan love songs, but she doesn't speak Veriboldan, so the words are all wrong—" He laughed. "And then you would say I love the theater as much as you love your horses—"

"Would I? Yes, probably. You lose all your reserve, when you're there. It's refreshing."

"I feel at home around people who do nothing but lie for a living. Somehow I find it more honest than the real world."

"That's an interesting way to look at it."

"If you both know the other person is lying, in a backwards way it's like truth."

The carriage came to a stop, and Anthony assisted her down. "It's so much nicer not to be on display, don't you agree? May I escort you back to Mother's apartment, milady Countess?"

"Thank you for your consideration, your Highness."

He took her by a route she hadn't seen before, through a much older part of the palace that looked more like the Library's old stone and dark corners than like the polished and carpeted hallways she was familiar with. "You *do* know where you're going, right?" she asked. She glanced down a dark cross-corridor and told herself she was only imagining movement in its depths.

"Of course. I used to run around this place all the time when I was younger. Or…no, this doesn't look familiar…."

She swatted his arm. "You're not funny."

"You're laughing, aren't you? See, this hall leads to the east wing, and then it's just a few more steps to Mother's apartment." He spun her, with a flourish, to come to a stop at the foot of the slope that led up to the Dowager's door. Alison laughed again, then stifled her humor, conscious of the two guards just up the hall who thought heaven only knew what of that display.

"Thank you for your company, Anthony," she said, curtseying just a little.

"It was entirely my pleasure. No, Alison, wait a moment," Anthony said, putting his hand on her arm to stop her. He seemed to be searching for something to say, and eventually came out with, "You forgive me, right? For thinking only of myself and not of your feelings?"

"Of course," she said. "You made such an effort to redeem yourself, how could I not appreciate that?"

"Thank you. And thank you for telling me the truth tonight. I think people often tell me only what I want to hear. I'm glad there's one person who isn't my sister who'll tell me what I *need* to hear."

"I promise to always tell you the truth, if you'll do the same for me."

"Agreed." He kissed her hand and was gone almost before she could register the touch of his lips against her skin. She stood motionless until he disappeared around the corner, then walked slowly up the hall to the Dowager's door, removing her cloak and draping it over her arm despite the lingering dampness. The guards showed no sign they even knew she was there, but she nodded at them anyway. She felt drained now, as if she'd been doing something far more exhausting than watching a play and having an uncomfortable conversation. *You shouldn't have told him that,* her inner voice said, *he'll just use it against you,* but she was too tired to take that voice seriously. He'd apologized, and he'd really meant it, and he was nothing at all like she'd thought he was. He was her friend. And how glad she was that that was true.

Chapter Nine

"So, Alison, how long does a play last?" Elisabeth Vandenhout said, and scooped a tiny, demure bite of soft-boiled egg into her mouth. Alison took a long drink of her hot, milky, sweet coffee. Another two of these and she'd be ready to open her eyes. Just her bad luck that Elisabeth knew this and delighted in carrying on a conversation with her every morning across the Dowager's white and glossy breakfast table. She sent up a brief prayer to ungoverned heaven that Elisabeth would choke on her egg and be struck speechless for the next four months.

"Three hours, or thereabouts," she said, and sipped her coffee more slowly. Elisabeth was going somewhere with this, and it wasn't going to be somewhere pleasant. Her head was throbbing, as usual, and being polite to Elisabeth wasn't going to be easy.

"So you must have been out late last night," Elisabeth said.

"Yes, that would make sense, wouldn't it?" Alison smiled sweetly at Elisabeth. It had been even later than Elisabeth guessed; she and Anthony had spent nearly an hour after the performance arguing cheerfully about the ending of *Rapture Song*. She was right, of course, but Anthony had held his own, and they'd ended up laughing so hard the carriage driver had given them a very strange look when they'd finally emerged. She had no idea going to the theater in company could be so much fun.

"I just wonder," Elisabeth said, just as sweetly, "that you're spending so much time with the Prince. People are beginning to talk."

"Really? I wonder that *people* don't have better things to do with their time."

"Now, Elisabeth," the Dowager said, "surely you don't think Alison would be carrying on a secret courtship with my son, practically under my nose?"

Elisabeth went pink. "No, of course not, Milady. But I thought Alison should know, because of course she's concerned about how her reputation reflects on you. And after what happened at the Equinox Ball—"

"Elisabeth, your concern for Alison is touching, but I must remind you that *you* are not the keeper of her reputation, and isn't that fortunate! I'm sure each of us has enough trouble tending to her own affairs without worrying about those of our friends. And I think you may be exaggerating these rumors, because I have to say I haven't heard anything of the sort. It *is* my son we're talking about, after all." The Dowager's smile didn't reach her eyes, and Alison suddenly understood what Anthony had meant about his mother's displeasure. Elisabeth went from pink to red.

"Of course, Milady. Alison, I beg your pardon if I overstepped."

"Not at all, Elisabeth, and I'm glad you're so concerned." Alison glanced at the Dowager, who had gone back to spreading jam on a toast triangle. Granted that Elisabeth seemed to delight in finding ways to needle her, but how many other people might assume she and the Prince were romantically involved? Now that she thought about it, they *had* spent much time together in the last five weeks, and to anyone who only observed them at a distance, it probably did look similar to courtship. What kind of whispers were going around Aurilien about them?

She poured herself more coffee, mixed in cream and probably too much sugar, and helped herself to some melon chunks. There wasn't much she could do about those rumors, short of seeing Anthony less frequently, and that idea made her stomach, always a little sensitive at breakfast, feel sick. Well, if she couldn't do anything about them, there was no point in worrying about it. And she certainly wasn't going to let other people's low minds ruin her new friendship.

Elisabeth seemed to have felt the Dowager's rebuke, because she said nothing more, and Alison's headache diminished to the point that she could give the woman a pleasant smile before leaving the table. She dressed in comfortable old trousers and a soft shirt; the Dowager was paying calls that morning, and a quiet morning reading sounded like a wonderful idea. She sat at her vanity table, combing her hair and making a face at how frizzy it had decided to be that morning, when someone knocked at the door. She rose to answer it and met Belle halfway. "Milady the Dowager would like to see you, milady," she said.

The Dowager's dressing room was pale pink rather than white but still as gilded as the rest of the apartment. The Dowager sat in front of a mirror easily as tall as Alison was while a pink-uniformed maid brushed her short hair. "Thank you, Justine, that will be all," the Dowager said, and Justine bowed and left the room, leaving Alison alone with the Dowager.

"You wanted to see me, Milady?" Alison said.

"Sit down, Alison," the Dowager said, indicating a low stool a few feet away. Alison sat. "Now, tell me the truth."

"The…the truth, Milady?"

"Zara told me she'd released you and Anthony from the responsibility she put on you. Why are you still spending time with one another?"

"Well…we're friends, Milady. We both enjoy the theater."

"And that's all?" The Dowager's gaze was uncharacteristically sharp.

"What more could there be, Milady?"

"Don't be disingenuous, dear. Are you romantically involved with my son?"

Alison gasped. "No, Milady!"

"You needn't sound so shocked. Would it be so terrible if you were?"

"I—" Was she the only one who didn't think her relationship with Anthony was romantic? "I didn't mean to be rude, Milady, and

Anthony is…he's a good man, and of course…but no, we're not romantically involved."

"Oh. I'm sorry to hear that." The Dowager turned away and looked at herself in the mirror. "But I suppose he really isn't the sort of man…you know he's had a number of inappropriate affairs, it's common knowledge. I'm just so grateful none of them resulted in a child. An entailed adoption—such a nightmare. But you deserve better, I suppose."

"I don't think less of him for having made a few mistakes," Alison said. "And I don't know that I am such a perfect person as to only deserve someone else who's perfect."

"Oh, Alison," the Dowager said. "You are exactly the sort of woman I wish Anthony would fall in love with. I don't suppose you…you *are* friends, you say…that you might someday…?"

She remembered how serious Anthony had looked that night three weeks ago, apologizing to her, and how his face was transformed when he laughed, and felt terribly uncomfortable. "We're just friends, Milady," she said. "But I think your son is deserving of a good woman, whomever she may turn out to be."

The Dowager smiled and patted Alison's hand. "Thank you, my dear," she said. "You should go and fix your hair. Forgive me, but it's terribly frizzy today."

Alison returned to her own rooms and let Belle finish her toilette, keeping a blush off her cheeks through willpower alone. Romantically involved with Anthony. She barely dared call him friend, for heaven's sake. It probably should have occurred to her that Anthony's reputation as a romancer of women would lead others to think she was just another of his conquests. The thought made her feel terribly uncomfortable. They *were* together often, and she didn't think he was squiring anyone else around town, so maybe that made sense. Well, that and the fact that people tended to assume physical beauty was enough on its own to compel someone to fall in love. It was true

Anthony was the most handsome man she'd ever seen, but she'd learned from her past mistakes, and if she were going to fall in love with someone, she wanted that person to be kind and honest and funny and share her interests, and handsome was just a bonus. *He's kind and funny and he shares your interests,* her fickle inner voice told her, *and he was more honest than anyone you've ever met, after the play,* and she grabbed her book and flung herself into the sitting room chair. She was going to ruin everything if she couldn't keep her thoughts under control. And she barely knew him. And she wasn't interested in falling in love, anyway.

Someone knocked on the door, then opened it without waiting for a response. "Sorry to interrupt," Anthony said, "but if you aren't doing anything important, I thought you might like to tour the palace. It's more interesting than it sounds."

"I'd like that," she said, setting her book on the arm of her chair, then clutching it to keep it from falling off the padded, curved surface. "I was just reading."

"Did you borrow a book from the Royal Library, then?" Anthony lounged in the doorway while she found a pair of shoes. She'd never seen him dressed so informally before, in a buttoned, collarless white shirt with loose gray trousers instead of his formal fitted frock coat and satin knee breeches.

"No, they don't loan them out. This one came from my library at home. It's an old favorite."

"Why would you read a book more than once? Or is that a stupid question? I'm not much of a reader."

They crossed the white-carpeted antechamber and Alison waited for Anthony to hold the door for her; it wasn't a custom she really cared about, but it seemed to matter to him, so she never made an issue of it. "It's not a stupid question," she said. "I've always thought it's because you're a different person, every time you re-read a book, and you learn things your earlier self wouldn't have noticed or wouldn't have cared about. Or sometimes it's just because the story is an old favorite, and it's a comforting reminder of good things."

"I can understand that. There are places I go back to, more than once, because of what they mean to me. I'll have to show you some of them today." He glanced down at her, and added, "You know, you look very different without—" His mouth closed abruptly, and his cheeks went a little pink.

"Without what? You have the strangest expression."

"I was going to say 'without your dress'."

Alison started laughing. "You—" she began, and couldn't say anything else. "I don't know what to say to that," she finally said. "I'm so glad you didn't keep that thought to yourself."

"I'm glad you weren't offended at it," he said. "Obviously I meant you look very different in, shall we say, civilian clothes."

"I dress this way all the time, at home. I think I've worn more gowns in the last two months than I did all last year. Where are we going?"

"Out to the southwest wing, first. That's all guest quarters, but they've had a dual role as unofficial museums since before the Norths came to power—possibly before the Valants, too. Personally, I think we should put most of it in an actual museum, but that's a complicated project with a low priority. Through here." He pushed open a door black with age, leaning heavily on it to make it move, and waved Alison through.

The door opened onto a pillared, vaulted corridor tiled in squares the color of old blood, two feet on a side, some of them cracked, with black mortar dividing them as if someone had outlined them in ink. Marble pillars rose to support arches curving across the copper ceiling in which was reflected the wavy outlines of the floor tiles. Pots more than waist-high to Alison sat at the bases of the pillars, still filled with earth that smelled stale and dead and bare of plants. The smell of cedar rose from doors lining the hall between the pillars, each knob made of faceted crystal that looked dull with dust, as if they hadn't been touched in a hundred years. Light came from Devices set into the capitals of the columns, shedding a dim light that was probably filtered through more dust. "How are they still glowing?" Alison said.

"Someone comes in here once a year to renew the source," said Anthony. "Apparently that's all they do. Housekeeping is supposed to keep the entire palace clean, but it seems they're not as diligent in areas they know aren't being used. Hard to imagine this place used to be thronged with people. Now that the royal family is reduced to just Zara and me, it echoes. And I don't even live here."

"You don't?"

"I have a townhouse. Much more convenient for parties and card games and the like." He put his hand on a doorknob, made a face, and wiped his palm on his trousers. "I promise it gets nicer."

"I've never been bothered by a little dust."

Anthony opened the door and showed her into a room almost entirely filled with a four-poster bed. Its pink counterpane and pillows showed their original color of deep magenta in their creases. "I thought this might interest you," he said. "Landrik Howes stayed here for six months, supposedly while he was writing *Death and the Countess.* So doubly interesting, though I doubt you'd like Death to come for you."

Alison moved around the bed and ran her fingers along the dresser's narrow surface, then opened the top drawer. It was empty. "That's one of his most famous plays," she said. "Do you suppose the Library has the folio?"

"I don't know. It's possible. Come, let me show you something else."

For someone who didn't live in the palace, Anthony was remarkably knowledgeable about it, as if he'd spent a great deal of time roaming its halls. The southeast wing truly was a museum, filled with marble and olivewood statuary and gold-framed paintings Alison agreed would be better off on public display somewhere. There were bathrooms with sunken tubs the size of a small country and tiny nooks with windows that looked out over unexpected parts of the palace and disused ballrooms with mirrored walls that looked as if they went on forever. One room held rows of green shelves upon which sat cloisonné urns with golden lids. "Former royal pets," Anthony said, and Alison made a face. "Don't look like that. It was quite the tradition, years ago. They have nameplates and little pictures to say what kind of animal it was."

Alison looked closely. "Someone had a pet rat?" she said.

"And someone else had a pet crow. To each his or her own, I suppose."

They walked a long, narrow corridor with round windows near the ceiling that was lined with portraits of the kings and queens of Tremontane, all the way back to the semi-mythical Kraathen of Ehuren, who'd united the three warring tribes and made the first bond between man and ungoverned heaven. Alison stopped for a long time in front of Queen Zara's portrait. "She looks so young," she said.

"Zara's always looked young for her age," Anthony said. "It was a struggle for her to command respect from the Council after our father's death because most of them still thought of her as the child they'd known all those years. But she's strong and ruthless. She really hates this painting. Says it makes her think of a memorial, as if she's already dead."

"It's a good likeness, though."

"Very. Shall we go? There's one last thing I wanted to show you."

They passed the wide central corridor that led to the north wing and ended up in a familiar hallway of dark, dimly-lit stone. "I've already been here," Alison said.

"I was hoping we could see a little more," Anthony said, and opened the scriptorium door for her. It was far emptier than she'd seen it before, with only two people reading at the desks and a lone apprentice sharpening pencils at the end of the librarian's desk. The skeletal man—Bancroft, she really ought to call him Bancroft no matter how objectionable he was—was nowhere in sight. A librarian Alison knew as Baxter left off rummaging in the cupboards and came around the desk to meet them halfway to the catalog.

"Excuse me. The Countess and I would like to see the Library," Anthony told Baxter. The man glanced from Alison to Anthony and back again.

"Not allowed to see the Library," he said. "No one goes in but the librarians."

"Does that include you?" Alison asked. Baxter nodded.

"Then I'm sure if you accompany us it will be all right," Anthony said.

Baxter looked at each of them in turn again. "Don't think so," he said, but he sounded uncertain.

"What seems to be the problem?" Bancroft said from behind them. Alison cursed mentally. Someone ought to put a bell on him.

"Your assistant was about to show us the Library," Anthony said.

"He was certainly not. No one sees the Library."

"Master Bancroft," Anthony said, his voice quiet but intent, "I recognize your authority here. I also recognize that in a sense I own this Library. The lady and I simply wish to see the room. We have no desire to handle your collection or to intrude further on your time. I don't see that this is an unreasonable request. Can you not spare five minutes?"

"Your Highness, you may be this Library's sponsor—although I think it is more truthful to say your sister is—but I am, as you say, responsible for it. I cannot set policy aside for anyone, even you. Even for the Queen, should she ask it, which she never would because she respects my authority. If there is a book you would like to see, you may request it. Otherwise, I suggest you go elsewhere for your entertainment." He glared at Alison; she could clearly hear him thinking *No question who put him up to this.* She glared back at him. He was obnoxious and rude and had really poor personal hygiene, and maybe she could have put up with the latter if they were friends, but that was never going to happen and she was tired of being polite.

Anthony looked as if he was going to erupt. Alison laid her hand on his arm, saying nothing, and he took a deep breath and stepped back. "Thank you for your time," he said, and turned away.

He seethed all the way down the hall until Alison grasped his arm and made him stop. "You see how frustrating it is to deal with him," she said. "I should have let you hit him."

He looked at her, startled. "I wasn't going to hit him," he said. "I was going to start shouting. And then I was going to take his key away from him and open the damned door."

She covered her mouth to suppress a giggle. "Oh, that would have been lovely. And the Queen would have been furious with you."

"I don't care. It was supposed to be a surprise for you. I mean, I've been in there before, and I can tell you all about it, but I knew you'd appreciate seeing it better than I did when I was fourteen."

A warm tangle of emotions, pleasure and happiness and a pang of sympathy for him, filled her heart. "Anthony," she said, "that is without question the nicest thing anyone has ever done for me. Even if it didn't work out."

He made an exasperated face. "Alison, I don't understand why he won't let anyone in. The last Royal Librarian—no, the one before the skeleton's predecessor—he didn't have any problems with it. I was even required to see it. I think it's strange."

"I think there are a lot of strange things about that Library." She took his arm. "Tell me what it looks like."

"Big. Dark." He grinned at her. "I was fourteen. I don't remember much except that I was thinking about the new horse Father had bought for me and how I could be riding it if I didn't have to look at a bunch of boring books."

She laughed. "You must remember more than that."

"The windows are high, and I don't know how recently they'd been cleaned. It smelled like old paper and dust. And the shelves seemed to go on for miles."

"Wait—dust? Not dampness? Because the few books I've been able to handle have felt a little…it's hard to explain the sensation, but damp is a decent approximation."

"No. I remember because the Librarian said these were the perfect conditions to keep books, that dampness would ruin them. They have a Device that keeps it that way. Or should do."

"True." So what had changed in the last, how old was Anthony now, the last nine years?

"It was very tidy. I remember asking if he, the Librarian, knew where everything was, and he said he had a system."

"I wonder what it is. Oh, right, if I could go inside I'd be able to find out! Don't make that face, Anthony, that wasn't directed at you. Bancroft has his head so far up his ass he's practically looking out his own mouth."

Anthony let out a choked laugh. "Language, Countess!"

"Sorry. It's a measure of how frustrated I am with him. How did he even get appointed in the first place?"

"You don't know? The Scholia chooses the Royal Librarian and sends him to us when the previous one retires. It's always a him, too. I don't know why."

"Then it sounds as if the Scholia has their collective heads up their—"

"By heaven, Alison, you can be crude when you want to be, can't you?"

She sighed. "I know. It's one of my many flaws."

"I haven't been keeping track of them, but I don't think there are all *that* many."

"You haven't known me long enough."

They had reached the hall to the Dowager's apartment, but

Anthony kept walking. "Are you ready for dinner?" he said.

"I'm hungry, but at the risk of sounding uncivil, you didn't say anything about dinner or I would have changed."

"Oh. Yes. Well, I meant to ask you if you would have dinner with Zara and me, but I suppose I forgot."

Alison felt herself go blotchy. "If you'd said that, I would have changed into something *nice*."

"No need to be embarrassed. Zara's likely to be as dressed down as I am. Come, you don't want to go back and eat with all those chattering women, do you?"

Alison considered. "I suppose not. But you'll have to carry the conversation."

"Don't be so sure. Zara is good at drawing people out."

The east wing bore the marks of the Dowager's decorating taste. A large open space carpeted in a familiar blinding white was filled with couches upholstered in lemon yellow and spring green, outlined in gilt, and mirrors caught what little sunlight there was on that overcast autumn day and spread it around to make the room cheerful, if a little overdone and uncomfortably padded. "It's rather ornate for my taste," Anthony said as if he'd read her mind, "but Zara doesn't care enough to change it. Usually it's the Consort who does."

"Didn't the Queen...I'd heard she was thinking of marriage."

"Hah. Any time she meets more than once with a single man aged fifteen to fifty, that rumor goes around again. Stefan Argyll's a good man, but not nearly strong enough a personality to match Zara. Here, this is the dining room."

The dining room looked as if the Dowager hadn't ever set foot in it. It was paneled in dark oak with black moldings, and a floral carpet in tones of rust red and ochre covered most of the hardwood floor. The dining table, twice as long as the Dowager's, was set for three, but Zara wasn't there. Anthony held Alison's chair for her exactly as if they were dining formally, then sat down across from her. "Don't worry, we're just a little early," he said, putting his napkin in his lap. "I hope you're not too hungry, because despite my sister's instructions, chef won't send the food out unless she's here."

"Which I am, now," the Queen said, coming out of a concealed door behind the table. "It's good to see you, Countess. Thank you for joining us." She was dressed even less formally than her brother, which eased Alison's mind.

"Thank you for inviting me, your Majesty."

"You will call me Zara, Alison Quinn. Don't make me make it a royal command."

"Very well, Zara." She cast an embarrassed look at Anthony, who looked amused.

"I wish I'd thought of that. It took me weeks to get her to call me by my name," he said to his sister.

"You aren't as ruthless as I am, Anthony." She sat back to allow the server to set out the first course, then helped herself. "We don't stand on ceremony for these dinners, so please serve yourself whatever looks appetizing."

"Thank you, your—Zara."

Zara glanced at her brother. "You weren't joking about how formal she is."

"Would you both stop talking about me as if I weren't here?" Alison said, annoyed. The Queen looked at her. Her mouth twitched just a little. Alison stared, then began to laugh. "You *are* ruthless, aren't you?"

"It's one of my better traits," Zara said. "Did Anthony show you the palace?"

"Most of it, I think."

"Not the most important part," Anthony growled. "Zara, did you know that librarian who looks like a walking skeleton wouldn't let us into the Library?"

"Why not?"

"Because he has his head stuck up his—"

"Anthony, if you don't like me saying it, I don't think you should either."

Anthony gave Alison a sour look. "His only reason was 'because I said so'."

Zara took another bite of salad. "That's odd. Alison, why might he refuse someone entrance?"

"Why do you ask me?"

"Because of the three of us at this table, you are the expert on this subject. Is there some reason it might be necessary to protect a library from outsiders?"

"If you were worried about vandalism—but that would only mean restricting access to people who knew how to handle the books, and I think I'd qualify for that latter category." Zara nodded. "The possibility of theft. A decaying collection that shouldn't be handled, but even then you could permit access under supervision. It sounds to me as if Bancroft just wants control. Some people are like that."

"Indeed." Zara took another bite. Alison applied herself to her food and cast about for something she could say to royalty. She glanced at Anthony, who made a face at her. She nearly choked on her mouthful of food and had to cover her mouth with her napkin, thought about kicking him under the table, and realized her nervousness was beginning to evaporate.

"I'm interested in the Library's new acquisitions," Zara said abruptly. "I understand the publishing industry has made great strides in the last thirty years, since the development of the new printing Devices."

"It's true. Quinn Press alone will publish almost five hundred new titles this year thanks to the new Devisery. And we expect that number to grow exponentially as we improve our processes."

"Is that what you do, then? Processes?"

"No, I'm an editor. And I handle odd jobs for my father."

"And yet I understand you studied at the Scholia. Why not take the robe? You seem more than capable of the work."

"Thank you, Zara, but there's more to it than the studying." How to put this politely? "The Scholia is as much a political entity as a scholastic one. Taking the robe means...knowing the right people. Having the right opinions. I was interested in becoming a librarian, yes, but not at that cost. I just loved books and wanted to share them with others. So I became an editor."

"I suppose being in and out of your father's business all your life had something to do with that," Anthony said.

"Probably. And there's a certain pleasure in being able to shape someone else's words."

"Not control them, then?" Zara asked.

"Some editors do. Some authors need that. I like having a partnership with my authors. Though sometimes that's just not possible." She rolled her eyes at Anthony, who laughed.

"I'm missing something," Zara said.

"The playwright I told you about," Anthony said. "Alison is his editor."

"Forgive me," said Zara, "but would there even be an interest in reading plays as opposed to seeing them performed?"

"There's a great deal of interest here in Aurilien, where there are so few real theaters. People don't often have the chance to see performances, but the plays are still powerful literature."

"Zara, I still think you should sponsor a theater," Anthony said.

"I said I'd consider it. I do have other things to worry about, brother. Alison, would a book of plays by this man be something the Royal Library should acquire?"

"Oh, definitely," Alison said, then added, "provided you could convince Bancroft they were worthy literature. Access to the Library isn't all he controls. They haven't bought a new book in two years."

"Really." Zara pushed her plate away. "How strange. The Royal

Library is supposed to acquire new books all the time. I wonder that Bancroft's standards are so high." She tapped her finger against her lips. "Very strange."

"It's not all that's strange," Anthony said. "Alison says the environment is all wrong for storing books, and there are books missing from the catalog."

Zara looked Alison's way. "Are there," she said in that same tone. "Missing, or destroyed?"

"They say destroyed. But I suppose some may have gone missing over time. It's a very old library."

"But ten years ago the environment was perfect. How could it have changed?"

"I don't know. I haven't been inside to see."

"Maybe I should look into this." Zara signaled to the server to bring dessert. "I feel I've left the Library to the care of the Scholia Masters without taking a personal interest."

"I'm sure you have so many other things to think about," Alison said.

"We're the caretakers of the oldest collection of literary history in the country. I should at least be aware of what's going on inside it. Alison, thank you for bringing this to my attention."

"I—it's my pleasure."

Zara cocked an eyebrow at her. "I know perfectly well you simply care too much about books to let this go. I'm surprised I haven't had a complaint about you from Bancroft, given what I've heard about how persistent you are. No, don't be embarrassed, it was a compliment. I don't like the man much myself." She finished her dessert and waved away the server's offer of coffee. "I have to go back to work. Please stay as long as you like." She exited via the same invisible door she'd come in by.

Anthony and Alison looked at each other. "She's like a force of nature," Alison said.

"Yes, a tidal wave sweeping everything in her path," Anthony agreed. "Will you take coffee?"

"Please."

They chatted about trivialities for a while, then they rose and Anthony escorted Alison back to the Dowager's apartments. "Thank you again for the tour, and dinner," Alison said. "And I still think trying to get me into the Library was the nicest thing anyone's ever done for me."

"Think how much nicer it would have been if it had worked," Anthony said, his eyes twinkling with good humor. He took her hand and kissed the back of it, lightly. "I'm going into the country for a few days, but would you like to go riding again next week? Before the weather turns too cold?"

His hand was warm and dry in hers and she had a moment's inexplicable discomfort that passed so quickly she barely had time to acknowledge it. She was suddenly conscious of the guards, both female, standing sentinel on either side of the Dowager's door. "I would like that very much," she said.

"Then I'll see you next week," he said, releasing her, and held the door for her. She stood in the antechamber, which was empty, for a few seconds, breathing in the scent of poppies arranged in the tall vase in the center of the room. It was irrational for her to feel bereft just because she wouldn't see her friend for a few days. It was a mistake for her to depend so much on one relationship for her entertainment. Well, she didn't, though, did she? She had the other ladies, they were friends, and the Dowager had turned out to be so kind and understanding. And it wasn't as if she would have nothing else to do: she would make calls with the Dowager day after tomorrow, and then the Dowager was hosting a supper for her friends and she would…oh, no, she would have to make conversation. But they were all going out tomorrow…to a concert, something awful with people tooting horns or flutes. And the Queen's birthday gala was in five days, and that meant wearing full court attire, with the rigid frame under her silk skirt that made it stand out two feet in every direction and swayed like a bell with her legs for the clapper. She went into her room and shut the door hard behind her. It seemed the only thing she had to look forward to in the near future was going to the theater to talk business with Doyle, and even he would want her to go over investment proposals she didn't want to consider right now. She thought about riding in the Park with Anthony, of sweet little Ebon Night and how wonderful it felt to race in the crisp cold air, and wished next week would arrive tomorrow.

Chapter Ten

Alison sat in Mirabella d'Arden's salon, a poorly lit room draped in blue gauze, and tried not to fidget. Her gown of mint green silk patterned with pink rosebuds was a little too thin for the chilly room. From what the Dowager had said of Lady d'Arden — or, more accurately, what she *hadn't* said — Alison gathered that Lady d'Arden believed in the healthful properties of cold air and had only installed heating Devices in her home when her husband protested. Alison was sure the Devices were turned to their lowest setting now. She tried to focus on the poetry reading, which was actually very good; she should suggest to their father they court the author away from Struthers & Fine. Shereen Wilson was a better poet, but it wouldn't hurt for Quinn Press to cultivate more than just the one.

Two seats away, Elisabeth Vandenhout stifled a yawn, which forced Alison to stifle a smile. Elisabeth didn't like readings, and Alison rather guiltily found the woman's discomfort enjoyable. It was even better tonight, because yesterday morning Elisabeth had said something catty about Alison and her nonexistent romantic relationship with Anthony North, and Alison, caught off guard, had blushed and stumbled over her words in response, and then everyone had begun teasing her until the Dowager suggested gently that perhaps they could find better things to do with their time. The other four ladies hadn't taken it any further, but Elisabeth had found several opportunities to needle her since then, infuriating Alison. She felt at a loss to know how to respond. No, she wasn't in love with Anthony, but it felt so...wrong...to vehemently deny it, as if that denial was a repudiation of the relationship they *did* have. Worse, every time Elisabeth brought up the topic, Alison was reminded of the fact that her friend was gone and she missed him more than she'd expected. She'd begun counting the days until he returned, though doing so made her angry at herself for being so needy and sentimental. She turned her attention back to the poetry, which was robust and non-sentimental. It had been a surprise to her that the Dowager counted this poet among her favorites.

The lights came up just a little, enough to indicate there would be a short break, and Alison stood and tried to stretch without actually stretching. She left her place and wandered around the room, looking at the artwork Lady d'Arden had on display, portraits of d'Ardens throughout history.

"Milady Countess, how good to see you again."

She turned to find Alexander Bishop at her elbow, his long, sneering face attempting a pleasant smile. "Hello, Mister Bishop, and how are you this evening?" Alison said, hoping her smile looked more genuine than his did.

"Much better, now," he said, taking her half-heartedly offered hand and bowing over it. *Anthony would want me to be polite to his friend,* she reminded herself, and kept her smile as friendly as she could manage. "Do you enjoy poetry, then?" he continued.

"I do, though I prefer novels. I understand his Highness is in the country; did you not choose to join him?" It was the only conversational gambit she could think of, though saying it gave her the same empty feeling that always struck her when she remembered Anthony would be gone for another three days.

"Tony knows I dislike the country," Bishop said, taking her arm and beginning to circle the room without asking if she cared to join him. "I'm a creature of the city. Never go into the country except on business. What of you?"

"I…yes, I prefer the city myself," Alison said, "or at least I don't mind visiting the country at times, but there are so many more things to do in cities."

"Like the theater?" Bishop's sneering face turned his smile into something nastier, as if enjoying the theater was something only naïve, unsophisticated people did. The empty feeling turned cold.

"I do enjoy the theater, yes. Have you never attended a performance? Perhaps it is something you would like."

"Possibly. You've certainly turned Tony into an aficionado. Haven't heard him so enthusiastic for years. Not since he was squiring Lydia Brown about town. Now *she* kept him on his toes."

The cold feeling turned to ice. "I'm afraid I'm not acquainted with Miss Brown."

"Well, you wouldn't be, would you? Not really your sort of people. Tony thought he was in love with her, for a time. Kept her in good style. Good thing for him his grand passions never last long. He's always choosing the least suitable women to bestow his affections on."

"Is he?" It was hard to talk through the frozen mask.

"He's just very good at knowing exactly what a woman wants to hear," Bishop said, lowering his voice as if it were a profound secret. Then his expression went guilty. "I apologize," he said. "I should not have said anything so indecent to you. Please forgive me."

"I was not offended, Mister Bishop," Alison managed. "His Highness's personal life is of little interest to me. As his friend, of course I don't feel I should pass judgment on any mistakes he might have made."

"Very generous of you. I'm surprised you can call him a friend. I don't think Tony's ever had a female friend he wasn't trying to—that is, his interest in women has always been romantic."

"I suppose nothing is impossible, is it?" She had a terrible urge to slap him, and thought wildly, *Zara might make me appear in public with him*, and had to hold back a laugh. A look of anger crossed Bishop's face briefly, then the sneering smile reappeared. "We do have more things in common than I believed two months ago," she added.

"Obviously," he said, then looked around as the lights dimmed again. "May I escort you back to your seat?"

"Thank you, Mister Bishop, I would appreciate that," she said, but

125

when she was again seated she watched him walk away and tried to keep from freezing over entirely. That guilty expression had been fake, she was certain of it, and everything about that conversation had been carefully planned by Bishop. He'd wanted to make her uncomfortable, though why he'd thought telling her about Anthony's affairs would discomfit her, she wasn't sure. Possibly he'd thought her the kind of simpering maiden for whom any discussion of sex, any mention of illicit affairs that strained someone's family bonds, was embarrassing. Besides, why bring up something that was in the past? She hadn't heard of Anthony having any sexual affairs recently, but then he wouldn't mention anything like that to her, would he? And even if he did, it wasn't as if she'd stop being his friend, much as the idea appalled her.

Wait. That was what Bishop wanted. He wanted her to be horrified by Anthony's affairs and shun him. Why under heaven would Bishop do something like that? Was he really so threatened by her friendship with Anthony? Apparently he was one of those people who couldn't bear their closest friends to have any other friendships, as if friendship were something that was diluted the more friends you had. Alison looked across the room at where Bishop sat, looking with some interest at the reader, and felt her dislike of him flower into hatred. She had one true friendship in Aurilien and he was trying to destroy it out of spite.

She tried to listen to the reading, but couldn't stop picturing his sneering, ugly face, speaking those ugly words. Whatever Anthony might have done in the past, she was certain he'd put it behind him. Mostly certain, anyway. Certain enough that she wasn't going to hate him for it now. If she were going to be angry with Anthony over anything, it was that he held this awful man in such high esteem. He couldn't know what Bishop was really like, or he would sever the connection. And *she* certainly couldn't tell Anthony the truth, because he'd just become angry with her the way he had on the way home from the races. The poetry was flat and uninspired now. How strange that she'd ever found it appealing.

She sat, hands clenched in her lap, until the reading was over, then contributed to the discussion on the way back to the palace with frozen, curt responses. The Dowager and Elisabeth were both riding in the other carriage, for which she was grateful; the Dowager would know something was wrong, and try to coax it out of her, and Elisabeth would needle her until Alison snapped. Finally safe in her own suite, she dressed for bed and took the comb from Belle's hand to comb her own hair until she felt calm enough to sleep. It wasn't true. Anthony wasn't like that anymore. He wasn't the man she'd slapped at the Equinox Ball; that was a face he'd worn out of habit, concealing his true self, kind and honest and a true friend. She clung to those thoughts as she climbed into bed, then slept, and had disturbing dreams she only remembered filmy shreds of when she woke the next morning.

Alison held her arms slightly away from her body and tried not to inhale as Belle tightened her corset strings a little more. The bodice of her court dress stood on the bed opposite her, actually stood thanks to its heavy blue and gold embroidery and the thousands of tiny gold beads stitched in patterns all across it. The sapphire blue skirt, also covered in starburst patterns of gold beads, stood next to the bed. Its rigid frame of thin wood kept it as upright as she was constrained to be by the corset. The whole ensemble was stiff and formal and she wished she could send it to the ball in her place.

Belle dressed Alison's hair in the equally stiff and formal style traditional for this garb, though she let one curly tress hang over Alison's right shoulder in defiance of tradition. The bodice was cut a little too low for Alison's comfort, but she had to admit she looked very good in blue. For the first time in years, she wore her Countess's tiara of twined silver and gold wire framing a cabochon-cut fire opal that didn't strictly match the rest of her attire, but it was, again, tradition.

"Oh, milady, you are so beautiful," Belle whispered, as if Alison's beauty might disappear if she spoke too loudly.

"Thank you, Belle. I love what you've done with my hair." Alison touched it gingerly and felt it move not at all. "I don't know if I'll be able to dance in this dress."

"You could just stand and be admired," Belle offered.

"That would be a nightmare. Don't wait up if you're tired, I'll wake you. And thank you again."

Simone was the only other woman in the antechamber. She looked up at Alison's entrance and her eyes went wide. "Sweet heaven," she said. "Don't stand anywhere near me, please. I'd like to have a few partners tonight, and no one will even look at me if you're there. Even if you blush like that."

"I think there was a compliment in there somewhere," Alison said, but inside she cringed. Her body was the only thing anyone was going to see of her tonight, especially with the corset exaggerating her figure.

"Oh, definitely," Simone said. "Carola, Marianne, come and look at Alison's gown. I wish I'd thought to have the dressmaker do that pattern with my pearls."

"Look at how beautiful we all are!" Carola said. "We will all have any number of partners, I'm sure."

"I imagine your *friend* the Prince will admire you greatly," Elisabeth drawled. "Was that your intention?"

"The Prince is still out of town," Alison said, fighting an urge to slap the woman, "and I'm sure he would admire me as much as *every* other man will." Elisabeth's smile disappeared.

"Now, ladies, remember this evening is to honor your Queen," the Dowager said. Her short dark hair was topped by the coronet the Dowager Consort was entitled to, and her gown was wider and more ornate than any of her ladies'. "Being admired is very nice, but our appearances are intended to show how much we respect her. Though, just between us, Zara has always said she wished her birthday celebration were not quite so formal. Still, things are what they are, and I hope you will all remember to behave yourselves." Everyone except the Dowager looked at Alison, and she blushed hotly. The scandal might have died down outside the palace, but it was unlikely her fellow ladies-in-waiting would ever forget what she'd done.

Alison paused at the top of the ballroom stairs to admire the transformation. Thin, nearly transparent navy blue silk and silver toile draped the walls, making it look like an underwater fantasy. The Device-lit chandeliers had been lowered and their lights softened to provide a brighter, cooler light across the floor. Alison had to look away from that quickly because the effect made the imaginary curve of the floor steeper. She saw no chairs, which was probably a concession to the ladies and their rigid skirt frames, only tall tables that stood at exactly the right height for someone to set a wine glass on temporarily. That probably meant they would be just a little higher than was comfortable for someone her height. Well, she was accustomed to being the short one.

The sweet scent of lilacs came faintly to her nose, and as she reached the foot of the stairs she saw vases bearing white lilac bushes at intervals throughout the room, blooming out of season as if Zara were powerful enough to command the trees. Alison had no doubt the Queen could manage it. They must have come from a greenhouse somewhere in the palace—no doubt Anthony knew where it was, and he might show her. When he returned. The thought dampened her spirits further, and she pushed it aside and exerted herself to be cheerful. She already knew so many men, and none of them had made her feel awkward, and she would eventually be able to dance comfortably in this awful skirt, and she refused to feel miserable and frozen.

She had to walk a little faster to catch up with the Dowager and the rest of her ladies, who'd kept moving while she dawdled to look at the flowers. The silence that arose as she passed made her blush, though it was likely the rest of the guests were responding to the ladies as a group rather than to her as an individual. She ascended the three shallow steps of the dais to make her low curtsey to the Queen, who sat in a high-backed chair upholstered in red velvet and carved with spirals, its back topped with the triple peaks of Tremontane. Zara wore North blue velvet trimmed with silver and a choker of silver leaves, with a slimmed-down version of the Tremontanan crown in silver and sapphire. She gazed at them all, unsmiling, and nodded once to indicate they could rise, then came forward to embrace her mother. Over the Dowager's shoulder, she caught Alison's eye, and Alison nearly choked when the Queen winked at her, the barest droop of an eyelid.

Having made their obeisance, the ladies separated to drift through the ballroom on their unmoving silken skirts. *Now* people were staring at her. She felt like a jeweled butterfly, with the eyes of a thousand lepidopterists on her, waiting for her to alight so they could pounce and carry her away for their collections. She saw no one she recognized, and the few men whose eyes she met had the all-too-familiar expressions that made her wish she could cover herself or run and hide. There was no way she could leave the ballroom without being noticed, in this dress that stood out from her body by a hundred feet. She walked a little faster, hoping she might meet someone she knew, but the Dowager's party had arrived early, and by the look of these strangers' formal dress, most of these people were minor nobles from the outlying regions of Tremontane who would have traveled for days to arrive here and would not have wanted to miss one second of the gala. She neared the bottom of the stairs, turned left—sweet heaven, one of them was approaching her, a too-appreciative smile on his lips, his eyes fixed on her bodice, and she couldn't think of a reason to politely avoid him—

"Surprise," said a wonderfully familiar voice, and she spun around so fast she made her skirt swing wide around her legs. "I think you might be able to sweep the floor clean with that skirt," Anthony said, taking a step backward to avoid it. He looked wonderful in his formal knee breeches and waistcoat of North blue and the fitted black frock coat that hugged his broad shoulders and made him look taller than he was.

"I thought you weren't coming back for another two days," Alison said. The lump of ice in her chest melted like snow on a hot stove.

"No, didn't I say? Zara depends on me to take some of the social burden at this thing, what with all the foreign dignitaries. I am assigned to squire Prince Takjashi Kerish's harem tonight. The entire harem. Not one of them younger than forty and all of them filled with questions about the history of the palace. It took some doing to escape them, but I think it was worth it."

She knew she was smiling too broadly, but she felt so happy at his appearance that she didn't care. "I can't imagine anyone better qualified to answer those questions," she said. "But it seems a little hard, you having to spend the whole evening playing politician."

"Oh, never fear, I intend to dance with at least one woman here tonight, if she will promise not to slap me."

"If you will promise not to deserve it, I think she could control herself for the length of one dance."

Anthony laughed and clasped both her hands in his. "Then I will see you later, milady Countess, and no more despondent face, if you please. It's a celebration, after all." He was gone before she could reply to that, his broad back swallowed up by the increasing crowd. She couldn't stop smiling. He would return eventually, and his eyes hadn't left hers the whole short time they'd spoken, and she began to feel she could endure this evening after all.

"I must say, you're the most beautiful thing in this room," someone drawled at her, and she turned to see the man who'd been approaching her before Anthony appeared. He held two glasses of wine and offered one to her; she took it automatically. He smiled, and made no secret of the fact that he was examining her body. He was tall, and lean, and handsome in a tall and lean way, and she looked back at him—and laughed.

"Excuse me, sir, but do you know who I am?" she said, kindly.

He looked a little startled, and shook his head. "Just that you're the woman I'm going to dance first with tonight," he said.

In her memory, Anthony smiled at her again, and she felt buoyed by it. "What is your name, sir?" she said.

He bowed. "Bartholomew Lester, milady."

"Good evening, Bartholomew Lester. My name is Alison Quinn, and I am the Countess of Waxwold," she said, and watched the poor man go white. "That's a title you recognize, isn't it? Well, sir, I would be happy to dance with you, because I can tell you thought you were being charming just now, and I won't hold it against you. But I dislike being referred to as a thing, and I dislike more the way you just looked at me, and if you persist in doing either of those actions I will personally tell every woman in this room you have sweaty palms and a tendency to pass wind at both ends. Now, I hear the musicians tuning up; shall we dance?"

She removed the glass from his hand and set both glasses aside, then held out her arm, and he took it automatically, his eyes wide and his mouth hanging open the tiniest bit. She patted his hand. "I'm really not offended, Bartholomew Lester," she said. "And just think how good you'll look hanging on my arm."

Lester was a good dancer, though Alison took more pleasure in his stunned expression than in the dance, and at the end he bowed to her and said, with a self-deprecating smile, "You are far more gracious than I deserve, Countess," before walking away. She danced the next three dances with men she had met before, then the next two with strangers, all the time trying not to search the ballroom for the one person she truly wanted to see approaching to solicit her hand. By the time the tenth dance had come and gone, and she had accepted a glass of sparkling wine from her latest partner, she began to suspect Anthony's harem was rather more demanding than he'd expected, and he might not be able to dance with her at all. She smiled and laughed at a joke her companion told and tried not to feel disappointment. She would almost certainly see him tomorrow, and they could go for that ride, or look at the greenhouses.

She finished her wine and was swept away by her next partner for a dipping, swaying dance that, combined with the wine, left her feeling a little dizzy. Perhaps just one more dance, and then she should leave. She had no idea what time it was; after midnight, probably, and she was tired and a little low in spirits. She smiled as brightly as she could at the next man who approached her, and held out her hand toward him.

Hands grasped her about the waist and swung her away from her would-be partner. "Sorry, friend," Anthony said over his shoulder, "but the lady is engaged to dance this one with me," and he carried her a few steps and set her down to clasp both her hands just as the music started. She laughed with delight.

"That poor man," she said. "Losing his partner like that."

"Oh, he'll find someone else. And who's going to argue with the Crown Prince?"

"So high-handed of you."

"I've sacrificed my evening to my sister's government. I intend to have at least a little pleasure tonight." He led her through a set of complicated steps, then handed off the lead for her to do the same for him. "I hope you don't mind that I kidnapped you."

"I was beginning to wonder where you were," Alison said. "Was your harem—excuse me, I don't think this gown is compatible with this dance." The steps of the dance had brought them close together, pushing Alison's skirt back so the whole frame flew up three feet and exposed her petticoats. Anthony took a few hasty steps back.

"This really is a ridiculous costume," Alison said. "I wish the

Queen would declare a new fashion for court apparel."

"I'm pretty sure she told you to call her Zara. And it has its merits."

"It does? What are they?"

"I'd tell you, but you despise compliments."

"Only the insincere ones. I think I can trust you to know the difference now."

"Can you?" Anthony said. "Trust me?" He'd been smiling at her, but the smile fell away, leaving him with a serious expression that made her uncomfortable. She made herself smile, and nod, and say, "Of course."

He looked away from her, across the ballroom, and she waited for him to speak, but he was as silent as if they were strangers who just happened to be following each other through the complicated steps of the dance. She waited, growing more nervous as the seconds passed, and was about to speak when he spun her away from him, drew her back, and said, "That dress makes you the most beautiful woman I've ever seen, and if I have any regrets about this evening, it's that I didn't wait for a dance that would let me put my arms around you, because I can't imagine anything else in the world that would make me happier than I am right now."

She nearly tripped over her own feet. He'd gone from looking away from her to being fully intent on her face, with a look in his eyes that said he was waiting for some response from her. She felt, not frozen, but numb, her thoughts in confusion, incapable of understanding what he wanted. *Most beautiful woman—let me put my arms around you—make me happier* replayed in her memory, clear and unambiguous as her own thoughts were not. That intent look, so serious, made her wonder what she looked like, circling around him with her eyes wide and her mouth open in astonishment. He was waiting for her to say something. She had no idea what that should be.

The music ended with a flourish, and all around them, men and women bowed to each other. Anthony had hold of both her hands and made no move to bow. Alison stood unmoving, unable to look away from those blue eyes. *No,* she thought, *I refuse,* and she pulled her hands free of his, curtseyed, and walked away at a normal pace, merging with the crowd and then walking out of it, putting one foot in front of the other until she reached one of the little doors shrouded in blue and silver mist, went inside, and closed it behind her.

The room was dimly lit by a pair of Devices in sconces on the wall. There was probably a switch somewhere to turn up the lights, but the darkness was comforting, like a blanket during a thunderstorm. She felt as if she'd been in a thunderstorm, been struck by lightning and barely lived to walk away from it. A sofa and a wingback armchair stood perpendicular to each other, their upholstery dark gray in the low light. She sat in the chair and felt the wooden frame of her skirt bend and pop, so she quickly stood and walked a few steps until she was in the center of the room with her back to the door. She hugged herself tightly and closed her eyes. That was no good. She could picture him still, the way he'd looked at her, and she still didn't know how to answer the question that had been in his eyes.

That hadn't been flirtation. He'd been entirely serious. He didn't want friendship from her.

And she didn't want friendship from him.

How embarrassing that she'd lied to herself so successfully. She'd actually believed he was just a friend. Of course she'd been unhappy while he was gone; of course she felt content when she was with him. Apparently her too-trusting heart had found a way to fool her sensible, cynical brain. *You can't trust him, you know what will happen, he's no different from the others and you are telling yourself a damn lie if you believe otherwise,* her horrible inner voice said, and she couldn't convince herself it was wrong. She didn't want to fall in love. It had only ever brought her misery. She didn't have love, and now she didn't have friendship, either.

The door opened behind her, then shut, quietly. "Alison," Anthony said, and she felt tears come to her eyes that she blinked away, hard. "Alison, I'm sorry. I'm sorry. I should never have said that, but I thought—you looked so happy to see me tonight, I hoped it meant you felt…I'm sorry. I've ruined everything."

"You weren't wrong," she said, a little thickly because the tears were falling faster now. "I was stupid not to understand why I missed you so much. But I can't love you. You can't ask that of me."

She heard him take a few more steps. "I thought of you every day I was gone," he said. "There was always something I wanted to ask you, or show you…it took me three days to realize why I felt so bereft all the time. I love you, Alison. I love how your eyes light up when you get excited about something and I love the sound of your laugh and I love that you don't blush well and it doesn't stop you from crying at the theater where everyone can see you. I wish to everlasting heaven I'd never been crude to you when we first met, because I want to tell you how beautiful you are and how much I love the way you walk, like you're about to take on the whole damn world at once, and how much more I love your wonderful, vibrant spirit that makes you who you are. That makes me want to be a better man. So tell me why you can't love me, because I will do anything to make that change."

She turned around. He was standing about five feet away, leaning on the balls of his feet as if he wanted to close that final distance but was afraid to. "There's no point," she said in a low voice, and wiped away tears. "There's never any point. Falling in love has only ever made me miserable. It's not going to happen again."

"I swear I'll never make you—"

"That's what they all said." She turned away again. "'Oh, Alison, you're so beautiful, you're a wonderful woman, I love you.' And the only thing they really loved was what I could do for them. Make them my consort. Give them my money. Let them—" She couldn't bring herself to say *With a body like that, you can't expect a man not to think of you naked in his bed,* even though she'd never forgotten those words or Eric's face when he'd said them.

"You know I'm not like that." He was close now, right behind her; she could feel his nearness like a brand threatening to scorch her flesh.

"Do I? How well am I supposed to know you after only eight weeks? I don't even know what you want from me."

"I don't want anything, except to be allowed to make you happy. Alison, listen to me." He put his hands on her shoulders and turned her around, gently, so she could look up at him. "I'm not those men, Alison. I don't need your fortune. I have a better title than you do. And at the risk of sounding vain, I'm by far the most handsome man you're ever going to meet, so maybe I should be worried *you're* only interested in *me* for my body." He gave her a crooked, self-deprecating smile that was so comical it surprised a smile out of her. The crooked smile turned into a real one, and he wiped some of her tears away with his thumb. "I can't promise to be perfect," he said, "but I can promise I won't betray you. And I can promise my heart is entirely in your keeping."

She blinked up at him. "I love you," he repeated, and caressed her cheek again, then slid his hand around to the back of her neck and stroked her skin, so lightly. Slowly, he drew her close to him. "Tell me if this isn't what you want," he said quietly, and lowered his head to kiss her.

It felt as if he'd knocked all the air out of her, as if that thunderstorm had returned for a second performance. She felt as if she were falling, and put her arms around his neck to keep her balance, and he kissed her again, his lips lingering on hers, and then she was kissing him and she couldn't remember why she'd ever thought this was a bad idea. His arms went around her waist, holding her up, and she felt the awful skirt swing up and away from her as she was pulled deeper into his embrace. *He loves me,* she thought, *he loves* me, and a knot of pain she hadn't even realized she was carrying around broke free inside her and left her feeling as if she might float away if Anthony weren't holding her so closely. She felt enveloped in his arms, protected, and it was such a good feeling that she clung to him and willed him never to let her go.

He moved to kiss her cheek, her forehead, then back to her lips, murmuring, "I don't think I'll ever get enough of this." She nodded in agreement, and her chin brushed his cheek as he moved to kiss her throat. She laughed, and Anthony drew back just enough that they could look at each other. "You're still crying," he said.

"These are just leftover tears. They'll dry soon enough."

"I hope so. I would hate for you to be trapped in this room all evening by a blotchy complexion."

"It's a nice little room. And the company is excellent. Did anyone see us leave?"

"You made a very demure exit this time. I probably looked like a man sentenced to die."

"I'm sorry. I didn't know what to say."

"In retrospect, I realize the middle of the ballroom probably wasn't the best place to make a declaration of love. I'll remember that for next time."

"You expect there to be a next time?"

He smiled at her, that crooked, self-deprecating smile again, then kissed her, a slow, wonderful kiss that left Alison out of breath. "No," he said. "But I intend to show you, every day, that I love you."

"I look forward to it. I wish we could sit down together and be more comfortable."

"I think, if we were more comfortable, I would have trouble stopping at kissing you."

"Oh."

Anthony held her close again. "I know what that sound means," he said. "Would you like to know the truth about my sordid past?"

Alison hesitated, then nodded, cautious of her rigid hairdo.

Coming out of this room looking mussed, followed by the Crown Prince, would cause the kind of scandal even Zara would have trouble hushing up.

"All right," Anthony said. "When I was seventeen I had an affair with a much older woman that lasted about a month. She broke it off—I think she was using me to make a point to her husband. The next year I spent a week with an equestrienne who came through Aurilien with a traveling circus from Veribold. When I was twenty I had a woman in keeping for several months until we tired of each other and parted company. During those three years I spent the night—just one night, I mean—with maybe a dozen other women. And the reason I'm holding you so tightly is I'm afraid you're going to flee in maidenly distress, but I want to be honest with you. I hope you don't think I'm proud of any of that."

"I can tell you aren't, and I'm not going to flee." His matter-of-fact recounting gave her a little pain, but that was blotted out by her relief that the truth was so much better than what she'd imagined. "What made you stop?"

"When I'd been with Lydia—my last lover—for several months both of us started to feel as if we were being torn in several directions. It seems that's what happens when you abuse your family bonds by sleeping with someone who doesn't share them; you start to lose connection not only to your family, but to the world around you." He laughed. "And Zara threatened to cut off the relevant bits of me if I didn't stop."

"She did not."

"You've met her. What do you think?"

"Good point."

"Anyway," Anthony said, relaxing his grip just a little, "I'm sorry I haven't always made good choices, and I hope you won't hold it against me."

"I won't." She drew his head down so she could kiss him. "You're far too tall for me," she said with a smile.

Anthony put his arms around her waist and lifted her, making her shriek a little with laughter. "You're right, I am," he said. "I'll just have to stop loving you and find someone taller."

"Don't you dare." She kissed him again. "Am I still blotchy? Because I think I would like to go out there and dance with you again where everyone will see us."

"You look wonderful." He hesitated. "Would you mind terribly if we didn't make our relationship public just yet?"

"Why not? Are you ashamed of me, Anthony North?"

He grinned. "People have only just stopped staring at us because of our scandal. I'd like to go a little while before they start again, even if this time the staring would be less humiliating."

"That's...actually, I like that idea. How long?"

"Until Wintersmeet? Five weeks? We can pretend to be merely friends, and then every time we meet will be a secret pleasure."

"I think I can last that long. And secret pleasure sounds lovely." Alison took Anthony's hand and pressed it to her cheek. "I love you. And I trust you."

"I promise to always be worthy of that trust," Anthony said. "One more kiss, and then I think you should leave first."

"Mmmm. Maybe two more kisses."

"If it's going to be two more kisses, it might as well be half a dozen."

"Or a dozen. Oh, Anthony, I do love you."

Eventually Alison tore herself away from his arms and peeked out the door. The shrouding blue and silver mist made it easy for her to sneak away and circle the ballroom to where she could watch Anthony emerge. He truly loved her, and she loved him, and it was going to be all right. Everything was going to be all right.

Chapter Eleven

The dark gray stones might as well have been made of ice, as cold as the Library passage was. Alison blew on her fingers and then shoved her hands deep into her trouser pockets. She should have worn a heavier coat, but she'd foolishly convinced herself that since she wasn't going outdoors, of course she didn't need more than her quilted jacket. She shouldn't have needed a coat at all, but the old parts of the palace not only didn't have Devices to heat them, they had been built to keep out the heat of an Aurilien summer, which meant in winter the ink probably froze solid.

She quickened her step. Bancroft sometimes closed the Library early, no matter who might want to use it. Or, possibly, he did it on purpose to inconvenience her. Though it was true the cold seemed to keep most people away. The last time she'd visited, she had been the only person there who wasn't a Scholia employee, and Baxter had given her a more sour than usual look. He'd had a large wrapped bundle of books on the desk when she requested *Wonders of Eskandel*, and when she'd peeked at the bundle—just a little peek, curiosity was natural—he'd almost bitten her hand off, then curtly explained he was taking them to the bindery for repairs and she had better not damage them further. His customary abruptness left her groping for a response, so she'd said nothing, but privately resolved to find the bindery and look at its Devices. Anthony would probably know where it was.

She'd seen Anthony only four times in the two and a half weeks since Zara's birthday gala, once when he joined his mother and her ladies for dinner, twice at informal parties which they did not attend together, and once, blissfully, when they went to the theater and secretly held hands during the performance and kissed madly in the privacy of the royal carriage. That had been a wonderful ride, and thinking of it now made Alison's cheeks, and other parts of her, heat up enough that she didn't much mind the chill of the passage. As unhappy as she was about seeing him so infrequently, it was probably just as well, because she was very bad at behaving as if Anthony North were nothing more than her good friend, thanks to her blotchy blushes of guilt and excitement whenever he walked into a room. He, damn him, always looked indifferent to her, sometimes indifferent to the point that she felt a pang of fear that she'd misunderstood him, he didn't love her and it was all a mistake and she'd made such a fool of herself by believing otherwise. Then he would catch her eye when no one was looking, and smile, and everything he couldn't say was in that smile, and she would remember the touch of his hands and his lips and her fears shrank into laughable caricatures of themselves.

She pushed open the door to the scriptorium. It was empty except for Edwin, who as usual turned bright red when he saw her. At least one person in the palace blushed even more dramatically than she did. "I'd like to see *Wonders of Eskandel* again, Edwin," she said when she reached the librarians' desk.

"Just one...I'll go get it, milady Countess," he whispered, and Alison sat at what she'd begun to think of as her desk to wait. She donned her thin cotton gloves—she'd had to provide them for herself, which was just another of Bancroft's shortcomings; it was appalling that he'd let people handle four hundred year old books with their bare hands—and waited. The book was in terrible shape, and handling it, gloves or no, made her nervous, but she was enjoying it far too much to simply leave it alone.

Edwin carefully laid the book down in front of Alison, nodded, and backed away quickly. Alison ignored him and turned the pages to where she'd left off reading. *They ought to at least re-stitch the binding,* she thought, wincing at the way the pages shifted as she turned them. This one was very loose—

She squeaked as an entire signature came away in her hand. Broken threads waved from its ends and trailed across the book's remaining pages. "Edwin," she said, "come and look at this."

Edwin began breathing heavily when he saw the damaged book. "This is terrible," he moaned, and gathered the book into his arms like an infant. Alison followed him to the long desk with the loose pages. "Terrible," he repeated. He put the book away somewhere under the desk, gasped when he saw what Alison was holding, and snatched the signature from her hand and stuffed it carelessly inside the tooled leather cover.

"It's not that terrible," Alison said.

"You damaged a book. Master Bancroft will never let you in here again," Edwin said in a whisper.

"*I* damaged the book? It came apart in my hands because no one here bothered to care for it properly. You can even see where the binding threads were frayed!"

"Master Bancroft will never believe it."

"Edwin, you are such a...never mind. Just take it to the bindery and fix it. I'd love to see the Devices in action."

"We're not allowed to take the books out of the Library. Master Bancroft's orders."

"I saw Baxter taking books to the bindery just a week ago. I'm fairly certain Ban—Master Bancroft didn't mean *you* weren't allowed."

"Baxter didn't—I mean, only Master Bancroft uses the Devices for binding. I'm not allowed."

"Sweet merciful heaven, Edwin, bring me a needle and a spool of strong thread and I can have it fixed in ten minutes, if it's that dire an emergency!"

Edwin shook his head. He was starting to look terrified. "I won't tell him," he whispered. "I don't want you to get into trouble."

Alison stripped her gloves off and stuffed them into her coat pocket. "Fine," she said. "But I would think a librarian should care more about the books than he does about upsetting his superior." She turned and left the scriptorium, wishing she had something to kick.

Bancroft was arrogant and territorial, Baxter was a bully, Edwin was a coward. Nobody associated with the Royal Library seemed interested in it as anything but a way of exercising power over people. How long was a Royal Librarian's tenure, anyway? Maybe Bancroft's was nearly up. Maybe the Scholia would recall him and send someone a little less fond of his own privilege and more lenient in his policies. Though the way Alison's luck had been running with regard to the Royal Library, the Scholia would recall Bancroft the day Alison's term of service was up.

That thought made her stop in the middle of the hall. What would happen when it was time for her to leave? Anthony couldn't follow her back to Kingsport, and she couldn't stay in Aurilien—she had too many responsibilities back home. Could they continue to love each other under those conditions? *Should* they continue to love each other? Alison began to feel ill. That her tender, newborn love affair, still finding its bearings, might be destroyed filled her with horror. Right then she wished she could run to Anthony and remind herself she wasn't lost and alone, a wish she indulged for two seconds before mentally slapping herself. She wasn't alone, Anthony loved her, and there would be plenty of time to worry about what-ifs when spring came. *But*, she thought as she continued on down the hall, *I wish Wintersmeet were here and gone already.*

"Another note for you, milady," Belle said, her hand outstretched. "Certain sure you're not courting with the Crown Prince?"

"I'm certain," Alison lied, in the same teasing tone Belle had used. "Besides, I think this one is from the Queen. She's inviting me to dinner in the east wing tomorrow." Alison tried not to let her excitement show. *I can see Anthony. I have to pretend he's no more than a friend, with his sister sitting right there between us. This is going to be terrible.*

"Good afternoon, Alison," Zara said when she entered the east wing dining room. "Thank you for joining us. Won't you sit down?

Anthony seems to be a little late, but I don't think we need to wait for him."

"Thank you, your—Zara."

Zara smiled, a tiny smile that barely stretched the corners of her mouth. "It gets easier," she murmured. "Try some of the soup. It's a tomato bisque the chef learned to make in Veribold."

Alison nodded and sipped her soup. Anthony ought to be here by now. She was prepared; she wasn't going to blush, or refuse to meet his eyes, or anything stupid like that. But her emotional self-control was slipping away from her. "I'm looking forward to the Wintersmeet celebrations," she said. It was the only topic she could think of. "I'm told they're quite elaborate."

"The ball is certainly the biggest social event of the year, much less religious than Midsummer," Zara said. "And it's exhilarating to be a part of such a large crowd when the season shifts and the lines of power react to that. I imagine, knowing my mother, that you and her ladies already have your gowns."

"We have final fittings tomorrow," Alison said, then heard the door open behind her, and her heart began to pound. *Don't blush, don't blush!*

"Sorry I'm late, sister mine," Anthony said. "Good afternoon, Alison."

"Good afternoon," Alison said. *No blushing!* "What have you been doing?"

"I'm afraid I only just rose an hour ago," Anthony said. He spread his napkin over his lap and helped himself to a slab of glazed ham. "Very late night. Don't look at me like that, Zara, it was just a party with some friends. Very quiet."

"I'm sure," Zara said drily. "How much did you lose?"

"I won, actually, and you're going to give the Countess a bad impression of me."

"Worse than the one she no doubt already has?"

Good heaven, the Queen is teasing him. I had no idea she could unbend that much. "I think Anthony isn't so terrible as all that, and at least he can afford to lose occasionally," she said, and warmed at his smile.

"You're very generous of spirit, Alison." Zara tore a roll apart and, to Alison's astonishment, dipped a piece into her soup, completely unselfconscious of her breach of good manners. "Tell me, has your experience with the Royal Library improved since last we spoke?"

"Not really. At least I've been able to see more of the books. But Bancroft—Master Bancroft still hovers over me when he's there, as if he thinks I'll try to smuggle a folio out in my trouser pocket." She cut a piece of ham and bit into it with some ferocity. "I don't know what to think anymore. I'm just tired of not having access to the Library. Back home, I belong to two different lending libraries and I have access to new books not only from our own press but from several others we have business relationships with. And I can visit the library at my manor any time I want. This is stifling."

"How many books do you actually need?" Anthony said, amused.

"Who says it's about need? I love having my own library. It gives me pleasure to walk through a room full of books and know that one of them might be the next story I fall in love with. A new book—it could be anything. It could be awful. It could be magnificent. And some of them are simply beautiful, physically I mean. That's part of why it would be such a great loss if the Library collection really is damaged."

Anthony leaned on his chin and gazed fondly at her. "I take it back," he said. "You love *books* far more than I love my horses."

Alison blushed. "I seem to have been rattling on a bit, haven't I?"

"No need to apologize," said Zara, finishing her roll. "People who have a grand passion are either tedious about it, or they have a gift for making others understand that passion themselves. I'm happy to say you're one of the latter, Alison." Zara stood and pushed her chair in. "And speaking of passions, I have no idea why the two of you are trying to keep yours a secret, but with the way you look at each other, it won't stay secret long."

She disappeared through the invisible door, leaving Alison and Anthony staring at each other. "Was it that obvious?" Alison said. *Now* she was blushing.

"Zara's just far too observant for everyone else's comfort," Anthony said, wiping his lips. "And since she both knows and is no longer in this room, why don't you come over here and sit with me?"

Alison hopped up and almost ran around the table, then squeaked as Anthony grabbed her arm and pulled her down to sit on his lap. She put her arms around his neck and kissed him. "Oh, how I've missed that," she murmured.

"So have I," Anthony said. "Just a little more than two weeks now."

"I'm having such trouble keeping this secret. What would it hurt to be together in public now?"

"We've made it this far, haven't we?" He kissed her and twined his fingers in hers. "It's not that much longer. And I'm going into the country again in two days, so I won't be here to throw you into confusion the way I did yesterday at the Hantfords' salon."

"Yes, that was nearly a disaster."

"I'm sorry." He laid his cheek against hers and took a deep, satisfied breath. "I have an idea that might help satisfy that passion of yours. My townhouse has a library—it's small, only a few hundred books, but it's supposed to be fairly valuable and I have no idea what's in it. I don't suppose you'd care to take a look?"

"Would I? That sounds so exciting! I—"

He stopped her with a long, slow kiss. "Sorry to interrupt you," he said finally, while Alison tried to get the world to stop spinning, "but you get this light in your eyes when you're happy about something, and I couldn't help myself."

"And how do I look when I look at you?" she asked with a smile, touching his cheek.

He smiled back at her. "Joyful," he said. "You see me as a better man than I know myself to be."

"I see you for who you are."

"Then I must be a *much* better man than I thought."

She kissed him again, then rose, though she didn't remove her hand from his. "I have to return to your mother soon," she said, "but can I look at your library tomorrow?"

"I'll call for you just after dinner. That will give me time to find a spare key for you. No sense you having to wait until I return from my estate." He squeezed her hand. "I love you, you know."

"I can tell. You just gave me a library. Let's have coffee, and you can escort me back to the Dowager's apartment."

"With pleasure, Countess."

By comparison to the rest of the townhouse, which was decorated in the most modern style, pale woods contrasting with rich jewel-toned colors, the library looked like the set of a historical melodrama. Its heavy bookcases and the claw-footed desk looked like someone's idea of a library, right down to the hooded brass light Device on the desk and the portrait hanging on the wall behind it. Alison, her hands on her hips, looked up at the painting. The man looked back at her with a smile that said he knew a secret, and he wanted to share it with her. She walked around the desk and saw the chair, in contrast to the rest of the furnishings, was a plain office chair on casters that rolled smoothly over the plank flooring when she pushed it. Unexpected. She looked back up at the previous owner. Now he seemed to be smiling in delight at her surprise. She wished she could have known him.

"I didn't realize it was this dusty," Anthony said swiping a finger across the fireplace mantel. "I'll have Josie clean it up before you start. I don't think I've been in here more than twice since I bought the place last year, contents intact."

"Why didn't the owner take it when he left?"

"It belonged to a man who passed away leaving only one heir. She was only interested in the profit she might make from it, and I thought—you're going to think me terribly shallow—I thought all those books looked distinguished. At the time I was only concerned about impressing the ladies I flirted with."

"Well, *I'm* impressed. This is a real collection, not just a bunch of books someone bought as a job lot because the spines all matched. Oh, I love this one!"

"There's that light in your eyes again," Anthony laughed. "I take it this was a good idea?"

"It was an *excellent* idea. What would you like me to do with them? Reorganize? Value the collection?"

"I would like you to do whatever satisfies you. Though if you find anything interesting, I'd like to hear about it. Zara's right that you have a knack for getting other people interested in your passion. I want to know about the things you love."

"I'll try not to be boring." She laid the book aside and took his hand. "Are you sure you need to leave?"

"I've already put it off for a week because there's this incredible woman I keep seeing around the city and I was hoping I could convince her to kiss me."

"Anthony, we can't let the servants see us. They're as prone to gossip as anyone."

He put his arms around her waist. "Then we'll just have to be very, very careful."

Chapter Twelve

Alison wrapped her fur-lined cloak more tightly around herself and wished the heating Device embedded in the coach floor were a little more powerful. Outside, light snow covered the road and the shops lining it, though with the sun shining as brightly as it was, the snow probably wouldn't last past noon. Across from her, Carola shivered a little; she was wearing fashionable shoes that were too thin for the weather. Alison's own shoes weren't much better, but it was ridiculous to wear boots for such scant snow.

The shop bell jangled, and the Dowager emerged, trailed by a pair of shop assistants carrying parcels. The Dowager climbed the two short steps into the carriage while the assistants stowed the packages securely atop it. "Thank you," the Dowager said, tipping them both, and then the coach jerked into motion and took them away down the street.

"I do appreciate your assistance, ladies," the Dowager said. "It is so difficult to choose Wintersmeet gifts without help, don't you think? And I so enjoy shopping. I hope it is not too tedious for you."

"Not at all, Milady," Simone said, putting down the hood of her white velvet cloak trimmed with ermine. "It's fun to buy things for other people, don't you agree, girls?"

Alison nodded, though privately she thought it would be nice to pay someone to do her shopping for her, at least for the people she didn't care about but felt obligated to give to, like Elisabeth Vandenhout. She'd already sent her father's gift by post a week ago, and yesterday a very special gift had arrived from Quinn Press, one she'd had to hide under her bed because she couldn't explain why she'd ordered something so expensive for Anthony North. He'd been gone six days and they had been six surprisingly peaceful days, despite the whirlwind of shopping and social calls the Dowager was permanently at the center of. It was a little embarrassing that her longing for him could be so blunted by her enjoyment of his library. She went almost every afternoon for the few hours of the Dowager's nap time to remove books from the shelves, clean them, and rearrange them by the system she'd learned at the Scholia from Henry Catherton. His system had the benefit of being simple to learn and simple to understand, and if Anthony ever decided he wanted to take up reading, he would have no trouble finding the books he wanted. And it was good practice for her.

They returned to the Dowager's apartment, put away their purchases, and joined the other ladies for dinner, then Alison changed out of her morning clothes into an old shirt and trousers she didn't mind getting dirty, tied her hair back, and threw her fur-lined cloak over the ensemble. It made her look very odd, like a charwoman trying on the mistress's clothing, but it kept her warm and the day was far colder than she'd expected. If she could finish one more bookcase today, the entire job would be done before Wintersmeet. That left her feeling both pleased and a little empty, the way she always felt when a project was nearly completed. Though it would be nice to show her work to Anthony, even if he wouldn't fully appreciate it.

The townhouse was silent and a little cold; Anthony hired his household staff from a local agency and didn't keep them on while he was away. Alison turned up the light and heat Devices in the library, threw her cloak over the chaise longue, and set to work. The more time she spent with the books, the more fervently she wished she could have met its owner. It didn't have a lot of intrinsic value, though she'd made some remarkable finds and had set aside a rare second edition of *Campanile* for her father to value; he was the expert on early block printing. But she suspected it would have been of great value to the owner. She was beginning to get a sense of the kind of man he'd been, someone who loved to travel (Vernon's *South of Nowhere*) and was fascinated by people (two copies of *The Courts of the Veriboldan Queens*,

151

both editions) and a great lover of the contemporary novel, with whole shelves of books she herself loved and owned. She climbed onto the arm of a chair and reached high up to put away *Heart of Steel*, one of her favorites, shame the rest of the trilogy was out of print, and heard Anthony say, "Surprise."

She staggered, missed her footing, and gave a little shriek as she fell. Anthony darted forward and caught her. "Sorry," he said. "That was stupid."

"Just give me a moment to catch my breath," she said. He set her down on the chaise longue and took her hand. "That was certainly a surprise."

"I'm sorry."

"That's all right." She drew a deep breath. "I know you never said, but I was under the impression you weren't coming back until Wintersmeet."

"I couldn't bear not seeing you one day longer. Besides, the city's much more fun this time of year than the country, all those parties. How have you been?"

"Busy. Your mother knows so many people, and they all must have gifts. So I've done a lot of shopping. And a lot of work on your library."

"I can see. Alison, I didn't realize reorganizing the library meant taking it to bits."

"Sometimes building something new means tearing the old apart first. This way is better than trying to sort out what needs to change, a little at a time." She plucked a few strands of hair out of her mouth and pushed them behind her ears, discovered her hair had come down entirely on one side, and removed her hairband and tried to comb through the curly tresses with her fingers. She just had too much hair. This would have to do until she could get back to the palace and find a real comb.

She glanced up to see Anthony watching her with an unreadable expression. "May I?" he said, and without waiting for permission he slid his hands through her hair and began finger-combing the tangles. It felt wonderful. She closed her eyes and smiled at his touch, even when his hands caught on a knot and tugged a little. Pity she couldn't have this every day.

His hands paused, and she felt his breath warm on her face just before he kissed her, gently, sliding his hands from her hair to cup her face. She put her arms around his neck and kissed him back. Oh, how she'd missed this, his lips on hers, the spicy smell of his cologne and the slight roughness of his cheeks against hers. She kissed him more deeply and he responded by putting his hands on her shoulders and easing her back to lie against the sloping arm of the sofa. He was leaning over her, his chest barely pressing against hers, and she was very aware she wasn't wearing anything under her work shirt but a thin silky half-slip that did nothing to contain or support her breasts, and she wanted to feel his hands on them so badly her body ached.

As if he could read her mind, he leaned more heavily on one elbow and slid his other hand under both shirt and slip to caress her breast, his gentle fingers sliding along its curve and grazing her nipple. She made a sound she never dreamed she'd hear herself make and tore at her shirt, desperate to get it out of the way, it was in the way of his hands and she couldn't bear it any longer. Anthony helped her free herself from the fabric and touched her, still so gently, then he bent to kiss her breasts and she cried out because she had never felt anything like this in her life and she wanted more of it.

Her cry seemed to trigger something in him, because he moved from kissing her breasts back to her lips, and he was tugging at the buttons of his shirt until he could remove it and throw it across the room, where it landed on the desk corner and then fell to the floor. He put his arms around her and pulled her close to him, skin against skin, and they kissed desperately, wildly, until Alison felt her breath coming in short gasps and she clutched at him, unable to touch him enough to satisfy her need.

He kissed her neck, her shoulder, then her lips again, and she moaned and thrust herself against him, wanton and not caring about it. He put his hand between them, pushing her away, and she felt a pang of fear that she was doing something wrong, but he was only fumbling at the buttons of her trousers one-handed, his other hand tangled in her hair. She almost started to help him with the finicky buttons, but from some distant rational part of her brain came the awareness that they were on a chaise longue in his chilly library, and they didn't share a bond, and she thought, *Not this way. Him, only and ever him, but not this way.* So instead she took his hand away from the buttons, turned her face away from those devastating kisses, and used her other hand to push at his shoulder. "No," she said.

Unable to reach her face, he nuzzled her shoulder. "Alison, *please,*" he groaned, and despite herself she shivered at the passion in his voice.

"This isn't right," she whispered, "we both know it isn't right. No, Anthony."

He shuddered, then dropped his head to rest on her shoulder, silent. Then he released her and went to retrieve his shirt, still without speaking. Alison felt cold from more than just the chill in the air. She found her shirt and her slip and put them on. He wasn't looking at her. He was angry with her. She remembered tearing off her clothes, thrusting her body against him, and burned with shame. She'd led him on and then made him stop, and now he hated her. She couldn't find her hairband. Her loose hair had started the whole thing. Maybe he would think she was being a tease, leaving it down, when it was just that she couldn't find the damn hairband.

"I'm sorry," she said in a small voice. There it was, under her leg. She tied her hair back, roughly, not caring whether or not it was messy.

"Why are *you* sorry? I'm the one with no self-control," Anthony said.

His voice sounded so bitter, so disparaging of himself, that her heart was filled with compassion for him. "You stopped when I asked you to," she said, looking for the right words to reassure him.

"I shouldn't have started in the first place," he said. He still wasn't looking at her. She put her hand on his knee.

"You make it sound as if I had nothing to do with it," she said. "I might as well say I shouldn't have responded to your touch like that. Or are you suggesting I'm some kind of Device-driven doll with no volition of my own?"

"Not that. But I'm aware of what my reputation is and I don't want you to think you're just…the one who's available."

"I didn't think that at all. Honestly, I don't think I was *thinking* at all. It was…wonderful. But I'm just not ready and I don't think you are either."

He laughed and put his hand over hers. "I certainly felt ready." He kissed her cheek. "But I think you're right, and I also think we shouldn't be in this house alone together anymore. When do you come here?"

"From twelve-thirty to two-thirty. It's the only free time I have."

"I'll stay away until three, then. Just over a week, and we don't have to be a secret anymore."

"And we won't be so desperate because we can't see each other."

"True." He kissed her again. "I love you."

"And I love you. Now I'm going back to the palace to comb my hair and pin it up where it can't drive either of us mad with desire. I had no idea it had such unholy powers."

The next day, Anthony kept his word and didn't appear, though Alison did see the butler and the maid, Josie, which told her he was still in town. She made her way through a few more shelves, got distracted by some interesting novels, and left with a regretful glance at the chaise longue. What would it hurt, really, if they slept together? It wasn't as if it would be casual sex—no, it would definitely be the polar opposite of casual sex. Her body still tingled when she remembered how he'd touched her and kissed her, that look in his eyes of such delight and triumph. She wrapped her cloak more closely around her and trotted down the townhouse stairs to the coach the butler had summoned for her, and settled in for the ride back to the palace. She needed to stop entertaining those fantasies if she wanted to keep her composure when she read to the Dowager and the ladies that afternoon.

Another day, and she managed not to be distracted by some interesting histories of Tremontane to finish all but three shelves. All the lifting of books had left her a little achy. She clearly needed more exercise. She sat in a chair at the window, drinking some hot tea the maid brought her, and looked out over the street. Small gray heaps marked where people had shoveled snow off their walks and into the depressions between the pavers where trees had been planted. They looked as weary as she felt, their leafless branches sagging a little despite their bearing so little snow. Low gray clouds suggested another storm was coming, bringing snow to cover the dispirited streets and make everything look so beautiful. She swallowed wrong and coughed to clear her lungs. Coughing made her aches worse. She set her tea aside, stretched, and put on her cloak. She would be able to finish tomorrow, probably before the Dowager's nap time was over, and she could get some rest herself.

She stopped to consider the chaise longue more seriously this time. Suppose she didn't leave. Suppose she was still here when Anthony returned. It didn't have to be the chaise longue; he had a bedroom. She could wait for him there, wearing nothing but the cloak—*no*, she told herself sharply, *you'd both hate yourselves afterward*. But it was an image she had trouble shaking.

That evening, the Dowager and her ladies gathered in the Dowager's sitting room and wrapped Wintersmeet gifts. Alison sipped champagne and ate tiny cakes and giggled with the other women, even though she wasn't normally a giggler. "And I've already received three Wintersmeet gifts," Carola exclaimed, "one from each of the three B's! I don't know what to do about it!"

"You really should only accept a gift from a man you're truly interested in," Marianne said. "So which is it? Brian, Boris, or Bearn?"

"That's the problem—I like them all! They're all so sweet, and they dote on me, and they're ever so handsome. I don't know how to choose between them!"

"Perhaps you should draw lots," Elisabeth said, sounding bored.

"You should set them impossible tasks, and see who succeeds first!" Simone said.

"If they're *impossible*, how could anyone succeed?" said Elisabeth. "I know I would be embarrassed to receive a Wintersmeet gift from a man I wasn't betrothed to. It would be so awkward."

Excellent way to cover the fact that no man's likely to give you one, Alison thought. "There must be some way to choose, Carola," she said. "Something that sets one above the rest."

"Interesting advice, Alison," Elisabeth said. "I imagine *you* must have scores of men fighting for your affections. How do *you* choose?"

"I'm afraid I'm not expecting any gifts from a beau," Alison said, trying not to laugh at Elisabeth's spitefulness. She had put so much effort into finding a gift for Anthony that she hadn't really considered what he might give her. Something wonderful, she hoped. She coughed, covered her mouth delicately, and added, "Though I wouldn't reject one if it came!"

"Particularly from that special someone, yes?" Elisabeth said.

Alison paused in her wrapping and took another drink. She was already feeling a little light-headed. This should probably be her last glass. "Aren't gifts always better when they come from someone you care about?"

"Elisabeth, you really need to stop teasing Alison about the Prince," Philippa said, a little sharply. "It was only funny for a little while, and now it's just annoying. I'd rather talk about what I hope to get from my mother. She keeps promising to send me her ruby bracelet that belonged to my great-grandmother."

"Yes, dears, let's all try to be more generous of spirit with one another," the Dowager said. "This is a time of year to celebrate how we're all joined together, and it's hard to celebrate unity if you're niggling at one another. Alison, dear, I have just the ribbon to match that paper."

Alison coughed again, a little harder, and accepted the ribbon from the Dowager's hand. She'd lost count of how many days it was until Wintersmeet. Soon, now, and wouldn't it be funny to see the faces of the other ladies when they discovered Elisabeth had been right all along?

She woke up with a terrible headache. It was probably due to the champagne; she wasn't sure how much of it she'd drunk, but then she didn't have much of a head for alcohol. She had her morning coffee, but it didn't help. Headache from the wine, muscle aches from lifting the books—she had trouble not snapping at people, particularly Elisabeth, who looked a little hung over herself. The Dowager, far from being offended at Alison's irritability, excused her from morning activities so she could rest. "And don't exert yourself too much over that library of Anthony's," she said with a smile. "I'd tell you to leave it until you feel better, but I know you won't heed that advice as long as you have work left undone."

Alison rested on her bed for a few hours until her headache was mostly gone. She wasn't very hungry at dinner, but she made herself eat something, then put on her cloak and took a carriage to Anthony's townhouse. It would only take an hour to finish, probably, and then she could return and have more coffee and try to rid herself of the last remnants of this headache.

She worked slowly thanks to her throbbing head and aching body. It was just so hard, today, to put the books on the shelves. She stopped once to survey what was left to do, and had to steady herself on the back of a chair because she was momentarily dizzy. This wasn't sore muscles and a hangover, this was the beginnings of a nasty cold. She thought briefly about leaving the rest for now, going back to the palace to sleep and returning when she'd recovered. *It's just a few books*, she thought, *and who knows how long this cold might last?*

She wearily picked up another pair of books—her arms hurt too much for her to manage a whole stack—and placed them on the shelf, focusing idly on the titles embossed on the spines. Immediately her head cleared, and she snatched up one of the books. *Hearthsfire*, second volume of the trilogy beginning with *Heart of Steel*. Out of print and impossible to find—not only had she never seen it, she'd never known anyone who had. She laid it gently on the shelf and searched through the remaining volumes stacked on the floor. No *Starfall*, the final volume, but that would have been too much of an early Wintersmeet gift for heaven to bestow upon her.

She picked up *Hearthsfire* again and turned the pages reverently. This one book alone was worth the entire rest of the collection. She took it to the chair by the window and opened it to the beginning. Just a few pages; how could she resist? She shivered, got up and wrapped herself in her cloak. Snow had begun falling like sifting sugar crystals from the low gray clouds, wrapping the whole house in cotton wool silence. Just a few pages. She shivered again. A cup of tea would be nice, but this was not a book you read with any kind of food in hand. Just a few pages.

The sound of the front door opening brought her back out of her fictional world into the real one. She glanced up at the clock above the door, which made only the barest ticking sound because Anthony didn't like clocks that rang the hour, let alone every quarter of it. 3:35. She was late for reading time, and Anthony was home—well, it wasn't as if they couldn't see each other at all. She set the book on the broad arm of the chair and stood. Her head swam, and she had to grab the back of the chair to keep from falling. Maybe the Dowager wouldn't be so angry if she saw Alison was ill. She left the library and went to the top of the stairs. Two voices. Damn. Anthony had company. It could ruin everything if the wrong person saw her in his home. She carefully removed her shoes and looked over the banister. The sound of footsteps came down the hall toward the stairs, two men approached, Anthony and someone with curly hair. Alexander Bishop. Alison ground her teeth. It was Anthony's one character flaw — well, all right, he did have others, so this was his one *major* character flaw, that he couldn't see how awful Bishop was. Too bad there wasn't anything she could say that would make him drop the connection.

The footsteps went silent. Anthony and Bishop must have gone into one of the rooms lining the downstairs hall, the study or the billiards room, probably. Alison crept down the stairs to the first landing and looked down the hall toward the front door. The door to the billiards room was open a little, and light spilled out through the crack. She heard the distant murmur of voices. If she stayed close to the opposite wall, far from the doorway, and moved very quietly, she could probably make her escape.

Her unshod feet on the thickly carpeted steps were noiseless, the sound of her trouser legs rubbing together the only sound she made. Their conversation was louder now, but still unintelligible. She could hear the *tock* of billiard balls striking each other. She wished she'd thought to bring *Hearthsfire* with her, Anthony wouldn't mind if she borrowed it, but it was too late to go back now because she was at the foot of the stairs and creeping along the far wall like a mouse sneaking up on a piece of cheese.

She was nearly opposite the billiards room now and halted briefly to catch her breath. She couldn't cough now, that would be disastrous. The sound of their voices was clearer now. She knew she shouldn't eavesdrop, but she couldn't help it if she happened to be outside the room while they were speaking. It wasn't as if she'd come here on purpose to listen to them. She tried to move a little more quickly.

"...by Wintersmeet Eve." That was Anthony.

"Are you coming to Agatha Tompkin's party that night? No, I forgot, you're attending that dreadful frozen ball."

"That's the price I pay for being royalty," Anthony said. His voice sounded different, lazy and drawling, much more like the way he'd spoken when they first met, and it puzzled Alison enough that she paused to listen. Anthony had said he enjoyed the Wintersmeet Ball. There was another soft *tock*.

"That's not the price you're *going* to pay, if you don't start taking this seriously," Bishop said. *Tock tock*.

"You're not going to start on that again? Honestly, Alex, every time we meet it's the same thing. I'm tired of hearing about it."

"I just want to know —" *tock* " — you're taking this wager seriously. I'm starting to feel like I'm taking your money under false pretenses."

Anthony laughed, and the sound sent a chill through Alison's spine, because it had a nasty edge to it. "I won't say it hasn't been harder than I thought. It's taken a lot of work to get her this far. Not your kind of girl, Alex, quick to flip up her skirts."

Something about his words made her throat begin to close up. *Which girl? Got who this far?*

"I don't believe it," Bishop said, and there was a long string of intermittent *tocks*. "A woman who looks like that, she knows exactly what she's doing. She's just playing with you now, and you're too timid to take control. If I'd been in your shoes the bitch would have spread her legs for me long ago."

Anthony laughed again. "But you're not in my shoes, are you, Alex?" he said in that lazy drawl. "I'm the one who wagered I could seduce the Countess by Wintersmeet Eve. And I will. I'm still in control."

Chapter Thirteen

The words made no sense at first, as if Anthony had begun speaking Veriboldan. Then the icy mask she hadn't felt in weeks descended over her face, sealing her lips and her eyes and blinding her so she couldn't even blink.

"You don't have much time left," Bishop said.

"I don't need much time. Stop being such an old woman, Alex. I told you, I'm still in control."

Alison fumbled until she found the wall, then felt her way along it. The grayness around her vision began to fade, and she could see the front door too far ahead. "I'm also in control of this game," Anthony said, distantly, and then the roaring in her ears and the pounding in her head swallowed the rest of his words. It hurt so much to move; how could it hurt if she were frozen? The butler ought to be here to summon her carriage, but the hall was empty. Good. She couldn't bear to see anyone right now.

She reached the door and slowly turned the knob, pulling the door open just enough for her to slip through the crack, then closed it as quietly as she could behind her. The stairs were slippery with a light powdering of snow. She took a few careful steps before remembering her shoes were still in her hand. She held the stair rail and slipped them on, and felt snow melt off her feet into them. It didn't feel cold, it felt burning hot. That was probably because she was still frozen. She tried to pull her cloak around herself and realized she'd left it in Anthony's library. No way to get it now. Besides, she hardly needed it. And he wouldn't know how long she'd been there, just from the cloak. He wouldn't know what she'd heard.

She began walking along the sidewalk, putting one foot in front of the other like an ancient Device that hadn't been used in a century. She had to go home. No, she had to go back to the palace. Her face felt stiff from the frozen mask that still covered it. Snowflakes fell into her face and caught on her eyelashes, and she blinked until they floated away. She was too cold even to melt snow. She coughed, and it tore at her chest like a burning knife with a ragged edge. She hurt so much, and she wasn't sure how to get to the palace from here, so she kept walking because she couldn't think of anything better to do, and every step took her farther away from *him*.

A carriage, its horses' hooves muffled by the snow, passed her, then came to a halt. "Miss, are you all right?" said the driver, hopping down from her seat to put her arm around Alison's shoulders.

"I need to get to the palace," Alison said, and then doubled over as a coughing fit struck her with more force than before. She whimpered a little when it was over, and hated herself for her weakness.

The woman put her coat around Alison's shoulders. "Here, climb in, and I'll take you there," she said, and Alison curled into a corner of the carriage and tried not to cry out in pain when it bounced too hard on the rough road. She was so cold. Surely, if you were frozen, you wouldn't feel the cold. Everything was all wrong. Her head hurt. She was ill. The confusion, that had to be her illness. She'd sleep and in the morning everything would be fine. *Good thing you didn't have sex with him,* her inner voice told her. *Good thing no one knows how he tricked you. You desperate, pitiful creature.*

She put her hands over her ears to block out the voice, forgetting that it came from inside her own head. *He learned what you love and he turned it against you.* She shook her head, feeling the ice crack. *He made himself into someone you could trust.* Her head was pounding. Her brain was trying to burst out of her skull. *He said what you wanted to hear and you were so very ready to believe him.* She closed her mouth on a scream that came out muffled, like a cat's cry. She was too frozen to weep.

No wonder he'd looked so triumphant when he had her naked beneath him. How frustrated he must have been when she'd told him no. Every interaction they'd ever had replayed itself with devastating clarity in her frozen imagination. His initial "courtship" hadn't worked, so he'd watched her, discovered how to make himself appealing to her, turned himself into her friend, and it had worked. He'd found a way inside her defenses and she'd opened herself to him. And he'd done it all not for the sake of her money, or her title, or even the body he'd so openly admired, but for a sick wager. She covered her mouth to keep in another scream. How lonely had she been, that she'd been so easily fooled?

The carriage stopped, and the driver came to open the door. "Miss, you don't look well," she said, and helped Alison climb the stairs of the palace until she could be handed off to someone else, who took her through the halls of the palace to the Dowager's apartment. Dimly, Alison was aware of the guards breaking their usual impassivity to help her enter. *But suppose I'm a dangerous assassin?* she thought, and wanted to laugh at the implausibility of that scenario.

"Oh, my dear Alison, whatever is wrong? You, bring her to her bed," the Dowager said, and Alison realized she was being carried just as she was laid on the bed. Someone removed her shoes and the driver's coat and covered her with the white and gold counterpane, and someone else laid a burning cold hand on her forehead, and she flinched away. So she could feel pain, after all. "She has a terrible fever," the Dowager said. "Someone send for Dr. Trevellian." But the quilt was heavy, and she could feel the ice melting, and soon she felt warm enough to sleep, so she did.

She woke to find a short man in a doctor's tunic and wide-legged pants bending over her. "Ah, you're awake," he said. "Don't worry, there's nothing wrong with you that a few months won't cure."

"A few months?" Alison said, confused.

"Why, you're pregnant, my dear," the doctor said.

"But—I never—"

"Didn't you?" said Anthony. "You helped me win the bet. I should probably give some of this to you." He waved a large clinking bag in front of her face. "You were so eager for it, I almost didn't have to do—"

She woke to find a short man in a doctor's tunic and wide-legged pants bending over her. "Ah, you're awake," he said. "Don't worry, I think I've removed almost all of it."

Alison's head hurt. "Of what?"

He held up something that reflected the light like crystal. "The ice, of course," he said. "I'm sorry there's not much left of you, but you were ice all the way through and you wouldn't let it thaw."

"It was to protect me," she said. "If I freeze, it doesn't hurt."

"If you freeze, there's not much point to living, is there?" the doctor said. "I think you'd better—"

She woke to find a short man in a doctor's tunic and wide-legged pants bending over her. "Ah, you're awake," he said.

"Are you real or are you my mind torturing me?" she said, her voice hoarse from disuse.

He smiled. "Real, fortunately for you. You were trying to develop a nasty case of pneumonia. Did you have hallucinations?"

She nodded. "I thought they were bad dreams."

"They're a side effect of the treatment. The good news is you should be well in just a couple of days. You'll certainly be kicking up your heels at the Wintersmeet Ball, I'm happy to say."

"What treatment?"

He held up his left hand, and she saw a shimmer around it, like heat haze. "Healing magic. Inherent magic. I hope you don't have objections to it, because I can't put the illness back into you." He smiled and winked at her, and she smiled back, the muscles around her mouth tense as if she'd forgotten how.

"I don't see how anyone could object to anything so useful. Thank you, doctor."

"You'd be surprised how irrational people can be about inherent magic. It's not uncommon for people to be lynched just because they're suspected of being able to move things with their minds or, heaven forbid, see the future. Two hundred years since the Ascendants were defeated, but we haven't forgotten their powers." He crossed the room and put his fingers on her wrist, then laid the back of his hand against her forehead. "Pulse is normal, temperature is fine, and if you'll allow me—I'm sorry, this is a bit invasive—" He pushed up her shirt to just below her breasts and put a wooden cup to her chest on the left side, and laid his ear against it. "Breathe deeply, please...now the other side...thank you." He pulled her shirt down over her belly. "Lungs sound fine. I do excellent work, if I say it myself." He winked again, and she laughed, then had a fit of coughing so intense the doctor had to help her sit up so she could breathe.

"My goodness, that sounds awful. May I come in, Dr. Trevellian? Is she all right? How do you feel, my dear? I feel simply terrible at being angry with you for being late." The Dowager sat on the bed beside Alison and patted her hand. "Where did you go, dear? Anthony said you had already left when he returned home. He was quite disturbed to discover your cloak in the library."

"I...don't remember," Alison said. "I must have been confused and wandered a bit."

"Well, we're all glad you're home safely. Dear Zara sends her regards. And Anthony really was distraught. He blamed himself for not arriving before you left."

"I'm sure I'm grateful for his concern," Alison said, feeling the ice spread over her face. "Milady, would you mind terribly if I slept? I feel so weak still." It was true, but she didn't think she dared sleep, if she were going to find those dreams there.

"Yes, sleeping is a good idea," Dr. Trevellian said. "Your body has essentially experienced most of the illness at an accelerated rate. It's a draining experience. The longer you rest, the sooner you'll be back to normal. And it might be a good idea not to have any visitors for a while, other than perhaps Rowenna." It took Alison a moment to remember that was the Dowager's given name. She really wasn't well yet.

"Oh, of course, my dear. Are you hungry? No? Have Belle let the servants know when you're ready to eat. Sleep well." The Dowager patted her hand again and withdrew.

Dr. Trevellian packed his things into his bag and made to follow the Dowager, then stopped with his hand on the door. "May I tell you something you may consider impertinent?"

"I imagine you've already seen most of me during my treatment, so I can't imagine what more you might consider impertinent," Alison said with a wry smile.

The doctor didn't smile back. "You said...certain things...in your delirium I could not help but overhear. I want to assure you I won't share your secrets with anyone, including the Queen. But I think you could do worse than to confide in her." He nodded and left the room.

What did I say? She must have talked about Anthony's betrayal. She believed she could trust Dr. Trevellian not to speak, but...what did he think Zara might need to know about? The thought of telling anyone, even the Queen, about the humiliating wager made her freeze up again.

What was she going to do? Confront Anthony? Let him mock her further? She didn't understand what he was doing. It was...how long had she been ill? What day was it? At the most, if it was still the same afternoon, there were only four days until Wintersmeet; when did he think he'd have the chance to seduce her, particularly if she was going to be confined to bed for at least a day? Was he really so confident of his hold over her? And whether he lost or won, would he or Bishop publicize the wager? She pulled the pillow over her head. She was too frozen to cry. She'd let him touch her breasts, considered letting him do more. Let him into her heart when she should have known he was no different from the rest. She almost wished Dr. Trevellian had let her die.

She ought to tell Zara. It was impossible that she knew about the wager. Nor could his mother, come to think on it. Zara would be furious to hear her brother had made such an infamous wager…but, really, what could Zara do about it? Whether or not he won was irrelevant. The fact that he'd thought it acceptable to seduce her for the sake of a bet wouldn't change. He'd already humiliated her. Betrayed her, after he'd promised he wouldn't.

A knock at the door heralded Belle's entrance with a handful of sealed notes and envelopes. "Quite a lot of people wish you well," she said, handing everything to Alison. It warmed her frozen heart. Notes from former dancing partners, and the Dowager's card-playing friends, and there was even a tentative message from Edwin. *So daring of him,* she thought. Surprisingly, Zara sent a few lines of comfort and well-wishing. She hadn't realized how many people cared what happened to her.

One message, sealed with the North family sign and shield, she set aside, then, when she'd opened all the others, she returned to it and turned it over and over in her hand. He'd written her name in his carelessly graceful handwriting, so familiar to her from all the invitations he'd sent. Three times she started to break the seal, three times she stopped herself. She finally threw it into the fire, unopened.

Chapter Fourteen

"Marianne, I think your dress is the nicest," Simone said. "I love how the bodice fits."

"Well you, as usual, look radiant in white," Marianne said. "Alison, don't you think Simone looks wonderful?"

"She does," Alison said. "I think we all look amazing. Just think how many jaws will drop when we all enter together."

"They will certainly drop if you go dressed as you are now, Alison," Elisabeth said archly. "Do you plan to put your gown on, or are you going to go in nothing but your corset and petticoat?"

"I've been distracted by how lovely your gown is, Elisabeth," Alison lied. "Please excuse me, ladies."

She returned to her room and contemplated the gown hanging from the wardrobe door. It was a dream of white silk and silver gauze, with a square-cut neckline, a fitted waist and silver train. She planned to wear her mother's diamonds with it.

She'd bought it for Anthony.

She'd thought how much he would love to see her in it.

She'd considered letting him take it off her.

It was no consolation he'd lose his bet, though she was still confused about what he thought he was doing. She hadn't seen him since that afternoon when her world had frozen and cracked into a million glittering pieces. He'd sent two more messages. She'd burned both unread. She would have to see him tonight and she had no idea what she'd do, or what he planned to do. She wished she didn't have to go to the ball. Dr. Trevellian hadn't done her any favors by healing her so quickly. Death by pneumonia would be a good excuse to get her out of this nightmare.

She'd decided she had to tell Zara. Unfortunately, the Queen had been too busy to see her, had sent a polite note inviting her to dinner sometime after the first of the year. This wasn't something Alison wanted to entrust to a letter. She wanted to face Zara and know the Queen hadn't played any part in her humiliation.

She sighed, and slid her gown over her head, and had Belle fasten it up, all those tiny buttons along her spine. She clasped her mother's diamonds around her neck and let Belle do her hair atop her head with a single ringlet falling over one shoulder, as she'd worn it that fatal night she'd told Anthony she loved him. How he must have rejoiced to hear that, sign that his seduction was working. She felt herself go blotchy from the memory.

"Milady, are you all right? Only your skin is—"

"I know, Belle. It will pass. How do I look?"

"Beautiful as always. You're going to break hearts tonight, milady."

Only the one. Only my own.

She rejoined the other women and felt a moment's pleasure at Elisabeth's jealous expression, then hated herself for her spitefulness. "Oh, my dears, don't you all look simply beautiful!" the Dowager said. She embraced each of her ladies in turn, holding Alison a little longer than the others and whispering, "I predict you will have an evening you will never forget, my dear." Alison made herself smile. The Dowager was almost certainly right.

They arrived late on purpose, the Dowager wanting her ladies' entrance to make an impression on as many people as possible. Alison didn't see the Prince. She didn't look for him either. Her frozen mask made it difficult for her to smile, but thankfully it wasn't necessary; her hand was claimed for the next dance immediately, a country dance in which she went down the line so often she had no chance to speak to or even smile at her partner. After that she made an effort never to be without a partner. Anthony was going to find her eventually, and this was simply delaying the inevitable, but it gave her the illusion that some things, at least, were under her control.

She knew it was him before she saw him, knew the touch of his hand as he took hers, standing behind her. She put on a frozen smile before turning to meet his blue-eyed gaze. His smile was much warmer than hers. "If I had known how popular you would be, I would have secured my dance a long time ago," he said, leading her out to the center of the ballroom.

"It's the glamour of having been so ill, I suppose," Alison said, trying for a light tone. "I had no idea how many people cared about me."

"Including me. I was worried about you. You didn't respond to any of my messages. I can't believe I took so long to come home that day. I'm so sorry."

"You only did what we'd agreed upon. And I'm well now, so no harm done." *Not from the illness, at any rate.*

"If you'd wandered the streets much longer, we might not be able to say that. When I think of how ill you might have become...Alison, I don't know what I'd do if anything happened to you."

His expression of worry and sorrow was extremely convincing. *He's good. He's very good. Maybe I shouldn't blame myself for believing him. No, I should have known better. So many times, so many men, why did I think he was any different from the rest?*

"You'd go on," she said with a smile she knew was unconvincing. So did he. He looked surprised, then concerned. "Do you think me that shallow?" he said.

"No," *yes*, "I'm just being realistic. You'd find someone else eventually."

"Alison, I don't understand. Are you feeling well? You're not still sick, are you?"

"I feel a little light-headed. Would you mind if we sat down?"

"Not at all." He took her to a seat and said, "I'll get you something to drink."

Alison kicked off her dancing shoes, which were a little tight, realized she'd have trouble getting them on again, then realized further that she didn't care. She watched the dancers whirl round the room and realized she *was* a little light-headed. She wished there were a clock in here, or that she had a watch. She would welcome in the new year, then return with the Dowager, pleading faintness. Anthony wouldn't bother courting her once the deadline was past, and all she'd have to do would be to tell Zara and leave it in her ruthless hands.

"I hope you like champagne," Anthony said, and handed her a tall glass. She sipped and smiled.

"You're not trying to get me drunk, are you?" she asked archly. "I might be a mean drunk."

Anthony leaned forward, not smiling now. "Alison, is something wrong? You're behaving very strangely."

"I had some bad news recently. I'm afraid it's left me out of sorts."

"Is there something I can do to help?" By heaven, he was handsome, and he looked genuinely concerned. She shook her head.

"I'm afraid it's something I have to deal with on my own. But it's sweet of you to offer."

She thought he looked a little relieved. Probably he thought he hadn't lost his chance to win the wager, though he was definitely running out of time. "Would you like to finish our dance?" he said. "Or, actually, have another one, since ours seems to be over."

"Oh, we can't dance two in a row, you know that. Wouldn't want to give anyone the wrong impression." She smiled and winked at him, and saw him briefly confused before he smiled and nodded.

"I'll be back later, then, to claim my dance." He leaned over and whispered into her ear, "You look so beautiful. I love you."

It took everything she had to give him a sincere smile. The rest of her froze solid at his words. What under heaven was he playing at? She was suddenly angry. How *dare* he toy with her like this? Was she really so pathetic, so desperate for love that she'd let him play this game, let him laugh at how easily he got inside her defenses? She put her shoes back on, found another partner and threw herself into the dance, laughing and flirting until she almost convinced herself she was having a good time.

She didn't see Anthony again until it was nearly midnight. He appeared as if from nowhere like a bad fairy from a children's tale, smiling and looking at her as if he really did love her. She allowed him to lead her onto the floor and decided to play the game out; whatever he had in mind, she felt she had a right to be there when he failed. Her smile was growing a little tattered around the edges, but Anthony didn't seem to notice. He seemed entirely too happy for someone who was about to lose a wager.

The dance ended, but when Alison would have reclaimed her hand, Anthony gripped it tighter, leaned close, and whispered, "I want to show you something." Before she could assent, he'd drawn her out of the ballroom and down a series of passages to one of the older sections of the palace. The stones here were a paler gray than those along the Library passage, and the hall was more brightly lit, but it all radiated the same chill, carried by a draft like the breath of some ancient dragon born of ice. Anthony opened a door only a little taller than Alison was to reveal a room about twelve feet square, its black stones so tightly fitted together that it looked as if it had been carved out of a single block. Narrow, steep stairs of unfinished wood constrained only by a slim iron rail spiraled up out of sight.

A lantern hung on a peg by the door; Anthony lit it and held it up to illuminate the room better. Its light reflected off the myriad rough planes of the stone like flashes of gold. "I'll go first," he said, and Alison had to follow him or be left behind in the dark. It was a long way up. Alison's sides burned, her chest ached, and before they'd gone a hundred steps she was breathing heavily. She tugged at the hem of Anthony's dress coat and said, "Stop."

"I'm sorry, love." Anthony came back down and put his arms

around her, supporting her, and she was too grateful for it to push him away. "I planned this before you got sick," he said, "but the doctor said you'd be well by now, so I thought it would be all right." He sounded contrite, the lying bastard. If this stairway came out into a softly-lit boudoir with an enormous bed, she was going to kick him all the way back down it.

When she'd recovered, he led on, more slowly this time. The stairwell continued chilly, but Alison didn't realize it opened to the outdoors until she emerged from the stairwell to find herself at the top of one of the palace towers. In the summer, it would be a garden; right now, at the heart of winter, it was a twisted mass of dead undergrowth and spiny, leafless bushes. In the center stood a brazier larger than Alison could put her arms around, burning with a bonfire that leaped toward the sky as if it wanted to touch the face of the crescent moon. The dead branches twined around its base, forcing it back to earth. Alison thought she'd never seen anything so depressing. Anthony seemed to think it was marvelous. "Do you remember when we drove up to Old Fort and I showed you the fire at the top of Willow North's tower?"

"This is usually a place where lovers go," you said. You were priming me to fall in love with you even then. "I do," she said.

"This is that tower. And this is Willow North's garden," he said. "I should bring you up here in summer, when it's beautiful. I know it's awful now, but we're not here for the garden." He took a deep breath. "This is the tallest tower in the palace, and—" The deep tones of the bell tower clock at the foot of the palace drive began sounding the hour. "—it's Wintersmeet Day now."

She could feel the shift of energy as the lines of power changed their alignment in response to the solstice. For the space of three seconds she could feel her bond to her father, and to Patrick and her other cousins, and, more faintly, her connection to more distant relatives, and she knew they could feel her presence here, all those miles away from County Waxwold. If she'd been home, the intensity would have been greater, more powerful, and she wished with all her heart she were home instead of standing at the top of this freezing, dead tower with a man who'd humiliated her for the sake of a stupid wager.

Anthony breathed out, a long, satisfied sound. "That's the most amazing feeling, isn't it?"

"It is," Alison said. Was this what he'd wanted? The new year had begun. He'd lost his wager. She didn't know why she was still standing here. She began to turn away, but before she'd moved more than a fraction of an inch, he took both her hands in his.

"Happy Wintersmeet, Alison. I wanted to give you my gift now, just at the first of the year. I hope it was worth waiting for." He pulled something small out of his waistcoat pocket. "Betrothal rings aren't in fashion now, but I thought, being who you are, that you might appreciate tradition." He took her left hand and slid a ring over her middle finger. "Marry me, Alison? And let me shout it from the tallest tower that I love you?"

Alison retrieved her hand from his and looked at the ring. It was set with a dark faceted oval stone that was black in the firelight, surrounded by a ring of small round diamonds. It was beautiful. She held her hand up closer to the light; still black. It certainly seemed real. Absently, she said, "This is an awfully long way to go to lose a bet."

Anthony went perfectly still. "What?" he said.

Still gazing at the ring, Alison said, "I still don't understand what you were doing. You were running out of time and you didn't even try to seduce me again when the first time failed. You had to know I was primed to fall into your bed—after all, it almost worked once."

She looked up at Anthony. "What were the stakes, anyway? Bragging rights? Or was it money? Come, Anthony, I think I have a right to know what my body was worth."

He looked as frozen as she felt. His mouth opened, but nothing came out. Alison looked at the ring again. It looked good on her finger. Pity it was too beautiful for her to throw it in his face.

"You were very good, you know," she went on when it became clear Anthony wasn't going to say anything. "The way you went from being a dissolute drunk to that whole vulnerable act—I'm ashamed to say I believed you. It's been a long time since I believed the lies any man told me. So maybe that can be a nice consolation prize—you won the heart of Alison Quinn through trickery and deceit. Possibly that's the only way it *can* be won." She added, "I wish I hadn't let you touch me so intimately. I'm never going to forgive myself for that."

Anthony said, "No. No, Alison, that's not—I swear I didn't lie to you about that—"

"You know something, Anthony?" Alison said, cutting him off. "If this were a play, I would have learned about your wager through some third party, and it would all be a huge misunderstanding, and we'd be reconciled in the end. But this isn't a play, and I—lucky me—I got to hear about it from your own mouth and that of your charming friend Mister Bishop. No misunderstanding. No comedy. Just me, standing in your hallway, hearing you say you'd wagered you could get me into your bed by Wintersmeet Eve. Obviously I'm happy you failed. But I admit to some curiosity about what you'll do next."

Anthony grabbed her by the shoulders. "Alison, listen, I can explain, just listen to me—"

"I'm so pleased! Yes, tell me everything. Especially what the stakes are. I'd still like to know that."

He shook his head. "No. No. Alison, listen, I swear to you I never meant to collect on that bet." He was breathing heavily, as if some creature had been chasing him. "It was the night you slapped me. I was already drunk and I went home and got drunker. I…said things I shouldn't have, and Alex said I should teach you a lesson. And I said…I don't want to repeat it, but I bet Alex I could make you sleep with me before Wintersmeet Eve."

"You can imagine how special that makes me feel."

"I want to be totally honest with you."

"You've said that before. Do you even know what that word means?"

"Please! Alison, don't...." He was crying now. "I had no idea Zara was going to throw us together. I thought, how convenient, I'll win this bet in two weeks. But everything I knew, all the ways I knew to seduce a woman, they just slid right off you. Then we went to the play and you were so different, you were alive and happy and I didn't know what to do with that. Every time we met, you'd do or say something unexpected. Then you told me, that night in the carriage, about how often you'd been treated like a prize instead of a woman, and here I'd been trying to do the same thing to you. I felt so ashamed. I knew I couldn't try to win that wager anymore."

"That's a lovely story," Alison said. "And yet you didn't call off the bet. Why was that? Too costly?"

He shook his head. "It was just a token. A hundred guilders."

"Oh, and now I don't feel special at all."

Anthony let go of her and turned away. "I didn't want Alex to know I couldn't bring myself to do it. He wouldn't ever have stopped taunting me." He shuddered. "And then I fell in love with you, and I *really* couldn't tell Alex. He would have said the most awful things about us, and I couldn't bear that."

"And yet you had no problem listening to him call me a bitch and tell you I'd have spread my legs for him months ago. I wonder what else he's said about me, all those times I wasn't listening in."

He groaned. "Alison, I've been so stupid. I can't begin to tell you how sorry I am."

She felt no pity, no sorrow, nothing but a distant echo of the misery she was sure would catch up with her soon. "So, you fell in love with me, you let your bastard of a best friend mock me and harass you, and you did...what? You let the clock run out? That's why we had to keep our relationship secret until now?"

He nodded. "I was going to miss the deadline, pay Alex, and marry you. And you were never going to know."

"Right up until Bishop told everyone how you failed to seduce me and wasn't that hilarious, and by the way, Countess, your husband thinks so little of you he can't even defend you to his friend. Did you really think losing the bet would make everything all right?"

Anthony groaned again. "Alison," he choked out, "I love you. I never lied to you about that. I wanted to make love with you because I love you, not because I was trying to win a bet. I swear on my life it's the truth."

She considered his words, considered his desperate face. Why was he continuing the charade, now that the deadline had passed? He should have just walked away. She replayed their relationship once more, examined everything he'd said to her, compared it to the story he'd told her just now. So. He'd been telling the truth about something. He really did love her. How sad that it didn't matter.

"I believe you," she said, and he looked at her with such hope it froze her right to the core. "It's a relief, actually. I don't have to hate myself for falling in love with a man who cared nothing for me. But it means the man who loved me exposed me to humiliation because he cared more about the good opinion of a degenerate bastard than he did about me." She took his hand, dropped the ring into it, and closed his fingers over it. "I might have forgiven you for everything else, even for being so juvenile as to wager on my virtue, but I cannot forgive you for that."

She turned and walked away from him, listening for the sound of him following her, but her footsteps made the only noise on that frozen roof. She imagined she could feel him watching her, his gaze weighing her down, and she thought about running down the stairs to get away faster, but she would probably fall if she did. *So I do care whether I live or die, after all.*

She thought about looking for the Dowager to tell her she was leaving, but decided she'd had enough of the North family for one night. Safely in her room, she let Belle unfasten all the tiny buttons, stripped off the gown and kicked it into a corner, then, wearily, picked it up and put it back on its hanger. When she got into bed, her toe bumped into something hard and sharp-edged. She reached under the bed and found the one Wintersmeet gift she hadn't wrapped. The first edition advance copy of Flanagan's book of plays. She couldn't bring herself to hurl it across the room, so she shoved it further under the bed and fell asleep, still tearless, her fist clenched on the pillow as if daring the nightmares to return.

She woke, dazed, to full sunlight. *I've missed breakfast,* she thought, and hurried through her toilette to burst into the dining room and find no one there. One of the servants pointed at the Dowager's dressing room and said, "Milady asked to see you when you rose."

Mystified, Alison entered the room and found the Dowager seated at her dressing table, having her hair brushed by one of her maids. She saw Alison in the mirror and turned, waving the girl away, then rose and crossed the room to embrace Alison.

"My dear, I can't tell you how happy I am for you both," she said. "I was so surprised—honestly, I had no idea the two of you were courting. I should be angry you kept it a secret, but I'm just so happy to welcome you to the family I can't find it in me to do so." She grasped Alison's hands and kissed her lightly on both cheeks, then looked at her hands in some surprise. "You're not wearing it?"

"Milady, I don't understand."

"My betrothal ring, dear. Anthony came to me yesterday morning to ask me if I wouldn't mind you having it. Don't tell me he forgot to give it to you!"

The Dowager's innocently pleased smile made Alison angry. He'd dared to involve his mother—! "Milady," she began, keeping a level tone, "I thank you for your generous gift, but I do not intend to marry your son."

"But—Anthony assured me your affections were definitely engaged. I may not approve of his lifestyle, but I have never known him to be mistaken in that regard. How could you treat him with such casual disrespect as to pretend to care for him?"

"Milady, if anyone has been toyed with, it is I."

The Dowager drew back, her eyes going cold. "How dare you suggest my son would treat you with disrespect? I have never seen him so joyful as he was yesterday when he told me how he loved you!"

"Three months ago your precious son wagered he could get me into his bed by last night. You have no idea how grateful I am that he failed!"

The Dowager's eyes went from cold to furious. "You *dare* make such allegations, you vicious...*harpy*!"

"Better a harpy than a fool who's too willfully blind to see the truth about her degenerate son! Maybe if you'd been a better mother, we wouldn't be having this conversation now!"

The Dowager sucked in an outraged breath. "Get out. Leave me at once."

"Milady, I'll be happy to leave. In fact, I'm going back to Kingsport immediately. Let the other ladies take what they want from my wardrobe. I won't need it. And if I never see another member of the North family again, I will die happy."

She stormed out of the room and slammed the door to the bedroom that would only be hers for the next few minutes. She changed out of her morning gown into sensible traveling clothes, packed up what few things she cared about, and gave Belle a severance bonus. "If you need references, write to me at Quinn Press in Kingsport," she told the girl. "Thank you for everything."

"But...why are you leaving, milady?" Belle said, her eyes wide.

"You'll hear about it soon enough," Alison said. "Just remember, Belle—if anyone asks, make sure to tell them he lost the bet."

She carried her own suitcase through the halls of the palace, trying not to think about why she knew them so well. In the yard, she asked for a carriage that would take her to the coaching station for Kingsport. In half an hour, she was on her way home. She still hadn't cried. She thought she never would.

Interlude

He stumbled through the dark hallway to what he hoped was the study door. Turning on the light seemed like too much work, and besides, there were mirrors there, and he didn't want to see his face right now. Anyway, he didn't need the light to find the liquor cabinet, which said a lot about his life, that and the fact that he could identify every bottle inside it by touch. *Brandy*, he thought, *that's the stuff*, and picked up the decanter and hugged it to his chest, then felt around until he found an armchair, fell into it, yanked out the stopper and had a good stiff drink straight from the bottle. It wasn't very good brandy, but it didn't have to be; all it had to be was alcoholic.

He'd killed something inside her. He'd seen it in her eyes, there in the moonlight. He'd done something to her you should never do to another human being, let alone the woman who'd trusted you with her heart. A woman who'd already been betrayed so many times. He took another drink. He'd tried to explain, and the thing of it was, she'd *listened* and then told him in so many words that she could never forgive him because he was weak and easily led and, basically, not a man. She hadn't shouted or sworn at him. She'd just walked away, leaving him standing on a cold roof holding a ring he'd hoped to see her wear. And he deserved it. He deserved every word she'd flung at him and a thousand others she hadn't. He drank again. The brandy wasn't working fast enough. He could still see her eyes.

The light went on, making him wince. Alex said, "I know you're disappointed at losing our little wager, Tony, but I didn't think you'd take it quite this hard. You planning to take that brandy to bed with you?"

"Damn you, Alex," Anthony said. He set the decanter down hard on the floor and went to the desk, yanking out the center drawer and rummaging in it until he found a small purse. He threw it at Alex, who fielded it neatly, his long dark face amused. "Count it if you like," he said. "You've won." He sank back down into the chair and took another drink. The world was starting to get fuzzy.

Alex poured the coins into his hand, then back into the purse. "Really, Tony, you're acting as if this wager mattered," he said. "Who cares that some priggish, stuck-up bitch won't sleep with you? Her loss, if I—"

Anthony hurled the decanter at Alex's head, which barely missed him to smash on the wall behind him, and followed it up by leaping out of his chair and shoving Alex backward so hard they both nearly tripped. Alex ended up pinned against the dripping wall, Anthony's arm pressed across his throat.

"*Shut up,*" Anthony snarled. "Don't say another word, Alex, or by heaven I will crush the life out of you."

Alex had gone limp when Anthony pinned him, but now he gave him a startled look, then began to laugh just as if Anthony's arm wasn't poised to crush his windpipe. "You fell in love with her," he chortled. "That's just rich, Tony. Set a trap for her and be caught in hers instead. Did she find out what you'd planned? Is that the reason for this death by alcohol poisoning you've embarked on?" He laughed again. "Oh, poor boy—"

Anthony pressed harder, and Alex's voice cut off. He grabbed at Anthony's arm, choking, but Anthony was taller and heavier and filled with brandy and rage. "Killing...me...won't...fix it," he wheezed.

Anthony released him. Alex, clutching his throat, slid down the wall to sit at its base. "Sorry, old friend," he said when he'd regained his breath. "Still, plenty of other lady fish in the sea, right? Let me take you somewhere, get you some real female companionship—"

"Get out," Anthony said. He leaned down to pick up the purse Alex had dropped and felt the world spin. It took him a couple of tries; the purse kept moving around. Anthony finally snared it and threw it at Alex's chest so hard it bounced. "Get out. And don't come back.

We're finished."

Alex looked surprised. He stood up, clutching the purse. "Now, you know you don't mean it. We'll talk when you're sober."

Anthony looked his former friend up and down. He saw a man several years his senior who tried to dress and talk like a younger man. He saw a lean face with early lines of dissipation etched into it. He saw a mocking mouth that, now Anthony thought about it, never had a kind word for anyone when a sarcastic, biting one would do.

"I said we're finished, Alex," he said. "I can't believe I ever thought you worth listening to. If I'd been strong enough to tell you the truth, I'd be with her now. I let you say things about her I never should have put up with because I didn't want you to mock me for falling in love. She might have forgiven me for the wager, someday, but she's never going to forgive me for caring more about what you thought than about her."

"And why shouldn't you? Who is *she*, anyway, compared to what we've been through together? When your father died—"

"My father would be *ashamed* to know how I've wasted my life since I met you. You're worthless, Alex, you spend your life battening on the wealth and hopes of others, always looking for a way to tear people down instead of lifting yourself up. I ruined my life, but you damned well helped me do it. Get out."

Alex's face had gone red during this speech. "And I suppose it's my fault you're a drunk and a womanizer? You think your precious Countess could bear to know everything you've done in my company? That she'd still love you when she knows who you really are?"

"Haven't you been listening, Alex? She doesn't care if I live or die. She despises me almost as much as I despise myself. You can't make my life any worse than it is. Now get out or by heaven I will throw you out."

Alex sneered. "So, you think I can't make your life worse? Wait until news of this wager gets around. And, my dear boy, you can be assured it *will* get around." He slammed the door behind him.

Anthony sank back into his chair. The air stank of brandy and Alex's noxious perfume. He wasn't nearly drunk enough yet. He went back to the liquor cabinet and found a bottle of a colorless liquid that didn't smell like much of anything. He took an exploratory sip and felt it burn the lining of his throat all the way down to his stomach. Oh, yes. This would do the trick.

"Anthony? *Anthony!*"

He groaned and lifted his head. His mother, blurry and dancing in the midmorning light, loomed over him. He found he was on the floor, leaning against the chair, the half-empty bottle of mystery liquor tipped over on the carpet beside him. The room still smelled of brandy and cologne.

"Is this true? Did Alison actually refuse you? Please look at me, Anthony. Must you always deal with disappointment by becoming too drunk to stand?" His mother reached down and tried to pull him to his feet. He used the chair to push himself into a standing position, then used the chair again to maintain it. He wasn't hung over, he was still drunk.

"I spoke with Alison this morning and she had the utter nerve to lie to me about why she'd refused your suit. I am so sorry you were mistaken in her, though I must say I didn't think her the type not to just say she didn't want to marry you—"

"Mother," Anthony said, desperately trying to get her to stop swaying, "she was telling the truth. There was a wager. I've destroyed everything. I betrayed her."

The Dowager went silent. Then she poked her son in the chest, making him wobble and sit down in the chair. "Explain," she said.

He told her everything. The wager, what had come of it, his change of heart, his inability to face Alex. What she said, what she did, how she'd walked away from him on that tower. And, in harsh detail, how he'd betrayed the love of his life.

When he finished, his mother continued to look down at him. He rubbed his hand over his face and said, "Mother—"

"Don't say another word, Anthony," she said, and her voice was like sharpened steel. "I have stood by you all these years. I told everyone I believed you had a good heart, even when you drank too much and gambled too much and got far too close to far too many women. And now I am so ashamed of you I almost want to walk out of this house and let you drink yourself to death. How dare you treat any woman with such callous disrespect? Your pride is hurt, and you think that entitles you to demean someone else? Let alone someone like Alison Quinn?"

Anthony groaned. "I know, Mother. You're not telling me anything I haven't told myself."

"Then let me tell you something new, Anthony. You need to grow up. You've spent the last six years since your father died in a state of permanent adolescence, and I let it slide because I loved you and I always told myself one day you'd wake up and realize you were tired of the drinking and the betting and the whoring. So some of this is my fault. But most of it is yours. You don't deserve a woman like Alison because you're just a boy in all the ways that matter. A man would have stood up to that awful Mister Bishop, whom I've never liked. A man wouldn't have made that wager in the first place." She prodded the bottle with her toe. "And a man wouldn't deal with his disappointment by diving face-first into a bottle."

Anthony felt tired, and sick, and his head spun. "Thank you for making yourself clear, mother," he said. "I'm going to bed now. I'll call on you later, if you're willing to receive me." He stood and staggered to the stairs leading to his bedroom. His mother didn't follow him. He fell, fully clothed, onto his bed, and was asleep seconds after his head hit the mattress.

He woke in the late afternoon, mouth tasting like stale piss, eyes gummy with sleep, head stuck to the mattress with a rope of saliva. *Finally I look as despicable as I feel,* he thought as he wiped his mouth and sat up. *Now* he was hung over. He staggered into his bathing room and stared at himself in the mirror. No one was going to call him handsome any time soon; no one was going to look at him as if he were the only man in the world, or whisper into his ear that she loved him. His eyes watered, almost certainly because the light was too bright.

He set about turning himself human again. He bathed, and washed and combed his hair. He dismissed his valet and shaved himself, carefully, his hand shaking a bit from his debauch. He dressed himself in semi-formal clothing and found a pair of boots that still had some polish left; he couldn't find the boot-blacking kit. He went to the kitchen, ignoring the staff, who all looked at him in confusion, and ate something out of the cold locker, even though the idea of food made him queasy. He found his greatcoat and eased into it, feeling like an old man. Then he went into the library.

She hadn't quite finished the job. There was an empty shelf, a few piles of books on the floor and tables, and a single volume sitting on a chair near the window as if she'd just gotten up to get a cup of tea before returning to her reading. He ran his fingers along the spines, looking at the titles. The new order was as meaningless to him as the old. He avoided looking at the chaise longue in the corner. The scent of her filled the air; if he closed his eyes, he could imagine her lying there, waiting for him. She'd thrown that intimacy back in his face, poisoned it with the accusation that he'd only wanted to make love with her to win that damned bet. No, he'd poisoned it himself. He remembered how she'd looked that day, the passion and trust in her eyes, the waves of blond ringlets spread out around her, her glorious breasts, and wished he'd drunk himself to death after all.

He left the house and walked to the palace. It wasn't that far away, and he needed to clear the last of the alcohol from his head. The palace guards ignored him as he went through the gate and up the stairs towards the north wing. He went to the reception desk and formally requested an audience with the Queen. The receptionist, a man about Anthony's age, seemed surprised that the Prince might need a formal audience, but put the request through. Anthony waited. Finally an older woman stuck her head out of a door and beckoned to him. She led him down a short hall to Zara's office and opened the door for him. Zara sat at her desk, writing. She didn't look up. "Yes?" she asked.

Anthony took a deep breath. "You already know what happened," he said. "You'll probably want to yell at me. Mother did. I deserve it. But I want to say something before that, so you can't say later that I only said it because you yelled at me."

Zara still didn't look up. She waved a hand as if to say 'get on with it.'

Anthony took another deep breath, let it out slowly. "I did all of this to myself," he said. "I was a fool. I was selfish. I was a coward. And I think on some level I knew all those things about myself, but I had an amazing woman who loved me and I thought that meant I must not be so bad after all. I didn't do anything to change, because I didn't realize I had to. I know she's never coming back. I know I hurt her too badly for her to forgive me. I'm not saying I can make her love me again. I just...I think I would like to become the man I should have been, the man she thought I was. I think he must be someone worth knowing."

He waited. Zara said nothing. He knew she could use silence like a weapon, so he continued to wait, not moving, until she raised her head. "Now that," she said, "is something I believe we can work with."

PART TWO

Chapter Fifteen

Three months later

Alison Quinn pushed open the door that read MARTIN QUINN, EDITOR and walked into her father's office, tapping a slim sheaf of papers against her leg. "You can't be serious," she said, waving the manuscript in her father's face.

Father set the document he was reading on a pile of other papers and looked at her with calculated innocence. "I don't know what you mean."

"Oh, you absolutely know what I mean. We can't publish this. It's dreck. I told you it was dreck when Shereen sent it in. And here it is with your chop boldly on the first page okaying it for publication. And *then* you have the gall to assign it to *me*."

"You've worked with Shereen on her other books. It was an obvious choice."

"Her other books didn't have recycled imagery and sentimental hogwash dripping from every line. It's embarrassing."

"We can sell it on the strength of her name alone. And before you tell me our reputation as a publisher is at stake, let me remind you that as successful as we are, we can still use the guaranteed sales."

"Can't we find something else? Something not made of sugar-coated treacle?"

Her father's eyes narrowed. "Alison, Shereen Wilson is a sweet woman who considers you a friend. Imagine how she'd feel if she could hear you talking right now. I'm tired of your bitterness spilling over into your work."

"It's not affecting my work."

"You haven't had a kind thing to say about any new manuscripts since you came back from Aurilien. You've changed, and not for the better."

Alison's face tightened. "I wonder why that is."

"Alison, the talk has died down. You're not the subject of gossip anymore, even if it was sympathetic gossip. You need to move on."

"As if it were as simple as that."

"It's not simple. But you're hanging on to your anger and pain. I can't bear to see you torturing yourself. None of this was your fault. Stop blaming yourself."

The frozen mask began to descend and she shook her head to dispel it. "You're right. I'm sorry, Father."

"Don't apologize to me. Just find a way to forgive yourself for whatever sins you feel you've committed." He paused, and added, "And stop being so isolated. That young man last night, Brenton something—"

"Brendan Videros. What about him?"

"He was interested in getting to know you better. You might have given him some encouragement."

"I wasn't interested in him."

"You barely spoke to him to be able to make that judgment."

"He was only interested in my physical attributes."

"That's unfair."

Alison sighed. "I don't understand where you're going with this. Do you think I should have pursued the connection? Am I supposed to encourage every man who pays me compliments?"

"Alison, damn it, stop being so flippant!" her father shouted, slamming his fist on the desk. "You wall yourself off from other people so thoroughly you are on your way to becoming a bitter, lonely woman. I know you've been hurt. That's the price we pay for living. Don't let this one bad experience—"

"*One* bad experience? Father, this is just the latest in a long line of bad experiences." She couldn't keep tears from welling up in her eyes. "I'm tired of trusting people who aren't worthy of it. What is so bad

191

about protecting myself?"

"Alison," her father said, running his fingers through his hair, "it's one thing not to allow people to take advantage of you. It's quite another to be so afraid of being hurt you never give people the chance to show they can be trusted. To let someone else give you happiness."

"You saw how well that worked out for me recently."

"Damn Anthony North and damn your pride too," her father said. "I'm talking about your future. You're not made to be alone, Alison. Somewhere out there is someone who will fill your heart with joy, and you're never going to find him if you refuse to trust anyone." He took a deep breath. "I loved your mother very much. Sometimes I hurt her, and sometimes she hurt me. But I have never regretted giving her the chance to do so, because it gave her the chance to love me. I think she felt the same."

The tears spilled over and ran down her face. She buried her face in her hands, wishing she could hold them back. "It's not worth it," she cried. "How am I supposed to know who to trust?" *I thought I knew. Clearly I was wrong.*

She heard her father come around the desk, then he put his arms around her. "You take chances," he said. "You trust your instincts. Are you telling me you don't know how to identify a fortune-hunter, or someone who sees you as nothing more than a beautiful body? You give people a chance to prove themselves, and you prove yourself to them."

Alison wiped her eyes. "I don't know how," she whispered. "Father, I think I'm broken."

"If you are, it's not irreparably so," he replied. "Do something for me. The next time a young man approaches you—an honest one—*talk* to him. Try to make a connection, even if it isn't a romantic one. Stop assuming any man who's interested in you has ulterior motives. It would be a good first step."

She smiled and sniffled a little bit. "I think I can do that." She took a deep, shuddering breath. "I promise I'll do that. Just—look, I'm sorry I was so harsh about Shereen. It was cruel. But I really think these poems are a bad idea. Shereen's going to be excoriated by the critics. Can't I work with her to find an alternative?"

The post boy opened the door. Father beckoned to him. "You can try," he said to Alison. "You may have a point about Shereen's reputation. See what you can do."

The boy staggered in under a sack of mail, a couple of parcels— and a long black scroll case. An address tag was tied around its middle, stark white against its blackness.

It was sealed at both ends with the sign and shield of the royal house of North.

Father reached out and flipped the tag over so they could read the address. ALISON QUINN, COUNTESS OF WAXWOLD.

Alison felt the blood drain from her face. "No," she said, "no, this isn't happening."

Father took out his belt knife and slid it under one of the seals, then tilted the scroll case to allow the parchment to slide out. It caught a little on the lip of the case and he had to shake it to dislodge it. He unrolled it and scanned the contents. Alison could only see that whatever message it contained was brief, barely covering half the page, and most of that was her full name and title. Maybe, if she didn't read it, she could pretend it hadn't arrived.

Father read it a second time, then passed it to her. Reluctantly, she read it aloud. "'*Alison Quinn, Countess of Waxwold, is summoned to attend Zara North at her offices in Aurilien at her earliest convenience. Send acknowledgement of receipt of this missive by return post.*' And it's signed by the Queen. I don't understand." An icy chill spread through her body. If this was with regard to *him,* surely Zara would have insisted on her return months ago. What else could she possibly do for the Queen? *What else can the house of North possibly do to me?*

"Cryptic, certainly," her father said. "What are you going to do?"

"Run away? Move to Veribold and live with the rebels? I have to go. I don't—Father, why would she do this to me?"

"Zara North never does anything without a reason, even if the reason is rarely clear to mere mortals," he said. "I don't think she'd want to humiliate you further, or expose you to...."

Anthony's presence hung in the air between them. Alison squeezed her eyes shut and said, "At one time I thought we might become friends. I wish I'd gone to her with my...problem... immediately."

"I thought we agreed you were going to stop torturing yourself."

"And yet here I am walking back into the scene of my torment." She opened her eyes and looked at her father. "I'll send the return message. I'll talk to Shereen. And I'll be back as soon as I can."

"Less than a week," Father said, but he didn't look certain about it. Alison didn't feel certain about it either. She rolled the parchment tightly and shoved it back into the case. Whatever Zara North had in mind, Alison doubted it would be so simple as to resolve itself in a day.

Alison didn't make an appointment. If the Queen wanted to see her, she would make time for the woman whose life she'd disrupted. Twice. She sat in the reception area, watching busy men and women come and go, and picked at the seam of her trousers. Would the Queen be offended that she hadn't dressed up for this summons? If she was, there wasn't anything Alison could do about it now, and maybe Zara would just send her home. She leaned back and tried to relax; she was sitting as stiffly as if she were wearing a corset—

"Do you even know how to slouch?" Anthony said—

Her spine stiffened again. She'd done so well, hadn't thought of him in...in days, and it was just that she was back in the palace that she'd slipped. She caught the receptionist staring at her and she glared at him until he flushed and looked away. She felt a little guilty about that, but being stared at put her on edge these days. There had been so many weeks when the staring had been accompanied by whispers whose content she could guess too easily.

"Milady Countess? The Queen will see you now," said a woman in North livery, bowing. The woman led her down a short hall to the Queen's office door, which was standing slightly ajar. Alison's heart pounded in her chest until it hurt. If *he* was in there, if Zara believed Alison had been in the wrong and wanted to punish her, if this was another colossal joke.... She pushed open the door and went in.

Zara was alone. She sat behind a desk piled with neatly organized paperwork, reading something in a folder. "Please sit down," she said, not looking up. Alison sat in the only other chair in the room, a comfortable armchair, not a hard kitchen chair, and waited. Eventually Zara put the folder down and looked at Alison with those sharp blue eyes. "Thank you for coming, Countess," she said.

"You asked so politely," Alison said without thinking, and blushed. Zara smiled.

"I'm glad to see in some ways, you haven't changed," she said. "I'll skip the formalities. I've summoned you here because I appointed you Royal Librarian five days ago." She reached into her desk and pulled out a shiny new key, definitely not the one Alison had seen Bancroft use. "Consider this your official investiture. There's really no ceremony, though I didn't think you'd want one if there were."

Alison gaped. "You can't do that," she said. "The Scholia—"

"The Scholia lost its say in the administration of the Royal Library five days ago, when Charles Bancroft was convicted of embezzling Library funds and stealing and selling books from the Library."

That struck her with a nearly physical pain. "No," she said. "That *bastard.*"

Zara grinned, a completely unguarded expression that startled Alison. "And *that* reaction is why you've now taken his place." She went from amused to serious in half a breath. "This will not be an easy task, Alison," she said. "Bancroft left the Library...well, you'll have to see it for yourself. There's little chance we'll be able to recover the missing books, let alone identify which ones are missing. I blame myself for letting it get this far. If you hadn't been so relentless about trying to get inside, I doubt anyone would have known there was a problem until there wasn't a Royal Library anymore. The Scholia continues to insist Bancroft's conviction is fraudulent, that none of their Masters could possibly lend himself to such gross dereliction of duty and certainly wouldn't try to line his own pockets with the proceeds. I need someone with Scholia training who is not a Master and I need someone who is passionate about books. You are the only person I know who meets both these qualifications. And I trust you."

Stunned, Alison said, "Thank you, your Majesty, that's…I'm overwhelmed. But I really must decline. I already have a job, and as I believe I told you once, I'm not qualified for the robe. Surely there must be someone better able than I to take this responsibility."

"Alison Quinn," said the Queen, "we could argue all day about your qualifications. I could point out that your position in your father's business could be done by many people, though perhaps not to your standard. I could remind you that you yourself told me taking the robe was more about politics than it was about librarianship. I could also make this a royal command. But I'm not going to do any of those things, because there is one key fact that makes all of that irrelevant. Ask me what it is."

"Uh…what is it, your—"

"I also told you to call me Zara. Nothing that's happened has changed that."

"What is it, Zara?"

"It's that the first thing that crossed your mind when I told you of your appointment was that *you want this job.* You had a vision of yourself as Royal Librarian and for that brief moment you wanted it more than anything. Yes, your mind immediately threw up objections, but they were all afterthoughts. You know you're qualified. You know you want to. So it's lucky for you I'm going to insist you take the position. It would be awful to have a Royal Librarian wandering around without a Library to take care of."

Alison stared at Zara in disbelief. Zara returned the stare with that blue-eyed glass-cutting gaze. Her mouth curled up at the corners, ever so slightly. Alison began to laugh. "Your Majesty—Zara—I hope you never decide to rule the world."

"I have enough trouble ruling Tremontane," Zara said. She pushed the key across to Alison. "I had the locks changed. Something about barn doors and horses applies here, but I didn't like the idea of Bancroft wandering around with the key to the Library still in his possession."

"He's not in custody, then?"

"Oh, he is, for now. The Scholia insists he be returned to them for justice, which would be the same as letting him go free. I haven't decided yet how far I want to push things. They're nominally under my jurisdiction, but in the spirit of free learning and inquiry—" she rolled her eyes—"they govern themselves in internal matters. And they're insisting that because his crime involved the Library, that brings it under their jurisdiction. It's nonsense, but Scholia Masters are positioned in key roles all over Tremontane, so the balance of power is sensitive. Well, at the very least I can squeeze most of what he embezzled out of him and his co-conspirators."

"I feel a little sorry for Edwin. He always seemed trapped between what he knew was right and what his superiors told him to do."

"I feel no such sorrow. He cared more about keeping his superiors happy than doing the right thing. Something I'm sure you can relate to."

Alison felt her face go blotchy, but with anger rather than humiliation. She lowered her head so she wouldn't have to look at the Queen. She hadn't believed Zara could be so thoughtless.

She heard Zara shift in her chair, and say, "I wonder if all our meetings are going to involve me apologizing for my brother."

"You don't need to apologize," Alison said, not looking up. "You didn't do anything wrong."

"Apparently I did," said Zara. "I neglected him as much as I did your Library. I let him go his own way after our father died and never considered that I was letting my heir turn into — well. I don't have to tell you."

"Are you trying to make excuses for him, your Majesty?"

"Are there any you would accept? I think there is nothing I can say that excuses what he did to you. I have had Anthony's full story, his part of it, and if there is anything I can tell you, anything I can do to ease your mind, I believe I owe you that. But I will never speak of this again unless you bring it up."

"I would rather not speak of it." She looked at Zara and saw compassion in her eyes, and had to look away again.

"Then we will not." Zara said. "Though I would like you to know I would have enjoyed having you for a sister."

Alison went blotchy again. "That was never going to happen."

"No? And if there had been no wager? As far as I can tell, loving you was the one thing Anthony never lied about. Which has made it hard for me to forgive him and might make forgiveness impossible for you." Zara cleared her throat. "But we've agreed not to talk about it, and I apologize for bringing it up. I would like you to assess the condition of the Library, make a list of recommendations, and make an appointment with my secretary for us to discuss what you've learned in, say, one week's time."

"I'll need time to put my other affairs in order. I have County business to attend to as well."

"That's what the post is for." Zara smiled wryly. "You may certainly have whatever time you need, but look at the Library first. I believe it will adjust your priorities." She drew a folder toward herself and busied herself with its contents. The meeting was over.

Alison picked up the key, shining steel rather than rusted and pitted iron. A rush of pleasure filled her from head to toe. The Library. *Her* Library. She felt something she hadn't felt in months. Joy. She smiled with pure happiness, opened the office door —

— and ran straight into Anthony North.

His left hand was raised in the act of knocking. His right hand held a sheaf of folders. "Excuse —" he said, then he said, "Dear heaven." He looked as utterly stunned as Alison felt. Her heart thumped once, painfully hard. *What cruel misfortune rules my life?* she wondered. *Of course he'd be here somewhere, but in Zara's office? He doesn't even work!*

"I beg your pardon, your Highness," she said, and stepped back to let him pass just as he did the same.

"No, please excuse me, Countess," Anthony said. She took a breath, then brushed by him without looking at his face again. She heard Zara say, "Anthony, stop hovering in the doorway and get in here," and then she was out of the office, out of the north wing, and standing on a third floor landing wondering what to do next.

So. She'd met him and she hadn't dropped dead of humiliation or had to endure more of his protestations of love and pleas to forgive him. Zara was right; Anthony had loved her. So what? He'd loved her and he'd still exposed her to Bishop's coarse comments and he'd still cared more about looking like a fool than he had about her. She'd been angry about it at the time and she was angry now. How could you even call that love? She realized she was standing in the middle of the hall, forcing people to step around her. What was she doing? Of course. Stupid. She clenched the key in her fist and tried not to run to the Library.

The scriptorium door still wasn't locked. No reason to. There was nothing in that room worth stealing. She pushed the door open and was startled to find two young men and one woman lounging about on the desks. "Who are you?" she demanded.

"We're the apprentices. Who are you?" the young woman retorted.

Encountering Anthony had left Alison in a heightened emotional state. The young woman's smug tone of voice was like stone scraping over raw skin. She held up the Library key. "If you're really apprentices, which I doubt, then I'm your new master," she said. "Who are you, and why are you in the scriptorium?"

The younger boy sprang up. "We really are the apprentices, milady," he said, and Alison realized she'd seen him in the Library before. "And you're the Countess of Waxwold who made such a fuss about getting into the Library."

"Guess you get your wish," said the other young man, pale and pale-haired like Alison herself, but with light gray eyes. He looked as if he'd been bleached. Alison glared at him. "What's your name?" she said.

"Declan," he told her, still lounging. He grinned at her impertinently.

"Declan. And how long have you been an apprentice?"

"Five years."

"And you need another two years to achieve a journeyman's certificate that will allow you to work at another library, or in some related field."

"Yes." He started to look a little uncertain.

"Interesting that Bancroft didn't take you with him. Oh, wait, that's because *he's in prison*."

Declan looked confused and a little worried. "I know that."

"So you might want to ask yourself, Declan, who's going to sign that journeyman's chit?"

The penny dropped. "Um," Declan said, "you are. Your ladyship."

"That's right, Declan, I am. Or, rather, I *might*. I suggest you take some time to think about what kind of behavior will earn you that certificate. Go ahead. I'll wait."

The young woman, a skinny redhead, sniggered. "And your name is…?" Alison said.

"Gwendolen Burns, milady. Of the Westover Burnses."

"I appreciate the information, Gwendolen. How long have you been an apprentice?"

"Three years, milady." Gwendolen had the look of someone who was doing everyone a huge favor just by breathing the same air as them. Alison's irritation increased. She tried to control it by asking the last apprentice, "And your name?"

"Trevers, your ladyship." She did remember him. He was a small, dark-complected boy who'd seemed eager to respond to the needs of the patrons.

"Trevers, you've been an apprentice how long?"

"Just one year, milady." And if she was any judge, he already knew more about the workings of the scriptorium than the other two. He'd be useful. The others…could she fire apprentices? She'd have to ask Zara, but she was willing to wager the answer was 'yes.'

"Where are the others? I know I've seen more than the three of you in here."

"They went back to the Scholia, your ladyship," Trevers said. He ducked his head. "They were Scholia students. We're just…." He left the sentence hanging in the air. Alison could guess what they were: local labor hired at no wages beyond room and board, promised a journeyman's chit if they did as they were told. No one a Scholia Master would consider worth expending effort on.

She took a deep breath and let it out. Sorting the apprentices out was interfering with what she actually wanted to do. "All right, you three. I'm going to take a look at the Library. I want you to put your heads together and make a list of all the tasks the librarians used to do, and all the tasks you were responsible for. There's pens and paper, yes?"

The three of them shook their heads. "Baxter and Edwin took a lot of things when they left," said Trevers.

"Weren't they arrested with Bancroft?"

"They convinced the guards they weren't important, that they didn't know anything about what Master Bancroft was doing. Then the Queen sent other guards to arrest them, but they were already gone."

Alison swore under her breath. "Fine. You just...just sit there quietly, and we'll talk when I've finished this." The Library was pulling at her so hard it was almost physical. "And don't go anywhere." She crossed the room with long strides—she had enough self-control not to run in front of the apprentices—slid the key into the lock, turned it, took another deep breath, and pushed the door open.

It was darker inside than the scriptorium. The high windows, dirty as Anth—as she'd been told, let very little light through. She stood at the top of a flight of stairs that descended into the darkness. She let her eyes adjust, scanned the room, and her mouth fell open.

The first thing she noticed was how big the room was. It was at least three stories high and might be bigger than the palace ballroom, though the lighting was so dim she couldn't see the far end of the room. She thought it might once have been a reception room of some kind, though the floor was stone rather than wood and was in bad repair. The bookcases, six or seven shelves tall, filled its vastness, lining the walls or standing upright in the center like dancers frozen in mid-step.

The second thing she noticed was the gaps on the bookcase shelves. Big gaps. Gaps that should have held books. Every bookcase she could see had at least one big gap and a handful of smaller ones. Piles of books lay on the floor, haphazardly, some tipped so the books slid off the pile to lie loose and disregarded on the floor. Some of them lay open. Some of them, to her disgust, lay open on their faces. She couldn't begin to tell how many books the Library still had.

The third thing she noticed was the smell. It was damp, and sour, and slightly mildewy. It was an unpleasant smell under any circumstances. In a library, it was a close second to the smell of smoke.

She cursed, a torrent of profanity spilling over her lips that she thought might fill the room. Fill it as the books did not. She descended the stairs. To think how she'd dreamed of how beautiful the place might be. This was more like a custom-made nightmare. She trailed her fingers along the spines, righted a couple of the piles, but it was all reflexive; her brain, unable to cope with the enormity of Bancroft's desecration, had shut down.

She came to a brass tank, corroded and stained, that was about six feet long and two feet in diameter and lay on its side in a cradle. She flipped open a hatch at the top and saw gears, wires, and coils. The Device that controlled the Library's climate. Not working. Not working for a while now, and that was just stupid, Bancroft would have benefited from keeping his cash cow in prime condition...no, it wasn't stupid. He couldn't afford to let a Deviser in here who might report on the Library's condition. She couldn't help it; she cursed again, a litany of furious insults to Bancroft's parentage and sexual preferences. She couldn't let him go to the Scholia for "justice." The Scholia Masters had to see this for themselves.

She wandered around until she couldn't bear it any longer. First thing, get the Device running and get some lights set up in here. She groaned. No, first thing was to get pen and paper so she could write down all the other first things. She cursed again, this time Baxter and Edwin, the latter of whom she was sorry she'd ever pitied. If she could get him alone she would wring his scrawny neck.

She went back upstairs, slammed and locked the door, then leaned against it and addressed the apprentices, who at least had done as she'd told them and stayed put. "Did any of you know about that?" she demanded.

They looked at each other. "We knew something was going on, milady," Declan said (good, he'd worked out politeness was a survival strategy), "but we weren't allowed inside. Is...is it bad?"

"It's bad," Alison said, "but it's not irredeemable. Did Baxter and Edwin leave *anything* behind?"

They had. Not anything useful, no writing materials, no glue— wait, that would be in the bindery, maybe they hadn't pillaged that. But they'd left a handful of bound volumes, long and thin, that turned out to be acquisition logs. Alison had no idea why they'd bother keeping those records, given that they wrote the same information in the same order in the catalog. Well, the acquisition logs just had titles and dates; the catalog would have more detailed listings.

Right. The catalog. She went to the lectern.

It was empty. The chain dangled almost to the floor, unattached to anything.

Alison's heart sank. "Where's the catalog?" she said.

The apprentices looked at one another. They looked guilty.

"*Where's the catalog?*" Alison shouted. They looked even guiltier.

"Milady," Trevers said, "they took it with them."

Chapter Sixteen

Alison sank down onto a chair, put her elbows on the desk, and put her face in her hands. "They took it with them," she repeated. "Did any of you see them do it?" Silence. She lifted her head and glared at them. "Did you?"

Declan said in a small voice, "They came back for it. They told the guards it wasn't in the Library so it was theirs. They took it away."

"You saw this? You didn't say anything? You all knew what it was!"

"Nobody listens to apprentices," Gwendolen said smugly. Alison itched to slap her.

"Gwendolen," she said, as calmly as she could, "is there a reason everything you say comes out sounding like 'I told you so'?"

"I'm sorry, milady, but I've been saying all along the Masters were doing something shady, and no one listened." There was that sneer again. Alison imagined smacking the girl so hard she fell on her skinny rear end.

"You have not," Trevers said hotly. "You only ever complain and brush your hair. Some days you don't come in at all." That was true. Alison had seen Declan and Trevers in the scriptorium, but she'd never seen Gwendolen before today.

"It's not like I have to be here," Gwendolen said. "My mother is Evangeline Burns. I can have any apprenticeship I want. This one isn't very interesting, anyway."

"Fine," said Alison. "You're fired."

Gwendolen stood up, outraged. "You can't do that!"

Alison still wasn't sure she could, but she didn't care. "I just did. Get to the apprentices' hall and get your things, then go back to your mother, whoever she is."

"You don't know who *Evangeline Burns* is? Of the Westover

Burnses?"

Alison's fingers curled up into a fist. She opted for verbal violence. "Gwendolen, I don't even know where *Westover* is. And I don't care. If you think you can swan around here on the strength of whatever connections you think you have, then I don't need you. And you don't need this job. So get out. Declan, pull out those acquisitions logs. Trevers, do you know where you can get paper and pen and ink? Good. Bring those here. It doesn't have to be a lot. Are you still here?" This to Gwendolen, who stood perfectly still with her mouth open in outrage, sputtering, unable to find words. "Look, Gwendolen, you're going to be happier somewhere else. Now get out before I have a guard throw you out." Was it acceptable to threaten violence to a girl no more than fifteen? Well, legally she was an adult, and Alison was in a temper. No catalog. Even a disorganized, inaccurate one. Alison wanted to cry.

Gwendolen came to herself, said, "I didn't want this apprenticeship anyway," and stormed out. Alison helped Declan bring all the acquisitions logs to a desk and organize them by year. Trevers returned with writing supplies. "Now, I'm going to make several lists, and you two are going to tell me everything you remember about your tasks and the librarians' duties," she said. "And then...we are going shopping."

It wasn't as bad as Alison first thought, which still meant it was nightmarish. She'd paged through the catalog often enough that she could attest to the accuracy of the acquisitions logs, though she wasn't sure how helpful that would be: title and date weren't nearly enough information, said nothing about edition or printing or anything useful, but at least they could match books with titles and possibly get an idea of what Bancroft had stolen. She tried not to think about how slender a thread she was grasping.

She felt as if she were floundering. She had to return to the north wing to make an appointment to see Zara next week, something she'd forgotten in her distress over meeting Anthony so unexpectedly, then had left again before she remembered she had no idea what the Library budget was, or even if there was one. She ground her teeth and made herself count to ten, slowly, to focus herself. It didn't matter for now. The Library might not have a budget, but Alison Quinn had plenty of funds, and she was sure she could be reimbursed. Somehow. She hoped it was with Bancroft's money.

She took the apprentices into the city with her so she'd have someone to carry things. Reams of paper, neatly cut and packaged. Boxes of self-inking pens, gallons of ink to fill them with. She borrowed a cart from one of the stationers and loaded it up. Bound notebooks. Pencils. Then they went to the Devisers' district to arrange for delivery of lights on tall stands, a portable heater and dehumidifier, and auto-focusing magnifiers. She didn't feel like haggling, but the men and women she dealt with spoke to her with great respect, even the ones who didn't know who she was. She felt filled to bursting with righteous anger. Maybe it showed.

"How long have you had that shirt, Declan?" she said while they waited at a Deviser's shop for the woman to check her inventory to see if she had enough self-inking pens to meet Alison's needs. Declan flushed and crossed his arms across his chest. "Declan, lift your arms." There was a hole the size of her fist in the seam under his arm. Alison ran her eye over both young men. Not only were their uniforms tattered, they were in Scholia colors and bore the black and red Scholia insignia. Alison lifted the hem of Trevers' tunic and tugged a thread that unraveled as she pulled. "Well, that has to change," she said.

She took them to a tailor's for fittings for knee-length sleeveless tunics and trousers in the Tremontane colors of forest green and walnut brown, bought shirts and socks and—without regard for their embarrassment—underclothing, and bought ready-made shoes and had them fitted for ankle boots. Someone in the palace would be able to put together a badge with the insignia of Tremontane on it. By the time she was done, she'd spent more guilders in a single afternoon than she'd ever spent at one time before. Her tension was almost gone. Spending money made things better.

"Now," she said when they returned with their booty, "we're going to put all of this away. You were never allowed in the Library, were you?" Both Trevers and Declan shook their heads. "Well, that's going to change. I don't know what Bancroft told you, but there really aren't very many rules about how to behave in the Library. No food. No fire. No running. And no touching the books until I say you can. Break one of those rules, and you'll be looking for a new apprenticeship. Any questions?" That righteous anger still surged through her, hot and fierce, and she was deeply satisfied to see how nervous they looked as they nodded understanding, though she was sure she'd feel guilty later about intimidating them.

It took them an hour to put everything away, and a lot of men came while they were working to set up the light Devices. When everything was stowed away, Alison set the apprentices free for supper and visited the bindery. It was awe-inspiring and depressing all at once. The bindery Devices were, to her surprise, intrinsically beautiful, most of them at least a century old and carefully maintained the way the climate control Device in the Library had not been. They were in perfect condition—for museum pieces. Modern books wouldn't even fit into their braces. It was the most depressing thing she'd seen all day—no, the image of that dangling, empty chain kept returning to mind, and she cursed Bancroft and Baxter and Edwin again, but half-heartedly, because the righteous anger was beginning to drain out of her, leaving her exhausted. Fortunately, nothing here had been taken. If they had a modern Device for binding books, they'd be able to make repairs to just about any damage the Library books had sustained. She'd have to ask the Deviser she'd called on to look at the climate control Device if there was anything that could be done to update the bindery Devices.

Her stomach growled. She looked at her watch and realized she'd missed her own supper. She was filthy from book grime and Devices and couldn't very well go to a restaurant looking like that. So she did the only reasonable thing left to her. She went back into the Library.

The Devices had dispelled most of the shadows. She really ought to have turned them off before going to the bindery. She wandered through the stacks, brushing her hand against the leather and cloth spines, smiling when she found old friends. When she reached the back of the room, she turned back and began putting out the Devices as she went. As the room darkened, she felt tension drain out of her, soaked up by the ancient stones. Zara was right; she wanted this job, and she was certain now she'd be good at it.

She went back to the inn where she'd taken a room earlier that morning so she'd have somewhere to put her luggage while she went to the palace. It wasn't too late for supper there, so she ordered a meal and then took a bath. *You wouldn't think librarian was a dirty job, but then you wouldn't think a trained librarian could so grossly abuse his position.* Her remaining outrage, and sorrow, and irritation all faded, soaked away by the hot water. Tomorrow, lots of letters home. Zara had been right; she couldn't put this second to anything else. Her cousin Patrick would be able to handle things for a few weeks. Tomorrow, find out if she could take chambers in the palace. Going back and forth from this inn would be inconvenient. Tomorrow…tomorrow everything.

She got out of the bath and got ready for bed, combing her hair until it was tame and then braiding it so it would stay that way. She hated her hair. They had loved each other, they really had, so she shouldn't feel ashamed to remember Anthony touching her hair, touching her…everything…but the memory was so tied up in his betrayal it made her cringe. She wanted to forget about it entirely, would succeed for a while, but then she would have the dream where she didn't make him stop and she'd wake up crying and hating herself for being so weak as to still desire him. She rolled over onto her side and clutched her pillow. *I'm not going to dream tonight, I'm not,* she thought, and she didn't.

She wrote a lot of letters the next day, mostly to her father, her authors, and her estate agent. She sent a message to the employment agency, inquiring about Belle's availability. She wrote to her heir Patrick to make sure he understood the situation. She had no idea how she would be able to perform her duties as Countess *and* run the Royal Library, but it couldn't be more difficult than serving on the Queen's Council would be, yes? A treacherous voice in the back of her mind whispered, *You know you already care more about that sad, gutted shell of a Library than you do about County Waxwold.*

After some thought, she wrote another letter and posted it with the rest. It was a long shot, but someone had to know where Henry Catherton had ended up, and she could use his advice if not his help. And she hadn't had a real friend since Tessa had disappeared with her husband.

Later, she watched the Deviser tinker with the climate control Device and reflected on her situation. The Library budget was probably big, but it wouldn't be big enough to replace the missing books, assuming they even could. And she'd need more laborers. People to haul books out of the Library and into the scriptorium for cleaning and title matching. People to remove the shelves and repair the floor. People to put everything back. Readers to match the books with the titles, and that would mean educated labor. More things to put on her list for Zara. She left the Deviser to his work and wandered through the stacks.

This time, she looked at the shelves with an eye toward seeing what the collection held. There were a lot of titles she didn't recognize and many more she did. *Ambler's Holiday,* not valuable in itself, but an excellent representation of Duforda's early work. *Binder of Two Worlds,*

A Fantasy, just what it said on the cover. And—she swallowed hard—*Hearthsfire*. First edition. All by itself, the rest of the trilogy absent. Anthony's copy had been in better condition. She took it down from the shelf and flipped through it, put it away hesitantly, then picked it up again and found the place where she'd left off reading when Anthony and Bishop came back that afternoon. She'd take it back to the inn that evening. Bancroft's no-lending policy was over, at least as far as her own borrowing was concerned.

After dinner she went back to the offices. "Chambers?" the woman at the desk said. "You want to go to Household." Household sent her to Domestics, who could assign her a maid but not a room for the maid to clean. Domestics sent her to Physical Facilities, who at least knew she should have quarters but not where they were. Physical Facilities sent her back to the front desk, which sent her to a tiny, dark office staffed by a wrinkled old man who apparently kept the entire blueprint of the palace in his head. He escorted her to a door near the Library she'd already passed half a dozen times that day, handed her the key and patted her shoulder. "They're all yours, milady Countess," he said.

The smell of rotten food and stale sweat that wafted from the Royal Librarian's chambers when Alison opened the door made her gag. She pinched her nose closed and stepped inside. The door opened on a small sitting room with two chairs drawn up to a fireplace that had been filled in and replaced with a shining brass and silver heating Device. It was the only clean thing in the room. Plates of rotten food and glasses coated with the dried residue of juice or wine were stacked on the floor and on one of the chairs, crusts and the rinds of withered fruits lay strewn across the old mantel, and limp, unlaundered clothing was heaped on the floor and kicked under the chairs. Alison nudged one of the piles of clothes with her toe and shrieked a little when a large beetle ran out from underneath it. She moved on through the suite of rooms. The bed in the bedroom was unmade, the sheets and the mattress beneath them were stained with sweat, and loose shoes were scattered under the bed and in the bottom of the wardrobe. The study table was also covered with dirty dishes; the bookcases were filled with books and papers piled haphazardly on the shelves. She couldn't bear to take more than two steps into the bathing chamber, which reeked of the clashing odors of five different colognes and the smell of a body that used that many colognes to cover the fact that he rarely bathed. Alison closed the door on it, shuddering, and leaned against it. Was she going to have to clean *everything* related to the Library before she could use it?

She went back to Domestics and wangled not one, but three maids to clean the apartment, instructing them to get rid of all the dirty clothes and bedding, throw away the food, and make piles of everything else. She thought about it further and told them to replace the mattress and pillows and remove the sofa cushions for cleaning too. She wandered from the bedroom into the study, staying out of the maids' way, and began poking at the books crammed onto the shelves. It would be poetic justice if she took them all for the Library, she told herself, and began sorting through them. It took her a moment to realize what she was holding. These were some very valuable books indeed. And every one of them was stamped with the mark of the Royal Library inside the back cover.

It was a pity Bancroft had already been convicted. Alison briefly fantasized about marching up to the court and spreading all of these books out for the world to see. How *dared* he steal from the people of Tremontane? How dared he steal from *her*? She clasped an octavo to her chest and took a few calming breaths. So she'd recovered a few of the missing books. Who knew how many more were still missing? She ran back to Domestics and came away with some crates and a couple of burly men to carry them.

Once she'd gotten the books safely put away in the Library — the Device was working now and she imagined she could feel the air drying out around her — she locked the door behind her and went back to the inn, took a bath, then put on her dressing gown and ordered supper, which she ate in her room. Fed, clean, and free of obligations, she lay back on her bed and stared at the ceiling. She felt tired, but not sleepy. She rolled over. She had *Hearthsfire*, but she didn't feel like reading. She looked at her watch, and considered. *Henrietta Magnificat* had opened at the Waxwold Theater three days before. If she hurried, she might only miss a little of the first act. She didn't have any gowns with her, but if she sat well back in her box, no one would notice. She combed her hair and had the innkeeper call her a carriage.

Doyle was in the lobby when she got to the theater. "Allie!" he exclaimed, not too loudly so as not to disrupt the performance. Then his face went wary. "What are you doing here?" he said, taking her arm and drawing her into his office. "I thought you weren't coming back to Aurilien for, you know, forever."

"It's a long story, and I really just want to see the show. I'm not too late, am I?"

"Curtain went up five minutes ago," Doyle said, shaking his head, "but you might want to reconsider going up to your box." He'd gone from wary to guilty.

"What's wrong with my box?" Alison said, alarmed.

"Nothing. It's just—" Doyle ran his fingers through his thinning brown hair. "It's just the Crown Prince of Tremontane is sitting in it right now."

Alison blinked at him. "*What?*" she exclaimed.

Doyle shushed her, took hold of her arm and drew her toward his office. "It's a long story, Allie, and you've already missed some of the first act, so how about we sit in here, and I'll get Marco to make us some tea, and we can tell each other our long stories until you calm down enough not to kill me."

She wrenched her arm away. "I'll kill *him* first. How dare he take over my box like he owns it? I'm going to throw him out—"

"During the performance? Make a scene like that? Not you."

Alison hesitated. "Damn you, Doyle."

"Too late for that. I don't know whether heaven will even take my soul, it's got so many liens on it." He guided her gently to a seat and went away to talk to Marco. Alison waited, tapping her foot furiously. Doyle didn't return. Her irritation began to fade, just a little, and she struggled to keep hold of it, but it slipped away until it was nothing but an echo. After enough time to make three pots of tea, Doyle finally pushed the door open. "So, what brings you back to town?" he asked.

"Oh, no. We are hearing *your* story first." Alison crossed her arms over her chest and went back to tapping her foot. Doyle cleared his throat and looked at his shoes.

"Well. You know we liked having the Prince around, even if we did have to keep up the whole 'Tony Sutherland' pretense. He was everybody's favorite audience, on stage and off. Then the whole scandal burst. Hard to winnow out the truth from the rumor, but the least of what we heard was bad enough we all felt badly used on your behalf, and nobody wanted to see Tony Sutherland again no matter what name he used.

"Then, maybe three weeks after Wintersmeet, the week *Splinter of the Heart* opened, he showed up at the gate and asked to see me. Told me who he really was—I can't believe he thought we were fooled by the false name—and apologized for lying to us. I was pretty frosty with him, still angry on your behalf, and he said he knew he couldn't make amends for that, he just wanted to buy a ticket for a box. I've never seen anyone so miserable in my life. He didn't try to make excuses, just said he wanted to get away for a while. And he had a lot to get away from. I felt...I'm sorry, Alison, but I felt sorry for him. I thought—well, that doesn't matter, but basically I took his money and then realized we only had the one box available. So I put him in yours."

"Doyle, how could you do that to me?"

"I don't see how it hurt you at all. You weren't using it. Nobody actually knows it's your box. And I looked up once or twice from the pit and I couldn't even see him, he sat that far back. So if you're worried about looking soft, don't. Nobody's going to think you've forgiven the Prince for…what exactly did he do? Like I said, rumor was pretty thick on the ground, and we didn't want to make assumptions except it couldn't have been as bad as it sounded."

"He bet someone he could get me into his bed before Wintersmeet Eve."

Doyle whistled. "I can see where you couldn't forgive him for that, but I have to say, Allie, that's a lot better than what we were hearing. I don't know who started spreading the rumors, but it must have been someone who hated him, because they were too vicious to have sprung up on their own."

Bishop, Alison thought, and felt a rush of fury tangled with an unexpected sympathy for Anthony. She might not be able to forgive him, and she'd never trust him again, but he didn't deserve to be the center of any calumny that degenerate bastard might have spread.

Marco brought a tray into the room that held mismatched mugs and a chipped teapot and sugar in a bowl that had started life as a greasepaint container. When the boy left, Doyle continued, "Like I said, I felt sorry for him. I don't know what punishment he deserves for hurting you, but nobody deserved being drawn and quartered like that. He left before the performance was entirely over. I didn't think I'd see him again, but he came back the next week, and I gave him your box again. That time, he stayed so long I went to see if he was still alive, and he said he was just waiting for everyone to leave. So I invited him backstage. You know how theater people are, Allie, attention span the size of a gnat's whisker unless it's about them. If they remembered anything about him, it was what he'd told them about their last performance. Jerald was furious he'd been away so long." Doyle took a long drink out of his mug, made a face, and dug out a bottle of whiskey from his bottom drawer. He poured in a generous measure, offered it to Alison, then put it away when she declined. "Then he just kept coming back. He made friends with Junia and got to know the props department, and got Caleb a line on costumes for *Wintersmeet Ball*, and of course you already know he's the only person in Tremontane, Eskandel, and Veribold who gets along with Jerald."

"You didn't have to be so nice to him," she said.

Doyle gave her a long, level look. "And you don't get to tell me how I should behave to anyone," he said. "I understand that you can't forgive him, Allie, and I don't know whether he deserves your forgiveness. But I think he's done a lot of things he's ashamed of and most of them aren't about you. You think your grievance is so great he should never be forgiven for anything else?" He took another long drink. "You never used to be this bitter."

"I never had so much cause before," she said.

He waved that away with his mug. "You want to hang onto your bitterness, doesn't matter how much cause you have, you're still only hurting yourself."

His words were so like her father's it stunned her. "You think I'm wrong not to forgive him?" she asked.

"I already said I don't know that he deserves your forgiveness. But I'm damn sure he doesn't deserve your hatred." He drank again. "He's changed," he said. "Still got that...still cheerful, but less chatty. He used to listen like, well, he did care what people were saying, but you could see him lining up what he was going to say next as soon as you stopped talking. That's gone. And...Allie, stop giving me that look."

"What look?"

"The look that says you stopped listening because you don't like what I'm saying."

"I don't need to hear you defend him."

"I'm not defending him. I'm just giving him credit for trying. Far as I can tell, it's got nothing to do with whatever relationship you have with him now."

"We don't have a relationship."

"*Everyone's* got relationships, even if they're the mortal enemy kind." Doyle drained his mug and wiped his mouth. "All I'm saying is I don't think he deserves to have his life come to an end just because he wronged you so terribly. He's part of this theater now, and, Alison? This is your theater, mostly, it's got your name over the door in lights, and if you tell me to, I'll send him packing. But I never thought I'd see you that vindictive."

Alison set her cup down, shocked. "Is that what you think of me?"

"I'm saying you might decide to go that route, yes."

His words shamed her. Doyle was right. Anthony didn't deserve her forgiveness, but he didn't deserve her hatred either. "Give me that bottle, Doyle." Puzzled, he pulled it out of the drawer and handed it to her. She took a healthy swig from it, shuddered, and handed it back. "I don't want you to kick him out," she said. "But I'm not ready to see him. And...he can keep using the box."

Doyle nodded. "I'm sorry if I was harsh, Allie."

"No, you were right. I was behaving like a spoiled child. Thanks for pointing it out." Alison wiped the whiskey from her mouth, then unexpectedly belched, making Doyle laugh like a madman. After a moment, Alison joined him, trying to remember the last time she'd laughed so unselfconsciously.

"All right, I won't be vindictive," she said as her laughter wound down, leaving her surprisingly relaxed. "I'm coming back soon, I'll be on time, I'll be properly dressed, but I don't want to find anyone in my box, okay? He can use it when I'm not here."

"Will do, boss," Doyle said. "You want to talk to Flanagan? He's got things to say to you about the book."

She shuddered. "Let the Prince deal with it, if they're such good friends." She wondered what had happened to the book she'd bought for Anthony's Wintersmeet gift and left under her bed in the Dowager's apartment. Had he ended up buying one for himself? She should retrieve it for the library, probably, but the idea of facing the

Dowager again filled her with weariness. They'd said such harsh things to each other, and the Dowager had been so kind to her, and had been so pleased to think Alison might become her daughter — she shied away from that line of thought.

She left Doyle and stood for a while at the foot of the stairs. Anthony had kept coming to the theater, even after she'd left. He'd made a place for himself here. No, he'd dared to intrude on *her* place. He should have had the decency to withdraw from everything they'd shared. *I'm not going to forgive him,* she thought, *he deserves to suffer,* but she remembered what Doyle said, about how vicious the rumors had been, and she felt a little ashamed at her anger. Anthony hadn't deserved to suffer at Bishop's hands. She felt an unexpected flash of compassion for Anthony that she crushed out of existence before it could take root. Maybe he didn't deserve to suffer like that, maybe she didn't have to hate him, but he'd hurt her as no one else ever had; he didn't deserve her compassion and he didn't deserve her forgiveness. Even so.... *You want to hang onto your bitterness, doesn't matter how much cause you have, you're still only hurting yourself,* Doyle said in her memory. He didn't understand anything. She wasn't bitter. She was just protecting herself. She gave the stairs one more long look, then turned and left the theater.

Chapter Seventeen

She slept poorly, plagued by nightmares in which carnivorous books pursued her through the halls of Waxwold Manor, and woke late. It was going to be one of those days. She fortified herself with what would probably turn out to be too much coffee and slogged toward the Library at nearly ten o'clock. She'd found another entrance that led directly to the Library and saved her ten minutes of walking from the main doors and down the stairs to the Library level. That it also avoided the east wing was irrelevant.

She turned the corner to the Library corridor and saw someone standing next to the Library door. Gwendolen. Alison's pace slowed for just a few steps, long enough for Gwendolen to realize Alison was approaching and turn to face her, shoving her hands into her trouser pockets. Alison increased her stride a little and saw Gwendolen twitch as if she didn't know whether to stand still or run away. She decided to ignore the girl. If Gwendolen wanted something, she would have to work for it.

"Your ladyship," Gwendolen said in a small voice, "I...."

Alison channeled her inner Zara and raised an eyebrow at her. "Yes?" she said, her hand on the door latch.

Gwendolen ducked her head. "Your ladyship, I...."

"Please stop repeating yourself. I have work to do."

"I want to beg your forgiveness and ask for my apprenticeship back." She said this all in a rush, as if she'd memorized it, though her emotion seemed genuine and not at all learned by rote.

"Do you? I was under the impression you didn't need it."

Gwendolen blushed. Funny, she did it as blotchily as Alison did. "Mother said...she wasn't going to keep finding me apprenticeships...and I have to prove I can stick with something."

"Your mother is right, but I fail to see why it's my duty to provide you with something to which you will stick. It sounds as though you've had plenty of apprenticeships already."

The blotches turned a darker red. "I lied," she said, "about this one not being interesting. I love to read. I wanted to work in a library, but the librarians wouldn't let us do anything but fill the inkwells, and Declan and Trevers took that over. I just don't like feeling... unimportant. No. I don't like feeling like a *nothing*."

It was the most honest thing she'd ever heard from Gwendolen. "And talking about how important your mother is makes *you* feel important?"

She looked away and nodded. Alison sighed. "That's a great deal of honesty," she said, "but it doesn't explain why I should retain you as an apprentice."

"You need at least three if the Library's actually running—"

"I can hire others. Others who actually want to be here."

"But *I* want to be here!"

"So you lied about that too?"

Gwendolen burst into tears. Alison felt she'd pushed the young woman a bit too far. "Stop crying, Gwendolen," she said, but gently. "Listen. If you can tell me one reason, one thing you can do as an apprentice that no one else can, I'll give you back your apprenticeship and I won't even cancel out your elapsed three years."

Gwendolen shuddered and wiped her eyes. "I know where the books went," she said.

Alison stared at her. "You *what?*" she shouted, and Gwendolen cowered, but Alison didn't care. "You mean you were going to walk out of here and leave me scrambling to find out what that total bastard Bancroft stole and all this time *you knew where they were?*" She slammed her fist against the door and tried to control herself.

"No, I don't know where they are now, but I know where they took them!" Gwendolen exclaimed, still flinching from Alison's wrath. "I can take you there!"

Alison made herself calm down, let her breathing return to normal. "Why didn't you say something before?"

Gwendolen raised her head and met Alison's eyes. "Because I was stupid and proud and selfish," she said, "and I thought it was my secret to keep. And I'm sorry. And I'm here now."

Alison closed her eyes. Gwendolen got on her nerves, true, but she'd also stood up to Alison and admitted her mistake. "You're provisionally accepted back as apprentice," she told the girl, who didn't seem to know whether to be happy about "accepted" or worried about "provisionally." "You will take me to wherever it was Bancroft and his stooges took the books. You will be polite and humble to me and to your fellow apprentices. You will do everything in your power to convince me you're useful. After that, we'll see."

"Thank you, milady," Gwendolen said. "Should we go now?"

"Where is it?"

"There's a sort of pawnshop at the bottom of Southgate, only it's just for books. I've been here since before Bancroft took over and I know he only started going there about a year ago. So he wasn't stealing the whole two years."

"How do you know any of this?"

Another blotchy blush. "They used to take me along...because I liked being in on the secret. It made me feel...."

"I get it." No sense punishing the girl for what was, after all, Bancroft's crime. "Let's just forget about all that and be grateful you *did* go along." She thought about it. She didn't know the city well, but she did know Southgate wasn't the best neighborhood. "I don't suppose the books are going to get any more lost if we wait an hour. I have some things to take care of, and then we'll see what we can do."

The streets of Southgate were narrow enough that the word "warren" came to Alison's mind—narrow, and overhung by the jutting upper stories of buildings that leaned together a little, making unexpected turns and cul-de-sacs the carriage driver seemed, fortunately, well familiar with. Passersby paid no more attention to their black, unmarked carriage than they did to any of the other traffic that thronged the streets. Most of the pedestrians seemed huddled in on themselves as if it were midwinter and not early spring; it did not seem as if Southgate noticed the passing of days. When Alison saw the pawnshop, with its upper windows boarded over and a tread missing from the steps, she wished she'd brought someone big and well-muscled to back her up. It looked exactly the kind of place where people were robbed and murdered on a regular basis. But Bancroft had come here often, and nothing had ever happened to him, such a pity. Well, she'd decided to try the nice way first. She could always come back with a squad of palace guards later if she had to. There must be some procedure for requisitioning a squad, yes?

Chimes rang as she pushed the door open, Gwendolen trailing in her wake. Gwendolen was right; it wasn't exactly a pawnshop, more a used book store, and it was packed to the rafters with books. Shelves groaned under the weight of tomes piled any which way, though none lay on the floor, Alison was glad to see, because the floor was dirty. Alison took a deep breath and smelled old paper and timeworn leather. She sighed, contented. Lack of organization aside, this was how the Royal Library ought to have looked, and smelled. The shelves formed a little maze she navigated, sometimes turning sideways to slide through narrow spaces between shelves. She wished she were here for pleasure, because there were a number of titles she wanted to look more closely at, but she resolutely kept her eyes focused on her goal, which was a wooden counter with a cracked glass top, also piled high with books. A bell stood on the counter. She rang it. Gwendolen stayed close behind as if trying to hide behind her skirts, which was absurd because Gwendolen was at least two inches taller than Alison was and Alison was wearing trousers.

"I'm coming," said an age-cracked voice. Alison waited. After a moment, a squat, white-haired woman came out of a back room, dusting her hands off on her skirt.

"You have something to sell?" she asked, eyeing the parcel under Alison's arm.

"Not exactly," Alison replied. She unwrapped the book and laid it on the counter—Simpkins' *Travels in the Rockwild*, not too valuable, but worth at least a little money. "What would you give me for this?"

The woman picked it up, felt the spine, riffled the pages. "Five staves," she said in that creaky voice.

"Interesting," Alison said, taking the book back. "I don't suppose *this* changes the value at all?" She flipped the book open from the rear and showed the woman the Library seal. The woman swallowed hard, but her face remained impassive.

"That supposed to mean something to me?" she said.

"I know you've seen it before, Mistress—I beg your pardon, we haven't been introduced. You are...?"

"Thelma Inkpen," said the woman, peering suspiciously at Alison.

"What a perfectly appropriate name! Mistress Inkpen, I am Alison Quinn, Countess of Waxwold and Royal Librarian." The woman blanched. "And I believe you can help me. I have this feeling, and tell me if I'm wrong, you've seen this—" she tapped the seal with her index finger—"before. And before you decide whether or not to lie to me, I want to assure you that you haven't committed a crime." This was a lie. Witting or no, Mistress Inkpen was an accessory to theft, and Alison was certain she was a witting accomplice. But Bancroft was in jail, and Alison wanted those books back more than she wanted Mistress Inkpen punished.

"I mean, really, Mistress Inkpen, you can't be expected to check the provenance of *every* book that comes across your counter," she continued. "It's not your fault you were taken advantage of by the previous Royal Librarian. Really, you're the victim here." Enough buttering up her victim. "So, with all that in mind, Mistress Inkpen, have you purchased any books with this seal stamped inside the back cover?"

Mistress Inkpen wrestled with herself, then nodded. "Not many," she insisted.

"That's just fine, Mistress Inkpen. Now here is the important thing, Mistress—do you currently have any books with this seal in your shop?"

More struggling, then Mistress Inkpen said, "I don't think I should lose out just because I was took advantage of by that smug git."

"I agree. In fact, I think you should be recompensed for *any* books with this seal that you can dig up for me." *But not by as much as you might want.*

The old woman scowled, then said, "Wait here." She went into the back room and returned after several minutes with four small volumes balanced on an outsized folio and set them none too carefully on the desk. She brushed past Alison into the store itself. Alison eagerly flipped open each cover. Five seals. A set of Marusel's *Vondark Legacy,* volumes one through three and volume seven, and an illuminated encyclopedia of Tremontanan birds with the illustrations hand-tipped. Mistress Inkpen returned with another stack of books and set them next to the first pile. "That's it," she said.

"You've sold all the rest?" Alison exclaimed.

"This is a bookshop, milady Countess," the woman said smugly. "I buy books. I sell them again."

"Do you know who buys your books?"

Mistress Inkpen drew herself up to her full four-foot-ten height. "I got customer privacy to worry about," she said. "Can't tell you those things or I'd have no custom."

Alison controlled herself. "I respect that, Mistress Inkpen," she said. "But I would really like those books. Here's what I'd like you to do. I'd like you to put the word out that the Royal Library will pay for any books with that seal on them, no questions asked. And if you receive any more, the same deal applies to you."

"Don't know that you'll get many takers," the woman said. "Collectors don't like getting rid of what's theirs."

"Oh, I think it's worth a try, don't you, Mistress Inkpen?" Alison leaned over as if to share a confidence. "And I think you should definitely try, because if I don't see results, do you know what I'm going to do? I'm going to come back with a squad of guards and a letter from the Queen herself that says I get to take your records and do whatever I like with them. But that would be *so* taxing and I think it would put a strain on our new friendship, don't you?"

Mistress Inkpen looked scared and angry at the same time. "You can't hold me responsible for what other people do."

"Oh, Mistress Inkpen, I just think you know your clients so much better than I do. I think you know best how to explain to them that those books really are better off back in the Library. I think you don't want your customers knowing their privacy might be violated. That would be a shame." She patted the old woman's hand. "Would you mind setting these aside for me? I'll return this afternoon and pay you for them—oh, and for any others you might have acquired in the meantime? Thank you *so* much for your help, Mistress Inkpen, it's been a delight. And I'm sure I'll return on my own time in the future. You have a lovely store."

She sailed out, clasping her hands in front of her to conceal their shaking. What had she just done? Threatened an old woman with confiscation of her property and terrified her into demanding the return of books that almost certainly were owned by people who didn't want to give them up? Yes, she had. And, nerves aside, she didn't feel one bit guilty about it.

"I think that's everything, Zara," Alison told the Queen, who'd listened to her report in silence. "It's going to take a lot of labor, and I haven't decided what to do about the missing catalog. Baxter and

Edwin have probably gone to ground in the Scholia, and though stealing the catalog was just adding insult to injury, I'm sure the Masters won't give it back."

"And I wouldn't demean myself by asking for it," Zara said. "From what you've said, it seems it was nearly worthless anyway."

"But better than nothing. I'm ashamed to say I've put off dealing with it."

"Plenty of other things to deal with first." Zara ticked off items on the list Alison had made for her. "Talk to Physical Facilities to get the windows cleaned and the floor and walls scrubbed. Personnel can give you laborers for the heavy lifting, but you'll have to hire scribes and readers yourself. Talk to Finance about your budget. I'm afraid it's rather straitened thanks to Bancroft's thefts, but there should be something there. Have you reclaimed any of the lost books?"

"More than I'd hoped." People, servants mostly, had showed up in a steady trickle since Alison had threatened Mistress Inkpen and were sent away with payments calculated by the Royal Librarian, who was not inclined to be generous, but decided a slightly-better-than-fair rate might ensure that the trickle kept flowing.

"Good." Zara pushed the paper away, laid down her pen. "One week, Alison, and you've already done more than I imagined. Still want to argue that you shouldn't have the job?"

Alison laughed. "I won't doubt your wisdom in the future."

"You probably will, but it's nice to hear you're trying." Zara stood, indicating the meeting was over. "May I ask you something? It's about Anthony, so feel free to say no."

Alison froze. "What is it?"

"Do you know what he's doing when he slips away, once or twice a week, and goes into the Humboldt district? I haven't wanted to follow him, but...and I recall he used to go with you, so I thought I'd ask."

"Oh. He goes to the theater. I took him once, early on, and he decided he likes it. Doyle — the manager — tells me he's quite involved with their productions these days."

"I see." Zara now looked relieved. "I'm glad to hear he's become so responsible. After he broke with that despicable friend of his, and sold his townhouse to move back here — "

"He sold the townhouse?" Alison's heart sank. "He sold the *books*?"

Zara smiled. "He sold the house. He did not sell the books."

Alison blushed at how intent she'd sounded. "But...what happened to them?"

"He had them boxed up and brought to the east wing. As far as I know, they're still there."

"Oh," Alison said lamely. Why had he kept the books? Sentimentality? It certainly wasn't because he liked reading. *Some reminder of me, no doubt,* she thought, and it made her feel uncomfortable and a little angry.

Zara said nothing about Alison's abrupt silence. "Thank you for relieving my mind, Alison. I suppose I should take in a play sometime. Both of you are so avid, it makes me curious."

"I'd be happy to have you join me, or perhaps it might be better if you went with Anthony," Alison said, and then was surprised at how easily his name left her lips. It made her a little angry, as if she'd betrayed herself, and she ground her back teeth together.

"I think that is a splendid idea," Zara said. "I'll check my schedule and we can set a date." Alison nodded, opened the door, and nearly walked into a young woman poised ready to knock. It reminded Alison so much of her encounter with Anthony in this room that she shied away more dramatically than was warranted, and then felt ridiculous about it.

The girl didn't seem surprised at all. "Express letter for you, your Majesty," she said, reaching past Alison to hand the Queen a sealed envelope. Zara turned it over and her lips tightened.

"Wait just a moment, Alison," she said, beckoning to her to come back into the room and shut the door. Zara picked up a letter opener, slit the envelope, and removed its contents with two fingers as if it were a dead rat. She scanned the paper quickly, then held it out to Alison. "You might as well read this," she said.

Alison read it, then read it a second time. "The Scholia Magisters are coming here," she said. "To challenge Bancroft's conviction."

"And to reinstate him as Royal Librarian, unless I'm mistaken," Zara said.

"I don't understand. How can they do that?"

Zara stabbed the top of her desk with the letter opener, which stood quivering in it for a moment before falling over. "They can make a legal challenge on the grounds that the evidence against Bancroft is circumstantial, that there are no witnesses against him since we can't produce Edwin or Baxter to testify. But that's not what this is about. This is a challenge to the power of the Crown over the sovereignty of the Scholia. They want to be an independent entity operating within the borders of Tremontane, self-governing."

"But that's not possible."

"I wish that were true." Zara leaned against her desk. "I have no idea how many Scholia Masters hold positions of authority throughout the country, but there are many—far too many for my comfort, now— within the government. The Scholia has hinted that these men and women owe allegiance to the Scholia that overrides their allegiance to the government and that one word from them will recall all those Masters—that they would abandon their responsibilities without question. The Magisters might be bluffing, but if they're not, it would cripple us. We've stayed in balance this long because the Scholia's primary source of funding is the Crown, and because I can cry treason against anyone who forsakes their oaths in favor of the Scholia's command. But if enough people go, it would be impossible to enforce that dictum." She picked up the paper knife and ran her thumb along its blunt edge. "It's disturbing, questioning the loyalties of people who've served the kingdom faithfully all this time."

"That's far more serious than I believed." Alison hesitated. "Why are you telling me this?"

Zara gave her the blue-eyed stare. "Because your appointment is the fulcrum upon which all this swings. I usurped Scholia authority by naming you Royal Librarian. They're using that to challenge me."

Alison swallowed. "Maybe…maybe you should rethink that decision," she said. "If it's going to make you so vulnerable." The idea of losing the Library filled her with dread.

The blue-eyed stare sharpened. "Alison Quinn," Zara said, "my decision is final. Their complaint is a pretext to fight a battle that's been brewing for longer than I've been Queen. I'm warning you because you're going to come under fire too. I have no idea what power the Scholia can bring to bear on you, but they have far too much influence for a scholastic institution and I have no doubt they will use it to make their point. Control of the Royal Library is symbolic of their power. Be prepared to fight this battle."

Alison nodded. She looked at the paper in her hand. Such an innocuous thing to bear such dire tidings. She handed it to Zara, who balled it up and tossed it into the cold fireplace. "Get back to work," she told Alison. "The Masters will be here in three days. Heaven only knows what will happen then."

Chapter Eighteen

"I can't believe the difference water and soap makes," Alison said. Spring sunlight poured through the clean windows, through which she saw a pale blue sky and a pair of birds tracing out an intricate dance across it.

"Water and soap and a particular Device, milady," her crew supervisor said. "Easier than trying to get workers up there, I'll tell you, and it's more thorough as well." The Device was a brass mop head attached to soft fibers that made a spinning disc when the Device was activated and went whirring around the windows, making a sound like a hundred bees vibrating against the glass.

"It must go through a lot of source, as fast as it goes," Alison said.

"Not a problem," the man said. "There are a lot of lines of power running through the palace, good thick ones too. Probably why they built it here in the first place. My Devisers say imbuing the motive forces that run those things is as easy as sniffing out a nexus, or listening for one, or however it is a particular Deviser senses source. I'd almost call it magic, if I didn't know better."

Alison knew the source that powered Devices *was* a kind of magic, but she said nothing. Devices were safe. You could turn off a Device, control it, but raw magic, even the kind of inherent magic Dr. Trevellian had, was a little frightening — too much like the power of the long-dead Ascendants who'd once dominated Tremontane. She and the supervisor stood at the top of the stairs, looking out over the Library. At ground level, the aforementioned workers scrubbed and repaired the stone floor from which Alison had removed all the piles of books. The scriptorium, with all the books she'd moved into it, was starting to look like a library itself, and she'd had a lock installed on that door as well.

Yesterday she'd finally faced the cruel reality that the catalog wasn't coming back and that she was stuck with recreating it. She'd gritted her teeth and examined the stacks in detail, trying to work out the system Bancroft had used to organize it, but nothing rational emerged. Pacing between the shelves, she'd cursed him again, but her heart wasn't in it. She knew from her time in the Scholia that librarians sometimes invented odd ways to organize their libraries, but she considered that selfish because it invariably meant the librarian was the only one who could find anything and therefore became indispensable. And if the librarian died or ran away or got arrested for embezzlement and theft, the system was useless. She briefly considered asking Bancroft, still locked in his tiny cell, what his system was, but decided she would rather chew glass than go crawling to him. After half an hour, she gave up. She would have to start from scratch. She tried not to think about how long that would take.

Today she left the workers to their scrubbing and returned to the scriptorium, where Declan and Gwendolen were running the heater/dehumidifier Device and Trevers was vainly trying to match books to the acquisitions logs. "Give me your attention for a moment, please," she said. "Trevers, you've been doing a wonderful job, but it's time to direct our efforts elsewhere. Declan, if you wouldn't mind moving the Device to the librarian's desk, and Gwendolen, take that book you're working on." They were irradiating the dampest and most mildewed books, a process Alison hated because it further damaged the books, but she reasoned it was better to halt the destructive process of the damp than worry about heat damage.

"I'm officially giving up on trying to determine which books Bancroft stole," she said. "We're moving forward, and that means working out what we still have. Which of the three of you is the best reader? Good at deciphering handwriting?" They glanced between each other, and Gwendolen raised her hand. "Gwendolen, give Trevers that book. You men gather up the ones that need treatment and move them to the librarians' desk. Gwendolen—thank you—get paper and ink and a couple of good pens. We have to start sorting."

Once she had something to focus on, the job went quickly. Group by subject. Group by author, if possible. Make a judgment call when the subject wasn't obvious. Divide fiction from fact and poetry and drama from both. Alison and Gwendolen hauled book after book to desk after desk. Alison tried not to think about how many books the Library had, but her mind insisted on doing calculations and coming up with absurdly high numbers. This was going to take *years*. Alison wiped sweat from her forehead and surreptitiously scratched under her arm. The workers, finished now, trooped through the scriptorium. She probably should have kept a few to do the hauling. She wiped her forehead again and stopped to free her hair from its band and bind it more securely out of the way.

"I must say, Alison, I didn't realize you thought being a librarian meant taking the books for a walk," said a voice from the doorway. Alison spun around. She knew that voice.

"*Henry*," she said, and flung herself at him, not caring that the apprentices were all staring at her open-mouthed. "Sweet heaven, it's good to see you. You got my letter."

"Eventually," Henry Catherton said. She released him and stepped back to look at her former professor and friend. His dark red hair had some gray in it, as did the short beard he'd grown since she last saw him, but he was as lean and, as she knew from their embrace, as strong as ever. "Your vague missive left me so curious I had to come," he continued. "Little Alison Quinn—" she punched him on the arm, and he grinned at her—"all grown up and running the Royal Library."

She grinned back. "You want to see it?"

It looked so much nicer now than it had when she'd first seen it, brightly illuminated thanks to the clean windows and the light Devices, with the floor washed and repaired and the piles of books on the floor removed. "It's still a mess," Alison said, looking at Henry's dismayed face; some of those piles had been dumped on whatever shelf was handy rather than being removed to the scriptorium, and a lot of those big gaps hadn't been filled. She felt defensive, ready to counter whatever criticism Henry might have of her beloved Library, but he only sighed.

"I don't mind telling you I never liked Bancroft," he said. "He only took the robe because his sister donates heavily to the Scholia. No surprise his only interest in books turned out to be financial. Have you gotten any of them back?"

"A few. No way of knowing how many are still missing. I've decided to give up on finding them for now, since I have to recreate the catalog anyway."

"Why?" She explained. He cursed. "Alison, that is…I don't know if you realize how much of a challenge that will be."

"I don't want to know, because it has to be done. I don't mind telling you I'm out of my depth," she said. "I could use your advice. The position of assistant librarian is open, if you want it."

"I want it. I've been working as a translator for Struthers & Fine for the last year."

"You were in Kingsport this whole time and I never saw you?"

"I didn't want any reminders of who I'd been." He gazed out over the stacks. "Tessa's dead, Alison. Died in childbirth two years ago."

She caught her breath, her chest tightening as if she'd been punched. "Henry, I'm so sorry." Once Tessa had been her best friend, her confidante. Alison had been there when Tessa and Henry fell in love, had suffered with them when Henry had lost his robe and been booted from the Scholia for marrying a student. She didn't know how her friendship with Tessa had faded, but she regretted more than ever not keeping up the connection. "I wish I'd known."

Henry shrugged. "There are a lot of things I wish I'd done differently." He smiled ruefully. "But I've come to terms with her death and…honestly, Alison, I never thought I'd have a chance at my real profession again. You're sure the Queen understands what it means that she's hiring non-Scholia librarians?"

"Zara understands it better than either of us, I imagine." She turned and went back into the scriptorium, Henry following her. "And I've decided to leave fighting that battle to her for now. She's…well, wait until you meet her."

"Good heaven, Alison. Royal Librarian and on first-name terms with the Queen. If you told me you were secretly the heir to a Veriboldan fortune, I'd believe you." He took her arm and swung her around to face him. "Do you love it? All this?"

Joy replaced the tightness in her chest. "I do," she said with a brilliant smile, "I really do."

Henry's smile widened to match hers. "It suits you," he said. He let go of her arm and said, "Put me to work, chief."

Alison surveyed his clean trousers, fine white shirt and waistcoat. "First I think we should find you a place to stay, and a place to change out of your nice clothes. This is a much dirtier job than I'm sure you're used to."

Henry swiped his thumb across one of her cheekbones. "I can tell," he said, displaying a smudge.

The process of finding quarters for Henry went quickly, now Alison knew whom to go to. She left him to settle in and decided to formalize his appointment by arranging to draw his salary from Finance. Henry would never complain, but as clean as his clothes were, they were also three years outdated and somewhat worn. She decided to try to get him a hiring bonus as well.

"Assistant librarian? Certainly. But the budget still hasn't been finalized, after the whole…" the Finance department chief's secretary said. He looked as if he'd bitten into an apple and come up with half a worm. "So you'll need Mistress Unwin's signature for a lump sum withdrawal." He pointed down the hall. "She's handling business right now, but I'll ring her and let her know you're waiting, if you'll just go down there."

The waiting room was larger than Zara's office, lined with fifty-year-old wingback chairs that had been reupholstered five years ago, judging by the pattern of the lime green brocade. Alison was the only person in the room. She sat and kicked her heels against the chair's thick legs, feeling bored and slightly regretting her impulsive, generous decision. Henry might see it as charity. He'd always been a proud man, one who stuck to his principles even when it meant he lost the job he cared about more than almost anything in the world. Maybe this was a bad idea.

She stood to go, took three steps, and saw Anthony at the other end of the hall, talking to Unwin's secretary. Alison threw herself back into the shelter of the wingback chair and pressed herself as far back into it as she could. He probably wasn't going to come down here. He was just having a few friendly words with the secretary. She heard boots tapping along the polished floor of the hallway and a blush of embarrassment began spreading across her face. She furiously willed herself calm. Damn her skin anyway. Who knew what he'd think she was blushing about?

She kept her eyes resolutely forward. *Don't be silly*, she told herself, *he's going to walk right past you, you can't turn invisible*. She was still blotchy. The boots stopped. "Good afternoon, Countess," Anthony said. He didn't sound embarrassed or upset. Damn him.

"Good afternoon, your Highness," she replied, glancing at him briefly. He was looking out the narrow window, the light coming through its blue and green stained glass making him look washed out.

"Are you here to see Mistress Unwin?" he asked.

"I am."

The silence stretched. Finally, Anthony said, "Thank you for the loan of your box. Now you're in town, I will be sure to engage my own."

"I'm pleased you made such good use of it," Alison lied. She added, after a moment, "Doyle says you've become quite the fixture at the theater."

"I enjoy the company," Anthony said.

Silence descended again. Alison stared at Mistress Unwin's door. What was the woman up to in there? Having her dinner? Taking a nap? "Are you waiting on Mistress Unwin as well?"

"I have some reports for her. She's my chief."

"I didn't realize you were working in Finance."

More silence. Alison turned her head just enough that she could see his hand, hanging by his side —

— *his hand, gentle on her face, wiping away a tear* —

and she stood abruptly and walked away from him, moving as if to examine the stained glass windows, furious with herself for being so weak. If she were going to remember anything about their time together, it would be that cold afternoon and his cruel, drawling voice. She was fairly certain he was looking at her now. What did *he* think, when he looked at her? Did he remember how close they'd been once? Was he remembering how she looked naked? She felt the blotches rise again and folded her arms across her chest, trying to stop them from spreading further.

"Zara's asked me to take her to the theater," Anthony said. "*Henrietta Magnificat* is still playing for the rest of the week. Have you seen it?"

"No, not yet," *because someone took my box,* "but I hope to go soon."

"It's an excellent performance." She heard him take a breath to say more, but just then the door opened and Alison turned to see a broad, short woman with silver-shot black hair and rosy cheeks. She looked from Anthony to Alison and came back to Anthony.

"Good," she said, "I've been waiting for those reports. Come in, Anthony."

"The Countess was here before me," Anthony said.

"No, please go ahead, I can wait," Alison said.

"Really, I insist," he said.

"No, I—"

"Countess, come in before your display of politeness keeps us here all night," Mistress Unwin said affably. "Anthony, have a seat."

Alison had trouble focusing on her brief conversation with Mistress Unwin and the chief's approval of Henry's hiring bonus. *He lied to you, he betrayed you, he doesn't deserve an ounce of consideration from you,* she told herself, but her traitorous body insisted on bringing up disturbing memories. She crushed them into oblivion. Those memories didn't change anything. Every one of his kisses had been a betrayal, and she refused to think of them with any amount of pleasure.

She thanked Mistress Unwin and left the office. Anthony rose from the lime-green chair and nodded at her as she passed. She nodded in return. This would be easier if she never had to see him, but they couldn't avoid each other entirely, especially if he intended to spend much time at the Waxwold Theater. She'd as much as promised Doyle she wouldn't let herself be vindictive and hateful toward Anthony, but she certainly wasn't going to treat him with kindness and definitely not with love. Polite. She could manage polite. Even if her angry heart felt otherwise.

She took the long way back to the Library, trying to calm herself. The long way took her past the east wing, but since Anthony was with Unwin, there was no reason to avoid it. A door opened somewhere ahead of her, down a cross-corridor, and Alison just had time to realize it was the hall leading to the Dowager's apartment before the Dowager herself appeared, saw Alison, and jerked a little in surprise. Alison stopped too, embarrassment and guilt once again filling her. Had the North family conspired to arrange these encounters today? Tension began building behind her eyes. Maybe she could just walk past. The Dowager couldn't possibly want to speak to her, after the horrible things they'd said to each other.

The Dowager stood looking at her, balanced lightly on the balls of her feet as if preparing to flee. She was gowned in simple white muslin like a girl and clutched a large book bound in dark blue leather to her chest like a breastplate. "Alison," she said.

"Milady," Alison replied.

The Dowager glanced at the book in her arms and hugged it more tightly. "One of the servants found this under your bed—your old bed," she said. "I thought—I decided to bring it to you."

It was Flanagan's book of plays. Alison swallowed past the unexpected lump in her throat. "Thank you, Milady," she said, "I'd forgotten about it." *She could have sent a servant. Why come herself?* She wasn't sure what else to say. She'd been so rude, and the Dowager hadn't been to blame for her son's behavior—

The Dowager cleared her throat. "I also came to apologize," she said. "I had no idea—I never would have believed it of Anthony, but I should have known you wouldn't lie to me—"

"Oh, Milady," Alison said, feeling tears slip down her cheeks, "I should never have said such things to you. I am so sorry. I was just so angry—"

"And you had every right to be," the Dowager said, and now she was crying too. "Can you forgive me?"

"If you can forgive *me*," Alison said, walking forward with her hand outstretched, and was completely startled when the Dowager dropped the book (*don't hurt it!*) and embraced Alison. Alison put her arms around the woman and hugged her. "I'm so glad you came," she whispered. "I was too proud, it wouldn't have occurred to me...."

"Someone always has to be the one to speak first, when both of you are wronged," the Dowager said. "And I've never regretted being that person. So much better than letting things fester, even if the other person can't forgive."

"I'll remember that," Alison said. They released each other, both of them laughing a little self-consciously, and Alison picked up the book, covertly examining it for damage and seeing none. "Thank you for bringing this to me," she said.

"I wondered why you'd left it, and why it was under your bed," the Dowager said. "It looks rather valuable. I—" she smiled, and blushed a little —"I admit I read it before bringing it to you. Such enjoyable plays!"

Alison laughed, more heartily this time. "I'm glad you enjoyed them."

"Well, it deserved better than to languish in the dust, and I'm appalled that my cleaning staff took so long to discover it. I've only had it four days. I hope you weren't too inconvenienced."

"Oh, no, it's not mine, it's—" Memory struck her so hard she couldn't breathe, how excited she'd been when she chose it.

"It's whose, dear?" She must look awful, for the Dowager to look so concerned.

"Just a friend," Alison lied. "She didn't know I bought it, so she'll be so surprised to see it now."

"That's fortunate." The Dowager embraced her again, making the hard edges of the book press into Alison's breasts. "I have an engagement now, but do come and see me, please? I miss your conversation."

"I will, Milady," Alison said, and the two of them parted ways. She felt lighter now, all her anger and confusion over meeting Anthony gone. It was so good to have made things right between her and the Dowager; it lifted a burden she hadn't realized she was bearing. She turned over the large book in her hands. It couldn't go to its intended recipient, so it might as well enrich her Library.

She handed Henry his hiring bonus with nonchalance, dismissing his concerns and insisting he not be ridiculous and refuse it. "I want to be sure you don't go anywhere else for employment," she pointed out. "I need you too much."

He laughed. "It's nice to be needed," he said. "Now, what exactly do you need me for?"

Alison looked around at her piles of books. "Tell me, Henry, do you know how to construct a mobile file catalog?"

Chapter Nineteen

Henry folded the banker's draft and put it inside his waistcoat. "You're sure you don't want to come?"

"You know more about the cabinets than I do," Alison said, "and I don't think it really needs two of us to order them. Besides, I still have books to sort."

"I'm a little concerned you're still paying for all of this," Henry said. "Shouldn't it come out of the Library budget?"

"The budget's not resolved yet, and all of this barely touches the interest on my income. And if I wait any longer to start on this catalog I'm going to go mad. The Magisters have been in Aurilien for two days and I have yet to see them."

Henry leaned against the librarians' desk. "Maybe that's good news."

"And maybe they're just trying to increase the tension. Zara said they would bring pressure to bear on me. Not knowing what kind of pressure that might be has got me so keyed up I can barely focus on my actual responsibilities. I wish they'd just get it over with."

Henry squeezed her hand. "You're stronger than they are," he said, "and I've never known you to give in to bullies. There's no sense worrying about something you can't control."

"You're so rational it's sickening. Go. I have to find space for the next batch of books."

She went down into the Library, but instead of bringing up a new pile of books, she wandered the stacks, letting her tension bleed out of her into the stones. If there were ever a day when the Library failed to calm her...she couldn't finish that thought. She pulled a random book off a shelf and paged through it. It was written in Veriboldan, so she only recognized a few words. Everything else on that shelf was in Tremontanese. Maybe Bancroft hadn't had a system at all.

"Milady!" Declan shouted. She heard him leaping down the stairs, then he came skidding around a corner and scrambled to stop before he ran into her. "Milady, they're here!"

Alison steadied the young man and looked up at the Library door. Maybe the Magisters would respect its dignity and stay in the scriptorium. Then she shook herself. They thought it was their Library. Of course they wouldn't. "Do I have any smudges on my face?"

"No, Milady. But what do we do?"

Alison drew herself up to her full height, which put the top of her head level with Declan's nose. "We keep working. They're no different than any other visitors." Having unsuccessfully lied to herself, she went up the stairs with what she hoped was quiet dignity.

There were four of them, all in full regalia, black hoods and gowns and stoles in shades of blue or red. The man in the red stole, poking around the piles of books wearing a pained expression, was merely a Master. The other two men, in blue stoles with black bands, were full Magisters, and the woman with seven black bands on her stole could only be Margaret Bindle, Magistrix of the Scholia. She was a pleasant-looking woman in her sixties with warm, welcoming brown eyes who walked with the help of a cane. She gazed around the scriptorium, at the apprentices working the dehumidifier, and at Gwendolen holding a stack of books, standing frozen in the great woman's path.

"Gwendolen, please don't stand in the Magistrix's way," Alison said, and Gwendolen snapped out of her trance and moved to put her stack down.

"Thank you," the Magistrix said. "You seem a bit old to be an apprentice."

Alison tried to relax her clenched jaw. "I'm not an apprentice," she said. "My name is Alison Quinn, Countess of Waxwold, and I am the Royal Librarian." Bancroft wasn't the only one who could pronounce capital letters. Alison lifted her chin and met the woman's gaze calmly.

"My mistake," the Magistrix said, though her eyes told Alison it had been no mistake. "Margaret Bindle, Magistrix of the Scholia. May I ask the reason for this untidiness? I was under the impression that the Library had plenty of room, but you seem to be overflowing."

Alison realized that in all her worrying, she hadn't given any thought to how she was going to handle the Magistrix. Blame Bancroft for everything? Challenge her on the missing catalog? She opted for breezy competence. "I'm afraid in the commotion surrounding my appointment, the Library catalog disappeared. An unfortunate situation, don't you agree? We're in the process of rebuilding it. Would you care to see the Library?"

The Magistrix and one of her companions were on their way through the Library door before Alison had finished speaking. Alison had to scramble to catch up. She stood on the landing as they went down the stairs and saw the Library with new eyes. The shelves were even barer than they'd been when she'd first seen them. The clean windows and floors dispelled the gloom that had made Bancroft's depredations look so much worse. Piles of books—on the shelves, not the floor, but still piles—ready for removal to the scriptorium made the room look untidy as well as ransacked. Alison imagined how it all looked to the Magistrix and felt guilty and embarrassed. Then she mentally slapped herself. She was repairing the damage the Magistrix's flunky had caused. If anyone had reason to feel guilty or embarrassed, it was the woman in the blue stole. Alison stiffened her spine and descended the stairs.

"This is quite the undertaking," the Magistrix said, "particularly for someone with no formal training."

"I spent four years at the Scholia, studying literature," Alison replied.

"Four years, and chose not to pursue the robe? Why is that?"

"There were other demands on my time."

"I see. Unfortunate." The Magistrix did not say for whom. "I don't recognize your organization system. Something you invented, no doubt?"

"I use the Catherton system."

"*Henry* Catherton? The name is familiar. Wasn't he expelled? I'm sure he was expelled. I'm not mistaken, am I, Darius?"

Her companion said, "No, Magistrix, you are correct. Henry Catherton was expelled for conduct unbecoming a Master."

"Yes, I recall now. Some business with a girl. And you choose to adopt his system. I don't remember it. Perhaps he never chose to present it for ratification."

Conduct unbecoming a Master. Some business with a girl. As if Tessa could be so easily dismissed, turned into nothing more than a black mark on Henry's record. Alison swallowed an angry retort and said, "All I know is that it's easy to use. Henry's quarrel with the Scholia isn't my concern."

"I'm sure ease of use would be very important to someone in your position." The Magistrix's soft brown eyes scanned the room, never resting on Alison. "This is such a big responsibility. I imagine you must feel overwhelmed."

Alison forced herself to remain calm. Losing her temper was what the Magistrix wanted her to do, so she could add lack of self-control to her list of Alison's other shortcomings: incompetence, inexperience, and lack of respect for Scholia standards. She still had no idea what the Magistrix planned to do with that list, but Alison was certain she would make it some kind of weapon.

She replied, "It *is* quite a large task, but I find it invigorating, don't you? Though I imagine in your position you don't have much time for actual library work." She put the slightest emphasis on *actual* and saw the Magistrix's brow furrow with annoyance briefly before settling back into its expression of pleasant concern.

"My opportunity to oversee *every* library is quite fulfilling," the Magistrix said, her emphasis on *every* not slight at all. "I only regret I haven't visited the Royal Library sooner. All this unpleasantness might have been resolved before it began."

"You mean Master Bancroft's using the Library as his personal collection."

"I mean Master Bancroft's failure to see what crimes his subordinates were committing."

"Bancroft stole Library property and sold it and kept the proceeds for himself."

"*Master* Bancroft's guilt has not been proven to the satisfaction of the Scholia. Our Masters have impeccable reputations. His conviction requires a higher standard of proof than that of a common criminal. We're convinced his subordinate Baxter sold the books and stole the money; he was, after all, in charge of acquisitions."

Alison chose to let this go. "I believe that's something you'll have to take up with her Majesty. I have enough to do running the Library."

"Yes, I imagine it takes all of your resources." The Magistrix ran her finger along an upper shelf and brought it away dusty. "I've seen all I need to see."

Alison followed the pair back to the scriptorium, matching her pace to the Magistrix's limping one. She disliked letting the Magistrix lead the way, implying she was in charge, but Alison didn't want to have those two at her back. In the scriptorium, the other blue-robed Magister was reading one of the books in a pile of dramas, the apprentices were standing in a corner, looking like a small flock of green and brown sheep huddling together against the storm, and the red-robed Master stood behind the librarians' desk, turning over pages of Alison's notes.

"Excuse me," Alison said to him, "those are private."

He looked up at her as if surprised she'd spoken. He had a round face with a fringe of black hair and pale gray eyes. "Library business is private?" he said. "Is there some reason you want your plans for the Library to be concealed?" He flipped over another page. "Or is it your naïveté you don't want on display?"

"You have no business behind that desk," Alison said, keeping a tight rein on her temper.

"More business than you," he said.

"Now, Arnold, there's no call for rudeness," the Magistrix said. "Countess, this is Arnold Gowan. He's here to relieve you of this burden."

"This burden? You mean the Library?" She could feel anger seeping out from the cracks in her calmness. "I don't see it as a burden."

"Come now, be reasonable," the Magistrix said. "You're untrained. You have no support staff. You have no experience in creating a catalog. You're using an unapproved, untested cataloguing system. And you no doubt have duties in your county that prevent you from giving your full attention to what is a demanding responsibility. You are unsuited to this position. The Scholia is grateful for your interim service, but it's time for you to let go."

The weapon struck home. For a moment, Alison wavered. Everything the Magistrix said was true. She was about to tackle a project whose enormity would have been daunting even to a trained professional. She had responsibilities as Countess she'd neglected. For a moment, she wavered. Then she remembered having this conversation with Zara. She *was* untrained. She *didn't* have experience. What she had was passion. She wanted this job. She was committed to this job. And she was damned if she was going to let some academic who was probably a political appointee take it away from her.

"I'm afraid that's impossible," she said. "Queen Zara appointed me to this position, which means it's not mine to give up. I realize I don't have the qualifications you believe are necessary, but at least I'm not a peculator or a thief. If the Queen has confidence in me, I wonder that you don't respect her decision. Now, if you'll excuse us, we have a great deal of work to do. As you so kindly pointed out." She turned to Gowan. "Get out from behind my desk or I'll have you removed."

Gowan set down the papers he was holding, his eyes never leaving hers. "You'll regret this," he said under his breath as he passed her. She raised her eyebrows at him, the picture of innocence.

"I'm sorry we couldn't make you see reason," the Magistrix said. "I'm sure we'll speak again, Countess." The four left the room and closed the scriptorium door behind them.

Alison let out a huge sigh and slumped against the nearest desk. They couldn't do anything to her as long as Zara supported her, and Alison had confidence that Zara would continue to support her past the point of reason. True, she could resign, but now that she'd met Margaret Bindle, she realized the woman wouldn't be satisfied with that. Zara was right; the Library was only a pretext. Alison wondered what the Magistrix really wanted. Why weren't they going to try to reinstate Bancroft? Had the Magistrix decided that was a battle she couldn't win? Was that a victory for Zara's side, or some subtle ploy?

"That man can't fire us, can he?" Trevers asked, sounding shaken.

"What? Of course not. Only I can fire you, and I won't do that so long as you do your job. Let's get back to work."

"But he said we weren't official apprentices, and the Scholia should replace us," said Declan.

"And he said girls don't belong in the Library," Gwendolen said. She was near tears, but with anger, not fear.

"I think he has his head up his—never mind. Gwendolen, if the head of the Scholia is a woman, I don't see how he can argue that girls shouldn't be librarians, though it explains why he thought he could be rude to me."

"I think you should have called the guards," said Trevers. His fists were clenched and he looked like he was ready to do battle.

"That might be necessary someday, but for today I'm just glad he's gone. Did you two finish irradiating that last book?" Declan nodded. "Then you can help Gwendolen sort. She'll show you what to do. I'm going to start bringing more books up."

But when she got back into the Library, she stood behind a shelf, where she couldn't be seen from the doorway, and wrapped her arms around herself to control her shaking. They weren't done with her. She wasn't sure what other pressure they could bring to bear, but once they realized nothing they could say or do would convince Zara to fire her, they'd undoubtedly do whatever they could to make her resign. She tried to tell herself she wouldn't give in, but deep down, she was afraid.

"Alison?" Henry called. "Where are you?"

"Here," she said, stepping out from behind the shelf. "How did it go?"

He came down the stairs toward her. "Fine. I commissioned one cabinet for us to test and made sure they could handle a larger order later. It should be ready in three days. I hope you don't mind that I paid for an expedited service."

"No, that was a good choice."

Something in her voice must have alerted him, because his expression became concerned. "What's wrong?"

"We had a visit from the Scholia contingency while you were gone. They want me removed from office."

Henry cursed. "The Queen won't acquiesce, will she?"

"No. But they want me to resign. They pointed out all my inadequacies and brought in my very rude replacement."

Henry put his arm around her shoulders and squeezed, gently. "You are already ten times the librarian any of them are. They're bureaucrats. They like power. Margaret in particular wants to see the Scholia in control of academia throughout Tremontane."

"You know her well enough to use her first name?"

"She was my thesis advisor, a million years ago. Obviously before she became Magistrix. I trusted her. That was the wrong move. She started the proceedings that lost me the robe and got me kicked out of the Scholia."

"I'm sorry, Henry."

"Don't be. It's true, I wish things were different. I loved teaching and I was good at it. But I wouldn't give up Tessa for anything." He released her and again met her eyes. "And I won't give up on you."

Something about his gaze made her uncomfortable, and she looked away. "Then why don't you haul a few more piles of books while I see about hiring scribes? I have to place some advertisements, and talk to an employment agency. Maybe more than one. We'll need several scribes."

"Lots of scribes."

"A gaggle of scribes."

"I believe the collective noun is actually a scribble of scribes."

"I'll add that to my vocabulary."

The next morning, Alison was awakened far too early by a knock at her door. Grumbling, she put on her dressing gown and found a page standing there with a note. She growled her thanks and shut the door in his face. Perfect. Zara requested her presence for breakfast in half an hour. She threw the note on the sofa and, still grumbling, dressed and picked up her keys.

It didn't occur to her that Anthony might be there until she was actually in the east wing. She tried to make her heart slow down. She shouldn't have to avoid him. In fact, she thought with growing indignation, *he* ought to be avoiding *her*. She squared her shoulders and pushed open the dining room door.

She needn't have worried. Zara was alone, though she did have a stack of papers next to her elbow. She pointed at the urn in the middle of the table. "Coffee first," she said. "Talk later."

Alison fell gratefully on the urn and poured herself a generous cup laced with equally generous portions of cream and sugar. She took a long drink, closed her eyes, and leaned back in her chair. Her mind was growing clearer already. "Another cup and I think I'll be ready to be civil."

"I take mine before I get out of bed," Zara said. "That habit has saved the life of more than one of my councilors, with whom I am frequently testy in the early morning." She frowned as she said this.

Alison took another long drink. "Do you often face your councilors early in the morning?"

"Only under extreme duress. Like a visit from the Magistrix of the Scholia." She continued to frown.

"Has she…has she made any demands?"

Zara looked up at her. "If you mean, has she demanded your head on a platter, yes. Not that Margaret Bindle would be so crass. She wants me to rescind your appointment and put her stooge in your place."

"I don't understand why she doesn't want to reinstate Bancroft. I thought that was at the heart of their challenge."

"I imagine the Magistrix realized we have a better than reasonable chance of proving Bancroft guilty, given that he actually *is* guilty and we've already done so once. Losing in court would weaken her case substantially. So she will appear to concede the point in order to get what she actually wants, which is increased independence for the Scholia and increased power for her. But she hasn't considered that I might actually care who runs the Library. I wouldn't allow Gowan anywhere near it even if you weren't involved. He had the nerve to be rude to me."

"I think it's his default state. He's a bully, too. Intimidated my apprentices. I had to threaten to throw him out."

"Maybe I should assign you a guard in case that becomes necessary." Zara turned over a few more pages. "I wanted to warn you that the Scholia intends to challenge Bancroft's conviction today. I want you there to testify to the condition of the Library and the stolen books."

"All right. Should I bring Gwendolen Burns? She accompanied

them on their selling expeditions."

Zara thought about that. "Do you think she'd be able to stand up to their questioning?"

"Um...probably not. She'd get angry."

"Then let's leave her out of it. This is a formality, anyway. They're going to lay the blame on Bancroft's subordinate and ask for Bancroft's release. Depending on what else they ask for, I might give him to them."

"But that would mean he won't be punished for his crimes!"

"I know. Unfortunately, we may have to give him up to gain a better position in this game."

"Do you see it as a game, then?" Alison asked, feeling a little angry at Zara's callousness.

"Politics is a game, Alison. The trick is to see more of your opponent's pieces than she sees of yours. Giving the Magistrix Bancroft may make her think she's regained a piece, when really we've lost a burden. Don't give me that look. Would you prefer I sacrifice you?"

Alison scowled. "I don't like it."

"Neither do I, but ultimately Bancroft doesn't matter. Eat something. Do you know where the Council chamber is? Be there at ten o'clock." She shuffled her papers together, still scowling, and left the room. Alison sat with a forkful of egg halfway to her mouth. The dark walls of the dining room seemed to loom over her, reminding her that she didn't really belong here despite Zara's—it had felt like a royal command, almost, and her eggs and toast looked unappetizing now. She finished her bite, took another drink of coffee, and wondered if she should leave. If Anthony was around, he could walk in at any moment, and that would be, again, awkward.

As if summoned by her thoughts, Anthony opened the door and looked inside without entering. He seemed unsurprised to see Alison. "Is she gone?" he asked without a trace of embarrassment. Alison nodded. He came in and shut the door behind him. "I take it she gave you your orders already," he said. "I've been avoiding her until she's in a better mood."

He seemed so matter-of-fact Alison didn't know how to respond. It was as if there was nothing between them, no betrayal, no dead romance, nothing but casual acquaintance. It made her feel even more awkward, as well as indignant that he could behave as if nothing had happened. "Why is she so out of sorts?" she asked, trying to regain her composure.

Anthony sat and began helping himself from the covered dishes. "Aside from the Magistrix's presence, she has Council problems," he said. "The chief of Commerce has been pushing, the last six months or so, to expand his portfolio. Since he's also a Master, his pushing of late has become more pronounced. All very correct, nothing she can call him on, but it's a strain on an already fractious Council. She's had me sounding the councilors out, to see who supports her and who's inclined toward Lestrange's side, but few of them want to commit to anything until they know what the Magisters will do."

"I don't understand. Isn't Zara the Queen? Don't they just, I don't know, counsel her?"

Anthony heaped scrambled egg on a piece of toast, bit, chewed. "Zara gets the final say in many things, but a lot of policies are determined by voting. It keeps the monarch from being too autocratic and keeps her in touch with the people, or something like that." He laughed once. "Three months ago I didn't know any of this and now I'm an expert."

"And I suppose she can't just replace, what was his name, Lestrange with someone favorable to her." *Three months ago there were a lot of things you weren't. Don't think I've forgotten.*

"Another policy backed up by law. Councilors serve their full term unless they're convicted of a crime or receive a vote of no confidence from the Council. And Lestrange may be a smug, self-righteous git, but he's law-abiding."

"No wonder she's in a bad mood."

"I just hope she gets over it before she has to talk to the Magistrix again." He took another bite. "We went to the theater last night," he said. "She loved it. I've never heard her laugh so loudly. I...took her backstage. I hope you don't mind."

"Why would I mind?"

"It's your theater. I thought...anyway. They were all very relaxed around her. I think half of them didn't realize she was the Queen. I'm afraid Eve told the pickle story. I couldn't stop her."

Alison put her hand over her mouth. "What did Zara do?"

"Laughed until she couldn't breathe. Really, the whole evening was a surprise. I wish—" He closed his mouth abruptly. "I'm thinking of investing in a theater of my own," he said.

"Really?"

"You did tell me once that having more than one theater benefits both. I have the capital and I'm starting to understand the business model. I just thought it might seem disloyal, somehow, after I've become a part of the Waxwold Theater...and suppose Flanagan jumped ship and followed me? I'd hate to rob you of that."

She shook her head, still contemplating the idea. "I ought to cultivate other playwrights," she said, "and there's a tiny—okay, very large—part of me that would love not to have to endure his ranting at me every time I arrive. If you're serious, Doyle might be able to suggest a manager and give you some ideas on assembling a company of players. It really would be nice to have a choice of plays. In Kingsport I could go to three different plays every week, if I wanted. I'd like Aurilien to be like that someday."

"I'm interested in being a part of that."

"I...if it's something you want to do, I don't see why you shouldn't." Had they just had a normal conversation? She tried to summon indignant memories and succeeded only in making herself feel ashamed. Why shouldn't they be able to discuss the theater? It didn't have anything to do with his betrayal. She could be polite about it. She pushed back her chair. "I should arrange for Henry to cover my work while I'm at the Council chamber."

"I'm acting as Zara's secretary, so I should probably finish soon." Alison was halfway to the door when he said, "I don't want to be your enemy."

Alison turned to look at him. He was so serious. She couldn't see any trace of the man she'd loved in his still, emotionless face. Her angry *You should have thought of that before you betrayed me* faded away. "I don't want that either," she said.

"Good," he said, then seemed to run out of words. He looked down at his hands. Alison looked at the floor.

"I'll see you in the Council chamber, then," she said, and fled the room.

He was so different. Serious. Interested in politics. The easy laugh, the gleam of humor in his eyes, both gone. What had happened, that he'd changed so much? She didn't think her rejection of him could have had such a profound effect. Doyle had said there had been nasty rumors; if Bishop really were involved, she could imagine how nasty they'd gotten. And he wouldn't have been able to defend himself against them because the rumor at the heart of them all, the story of what he'd done to her, was true. Despite herself, she felt sympathy for him. *No. No sympathy.*

Henry was kicking his heels against the wall when she finally showed up at the Library. "Haven't you heard of a work ethic?" he asked with a grin. "You're three minutes late."

"I had breakfast with the Queen and the Prince," she said, unlocking the door. "I think I can be excused a little tardiness."

Henry whistled, long and low. "Alison, you move in such exalted circles these days I feel I should bow in your presence."

She slapped him lightly on the arm. "Don't you dare."

He followed her to the librarians' desk. "But seriously, Alison, I'm a little worried about your closeness to the Prince."

"We're not close."

"You just had breakfast with him. I've heard some pretty awful things about what he did to you. I'm surprised you can be so friendly."

Alison sighed. "Henry, most of those rumors are false. You know how it goes. The truth gets lost in the lies. The truth is, we were...involved...and we had a very public falling out. He did some things I can't forgive him for, and we're not friendly, but I don't hate him and I can talk to him without throwing things or bursting into tears. Don't worry about me."

"I can't help it." His eyes on her face were disturbingly serious. Then he smiled and the look disappeared. "But I'm sure you know your own mind, and I have faith in you."

"Thank you, Henry. Will you be able to cover for me later? I have to testify against Bancroft."

"I thought he was already convicted."

"Not according to the Scholia. It should be interesting."

"I wonder at your definition of 'interesting.' I'll be happy to take over for a while, on one condition."

"You're technically my employee and therefore don't have a right to impose conditions."

"Let's go out to supper some time. I'd like to hear about what you've been doing these past four years. I'd like to tell you about Tessa. Say you'll come."

Again, there was something in his eyes that she couldn't read. She shooed away her discomfort. "I'd love to," she said.

Chapter Twenty

At five minutes to ten she walked into the Council chamber to find Zara and Anthony and a handful of people she didn't recognize already there. It was a windowless room hung with worn tapestries bearing the insignia of the eleven provinces, the house of North, and the triple peaks of Tremontane, their faded colors giving the room a depressed look. The center of the room was almost entirely occupied by a table formed from a round cross-section of a tree so enormous Alison could barely imagine what it might have been like before it had given its life in service to Tremontane. It was too big to fit through any of the doors, and looked old enough that it was easy to imagine that the palace had been built around it. Its surface was a deep, rich brown with darker rings circling the center like black water thrown up by a stone tossed into it. Cracks radiated from the edges across the grain, some as deep as three inches. It shone with a smooth finish that came not only from polish but from generations of hands running across its surface. Alison wished she dared touch it.

Zara sat at the table, facing a larger door than the one Alison had come in by, in a chair that looked remarkably like a throne. Anthony stood by her side. Another chair was placed directly opposite to her, across the table. More chairs were ranged in rows behind Zara, and several of them were occupied by the strangers Alison assumed were Council members. Zara beckoned to Alison to come forward and said, "Sit anywhere." She appeared calmer than she had at breakfast. Alison took the closest seat. It was only coincidence that it was the farthest she could sit from Anthony.

At precisely ten o'clock, the larger door opened and the Magistrix entered, followed by her colleagues. She approached the table and sat, leaving the others to take up standing positions behind her. Gowan looked annoyed; the Magisters looked indifferent.

"Thank you for agreeing to hear my petition, your Majesty," the Magistrix said, beaming at Zara with her soft brown eyes.

"I am nothing if not reasonable, Magistrix," Zara said. She didn't sound reasonable. She sounded distant.

"I ask that you reopen the case against Charles Bancroft. We deny that he is guilty of the crimes for which he was convicted."

"Much as I trust your word, Magistrix, your denial is not enough to exonerate him."

"We have the confession of Harvey Baxter, Master Bancroft's assistant librarian. He admits that he stole books from the Royal Library and sold them, and that in his capacity as acquisitions librarian he embezzled the money intended to buy books for the Library."

"And did you bring Master Baxter with you? If he admits to these crimes, he should stand trial himself."

The Magistrix looked sad. "I'm sorry to inform you that Master Baxter is no longer with us. He escaped custody and fled. I wish we could have presented him to you as a token of good faith."

"So do I." Zara steepled her fingers in front of her. "And what do you claim Master Bancroft's role was in all of this?"

"Simple incompetence," the Magistrix said. "Certain... irregularities in Master Bancroft's record with the Scholia have only just come to light. He should never have been appointed Royal Librarian."

"And who is to blame for that? Do you have another convenient scapegoat at large?"

"Your Majesty, I protest. We all make mistakes. We are here to correct one of them."

"Very well. I withdraw my comment. So you intend to present this new evidence at trial and request that Bancroft's sentence be reduced because he is guilty of incompetence rather than venality?"

The Magistrix laughed, a sound as soft as her eyes. "We would prefer not to put the Crown to the trouble. We ask that you remand

Master Bancroft to our custody. Let us discipline him rather than put a burden on the country."

"Interesting," Zara said. "I find your argument compelling. Very well. I will allow you to enact upon Master Bancroft whatever justice the Scholia feels is warranted here."

"Thank you, your Majesty," the Magistrix said. She smiled warmly at Zara, and Alison was reminded of the way a parent might smile indulgently at a child who'd just learned to print her name. "There is one more matter."

"I was under the impression that Master Bancroft's fate had been disposed of. What more is there?" Zara came close to sounding disingenuous.

"The disposition of the Royal Library, of course," the Magistrix said, sounding surprised. "Master Bancroft's unfortunate transgression has left it unsupervised. Master Gowan here is prepared to take up his duties immediately."

"I apologize for the misunderstanding, Magistrix, but we already have a Royal Librarian," Zara said.

"Tradition states that the Royal Library is under the direction of the Scholia. Naturally we are responsible for appointing its officers."

"Tradition is not law, Magistrix."

"No, but it should not be set aside lightly."

"I assure you, Magistrix, I have not made this decision lightly. It has been brought to my attention that the Crown has not been sufficiently interested in overseeing the activities of the Royal Librarian, as is evidenced by the unfortunate incidents recently uncovered. I plan to remedy this."

"Your Majesty is of course welcome to observe Master Gowan's work at any time. He is a skilled librarian and has many years of experience, which is why we've selected him for the position."

Zara held up a finger before the Magistrix could continue. "Countess, would you stand and describe the condition of the Royal

Library when you took office?"

Alison stood, conscious that every eye in the room except Zara's and Anthony's was on her, and let her memory of that first sight of the gutted Library fill her with hot anger. "The room was filthy," she said. "The windows hadn't been washed in months, perhaps years. Books were missing from the shelves or sat in piles on the dirty floor. The Device meant to regulate the climate in the Library had been broken for some time and the air was damp—"

"What is the purpose of this recitation?" the Magistrix asked, indignant.

"Thank you, Countess, you may be seated. Magistrix, I have investigated the Countess's report myself. While the peculation occurred exclusively on Charles Bancroft's watch, it appears the condition of the physical building has been as the Countess describes it for at least seven years, predating not only Master Bancroft's tenure but that of his predecessor. I am disturbed by your Masters' attitude toward the Library for which they are assigned to care. I believe that the Scholia has come to view the Library as belonging to it as opposed to a responsibility they owe the Crown. I appreciate the Scholia's many years of service, but it is my judgment that a new vision is needed."

The Magistrix stood. "Do you suggest, your Majesty," she said in a low voice, "that we of the Scholia are not competent to manage the Library?"

"I would never say such a thing," Zara said. "I suggest your efforts will be better directed elsewhere."

"That's insane!" Gowan exclaimed. Zara and the Magistrix both turned their glares on him at the same time, and he subsided.

"I apologize for my subordinate's language," the Magistrix said, her teeth grating.

"I accept," Zara said. "I am certain he is disappointed at not receiving the ripe plum you promised him."

"Your Majesty, if I may speak boldly, I believe you are making a terrible mistake you will come to regret," the Magistrix said. "Appointing a non-Scholia librarian means errors will creep into the catalog—"

"Which we no longer have, so you need not worry about that."

"Worse still, that a new catalog will be created by someone with no experience and little training. Acquisitions will be haphazard instead of conforming to our guidelines. No one will accept apprentices certified by her. The Royal Library is too important to be trusted to anyone but a Scholia-trained librarian."

"I appreciate your concern. Again, I thank you for your years of service, but my decision has been made. Alison Quinn has my full confidence." Zara stood, indicating that the meeting was over, but the Magistrix wasn't finished yet.

"So you refuse to accept our appointee?"

"I do."

"And you choose to insult the Scholia in this grave fashion?"

"I mean no insult. It's your choice whether to construe my actions as such."

"Then you are willing to accept the consequences of your actions?"

Zara turned her glass-cutting gaze on the Magistrix. "What do you suggest those consequences might be, Magistrix? Think carefully before you answer."

The Magistrix returned her glare for glare. "The Scholia is the preeminent educational institution in Tremontane. We guarantee the abilities of our students and Masters and receive commensurate respect for those abilities. If you refuse to accept our candidate, it might be seen as an accusation of non-confidence in the Scholia. I cannot guarantee our Masters will not feel insulted by it, nor predict what they might choose to do in that event."

"Do you threaten me, Magistrix?"

"Merely a warning. Consider it. If you decide to change your mind, no one will hold it against you."

Zara nodded once. "I appreciate the warning, Magistrix. I maintain a great respect for the Scholia. But I am not pleased at how our most recent Royal Librarians have treated their charge. Do not mistake my respect for you and your office for a willingness to allow that state of affairs to continue. Good day, Magistrix."

The moment the door shut behind the Magistrix, a man seated behind the Queen said, "Well, *that* was no surprise."

"I was surprised she didn't threaten you more overtly," a woman added. She stood and came around Zara's throne-chair. "She's in a strong position thanks to you giving her Bancroft."

"Bancroft is irrelevant, Fern," Zara said. She rose and turned to face her councilors. "As is the Library. You all know why the Magistrix is really here."

"The endowment," Clara Unwin said, her mouth twisted as though she'd just bitten a lemon. "You can't give it to her, Zara."

"Why not?" said the man who'd first spoken. His round, smooth, unlined face made him look like a doll carved of some fair wood. "If we support the Scholia, why not show that support? Give them the greater independence they want?"

"A former Master would be expected to have that outlook," Unwin said.

"Do you suggest I'm less than loyal to this Council?"

"I suggest that your perspective is different. Your support of the Magistrix is something else that is no surprise."

"Enough," Zara said. "Roger, your insights are valuable. Clara, protecting the kingdom's financial stability is your duty. I expect you to respect one another's views."

Unwin's lips thinned, but she nodded, a curt motion of her head. Roger said, "I meant no disrespect."

Zara waved that away. "We'll meet later today to prepare a strategy. Countess, thank you for your service to the Crown. Again, I assure you that you have my full support."

Thus dismissed, Alison walked back to the Library, deep in thought. Roger must be Roger Lestrange, chief of the Commerce department and Zara's main antagonist on the Council. He certainly made no secret of his partisanship. Alison was glad she only had the antagonism of the Magisters to worry about.

She spent the rest of the day hiring scribes and purchasing supplies, including thousands of little cards, pink and blue and white. While she was waiting for them to be delivered, she went from department to department until she found one that could provide her with a dozen wheeled carts, and led a procession of burly men pushing the incongruously tiny carts back to the Library. There she found the apprentices had cleared away the books from the desks and arranged writing utensils and stacks of cards on each one. Henry was sorting books again at the librarians' desk. He smiled when he saw her.

"You look like a duckling leading a line of mother ducks behind you," he said.

Alison thanked her helpers and watched them file out again. "I wonder how I could go on without burly men to do the heavy lifting for me? I can barely manage the books."

"Lift enough of them, and you'll have arms like your burly men." Henry hefted two large books in his hands and lifted them over his head.

"I'd rather not, thanks."

"I've made reservations for us for tomorrow night," Henry said. "I hope you haven't made other plans."

"No, I'm all yours for the evening," she said lightly, and was disconcerted at how her words changed Henry's expression again, if briefly. A thought dashed across her mind that Henry might be thinking of something other than a friendly meal. No, she was being foolish. She had never thought of Henry as anything but her best friend's husband, and she was sure he only saw her as a former student and friend. She had to stop believing that every man she interacted with had ulterior motives. She remembered what she'd promised her father. Henry wasn't exactly young, but he was a man and she didn't have to shut him out on the basis of what was probably a stupid, unfounded suspicion. Even so, she had to work at being normal around him for the rest of the afternoon.

Chapter Twenty-One

The next morning, she met Henry for breakfast and the two of them walked to the Library together. "I asked the scribes to arrive in about an hour," she told him. "Just in case there are any last things to arrange."

"You're excited about this," Henry said.

"I am. Is it silly to be excited about something as boring as a catalog? It's just that I keep reaching these landmarks that make me feel like we're *really* getting started. Cleaning the Library. Hiring an excellent assistant Librarian." She grinned at him.

"Yes, your assistant Librarian is remarkable, isn't he? You're probably not paying him enough."

"You're fortunate. I don't know if I'm being paid at all."

They turned the corner into the long hallway outside the Library. As they approached the scriptorium door, Henry said, "What's that on the floor?"

"It looks like—oh, no, sweet heaven, *no*," Alison said, and began to run, her heart pounding more fiercely than her activity warranted. She came skidding to a halt in front of the door and knelt, shaking, before it. The latch and the lock had been pried away from the door and lay shattered on the floor, twisted almost out of recognition. Alison put her hand on the scriptorium door and it opened without resistance. "*No,*" she repeated when she saw what lay beyond it.

Long streaks of ink painted the floor and the walls and striped the desks, and shards of empty ink jugs were scattered across the room. The apprentices' careful arrangements of writing materials lay torn and broken, the fragments of self-inking pens piled neatly on each desk as if some monstrous creature had sat there and calmly snapped each pen in half, leaving behind tiny puddles of ink and gleaming silver beads still imbued with source. The piles of books had been knocked over. Her

264

beautiful magnifying Devices were smashed into a million sparkling pieces of twisted metal. And the cards, thousands of them, lay in drifts across the floor and on every conceivable surface.

Alison rushed to the nearest heap of books. "They're undamaged," she said, then realized what that meant. "Those *bastards*," she breathed out.

"The Scholia," Henry agreed.

Alison kicked a mostly intact ink jug. "If they think they can intimidate me by making a mess, they are sorely mistaken."

"This is a really big mess, Alison."

She turned on him. "So? You think there's a point at which the mess becomes so big I should give in to them? Allow someone who can think this way take over my Library?"

Henry shook his head. "You're right." He bent to pick up an inkwell. "Margaret didn't do this, though. She prefers verbal manipulation and never wants to get her hands dirty. When I was fired, it was mostly because she whispered allegations about me until everyone knew how to think. But she's not above hinting to someone that she'd like you dealt with."

"I will bet you anything you like Gowan's behind it." She looked around, feeling despair despite her brave words. "Wait here for the apprentices. I'll get someone to help us clean up."

She headed toward Physical Facilities, anger surging through her, bringing tears to her eyes which she dashed away impatiently. There was no way she could prove who'd done it. She could get Zara to post more guards at the little door at the end of the hall, her shortcut out of the palace that didn't require her to go by the east wing, but that wouldn't help. They weren't coming back because they'd made their point: resign, or the Library suffers. Zara would believe her, but what could she do? She had her own problems. She blinked away more tears. Now the bastards had made her cry. She must look awful. Everyone she passed stared at her.

She realized that in her reverie she'd taken a wrong turn, cursed, and turned around, bumping into someone. "Sorry," she said, and the other person said, "Alison, what's wrong?"

She hadn't heard him say her name in so long it startled his out of her. "Anthony," she said.

Anthony said, "I've been trying to get your attention since you passed me in the hall back there. What happened?"

She scrubbed at her eyes again. "The scriptorium was vandalized," she said. "I need to get it cleaned up before the scribes get here."

He took her arm and drew her to one side, then released her all in one motion so swift she barely felt the touch of his hand. "The Scholia?"

He was quick. She nodded. "They left the books and the desks alone. No common vandal would have done that. It's a huge mess. There's ink everywhere. I need to get people from Physical Facilities to help clean it up." She moved as if to pass him, and he stepped into her path.

"Domestics is what you need," he said. "I'll get your labor. Go back to the Library and salvage what you can."

"Thank you," she said, and he smiled, and for a moment she saw the man she remembered, and smiled back at him. His smile vanished, leaving him completely expressionless. She blushed and had no idea why. "Thank you," she said again, and turned and ran back to the Library, feeling as if she were being chased by something she couldn't identify.

The apprentices had arrived while she was gone. Henry and Declan were moving books to whatever clean spots they could find, clearing the floor. Gwendolen and Trevers were busy picking up cards from the floor, discarding those too ink-soaked to be used. "They opened all the boxes, milady," said Gwendolen, who'd been crying her own tears of rage. "And all the ink jugs. And all the pens are broken."

Alison leaned face-first against the wall and quickly stepped back.

A smear of ink made a wide streak against her forearm. She cursed again, more eloquently, causing the apprentices to gasp and then giggle and Henry to say, "Don't corrupt the children, dear."

"They ought to learn these words while they're young or they won't know what to say when Scholia vandals break into *their* libraries."

A double handful of men and women entered, bringing buckets of water, mops, scrub brushes, brooms, and towels. They were followed by Anthony, who surveyed the room and said, "I didn't realize what you meant by 'huge mess'. Should I tell Zara?"

Alison hesitated. Finally, she said, "Would you? I know there's nothing she can do, but she ought to know they've started harassing me."

"Well, I don't know why they thought this was going to intimidate *you*," he said, still looking at the mess. "I imagine it just made you angrier."

"They don't know me at all," she agreed. "But it does make me worry about what they'll try next."

"I'll have someone see about replacing that lock with something a little more robust." He finally looked at her. "Tell me if you need anything else, will you? I can probably find whatever it is faster than you can, and you should put your energies toward taking care of the Library."

"I will. And thank you again." He nodded and left. Alison scrubbed at the streak of ink across her arm. They *didn't* know her. And he did. The thought made her angry again. She didn't need to be reminded of what they'd been to each other.

Out of fifteen boxes of cards, they salvaged two boxes' worth. Gwendolen was right; all the ink was gone and all the pens were broken. Alison ground her teeth and sent Henry and Declan back to the stationer's to replace everything. Then she and the remaining apprentices rolled up their sleeves and joined in the scrubbing.

She was so deep in her furious thoughts of what she could do to Arnold Gowan that she was surprised when someone said, "I'm here about the scribe position?"

She stood up and wiped her hands on her trousers, which were now hopelessly filthy and wet. The speaker was an attractive young woman dressed neatly in a scribe's smock with her long dark hair pulled back from her face. She looked at the room in dismay. She'd clearly come prepared to work; by her expression, she was not prepared for the sudsy, inky mess the scriptorium had become. Alison went to the door and held out her hand. After a moment's pause, the young woman took it. "Believe it or not, I'm the Royal Librarian," she said. "I apologize for the mess, but we've had a bit of a setback. Why don't we talk out here?"

In the hallway, Alison said, "Did you bring your credentials?"

The woman flushed. "I don't have anything. I was hoping to prove my skills directly."

"You don't have a reference from a previous job?"

"This is my first job." The woman looked at the floor. "I was a student at the Scholia for three years. I left because I wouldn't give my professor what she asked for." She looked up, and Alison was surprised at the anger in her eyes. "She wanted more from me than just essays, if you take my meaning. And the Scholia Masters took her side."

Alison nodded slowly. "I imagine you must hate them."

"I shouldn't say—"

"What's your name?"

"Danica Morton."

"Yes or no, Danica Morton. Do you have warm and loving feelings for the Scholia?"

"No, milady, I absolutely do not."

"Then you're hired. I won't have anything for you to do until we replace our supplies, so you're welcome to wait or, if you feel like it, join in with the scrubbing. Ah. It appears we have some more candidates." A group of five men and women were approaching them. "Ladies, gentlemen, may I see your credentials? Excellent. Now, are any of you affiliated with the Scholia? Harbor a great respect for them? Thank you for being honest, sir, you may leave. The rest of you—I'm sorry, did you want to say something?"

"I don't think you should discriminate against me just because I respect the Scholia," said the older man she'd dismissed. "I'm a good scribe."

"Sir, I am a non-Scholia librarian," Alison said, "and the Scholia Masters want me gone. I consider them an enemy. I will not tolerate the presence of anyone who believes I don't deserve this position, and I will not hire anyone who might be willing to work with them against me. Now, I'll pay you something for your trouble, and I wish you luck in finding another job. Which I'm sure will happen quickly if you're as good as you say."

"But—"

"Out. Now." Righteous anger surged through her. She probably shouldn't have taken it out on the poor man, but it felt good to have a target. Pity it wasn't Gowan.

More applicants trickled in over the next hour. She repeated her speech seven times but only turned away two other people, which surprised her. It surprised her even more how vehement most of them were about how much they *didn't* like the Scholia. Apparently the Scholia was quick to make enemies of more than just untrained Countesses who dared set themselves up as librarians.

It didn't take the workers long to complete their task. Dark streaks still showed on the desks where the ink had soaked into the wood, but the floors and walls were clean and the broken and damaged things had been cleared away. Henry and Declan returned about twenty minutes after the cleaning crew had left, towing carts filled with self-inking pens and boxes of cards. "It will take time to replace the other things," Henry said, "but we have enough to be going on with."

"Thank you, Henry. Ladies and gentlemen, if you'd take your seats, please. Mister Catherton, the assistant Librarian, will give you your instructions. This is a long-term project, so unless you prove incompetent you can plan on job security for a while." She saw a messenger enter the scriptorium and nodded to Henry to take over.

The messenger handed her a note addressed to her in a familiar graceful scrawl that made her traitorous heart beat faster. "Wait a moment," she told the boy. She opened the note.

Zara is furious but agrees there's nothing she can do aside from posting guards nearby. She says to remind you about horses and barn doors and apologizes. Invites you to supper to discuss options.

He hadn't signed it. Alison told the boy to wait again and snatched up a piece of paper and pen to write an acknowledgement and acceptance of the invitation. After the boy had run off, she remembered her supper with Henry. They'd just have to postpone, that's all. She leaned against the newly clean wall and listened with half an ear to Henry's instructions. Zara had to have some idea of what to do next.

Zara was alone when Alison entered the dining room. "Thank you for joining me, Alison," she said. "Were you able to salvage anything from the mess? Anthony said it looked like someone had shaken a giant bottle of carbonated ink and sprayed it everywhere."

"That's an accurate description. Yes, it's clean now, and I reordered supplies and we even had time to get the scribes started on the catalog. I'm actually grateful Gowan tried this now instead of a few days from now, when some of the books will be catalogued. That would have meant real damage. With a new, better lock and guards on that outside door, I don't think it will happen again."

"You believe Gowan is behind it, then?"

"Don't you? He didn't damage any of the things he'd need as Royal Librarian. And there was a nastiness to the vandalism that struck me as fitting his character."

"But you have no proof."

"No, damn it, and I have no recourse except to go on as if nothing has happened."

"That's the best policy." They ate in silence for a while, then Alison said, "I wish I could predict what they'll do next."

"So do I. I'm considering placing a guard on you."

Alison, surprised, said, "Me? Do you think I'm in physical danger from Gowan?"

"Possibly not. I don't know the man well enough to judge that. But it might be better to plan for the worst."

"I would really prefer not to be trailed by a bodyguard. It would interfere with my work."

"As I said, I'm considering it. I haven't decided yet. If you feel safe, then I'll table the idea for now."

"Thank you. And I appreciate your consideration."

"At the risk of bringing up a forbidden subject, I believe I told you before I would have enjoyed having you for a sister. I would be very upset to see anything happen to you."

Alison went blotchy all over. She turned her attention to her food. *Suppose you'd married him. Oh, yes, and then you would have found out what a weak, cowardly man you were oathbound to.* "Thank you," she said for lack of anything else to say. She reminded herself of the devastating conversation she'd overheard between Anthony and Bishop, always good for stopping memories she couldn't bear to think of. That reminded her of something else.

"Zara," she said, "what exactly were the rumors about what happened between Anthony and me? People have told me they were vicious, but they won't say what they were."

Zara laid down her fork and leveled her blue-eyed gaze on Alison. "There were many," she said, "but for a while it was common knowledge that Anthony had taken sexual advantage of you."

Alison's heart thumped once, hard. "They said he raped me?"

Zara nodded. "How have I not heard this?"

"It was buried in a host of conflicting rumors I started to head that one off," Zara said. "We both, Anthony and I, judged it better that it not go farther than Aurilien, to protect your reputation to the extent that was possible. I am nothing if not thorough."

"No wonder he always looks like a statue," Alison breathed. "Why didn't you stop it?"

"And make it look like there was something to hide? Rumors pass. Someone does something stupid and becomes the next topic of conversation. Your scandal is all but forgotten, now."

"But I would have come back—I would have told people the truth."

"Alison, the surest way to spread a rumor is to deny it. All that would have accomplished would have been to make you a figure of pity or, to those with low minds, a woman of no virtue. This was the best course."

"Damn Alexander Bishop." All Alison's anger was swept away for the moment by compassion. Anthony shouldn't have had to endure that, no matter what he'd done to her. No wonder he'd gone running to the theater to hide. No wonder his eyes didn't have their old gleam. "I don't suppose you did anything about him?"

Zara's mouth curled up in its calculating smile. "Let us just say that no one will ever see Alexander Bishop in Aurilien again, and leave it at that."

Alison shivered. "I won't ask."

"It's nothing so sinister. He just decided to take a permanent trip to Veribold." Zara sipped her wine. "He may or may not have had encouragement."

"I'm glad he's gone."

"So is Anthony. So am I. I don't think he'll be missed much, to be honest, except by his creditors."

The door opened and Anthony came in. "You started without

me," he said plaintively.

"And we are about to finish without you, too," said Zara. "What kept you so long?"

"You did, actually," said Anthony, laying his napkin on his lap. "That inventor you wanted me to meet with? He was late. But I was too interested in his invention to send him away."

"What invention?" Alison said.

He glanced at her before applying himself to his food. "Damn, this is cold. I know, it's my own fault. He has an invention that lets you instantly communicate with anyone, anywhere, provided you both have the same Device. He calls it a telecoder."

"Does it work?"

"It does, or at least his prototype does. It's quite impressive. I told him we'd give him the materials and space to put together a full-scale demonstration."

"Excellent," Zara said. She stood. "Send me word when it's ready. I'd like to see it myself. Good night."

Alison finished her meal in silence, painfully conscious of Anthony's presence. Anthony ate quickly and neatly and paid no attention to her until she pushed her plate away and stood, when he said, "Did Zara tell you she wants to give you a bodyguard?"

"She did. I turned it down."

"I think you should reconsider. Gowan acts like the kind of man who sees the world in terms of who will accommodate him and who will get in his way. I think he's ruthless enough to try to attack you directly if indirect means won't work."

"I don't think it's come to that."

"No, but it might."

"I appreciate your concern, but I think Gowan is going to stick to indirect threats for a while yet."

He shrugged. "I thought you'd say that, but I had to try."

"Thank you." She waited to see if he had anything more to say, but he just went back to his food, his attention fully on his plate, so she said "Good night" and heard his murmured reply.

She went to her chambers, which were so much nicer now that all traces of Charles Bancroft had been eradicated from them. She'd requisitioned—such a nice word; it was her new favorite word—new furniture, new bedding, even new curtains, and had most of her wardrobe packed and sent to Aurilien, trying not to think about what that said about the semi-permanent nature of her residence here. Now her chambers smelled of good things like bath soaps and new leather and her personal scent. She used the bookshelf to hold the Library books she borrowed and covered her bed with the red and gold quilt that had belonged to her mother. It made any place seem like home.

She sat on the sofa and thought about what Zara had told her. How had he endured the calumny? For someone who had been at the center of society, to be tarred with that vile accusation must have been devastating. *If you'd said yes, none of this would have happened,* her inner voice taunted her. *I was never going to say yes to him,* she told it. *Stop trying to make me feel guilty. He might not have deserved to be crucified like that, but he deserved everything else he got.*

But she had the dream again that night, and for a few blissful moments on waking wondered why Anthony wasn't beside her. Then she buried her face in her pillow and sobbed.

Chapter Twenty-Two

"You promise, no more changes of plans, yes?" Henry said.

"No changes. The two of us, supper, no excuses." Alison hefted another stack of books. "Unless *you* change *your* plans."

"I can't think of anything else I'd rather do than spend the evening with you." He sounded teasing, but his eyes were serious, and Alison had to look away, uncomfortable. Was he, or wasn't he, flirting with her? He'd never looked at her that way before, but what if she was imagining things? She decided to treat this as it appeared on the surface, just supper between old friends, nothing romantic about it. But...suppose he wanted it to be romantic? What then? It was strange, thinking of Henry in that light; he'd always just been her friend, and Tessa's husband, but Tessa was gone and Henry wasn't more than ten years her senior. Not a big difference at all. Mature men were attractive in a way younger men were not. Alison brushed those thoughts aside. Henry's attention probably meant nothing. But if it meant something, how would she feel about that? Not bad at all, she decided. Maybe Father's advice wouldn't be so difficult to follow.

Supper was enjoyable. They talked of old friends; they talked of Tessa, and found the subject not so painful as it once would have been. Henry talked about how much he missed teaching, and Alison told him how she regretted giving up her editing work. Afterward they walked back to the palace and her chambers slowly, enjoying the cool spring evening and continuing to talk of inconsequentialities. At her door, Henry turned to face her, took both her hands in his, and said, "Thank you for looking for me. And for the job. And...for your company." He kissed her hands, one at a time, his eyes intent on her. Once again, she felt a mix of emotions, discomfort and excitement and confusion, and she was afraid he might try to kiss her, because she really didn't know what she'd do then.

But he only released her, and said, "Good night, Alison, I'll see you in the morning," just as if nothing had happened. She stood watching him go for a moment before entering her chambers and shutting the door.

So. Henry was interested in her. *The man certainly does like younger women.* She ignored her snarky inner voice. The question was, was she interested in *him*? She liked the way he looked at her. She'd known him long enough to trust he didn't have any ulterior motives. And it was so...comfortable, really, to be admired by someone she was sure wanted her for herself. But she wasn't sure if she liked him, or just liked feeling desirable. It would be unfair to him if she pursued the relationship only to discover she didn't actually care about him. She banged the back of her head against the door three times, gently. Well, she certainly wasn't going to be able to sleep right away, not after all that.

Alison opened the first box and said, "Please stop breathing down my neck, everyone." The scribes and the apprentices took a few steps back. Alison reached into the box and drew out a brass magnifying Device with buttons and knobs all along its rim. She set it on the librarians' desk and adjusted the screws to keep it balanced, then pressed a button. The brass rim glowed softly, drawing a murmur out of the audience.

"They're self-focusing, milady?" Danica said.

"They are. And everyone gets one. Trevers, Gwendolen, help pass them out, please." Alison ran a finger along its smooth frame, then turned off the light. She remembered how the first batch had been destroyed, those beautiful Devices turned into twisted brass and glittering shards, and took a deep, calming breath. Days had passed with no word as to what the Magistrix and her party were doing or how Zara was handling her Council. Gowan hadn't tried anything else. Yet. The Library was purring along so smoothly it had almost become boring, but there was no sense in becoming complacent.

"These must have cost a fortune," Henry murmured in her ear.

"It's worth it to me," Alison said, feeling a little uncomfortable at how close he was. Nothing else had come of dinner with Henry. He treated her with the same friendly respect he always had, and she found herself disappointed by that. The trouble was she wasn't sure if she was disappointed because she wanted a closer relationship with Henry, or if she was disappointed because she liked the feeling of being courted and wanted more of it. Henry was attractive, and kind, and they cared about the same things, and they had a shared history, but did they have a...a spark? *Like what you had with Anthony,* her traitorous inner voice said, and she slapped it down, hard.

A page entered the scriptorium, note in hand, which he gave to Alison. "It's from my partner," she told Henry, and read *Come down to the theater when you get a chance.* Alison sighed. That was Doyle-code for "as soon as possible," but since he gave no specifics, it was impossible to tell whether or not it was important. Doyle had a habit of calling her down to the theater to confer on decisions he could, and should, make himself.

"Do you need to go now?" Henry asked.

Alison checked her watch. Almost time to lock up. "I think he can wait until I've had my supper," she said.

"Do you mind if I join you?" Henry was smiling at her, and there was that light in his eyes again. She thought about it for a moment.

"I don't mind at all," she said.

They took their time over supper. Henry's hand brushed hers more than once, though nothing else about his behavior told her whether it had been intentional or not, and she surprised herself by flirting a little and enjoying the look that came to his eyes when she did. Even so, she declined his offer of an escort and took a carriage to the theater, where she was early enough that the box office hadn't opened yet. She went through the foyer to Doyle's office and heard him talking to someone. She stood next to the door, listening not because she wanted to eavesdrop but to judge whether this was a conversation she could interrupt.

"…licensing…not really important…"

"I can't find anyone…stonewalling."

She recognized that second voice. Was she going to run into him everywhere she went? She pushed open the door. "Sorry to interrupt," she said to Doyle and Anthony, "but someone sent me an urgent message to get down here immediately."

"'Which I notice you interpreted as 'whenever I feel like it because I'm a Countess,'" Doyle said. Anthony stood and offered her his chair, which she declined.

"If you don't sit, no one will use it, because I won't sit while you're standing," he said with a wry smile.

"Oh, for heaven's sake, I'll get another chair," Doyle huffed. While he was gone, Alison raised her eyebrows at Anthony and said, "Don't tell me he summoned you, too? He really has no respect for the nobility."

"It's one of the many things I like about him," Anthony said, and there was that wry smile again. She tried to summon her anger that he could behave so normally around her, but felt only a distant echo of her old resentment. Maybe her relationship with Henry was changing her. "No, I came on my own. I've started the process of opening a theater, and I needed his advice on a problem I've run into."

"You're actually opening a theater? I'm so glad to hear it. Where?"

Doyle came back, dragging a folding chair as if it weighed as much as the palace, and Alison and Anthony both sat down. "Over in the Grayford district," Anthony said. "But it's much harder than I expected."

"Tony has the same problem we're facing, Allie," Doyle said, settling himself back into his seat and pulling out his bottle of whiskey. "Regulations. Twenty years ago you could do pretty much whatever you wanted with your business. Now there are rules for everything. What hours employees can work. How many employees we have to have." He took a drink and offered the bottle to them; they both declined. "Worse than that, entertainers are supposed to be licensed, but there's no licensing board for actors and no plans to create one any time soon. But that doesn't matter—they still have to be licensed. We're expected to comply with rules set up to govern businesses radically different from ours."

"My problem is I want to renovate an existing building, but I can't get the permits to do what needs to be done to turn it into a theater," said Anthony. "I want to install too many light Devices, according to the planning department. They're worried about a fire hazard, of all things, as if light Devices emitted heat. They want the building to have facilities of a certain size and they tell me I have to have more windows—in a theater! And there's much more. I hoped Doyle would know what to do, but he's dealing with the same nonsense. It feels as if someone's sending up obstacles to keep us from operating."

"Who could do that? And why?" Alison asked.

"Well, you're going to love this," Anthony said sourly. "This all comes under the department of Commerce. Zara said Lestrange was trying to expand his portfolio. I think we just found one of the places he's trying to weasel into."

"So that's who, but I don't understand why."

"Permits cost money," Doyle explained. "The more hoops we have to jump through, the more money goes into the Commerce department. Theaters are so new here in Aurilien that no one knows what to do with us, so I think someone in the Commerce department sees us as a money tree they can shake indefinitely."

"So what can we do about it?"

"That's what we've been talking about," Doyle said, taking another drink.

"Making decisions while drunk? That's a sound strategy."

"Stop being my mother, Alison, you're far too young and pretty."

"I'm telling your mother you said that."

"*Anyway*," Doyle said, glaring at her, "the first option is bribery. Find someone responsible for handing out permits, lay a little lard on our guilders and get him to look the other way while we go ahead with business. That's usually a short term solution, but we're only talking short term here." He ticked it off on one finger. "The long term solution is to petition for a sub-department for theater, or the arts, or whatever, so the regulations are made specifically to fit our kind of business. Lots of hassle, and it takes a while, but in the end you have stability." He ticked that off as well.

"But that second solution means my plans get put on hold indefinitely," Anthony said. "And I don't think I should bribe anyone. Even if it didn't get out and cause a scandal, Zara would be miffed, and I don't want her miffed at me."

"Which leads us to the third solution, which is that pretty-boy here goes straight to his sister and asks her to intervene."

"Which I refuse to do on the grounds that I want to solve this problem without taking the weak and spineless route."

"It's the best solution. Hand it over to the Queen. You said yourself she's concerned about what the department of Commerce is doing."

"Concerned, yes. Willing to solve my problems for me, no. She's made that clear."

"What if *I* tell her?" Alison said. "I don't have to ask her to intervene, but I think she should know about this. Theaters can't be the only new kind of business suffering. Suppose that man with the invention, the telecoder, tries to go into business? There's nothing to govern that either."

Anthony nodded slowly. "That's a good idea," he said. "She'll listen to you."

"She listens to you, too."

"Not the same thing." He didn't elaborate.

"Will you talk to her, Allie?" said Doyle. "Yes, I'd love it if she swooped down on the licensing department and made them squawk, but I think telling her about the problem will get her to come up with a solution none of us have thought of."

"I'll talk to her. But don't expect anything soon. I imagine she's preoccupied with the Magisters."

"That's an understatement," Anthony said.

"Really?" said Alison, but Anthony shook his head. "I should be getting back," he said.

"Me too," said Alison, rising as he did. "Thanks for letting me know, Doyle."

"Repay me by getting the government off my back, and I say that realizing that the two of you *are* the government," Doyle replied affably, taking another swig. "Now get out before the audience gets scared off by your scruffiness."

Alison looked down at herself, at her clean trousers and shirt, then looked at Anthony, who was dressed casually in a collarless shirt and trousers. "I think we look just fine," she said indignantly, and Doyle waved them away with the bottle.

On the street outside, Anthony asked, "Are you going back to the palace?" Alison nodded, and he added, "Would you like to share a carriage? There are things I couldn't say in front of Doyle."

Alison hesitated, just long enough that Anthony's expression went wooden. Guilt rushed through her. "I'm sorry, that was uncivil of me," she said, and something about her words echoed in her memory. "Please, let's ride together. I wondered what you were keeping back."

Once they were seated in the carriage opposite one another, Anthony said, "The Magistrix has been stirring up more trouble than we expected. She's been talking to councilors all week, trying to convince them to support her in the upcoming vote."

"Vote on what?"

"The endowment that will make the Scholia virtually independent of Tremontanan governance. That will make it self-supporting. They already receive great sums of money from the Treasury, but it's contingent on the yearly budget and it assumes the Scholia will get funds from other sources as well. For years now the Scholia has wanted the government to hand over properties and money enough for them to live off the interest and not depend on any other sources of revenue." Anthony leaned forward so she could see him more clearly. "It could mean financial disaster, as far as Mistress Unwin can see, and she's had a quarter century's worth of experience in the Finance department.

"And Zara has to put it up for a vote?"

"Financial policy is set by the Council. Keeps the Queen from running the Treasury as her own personal pot of gold."

Alison breathed out heavily. "How is her support?"

Anthony shook his head. "Hard to say. Lestrange is pro-Scholia, obviously. The Scholia is in County Cullinan, so their Countess supports them. Mistress Unwin backs Zara all the way and Albert Fisher in Transportation is an old friend of Zara's. Other than that, we have no idea."

"I'm glad it has nothing to do with me. I'm impressed you know so much."

"Zara confides in me, which I confess still feels strange, considering that I was just her wastrel younger brother only a short while ago."

"You were never a wastrel."

Anthony raised his eyebrows. "I'm surprised to hear you say that."

"I never called you a wastrel."

"I drank, I gambled, I wasted my time...maybe you should have done."

"I'd rather not have this conversation, if you don't mind."

"I apologize." He sat back so his face was in shadow.

They rode in silence. Finally, Alison said, "You've changed. At least everyone tells me you have."

"Do *you* think so?"

The question skirted the edge of what she was comfortable with, but she said, "You look different. Serious, all the time. And you care about politics now." She felt exposed, her face now shadowed, now lit by the street lights they passed.

"I never realized I had a talent for it," he said, "until Zara insisted I pay attention. She's training me to be her heir, I think."

"You already are her heir."

"It's about more than biology. If it were as easy as waving the scepter and spending money, I'd be qualified already."

"Don't—"He'd sounded too flippant, and she'd started to reassure him before embarrassment and anger stopped her tongue.

"Don't what?"

She considered her words carefully. "I think, if you really have changed, you shouldn't think so much about the ways you haven't changed. Whatever those are."

He shifted in the darkness. "I prefer not to forget about my failings, since I'd rather not fall into them again."

"I suppose that makes sense." She felt ashamed of her anger. Doyle was right; not everything Anthony was dealing with was about her. It was self-centered of her to assume otherwise.

They rode the rest of the way in silence. Anthony didn't offer to help her down from the carriage, for which she was grateful. Her peace of mind was disturbed enough already; she didn't need his touch to confuse the issue further. They walked together as far as the east wing, since they were both going the same way, and bid each other good night as if they were acquaintances and nothing more. It was surprisingly easy to be civil. *He's changed*, she told herself as she fell into sleep, *and maybe I have too.*

Chapter Twenty-Three

"We're going to start creating subject entries for the catalog," Henry said. Twenty scribes watched him pace in front of the librarians' desk. "These reference pages will tell you what to look for." Gwendolen went down the aisles, handing out printed sheets. "Each book contains a paper listing its subjects; you make one entry for each subject, on the white cards. Remember, you're not being paid by the card, but that's no excuse for sloth. Any questions? Good. Please stack each book neatly when you're done with it and put the cards in the basket. Thank you."

"It's almost like you're a real librarian," Alison teased as he came to where she stood behind the long desk.

"Funny how it all comes back to you." He leaned on the desk. "Have you seen Trevers? He was supposed to be here an hour ago, and Declan said he hasn't seen him since last night. Did you send him somewhere?"

"No, but I'm sure he'll be here soon. He's more responsible than Declan and Gwendolen combined. And now *we* need to be responsible and get to work."

"I'm at your service. What are your instructions, chief?"

"I feel as though you ought to be the chief. You have actual experience."

"But you have passion I never did. And I think you have a better eye for the quality of a book."

"I wish I could afford to indulge my passion in new acquisitions, but I think it would be better to determine what we have before purchasing anything new. Although I had an idea...."

She led him into the Library and to the back wall, where scroll cabinets took up much of the space. "Look at this," she said, drawing a scroll case out of its cubby and opening it. She gingerly slid the ancient, crumbling parchment out and unrolled it on the cabinet desk. It sent up a whiff of dust that smelled like history. "This is a long-form poem about the founding of Tremontane, maybe 800 years old. It's incredible that it's even legible. I've seen it referred to, but never read it. It must have been 'lost' in here for centuries."

"You want it copied out."

"Better. I want it *printed*. I want to see it published. I think we can set up an exchange, maybe not just with Quinn Press but with some of the others, to copy and print these for the public to read. Most of these documents are worthless, but there are some that are part of our literary tradition and ought to be preserved. They ought to be read. The originals are valuable, but what they contain might be even more so."

Henry said, "What did I tell you? Passion. I don't remember you being this passionate, Alison." He took her hand, his eyes serious, all his attention on her. She looked away, uncertain. His touch made her shiver, but she still didn't know if it was him or simply the novelty of being...courted? Was that what it was?

"I was much younger then," she said. "I didn't have anything to be passionate about."

"And now?" he said. "Is there anything else you're passionate about?" His voice was low. His thumb stroked the back of her hand. She closed her eyes briefly. What did she want?

"I don't know yet," she said. "I still have so many things to learn."

He put two fingers under her chin and lifted her face towards his. "Then let me learn them with you," he said, and kissed her.

She froze. He was a very good kisser, and she liked being kissed by him, but he was her friend, and her friend's husband, and something deep inside her cried out that it was all wrong. He sensed her stiffness and pulled away. "I'm sorry, that was inappropriate," he said. "I thought...but it was too soon, wasn't it?"

"Too soon," she agreed, and smiled ruefully at him. "Henry, I like you very much, and I won't deny I'm attracted to you, but I want to see how our friendship plays out before…more of that."

"I understand," he said, and released her hand. "Don't hold it against me, will you, that I wanted more of you than friendship?"

"I'm flattered that you did."

"Then I'm going to get back to work, chief. Let me know if you need anything from me." He winked at her in a way that suggested his double meaning shouldn't be taken seriously, and bounded back up the stairs.

Alison leaned against the scroll cabinet and took a deep breath. So. Kissing Henry hadn't cleared anything up. She still didn't know how she felt about him, other than conflicted. In some ways, this was worse than being courted for the wrong reasons; at least the response to a man who only wanted her body was obvious and uncomplicated. She struck the heel of her palm against her forehead as if to knock her confused feelings out of her head, and went back to the scriptorium herself.

She wandered around the room, trying not to hover over the scribes' shoulders. She opened a catalog drawer and flicked through its contents. She looked around the room, noted, not for the first time, the worn stone of the walls that would keep the room cool in the coming heat of summer, and reflected on how cold it had been in the heart of winter. She went back and looked over the Library from the landing. They were dependent on the Device to regulate conditions in this room that was, she realized, completely unsuited to housing a library. Would Zara consider relocating it? The idea of moving all those books again made her cringe. But if they were going to do it, if Zara agreed to the proposition, it was better to do it now while they were already in flux, before too many books made it back to the shelves. She tapped her fingers on the rail, a slim wooden pole whose stain had worn away years before. It needed renovation. The entire room needed renovation, more than she'd first realized. Something to ask Zara about. Better yet, ask the wrinkled old man who'd shown her the Royal Librarian's quarters. He would know if there was even a place the Library could move to. If she had a plan, maybe Zara would take her request more seriously.

She went back into the scriptorium and surveyed that room again. The idea of moving the Library had taken hold of her mind now to the point that she was disinclined to bring any more books up for cataloguing. Besides, the scribes had enough to do already. *Face it, Alison, you're bored*, she thought, and went over to the librarians' desk to see what Henry was doing. Shuffling lists. Boring.

The scriptorium door opened and a page entered. *Finally, something interesting.* The girl came straight to Alison and handed her a folded note. Alison opened it and read its brief contents. The blood drained from her face. She shoved the note at Henry, said, "Stay here, and don't let anyone leave." To the page, she said, "Take me there. Quickly."

The page interpreted "quickly" just as Alison had intended, which was a flat-out run through the halls of the palace. Alison had to work to keep up with the girl, despite all the exercise she'd gotten hauling books up and down stairs, and her legs hurt and there was a stitch in her side by the time they reached the infirmary.

She had expected a room full of beds, but instead she found some kind of waiting room, with a man at a desk and two doors on either side of it. She leaned against the desk and panted, "Trevers Stofford. Where is he?"

"Who are you?"

"His employer. Someone sent me a note that he'd been badly hurt."

"Wait here." He went through one of the doors. Alison paced. The man didn't return. She paced some more. Finally she cursed and flung open the door the man had gone through. It led directly into a well-lit room full of beds, about half of them occupied. A woman wearing a doctor's tunic stood next to one of the beds, consulting with the man from the desk and a woman wearing a nurse's smock. The nurse saw Alison and came to meet her. "You can't be in here," she said, taking Alison by the arm and attempting to lead her out of the room. Alison resisted.

"I'm here to see Trevers Stofford," she said. "Someone sent me a message, therefore someone wants me here. Where is he?"

"Who?"

"The apprentice who was beaten nearly to death."

"He's not able to receive visitors. He's asleep."

"Then will *someone* explain what happened?"

"Are you related to him?"

"No, I'm his employer."

"We should really speak to his parents first."

"He doesn't have parents. He's a singleton with no remaining family bonds. I'm the closest thing to family he has."

The nurse glanced back at the other two, who weren't paying attention to them. "Come with me," she said, and again took Alison's arm. This time Alison allowed herself to be pulled away.

The woman led her into what looked like a treatment room. "Trevers was beaten badly," she said in a low voice. "He managed to make it to the palace and was babbling something about the Royal Library before he fell unconscious. I don't know how he made it here. His left leg is broken in two places and he has three cracked ribs, just to name a few of his injuries. One of the other nurses must have sent word to you. You're sure he has no other family?" Alison nodded. "Too bad. Sometimes the presence of a family member strengthens that bond enough to ease pain."

"Is he asleep, or unconscious?"

"Dr. Wyatt put him into a narcotic sleep. We've sent for Dr. Trevellian." The nurse hesitated. "He'd better get here soon."

Alison's eyes filled with tears. "*Please* let me at least stand by him.

I swear I won't be disruptive. He's in my care. I don't want him to be alone even if he doesn't know I'm here." *And I'm positive this wouldn't have happened to him if he weren't working for me.*

The woman bit her lip. "Let me ask," she said, making a gesture for Alison to wait there, but after the woman left Alison pushed open the door and stood just inside. She watched the nurse speak to the doctor, who shook her head, saw the woman become more vehement and point in Alison's direction. Alison clasped her hands to keep them from shaking. Finally, the doctor shrugged and nodded, and the nurse gestured to Alison to join them.

Despite what the nurse had said, Alison wasn't prepared for Trevers' condition. His hair was matted with blood, he had bruises all over his face and a cut on his chin that hadn't completely clotted. His arms lay atop the blanket he was covered with, and his right hand was swollen painfully. Alison could only imagine what lay beneath the blanket. She closed her fists so tightly her nails cut into her palms. "Who would beat a child like this?"

She meant *what kind of person could do this*, but the doctor said, "He looks pretty well-to-do in that uniform. Might have been attacked and then beaten when they found out he didn't have anything on him."

"Maybe." *Or maybe someone's sent me another message. Bastards.*

"Excuse me, please—well, good morning, Countess!" Dr. Trevellian gave her a brilliant smile. "I'm glad to see you well. Now, if you'd all move back and let me take a look at this young man. In fact, could I ask you to leave the room? Myrna, give me a hand here."

Thus dismissed, Alison, the doctor, and the other assistant retreated to the waiting room. "Doctor, is there anything else you can tell me about the attack?" Alison asked.

"I only know what I observed when the boy was brought in," she said. "He was adamant we get word to you so you'd know why he was late."

Alison choked on a sob. Trust Trevers to care more about his job than the fact that he'd been beaten nearly to death. She pushed the door open a crack and peeked out. Dr. Trevellian didn't appear to be doing anything, but she could personally testify to his capabilities.

"Marcus and I have work to do," the doctor said, "but you can wait here if you like." They left the room and Alison sat, rocking back and forth in impatience. If Trevers died…no, better not think like that. Gowan was going to pay for this. She wasn't sure how, but she would make him pay. Could she hire thugs to go after him? Well, she had the money, so yes—if she knew where to find thugs for hire, which she didn't. How *dare* he involve a child? She now knew exactly what kind of man he was—a vicious, amoral bastard who would do anything to get what he wanted.

She stopped rocking and stood to pace again. If Gowan had moved on from vandalism to assault, everyone associated with the Library was at risk. If she resigned, the attacks would stop. But she couldn't give in to him, and not just for personal reasons. Giving the Magistrix control over the Library meant giving the Scholia one more hook into the government of Tremontane. On the other hand, could she ask Henry and the apprentices and all those scribes to risk violence and possible death for the sake of a principle?

Myrna pushed the door open. "Dr. Trevellian wants to speak with you."

Alison met the doctor halfway across the room. "I haven't woken him yet," Dr. Trevellian said in a low voice. "What do you know about what happened?"

"Nothing but what the doctor and Myrna told me, that he'd been set upon and managed to reach the palace before collapsing."

"Whoever beat him knew his work well," the doctor said. "It was no random mugging. All those blows were calculated to leave him alive but crippled. They just didn't account for how small he is. Does the boy have any enemies? Because I have to tell you this looks personal."

"Would you be willing to testify to all that?"

"Of course, but you'd need an independent witness to testify to the extent of his injuries before I got to him. Why, do you know who attacked him?"

"No. Just a suspicion. It might not matter." If Gowan was good, he'd have hired people who couldn't be traced to him. Maybe Trevers had seen something, but she wasn't counting on it.

"Will you wake him now?" she said.

"Come with me."

Trevers looked a thousand times better. The swelling in his hand had disappeared, the cut on his chin was gone, and his bruises were nothing more than faint shadows under his dark skin. Dr. Trevellian brushed the boy's hair away and laid the tip of his index finger in the center of his forehead. Trevers twitched, then his eyes opened as if he were waking from a normal sleep. "Milady," he said, "Am I late?

"Just a little," Alison said, blinking back tears. "I think you can be excused this once."

He smiled, then looked confused. "I don't remember why I was late. Why am I in bed?"

Alison's heart sank. "You don't remember being attacked?"

Trevers shook his head and winced a little. "I went out this morning to have my shirt mended and then I came back, and I was just past the bakery on Oloron Road, and then I was here."

So much for pinning this on Gowan. "Don't worry about it," she said soothingly, seeing that he was becoming agitated. "You were attacked, and you made it to the palace, and Dr. Trevellian fixed you up."

Trevers looked at the doctor, his eyes wide. "Dr. Trevellian for *me?*" he said, awed. "Was it that bad?"

Alison looked at Dr. Trevellian for guidance in what to say. The doctor said, "It was pretty bad, bad enough it's just as well you don't remember it. Don't worry about it. You're fine now."

"Did I break any pens? Only I remember breaking pens and

throwing them at Mister Catherton."

"Hallucination," Alison told him. "It happened to me when the doctor cured me of pneumonia. Just an hallucination."

Trevers' face cleared. "I was worried you might fire me because of the pens."

"Don't be ridiculous. Who would keep Declan and Gwendolen in line? Doctor, is he ready to leave?"

"You know how it works, Countess," Dr. Trevellian said. "Plenty of rest, preferably bed rest for a day, no hard labor for a while though it sounds like he's got a nice quiet job. Will you take charge of him?"

"I will. Thank you, doctor."

"My pleasure." He made as if to ruffle Trevers' hair, saw the matted blood and thought better of it. "I think a bath is in order." He nodded to both of them, took a few steps, then turned around. "I'm sorry for how things turned out for you, Countess," he said, compassion filling his eyes. Alison went teary-eyed again. She nodded her thanks, unable to speak, and watched him leave the room.

"Did something bad happen to you, milady?" Trevers said, sitting up.

"Nothing worth mentioning," she told him, blotting at her eyes with the back of her hand. "Let's get you back to the apprentices' hall and have someone draw you a bath."

She arranged for Trevers' care for the next few days, gave him strict instructions about staying in bed and not fretting over missing work, then went back to the Library. Free of concern for Trevers' health, she went back to being furious. Gowan's goons had beat a thirteen-year-old boy nearly to death and she had no way to prove it. She had no way of stopping him from trying it again. And she'd be damned if she was going to give in to his harassment.

She found she'd passed the turn for the Library and was heading for Zara's offices. Yes, Zara needed to know. But Henry—how long had she been gone? Henry had to be climbing the walls by now. She turned around and went back. Henry first, then the Queen.

Henry wasn't climbing the walls, but he was pacing the aisle and he pounced on her when she entered. "Is he all right?" he said in a low voice. She led him into the Library and shut the door, and described the state Trevers had been in when she first saw him. Henry clenched his fists.

"We can't do anything about it," he said. "Damn it, we're completely helpless against Gowan. I wish we could get Margaret to keep him in check. This can't be what she had in mind."

"I'm going to talk to the Queen. She might be able to see a way we can protect ourselves." Alison wrapped her arms around herself. "I'm almost glad Trevers doesn't remember anything. I can't stop thinking about how he looked, lying there—"

"You're not blaming yourself, are you?"

"Shouldn't I? That message was meant for me."

He put his hand on her shoulder. "It's Gowan's fault, not yours, Alison. Don't think like that."

She looked up at him. He was very close. His dark eyes had that serious look again. Before she could think, her hand slid around his neck and she pulled him toward her only to find he'd anticipated her. Their lips met, and this time Alison appreciated as she hadn't before the softness of his lips, the brush of his beard against her skin. She felt him smile just before he put his arm around her waist and drew her closer to him, his kiss growing more intense until Alison felt a little overwhelmed and stepped away. He looked a little uncertain, so she smiled, laid her hand on his cheek and said, "I wasn't planning on that when I dragged you in here."

"This time it was the right moment, wasn't it? Not just the stress of being under attack?"

"It was the right moment." She removed her hand and leaned on the rail. "I still don't know where this is going."

"Neither do I," Henry said, "but we have plenty of time to find out. It's not like I'll be leaving any time soon."

"I'm glad to hear it." They looked at each other in silence for a while, until Alison said, "I almost forgot. I have to see Zara."

"You should go. But—once more, perhaps?"

Alison smiled and stepped back into the circle of his arms. "Definitely once more."

In the hallway, halfway to the Queen's offices, Alison stopped and shook her head, violently, to clear her thoughts. What had she just done? She and Henry had to work together. What if this...whatever it was...got in the way of that? Or worse, if...whatever it was...went sour, what were they going to do? She still didn't know if she cared for him as more than a friend, or if, despite what she'd said, she'd only kissed him because she needed comfort. *Father, I don't know if your idea about me making a connection was such a good one.*

She reached the north wing and headed for Zara's office, only to be stopped by a sharp "You can't go in there, milady Countess, her Majesty is in a meeting."

Alison came back to the desk. "This is important," she told the receptionist, who shook his head.

"So is her meeting," he said. "You can wait here."

"But this really shouldn't wait."

"Sorry, milady Countess. It shouldn't be much longer."

Alison leaned on the desk. "Could you take a message to her? Please?"

The receptionist looked wary. "I shouldn't—"

"Just a message." Alison took a piece of paper and scribbled a short note on it, then handed it to the man. The receptionist sighed, went down the short hallway to Zara's office, knocked, and was admitted. He came back immediately and took his seat. "Now will you just wait?" he said.

"Thank you, I will—"

Men and women began emerging from Zara's office. They

sounded as if they weren't quite finished with what they'd been discussing, carrying the conversation trailing along after them. "Alison," Zara said, "inside. Now."

Alison shut the door behind her. Zara sat at her desk with her letter opener in her hand, tapping it on the desktop. Anthony sat nearby, a notepad on his lap and a self-inking pen in his hand. "Explain," Zara said, picking up Alison's note and waving it at her. Alison told the story, becoming angrier as she went until she was pacing in a tight circle in front of the desk.

"And there's nothing I can do about it," she spat, "because I have no *proof*. Gowan's going to keep trying until he makes me resign, and since I'm not going to do that, a lot of people could get hurt, and I know he's counting on me caring about that. And I don't know what to *do*."

Zara glanced at Anthony, then looked back at Alison. "We'll house the scribes in the palace for now," she said. "No more going out alone. We'll set someone to watch Gowan, discreetly. And *you* will have a personal bodyguard."

Alison protested, "I told you — "

"*This is not up for debate*," Zara shouted, startling Alison. "Someone is targeting the Library and it's only a matter of time before he gets to you. Did it not occur to you that if you were dead, Gowan's problem would be solved? Setting aside the tremendous personal loss that would be, I have no other candidate for your position. I would be forced to accept whomever the Scholia chose, and that would mean putting the man who killed you in charge of the Library. No part of that situation is acceptable to me. You *will* accept a bodyguard and you *will* go everywhere with him or her. Have I made myself clear?"

Alison looked at Anthony, who was even stiffer and more serious than usual. "Yes, your Majesty," she said meekly.

"Good. Anthony, please escort the Countess to Major Casson's post and explain the situation. Alison, Major Casson will assign you a guard and you are not to return to the Library until he has. Thank you for bringing this to my attention. Good day."

Alison left the office, still stunned, and Anthony shut the door behind them. "You've never heard her shout before," he said. It was not a question. Alison shook her head. The receptionist stared at her as she walked past, making Alison wonder if the man had heard the Queen shout as well. "She's on edge," Anthony added, unnecessarily as far as Alison was concerned. He went silent until they were out of the offices and into less-trafficked hallways, when he said, under his breath, "The Magistrix has suborned the Baron of Highton. Made promises to increase the number of Masters working in that county, which means increased trade because the Scholia's reputation is what it is. Gowan's attacks force her to split her attention, and she's uncertain how much support she still has in the Council, so she's short-tempered and not interested in arguing with people if she can make them do what she wants instead."

"Anthony, should I just resign? Wouldn't that make everything easier?"

He stopped and swung around to face her. "Don't you dare," he said. "Don't even think it. It would demoralize her more than you can imagine. She took a risk, appointing you, and if you resign it will mean that risk was for nothing. She will do whatever she can to protect the Library, and you need to repay her by not giving up."

The intensity in his voice awed her as much as the Queen's shouting had. She didn't know what to say, so she merely nodded, her eyes wide. Anthony opened his mouth to say something else, grimaced, and said, "Sorry. That was more serious than I intended."

"I think I needed to hear it. I hadn't thought of myself in those terms. A figurehead."

"Hardly that," he said, amused. "A rallying point." There was the old gleam in his eye, and Alison's heart began beating a little faster. *You could just kiss him,* her inner voice taunted, and she felt such a rush of anger and humiliation and pain that she wanted to run away and hide where her body wouldn't betray her anymore. And she'd been doing so well. She had no idea how much of that turmoil showed on her face, but the gleam left Anthony's eyes, and in an emotionless voice he said, "I apologize if I offended you, Countess."

"No, it wasn't you, I simply had a distressing thought," she said, feeling ashamed of herself. "Thank you for explaining the situation to me. It will help, the next time Gowan tries something."

"You're not the sort of person who can be easily intimidated. I just think you should know how important that is to other people, not just yourself." Anthony's voice was stiff; the moment in which he'd been himself again—that *they'd* been themselves again—had passed as if it had never been. Alison's guilt disappeared. She didn't want him to be so familiar with her. She could be polite, indifferent, she could even be kind, but he didn't deserve any more than that.

Anthony began walking again, and Alison hurried to catch up. They went in silence, Alison lost in her own thoughts, Anthony thinking heaven knew what behind that impassive mask. Alison felt daunted. That her resignation could mean so much to Zara was overwhelming and a little intimidating. *I'm not giving in, no matter what Gowan tries*, she thought. *I just hope he doesn't try something I can't face.* She refused to think about what such a thing might be.

Chapter Twenty-Four

The carriage with the triple-peak insignia of Tremontane embossed on its doors bounced along the cobbled streets. Inside, Alison looked at her new bodyguard. The woman was over six feet tall, had short-cropped hair, arms that looked like she was smuggling melons, and an expression that made her lovely face look forbidding. Even within the carriage, her eyes moved constantly, looking for threats. Her name was Elise, and she intimidated Alison to the point that she could barely speak. Upon assigning her to Alison, Major Casson had said, "It's probably better you have a female guard, someone who can go everywhere with you. And I imagine you'll be more comfortable with a woman around." In the three days since the major had assigned Elise to her, Alison had felt less comfortable and more awkward than she'd ever felt when appearing in public.

"The stationer's is in a good part of town," she offered.

Elise didn't stop scanning the street outside. "No guarantee of safety, if that's what you're getting at," she said. Her voice was surprisingly high-pitched. Alison had expected her to have a deep, commanding voice to match her physique.

"I just thought, if that makes your job easier...." Alison trailed off, feeling foolish. What did she know of what would make this woman's job easier? Elise didn't bother with a reply. Alison was afraid Elise didn't like her very much. *She doesn't have to like you,* she thought, *she just has to protect you.* And Alison had to admit she'd never seen anyone more likely to take on a small army than Elise.

The carriage pulled to a stop in front of the stationer's. Alison didn't move. She'd already learned Elise wouldn't let her get out until she was satisfied no danger awaited them. Elise stepped out and stood with her back to the carriage, looked around, then went to the stationer's door, opened it, and beckoned to Alison to join her. Alison moved quickly. Elise's presence and what it implied made her nervous of open spaces, though she didn't know what Gowan could do to her in broad daylight, in the midst of the crowd.

She went directly to the counter, hoping to conclude her business quickly and get back to the safety of the Library. Elise followed her, looming. Alison rang the bell and waited. In a moment, the stationer's assistant emerged from the back room. He started when he saw Alison and her oversized companion, and looked from Alison to Elise nervously.

"I just need to pick up my order," Alison said. "The cards. Alison Quinn?"

He glanced at her again, then silently went into the back room. After a moment, the stationer himself, a tall, broad man named Tom Jenkins, came to the counter. "What do you need?" he asked, eyeing Elise with suspicion.

"I placed an order five days ago. It was supposed to be ready today. For the Royal Library?"

Jenkins said, "Can't fill it. The supplies haven't come in."

"But you assured me you could do it."

"Sorry. It was an unexpected problem with our supplier." He wouldn't meet her eyes.

"So when do you expect to have my order ready?" This was going to set them back. They were almost out of cards.

"I don't know," said Jenkins. "I might not be able to fill it at all."

Alison frowned in puzzlement. "Not at all?" Then light dawned. "You have a Scholia account, don't you? I bet they're one of your biggest customers."

He glance sidelong at her and nodded, the tiniest movement of his head.

Alison ground her teeth. "You'd rather make an enemy of the government than anger the Scholia?"

He shrugged. "The Scholia has bought from me for ten years. I can't afford to lose their business."

"Then I'll just have to take *my* business elsewhere." She turned to go.

"You'll get the same answer wherever you go, milady."

"*Everyone?*"

The stationer turned red. "We have to eat, milady."

Anger filled her like a river piling up against a dam. She controlled the urge to let it break. "Look, Mister Jenkins," she said in a calm, polite voice. "I need those ten thousand cards. I know you have my order ready. Suppose you happened to set it down out back in, maybe, half an hour? No one would blame you if the boxes were stolen. And suppose I left you some money right here on the counter, as a little thank-you gift for your service to the Crown, enough to cover the loss of the theft. I wouldn't want you to lose your account with the Scholia by selling to me."

Jenkins looked painfully torn. Finally, he nodded, a curt jerk of the head. "There's a long alley that opens off Caterlon Street, you know," he said as if making conversation. "It's too far from this shop to be useful to me, but I've heard other businesses say it's nice and wide and good for deliveries."

"That's an interesting fact, Mister Jenkins," Alison said. "I won't see you again."

She summoned up her rage and stormed out of the shop, flung open the carriage door and threw herself into the seat, ignoring Elise's protests. "That was dangerous, milady," she said when she climbed in.

"More dangerous for Mister Jenkins if I'd looked satisfied," Alison said. She hadn't been acting. She was genuinely furious. Gowan had found another way to get at her, one less lethal but no less of a blow than attacking Trevers or vandalizing the scriptorium. Blackmailing her suppliers, was he? She really needed to strike back, but how?

When they reached the palace, Alison stormed up the steps ahead of Elise and off to the Transportation offices. She didn't bother dismissing Elise even though she was in the safety of the palace; when she'd tried it before, the first day, Elise had simply gone impassive and repeated "I have orders" to every one of Alison's arguments. Alison arranged for an anonymous cart and driver to be at the alley off Caterlon Street at the appointed time and went back to the Library, still seething.

"What happened this time?" Henry asked, then took an involuntary step backward as she approached at speed.

"Gowan got to our supply chain," she said. "I found a temporary solution, but eventually we're going to run out of materials."

"What are you going to do?"

"I hate taking my problems to the Queen, but she has a devious mind. We just don't have any hold on Gowan. No leverage. If we confront him, he'll deny everything and keep on striking at us. The only person who could make him stop is the Magistrix."

"And she probably put him up to it," Henry said. "I still say we should talk to Margaret. He's gone too far."

"You know she only wants one thing, Henry."

"She wants control of the Library. Maybe there's another way."

"What way? What else could there possibly be?"

Henry shrugged and shook his head. "Maybe she'd be satisfied with your compliance. She has to know by now the Queen won't fire you. Maybe she's ready for a compromise."

Alison was stunned. "Henry, you can't be serious. You think I should put myself under her orders?"

"No, I'm saying maybe we should think about some kind of middle ground, and that's one of the possibilities."

"She'd never accept me as Royal Librarian."

"You don't know that."

"I don't understand. I thought you hated her."

"I do. I'm only thinking of what might be best for you." Henry took both her hands in his. "I don't have to like Margaret to compromise with her."

"But she arranged for you to lose the robe. How can we trust her?"

"Back then, she had all the power. Now you're the one with the power and she needs something from you. It's a stronger negotiating position. And for all I despise her, I've never known her to go back on her word."

Alison met his dark, intense gaze. "I suppose it's worth considering," she said, though doing so opened an aching pit in her stomach. "But I'm still talking to the Queen."

"Of course," he said. He glanced around the room, then quickly kissed her, startling her so much that it was over before she could respond. "I want to make you happy."

She smiled at him, but it felt strained, as if it didn't reach her eyes. "Thank you for supporting me, Henry."

"Of course." He let go of her hands and stepped away from her. "Oh," he exclaimed. He picked up a folded note from the shelf below the librarians' desk. "This came for you. You looked so upset when you came in that I forgot."

Alison opened it. "How fortunate. Zara wants to see me in her offices in...oh, no, two minutes from now. I have to run. The cards will be here in about thirty minutes. I hope they'll last long enough for us to solve this problem." She ran out the door, causing Elise to make an exasperated noise and trot after her.

She reached Zara's office only about five minutes late, knocked on the door and was admitted. "Thank you for joining us, Countess," Zara said, raising an eyebrow. Anthony sat in a chair in front of the desk. "Your guard may wait outside." Alison saw Elise take up a watchful stance as the door closed.

"I'm sorry I'm late. I had a little supply problem."

"No matter. Have a seat." Alison sat next to Anthony and had a momentary recollection of the first time they'd sat like this, all those months ago when Zara had told them they would have to appear in public together. Rather than making her wince, the memory amused her. Who would have thought they would have ended up back here, in such very different circumstances?

"Anthony's told you some of the situation with the Council," Zara said, leaning back in her chair in exactly the same way she had on that fateful day. "I've spent the last two weeks meeting with my councilors, trying to make them see reason. We cannot afford an endowment like this, and it's a mark of how powerful the Scholia has become that the Magistrix has been able to convince some of my councilors that their best interests are served by following her lead. I need more support, and it happens I also need some changes to my Council. Alison, what you told me about the department of Commerce strong-arming new businesses disturbed me. Even if I didn't have issues with Roger Lestrange, the amount of power concentrated in that department would be a problem. So I'm creating a new department of Communications and I'm putting you, Anthony, at the head of it."

Anthony's mouth fell open. "Zara, you can't be serious. I have no idea how to run a department and I certainly don't know anything about communications. The Council will realize this is a ploy to artificially build your support."

"Anthony, I'm tired of your constant protestations of incompetence," Zara snapped. "I do not play games with my government. Yes, this move will benefit me, but I don't want Lestrange in a position to mandate regulations on this new telecoder Devisery. You know as much about it as anyone. You've been watching Unwin for months now and she tells me you are more than capable of taking charge of this department." Zara unexpectedly smiled. "What she actually said was you'd probably make a lot of mistakes, but you have the humility to ask for help when you need it. And you have my trust—no, you've *earned* my trust."

Anthony was the color of a brick wall and as inarticulate. "Then I suppose I should shut up and be gracious," he finally said.

"Yes. You should." Zara turned to Alison. "The theater problem is more difficult. I've learned the problems Davis Doyle faces at the Waxwold are just as bad in Kingsport and elsewhere. Theaters are being told to comply with regulations that do nothing to benefit them—regulations, I might add, that I feel benefit no one in any business. I am more disturbed by Commerce's requirement that actors be licensed. The policy has already encouraged mutual protection societies to spring up, which mandate for whom their members can work, and extort fees from theaters to allow them to hire from among their members." Alison let out a hiss of anger. "Precisely. What you may not be aware of is that others in the, let us say, artistic fields are facing the same type of interference with much the same results. I propose to strip these businesses out of the Commerce department and create a department of Arts to regulate and oversee the needs of our artistic community."

Alison's heart had begun to sink the moment Zara began to talk about the other arts. "Please don't say you want me to head up that department," she said. "Anthony is certainly qualified for his position, but I'm not, and there's no way you can justify putting the Royal Librarian over a bunch of theater people."

"You forget writing is also an art," Zara said. "I don't know what your father has told you, but publishing is almost certainly Lestrange's next target. Imagine publishers having to meet a list of criteria in order to be licensed—a list Lestrange would certainly tailor to benefit those publishers allied with the Scholia. Those who didn't comply could well be hounded out of business. As to your qualifications, you have charge of Tremontane's oldest archive of history and literature. The Library is supposed to collect and preserve our artistic endeavors. It is only a few short steps from there to justifying the Royal Librarian's natural right to protect those institutions creating such art."

It was Alison's turn to sit with her mouth open. "I—" she began, then couldn't think where else to go.

Anthony muttered, "Shut up and be gracious."

It was so unexpected she burst out laughing, and after a moment so did he. Zara smiled indulgently at both of them.

"It's true you're inexperienced," she said, when the laughter had died down, "and I will make sure you have an excellent support staff and well-qualified seconds. In fact, Anthony, I'd like you to see to that. Talk to the departments you've worked in and get some recommendations. I know Clara at least has some people she'd like to promote but doesn't have positions for. Your primary responsibility will always be the Library, Alison, but I think in the course of expanding the Library you'll naturally come into contact with those organizations under your care."

"You're taking an awful risk," Anthony said. "If the Magistrix succeeds, she may be able to force Gowan into the position, and he would abuse that power beyond recognition."

"You let me worry about that," Zara said. "Don't resign," she told Alison. "Start thinking of what you'd need to do to fulfill this new responsibility. I'll announce this to the Council today—you won't be present. I don't think either of you need to witness the reactions of my oh-so-reasonable councilors. You will be formally introduced to the Council tomorrow morning. Anthony, you have an office now; I suggest you use it to give Alison some idea of what to expect come the morning. Congratulations, both of you, though I think condolences might be more in order. Good day."

Alison found herself outside the office without really knowing how she got there. She looked at Anthony, whose lips twitched in amusement. Alison covered her mouth to hold in a laugh. "I can't believe *anyone* can stand up to her," she said. "How does the Magistrix do it?"

Anthony bent over until his breath tickled her ear. "Zara believes she is fueled by pure evil, but you didn't hear that from me," he whispered. Alison tried not to stiffen at his unexpected nearness. *I won't be ungracious,* she told herself, remembering his face when she'd refused to share a carriage with him. They were going to work together on the Council now; she couldn't be actively rude to him, and she felt a little guilty at the idea that she might.

"Where is your office?" she said.

"I have no idea. Maybe James knows." He spoke to the receptionist, who pointed down one of the halls. Anthony beckoned to her. "I'm glad to see you took Zara seriously about the bodyguard," he said, nodding at Alison's tall shadow.

"Elise goes everywhere with me. I can't say I'm exactly glad for her company, but I admit I feel safer."

"That's the idea. Well. That you actually *are* safer, not just that you feel safer." He opened a door for her and they both stopped short inside.

"This has to be someone else's office," Anthony said with dismay. The room was filled with stacks of paperwork. Alison turned over a couple of sheets.

"This is all related to the telecoder," she said.

Anthony looked at a few others. "The post service. Something about the message runners. This is insane."

"At least you know Zara was right about the need for a new department," Alison said.

Anthony began clearing his desk. "Let's just put these in the corner for now. I can't imagine there's anything here that won't wait. This upcoming vote is far more important."

Alison helped him move piles of paper until the desktop was visible. Anthony pulled his chair around to Alison's side of the desk, then rooted around in it until he found paper and pen. "I never thought I'd be so happy about self-inking pens," he said wryly, and began sketching. "Here's how the Council alignment breaks down. Zara's obviously voting against the endowment, and so are we. Mistress Unwin—good heaven," he said, laying down the pen and putting his head in his hands, "she and I are equals now. I'm never going to get used to that."

"We're equals with Lestrange too," Alison pointed out.

"That's different. I consider him my inferior in every possible way." Alison grinned at that. "Anyway. Mistress Unwin is against the endowment. Then Lestrange, Forsyte in Agriculture, the Countess of Cullinan and the Baron of Highton are all pro-endowment. The rest are unknown."

"I thought there was one other on Zara's side."

"Albert Fisher in Transportation. He and Zara have been friends for years, and until recently she believed he would support her, but now he seems uncertain. I don't know what hold the Magistrix might have over him, but Zara's doing her best to court him. The others are Godwinson in Internal Affairs, Delarue in Foreign Relations, Anselm in Defense, and the Countess of Harroden." He scribbled more names. "The meeting tomorrow is supposed to be for considering the Magistrix's latest proposal, but really it's for convincing these five to choose a side. And for the rest of them to intimidate you and me. I don't care what Zara says, no one's going to believe we were chosen impartially."

"We weren't, really. So what am I supposed to do?"

"Listen, mostly. See if you can work out who supports whom. Answer questions relating to your department but don't get drawn into an argument, especially with Lestrange or Cullinan."

"I'm starting to feel nervous."

"Don't be. I've never known anyone less likely to be intimidated than you."

His voice sounded strange all of a sudden, and Alison turned away from the paper to look at him. He was tapping the pen on the paper, leaving tiny dots. It occurred to her that he hadn't been stiff or distant at all since they'd left Zara's office. Neither had he been his old carefree laughing self. *He really has changed,* she thought, and at that moment, he turned his head and she was caught full force by the blue-eyed North gaze. He said nothing, merely looked at her as if he expected her to ask a question, but she was breathless, caught in a memory of him saying *You walk like you're about to take on the whole damn world at once* and the feel of his lips on hers, and she stammered out, at random, "Does the Magistrix have anything she can bring to bear on those five?"

"Good question," he said, looking away again. "Robert Anselm in Defense would lose a lot if the Masters pulled out of the armed forces. Monica Delarue votes based on some rationale no one's ever been able to figure out. She might see the Scholia's independence as an opportunity to treat them as a foreign country, which would give her more power. Belladry Chadwick of Harroden has sided with Zara often before, but she's fair-minded enough not to be influenced by the past, so it's impossible to say which way she'll jump. Godwinson *ought* to vote against the endowment because of the turmoil it would cast Internal Affairs into, but he might see giving in to the Magistrix as a way of maintaining internal harmony. And Albert...I just don't know."

"Can I take this with me? To study?"

"Go ahead. And I'll have recommendations for your department aides by the end of the week."

"Thank you. I appreciate your help."

"This is just me shutting up and being gracious. I'll see you in the morning."

Alison walked slowly back to the Library, clutching her paper with both hands. He'd changed more than she thought. She knew Anthony was intelligent, but she never would have guessed he was capable of all this...capability. And where had the reserve gone, the stiff statue's mask? It seemed he no longer felt awkward around her. She tried to summon up outrage, or even annoyance, at his presumption—how dare he forget his guilt?—but found only weariness at holding on so tightly to her anger. Polite indifference was so much easier. They were associates at the theater and now, it seemed, they would be colleagues on the Council; she couldn't afford to alienate herself from him. She could work with him without caring about him. She—

—*he was looking at her, so intent, saying* You forgive me, right? For thinking only of myself and not of your feelings?

—and humiliation and fury filled her, bringing her up short in the empty Library hallway with her eyes closed, angry tears leaking from them. *I can work with him, I can be polite to him, but I can never forgive him,* she thought. *And I will never forget.*

Chapter Twenty-Five

"What we seem determined to avoid," Clara Unwin said, "is the plain fact that this country cannot afford to give the Scholia the kind of endowment they're asking for." Her voice sounded strained, as if, Alison thought, she'd made this argument a hundred times before.

"What we can afford has always been an issue of the sacrifices we're willing to make," said Roger Lestrange, whose voice by contrast was smooth. "Giving the Scholia more autonomy means more and better-educated Masters, who then serve vital roles throughout Tremontane."

"Then why aren't those Masters contributing to the operation of their alma mater?" asked Belladry Chadwick, Countess of Harroden. "They're certainly successful enough."

"But not in a position to provide as generously as the Crown could," Lestrange said.

"And not as regularly," said Albert Fisher. Alison watched him closely. He was supposed to be Zara's old friend, but he seemed partial to the Scholia's argument. Though she had to admit when it came to government, friendship probably shouldn't be the primary reason for making decisions.

"It's a one-time payment as opposed to the annual outlay we already have," said Lestrange.

"'Payment' being the operative word. It sounds to me like extortion," said Unwin.

"That's a dangerous accusation to make," said Lestrange.

"What else can you call it, when Margaret Bindle has hinted at repercussions should we not comply?"

"*The Magistrix* has only pointed out what we've already seen. Many of the Masters have come to see the endowment as a symbol of Tremontane's trust in the Scholia and its graduates. Our continuing refusal to fully fund the Scholia may result in their choosing to find employment elsewhere."

"And you think the Magisters haven't encouraged that line of thinking?" Anthony said.

"I think some of us," Lestrange said, deliberately not looking at Unwin, "have been thinking of the Scholia as our enemy rather than our ally. The Magistrix is as concerned about the future of Tremontane as any of us."

"And it's precisely that thinking that has put us in this position," said Matthew Godwinson, head of Internal Affairs and one of those councilors Anthony had said was wavering. "This issue with the Scholia has spread beyond this room to affect the citizens. They respect the Scholia and dislike the conflict that's arisen."

"Is there a general feeling the government should support the Scholia?" Alison asked.

The other councilors seemed surprised she'd spoken. "Ah...I believe public opinion is divided," Godwinson said.

"Then you might as well say half the people harbor some resentment toward the Scholia. Shouldn't we consider why that is?"

"It's our responsibility to make the best decisions for the people," said Lestrange, smiling at Alison indulgently. "They lack the broader understanding that would allow them to see the whole picture."

"And yet it is *the people* who attend the Scholia, or not, and from whom new Masters arise. Their attitude toward the Scholia must surely influence our decision. Why fund an institution many people choose not to attend because of its policies?"

"The Countess makes a good point," Anthony said. "As much as we respect the Scholia, we shouldn't choose to fund it simply because of tradition."

Lestrange ignored him. "Countess, I'm certain you mean well, but I believe your current disagreement with the Scholia has influenced your attitude toward it."

"As I'm certain your position as Master has influenced yours," she shot back, for the moment forgetting Anthony's advice about not being drawn into an argument with Lestrange. "Would it not be better to say each of us has a perspective developed from our experiences? I attended the Scholia for four years and I have never regretted it. I respect the education I gained there. I simply don't believe Tremontane is served well by changing our current funding policy."

"If you were a Master, you would know much of the Magisters' time is spent on budget concerns," Lestrange said, losing the indulgent smile. "The irregularities of the Crown's current funding combined with our growing operational costs mean reorganizing Scholia spending drastically each year. This means the Magisters waste time on bureaucracy that keeps them out of the classroom where they belong."

You said "our." I think you just made a mistake, Lestrange. "Every business faces the same challenges. Income can vary dramatically from year to year, forcing changes in resource allocation. Should the Scholia be treated differently simply because its output is intangible?"

"As enlightening as this exchange is, Roger, Alison, I believe we need to return to the main question," said Zara. "Clara has made the point that we cannot afford this endowment. Roger says we can't afford *not* to fund the endowment. Let us suppose we take Roger's view, which would require cutting funds to other departments. Can anyone suggest areas in which funding may be reduced?"

Alison leaned back in her seat. She glanced at Anthony. He had his hand over his mouth, but his eyes were gleaming with humor. She looked away before she could start to laugh. Not ten minutes into her first Council meeting and already she'd been drawn into an argument. Good thing Zara had intervened when she did, because she was pretty sure Lestrange's next statement would have been about the impossibility of putting a price on the human mind, and that would have derailed the meeting entirely.

The councilors were mostly silent now. None of them wanted to suggest cutting their own budget, which was probably Zara's intent. Force them to face up to the reality of the endowment, and maybe they'd see sense. Alison watched faces. She still didn't know enough about her fellow councilors to tell how they felt, even the ones she knew were in the Scholia's pocket (aside from Lestrange, of course), but she had a feeling Albert Fisher was still on Zara's side. Why he might be playing the fence-sitter she didn't know, but although he hadn't said much, he watched Zara closely and she was certain she'd seen Zara glance at him. Of course, she could be wrong, and their exchanges might be wary instead, but she still had an instinct that Fisher's seeming uncertainty was part of a deeper game.

People began offering half-hearted suggestions for budget cuts, always in someone else's department. Zara listened to this for a while, then said, "Thank you all for your insights. In just over a week, the Magistrix will make her formal proposal to this Council, after which we will make a decision. In the meantime, I suggest you continue to discuss and consider the matter privately. Good day."

The councilors began to file out in silence. Alison was about to follow when she saw Zara make a tiny gesture for her to remain behind. Unwin exchanged a meaningful nod with the Queen, then left as well. When they were all gone, Anthony shut the door behind them and took a seat at the Queen's right hand. Zara leaned back in her sort-of throne and shook her head in despair. "Didn't you explain to her about not getting into an argument with Lestrange?" she asked Anthony.

Anthony grinned. "She sort of won," he said.

"Only because I intervened. Alison, sit down and stop hovering. Lestrange is a dangerous opponent. He would have turned your words against you eventually."

Alison sank into a seat and covered her eyes with her hand. "He made me angry," she said, a statement rather than an excuse.

"A specialty of his. Never mind. Between the two of us we

managed to make some important points that I do not think were lost on my councilors. Monica in particular seemed to be listening carefully, though I hesitate to mark her for our side because she's so unpredictable."

"Is Albert Fisher on your side?" Alison asked tentatively.

Zara's gaze sharpened. "What makes you say that?"

"Just a feeling."

"I hope no one else shares that feeling. Yes, Albert is on my side. He's my mole. And I thought he was doing a good job of concealing that. Albert tells me Matthew has decided to vote for the Scholia. Matthew's concerned about internal unrest and has decided maintaining the status quo will only inflame matters. He's usually so conservative that I think the Magisters have gotten to him somehow. Oh, well. With my vote, that still puts us ahead by one, and we still have seven days to sway some of the others."

"I'm afraid we've lost Robert Anselm," Anthony said. "He's worried about the effect on the armed forces if his Masters pull out."

"I'm handling Robert," said Zara. "You worry about getting your department into shape. Alison...don't let them get to you. Now, shoo. I have work to do."

Alison and Anthony exchanged glances. In the hallway, Anthony said, "She's not as confident as she sounds."

"Would it really be so bad if the Scholia got its way? I mean financially. Obviously it's bad in every other conceivable way."

"It would be bad. Mistress Unwin is already looking at options for shoring up the Treasury in the event of the funding going through. Robert ought to be more worried at the budget cuts the military will almost certainly endure. I don't know why he's not thinking that way. It's peacetime; he's already under pressure to reduce the armed forces. Well, maybe I'm wrong about Robert. I hope I'm wrong about Robert."

"I'm sorry I got into an argument with Lestrange after you told me not to," Alison said.

Anthony smiled. "I thought I was going to burst out laughing," he said.

"I saw. Was it really that amusing?"

"Nobody stands up to Lestrange. They've all been bested by him in verbal combat before. Half the councilors were cringing at your inevitable defeat. The other half were cheering you on. I almost wish Zara had let it go on a little longer."

"It was just as well she didn't. He would have started trouncing me in about a minute."

"But it would have been an outstanding minute. Where's your looming guard?" Alison pointed down the hall. "Then I'll escort you to her and hand you off. And remember, if you have any questions about your Council responsibilities, you can ask me anything."

"Thank you." *You see?* she told her snarky inner voice. *I can be polite. I can be indifferent.* She refused to think about how angry it made her that he was indifferent too.

"We really ought to be working," Alison said. "I have—"

Henry's lips on hers cut off whatever she'd been about to say. "Nothing that can't wait a few minutes," he murmured.

She gave in to his kisses. He was such a comfort to her, and not just because of stolen moments in the Library like this one, his hands tangled in her hair, hers stroking the lean muscles of his back. He was always there to give advice and comfort, or sometimes just to listen when she needed to vent her frustrations. His presence helped ease the tension of worrying about the Library and Gowan and her new Council responsibilities, the last of which left her nerves frayed to the point of wanting to scream. She'd made list after list of what she thought the department of Arts should do, what her responsibilities ought to be, and how to reverse the damage Commerce had done. Not that she knew the full extent of what Commerce had done, which provided her with greater tension. Anthony at least had stepped into a department whose structure had already been established. She'd started to doubt Zara's wisdom in creating this ill-defined one.

She put her hand between her mouth and Henry's. "Now I really do have to work, and so do you," she said.

He kissed her palm. "All right," he said. "But we're almost out of cards again."

Alison swore, making Henry's eyes widen in mock horror. "Such language, Countess," he said.

"It makes me feel better. Gowan hasn't tried anything for several days now and I can't stop worrying about what he'll do next. And there's no way to stop him, short of killing him, and I draw the line at assassination."

"We really ought to talk to Margaret," Henry said, taking a step away from her. "She could rein him in."

"Henry, don't you think the fact that she *hasn't* reined him in says something about where she stands on this issue?"

"She can't possibly realize what he's been doing. She just doesn't think that way."

Alison put her hand on the door latch. "I really don't think it's going to do any good. I'm going into the city to talk to a few more suppliers. They can't all have Scholia accounts. And then I have a meeting with the Arts department aides. I'm sorry to leave so much Library business to you."

"Anything I can do to help," Henry said, taking her hand and kissing it. "That's what I'm here for."

"I know," she said, smiling at him. "I'm glad you're here."

None of the suppliers would speak to her. All of them, coincidentally, had fresh damage to their shops, windows shattered, doors broken down. Alison didn't push. She rode back to the palace with the silent Elise, fuming and reconsidering her policy on no assassinations. The world would be a better place without Gowan in it. She got out of the carriage without waiting for Elise and snarled at the woman when Elise started to reprimand her. They were nearly out of supplies. The self-inking pens could go on for a few months, until their supplies of ink ran dry, but the paper would run out long before that.

Alison stopped in the middle of the hall. Paper. Of course. Now she just needed to find the right Device, and she was certain there was one somewhere in the palace. She struck out in the direction of Operations. What she needed now was a supply clerk.

Two hours later she returned to the Library, dragging a cart full of heavy paper and a strange-looking Device. Henry was already halfway to the door to meet her before he saw the cart. "What did you do?" he asked.

"Used my brain. Here, you pull this, my arms are tired. Elise refused to pull it on the grounds that she couldn't defend me if her hands were full. Really, you'd think they'd invent a self-propelled cart." Under her direction, Henry pulled the cart to the librarians' desk. Alison lifted the Device onto the desk and grinned at Henry. "We don't need cards, we just need card paper," she said. "The Device can be set to cut paper to any dimensions you want. Granted, I was only able to find white and blue paper, so we'll have to put off doing the author cards, but the apprentices can start cutting and we won't have to stop work."

"Alison, that's a wonderful idea, but I've found a way around our problem," he said. He drew her into the Library and shut the door behind them. "I spoke to Margaret."

Alison began to protest, but he cut her off, saying, "I know you didn't want me to, but with the supply situation becoming a real problem, I decided it was time to face it head on."

"Henry, I told you, nothing good could come of that."

"You're wrong, Alison. Margaret is reasonable and we were able to come to a compromise."

Alison's heart sank. "What compromise?" she said, trying to sound reasonable herself. Maybe Henry was right. It was worth hearing him out.

"First, Margaret swears she wasn't behind the attack on Trevers or the vandalism or anything, and I believe her. She only wants what's best for the Library."

"Except that her definition of what's best for the Library is a Scholia-trained Master."

"From her perspective, yes. And if you're honest with yourself, you know if you had more training, you'd be even better at this job."

"That's true, but I—"

"That's not all, Alison. Margaret had to admit you're doing an excellent job here. She doesn't think you ought to leave. All she wants is for you to have some assistance from a more experienced librarian. A sort of coalition, a union between the government and the Scholia. It would mean a new era of cooperation."

Alison thought that last bit was Margaret Bindle's words, but said nothing. "And how does she propose this alliance work?"

Henry looked a little shifty. "Well, the more experienced librarian would take precedence, of course. You'd still be assistant librarian, and you'd have charge of acquisitions, which I know is your real passion."

"And who would be the Royal Librarian in this scenario?"

He looked even shiftier. "Well, Margaret still has confidence in Gowan—"

"*Gowan*? The man behind all our problems?"

"We can't prove that."

"Henry, he had Trevers nearly beaten to death!"

"But he'll stop harassing us once he gets what he wants."

"What *us*? If I'm assistant librarian, where are you in all of this?"

This time, Henry both looked shifty and wouldn't meet her eyes. Alison's despondency turned to anger. "She promised you the robe," she said.

"She said she saw my ouster wasn't just. She said I deserved to be back at the Scholia. Alison, believe me, I'm not deserting you. I'll work to support you behind the scenes."

Alison's anger felt like ice, freezing her all the way through. "You want the robe. You've always wanted it. All your arguments mean nothing beside that one fact. She bribed you, and you leapt at it. And now you're trying to convince me to fall in line so you can have what you want."

"That's not true."

"Isn't it? You know everything you just told me is counter to what I've been trying to prevent. How is this a compromise, when I'm the one giving everything up?"

"You'll still be in the Library. You might even be Royal Librarian someday."

"Henry, you know damn well Gowan is a vicious bastard who won't put up with a non-Scholia librarian, even in a subordinate position. If I give in to this plan of the Magistrix's, he'll keep harassing me until I quit. I wouldn't even put it past him to try to have me killed if he can't get what he wants any other way."

"That's a vile accusation."

"Trevers, Henry. Are you still going to defend Gowan?"

"I did this for you, Alison. If you can't bend even a little bit—"

"This is not a 'little bit,' Henry, this is giving up everything I've fought for. I promised the Queen herself I wouldn't resign. The Magistrix's promises mean nothing beside that."

"I never thought you could be so stubborn."

"Then you don't know me at all." Alison flung the Library door open. "Get out. Go tell the Magistrix my answer is emphatically 'no'. Let's see if she keeps her promises to you when you've failed to get me to fall in line."

"You're making a mistake."

"I'm *correcting* a mistake. Elise, Mister Catherton is leaving. Perhaps you can show him out."

Elise approached Henry, who threw up his hands in defeat. "I wish things could have turned out better for us."

"I wish I'd known what kind of man...." She didn't want to finish that sentence in front of the whole scriptorium. Henry left the room without looking back.

Alison went to the librarians' desk and leaned heavily on it, staring blankly at its worn surface. She felt numb. Her anger had drained away, leaving her with only the frozen mask for her protection. She turned around to face the scribes, who weren't even pretending they hadn't heard that conversation. "Mister Catherton decided to throw in his lot with the Magistrix," she said. "He wanted me to give the Library to Gowan. Anyone who thinks that's a good idea may follow him out." No one moved. She looked from face to face and saw anger, resolution, and worry, but no fear. The mask melted away. "Good," she said. "I need to report this to the Queen. You three, start cutting. The rest of you, keep working. I'll be back in less than an hour. And...thank you for your support."

With Elise as her watchful shadow, Alison went to the Queen's offices and found she was in a meeting with some of her councilors. Alison decided not to disturb her. She might be convincing the fence-sitters to choose her side. She stood outside the office, feeling despondency creep over her. Just one more person who'd betrayed her. She had thought Henry an ally, thought he might become more than that. She was frozen to the core, unable even to cry out the rage and sorrow filling her chest. *Remember what Father said,* she told herself, *that you aren't meant to be alone.* She no longer believed it. She looked sideways at Elise, who made a better statue than Anthony ever dreamed of being.

She was halfway down the hall to Anthony's office before her conscious brain could stop her. Then she stood, unmoving, in the hallway while people dodged her, some of them giving her dirty looks. *He can tell Zara, and I won't be late for my meeting,* she thought. She refused to listen to the quieter thought that said *You have to tell someone or it will tear you apart.* If she needed a confidant, which she didn't, he'd be the last person she would choose. She knocked on his door, and heard a muffled invitation to enter.

Anthony had his head down over the inevitable paperwork, which Alison thought had increased since the first time she'd been in here. "Harriet, tell me you didn't—oh," he said, finally looking up and seeing her. "Do you need something?"

"Henry Catherton just went over to the Magistrix's side," she said, and found to her embarrassment she was trying to shed tears after all. "He wanted me to give up the Library to be Gowan's assistant librarian."

He grimaced. "Sit down," he said. "Just move that stack anywhere. Tell me what happened."

She described the entire encounter, managing not to cry tears of anger. "The Magistrix is never going to keep that promise to him," she said. "That makes me happy."

Anthony nodded. "What are you going to do? It sounds like you need an assistant."

"Yes, and where am I supposed to get another ex-Scholia Master? Come to that, why would I want one, since they're apparently so easily suborned?"

"Maybe you need someone who can be trained from the ground up. I don't want to be insulting, but from what I've heard from you it's not as complicated as the Scholia makes it sound."

"I don't know if I have the skill to train someone. I'm barely trained myself."

"You know what Zara would say if she heard you talking like that."

"Not exactly, but it would involve the kind of praise you can't believe you deserve."

"Precisely." Anthony clasped his hands in front of him and said, offhandedly, "I heard you and Catherton were...close."

321

"Not as close as we could have been." The tears threatened to come back, and this time they were tears of pain and betrayal. "I'm glad we weren't. I can't imagine how I would have felt if our relationship had been more serious when he betrayed me."

The words had left her mouth before she remembered whom she was talking to. Anthony ducked his head and stared at his hands. Alison felt a surprising rush of guilt. "I'm sorry," she said.

"Why should *you* be sorry?"

She didn't know what to say. For the first time, she remembered that night not with shame or anger but with regret. Regret that he hadn't been the man she'd thought he was. "I don't know," she said.

Anthony raised his head. "I never really apologized to you," he said in a quiet voice.

She blanched. "I didn't—you don't have to—"

"I was sorry then because I would have done anything to make you stay," he said, with a frankness that made her face go blotchy with embarrassment at the memory. "I should have apologized for what I did to you. I treated you like an object instead of a person, and you deserved better. I am truly sorry for that shameful wager, Countess."

There was nothing of the statue about him now. Alison had to look away from the sincerity in those blue eyes. "I accept your apology," she managed.

"Thank you," he said. "I would like…I hope we can be friends, someday."

"I—maybe. Someday. I don't know," Alison said. "Will you excuse me? I should get back to the Library."

"Of course. And…thank you for coming to me with this. I'll make sure Zara knows." He lowered his head and went back to his paperwork. Alison rose and left without looking back.

She walked through the halls quickly enough that even long-legged Elise had trouble keeping up with her. Had she really just forgiven him for wagering on her virtue? It was true, he'd been stupid and juvenile to make that wager, but if he'd confessed it to her himself—if, for example, the night they'd spoken so frankly in the carriage, he'd said *I've done something stupid, and I regret it more than I can say*, would she have forgiven him for it? Or even if he'd told her the first time he'd kissed her? To her surprise, she realized the answer was *Yes*. Yes, she would have been angry and hurt and humiliated, but a little honesty on his part would have done wonders for helping her move past that first reaction. Now she examined her heart and discovered she no longer bore him any malice for that careless, thoughtless act. The realization was a surprise to her.

But that was never the problem, was it? her inner voice taunted her. *He cared more about not being ridiculed than he did about doing the right thing.* Alison stopped in the middle of the hall and rocked a little when Elise bumped into her. It didn't matter. They might become friends, someday, might discover that their common interests could overcome their tainted history, but she could never forgive him for that. *And I don't want to,* she told herself, resuming her rapid pace and ignoring Elise's grunt of annoyance. *I don't want to love anyone, and to hell with what I told Father. I have the Library, and that's enough for me.*

The Library was as she'd left it. She sat behind the desk and watched the scribble of scribes go through stacks of cards, observed the apprentices working the Device, thought about what Anthony had said—the part before he apologized. "Danica," she called, and the young woman looked up from her work. "Come with me, please."

Inside the Library, the door safely shut, Alison said, "How many years were you at the Scholia?"

"Three, milady."

"I have a job opening. Assistant librarian. It's yours if you want it."

Danica's eyes and mouth opened wide. "Milady, I'm not qualified."

"You know, Danica, I'm starting to notice the qualified people don't care for this Library nearly as much as they care for their own comfort and prestige. I don't care that you're not qualified. You can learn alongside me. What do you say?"

Danica grinned. "I say 'yes.'"

Chapter Twenty-Six

The upcoming vote weighed on Alison like a lump of lead in her stomach, cold and unmovable, so she tried to ignore it by burying herself in work. There was certainly enough of it. Mysterious reports had begun appearing on her desk, reports on Commerce's activities with regard to the arts that had to have come from an inside source, and Alison was so grateful to have something on which to focus her efforts she didn't try to discover that person's identity. Their contents made her furious. What Commerce had done was only two steps from being outright extortion, but Lestrange had covered his tracks well enough that there was no way to prove his actions had been anything but completely legal. Alison would have rejoiced to find evidence of criminality that would get Lestrange removed from the Council, but she had to settle for being happy to finally know from which direction Commerce's next attack might come.

Where *Gowan's* next attack might come from was impossible to guess. Alison's suppliers still refused to deal with her, and although there had been no further assaults, Alison insisted the scribes and apprentices stay housed within the palace. It infuriated her to be so vulnerable, but she had no other recourse. Henry didn't return, for which she was grateful; nothing he could do or say would restore her faith in him, and she didn't want to endure another confrontation. She heard nothing from Anthony, and Zara didn't summon her. It all left her isolated enough that she could pretend there would be no vote, that her position in the Library was not in danger. She made lists, and scoured the city for supplies, and spent her evenings reading, and walked through the Library every night before she slept, letting her anxieties drain out of her into the stones.

Three days before the vote, she went to Waxwold Theater to speak to Doyle. It was a cold, rainy day better suited to winter than spring, and the gray, listless sunlight made Alison feel cold despite the warm cloak she wrapped closely around herself. Elise seemed not to be affected by the cold, though she wore a sleeveless shirt and neither cloak nor coat. She might as well be a Device for all she reacted to her environment, though Alison was sure even a Device would have trouble functioning on a day like this one.

At the theater, a shivering and wet young man stood on a ladder, putting up a new marquee sign. Alison ducked around him and into the theater, where she nearly ran into Doyle coming the other way. "Allie, what are you doing out on a day like this?" he said, taking her cloak and making a face at how wet it was. "I half expect to see dogs poling themselves around on rafts in the gutters."

"I didn't realize how bad it was until we were halfway here," Alison said, "and I'm so tired of the inside of the palace I didn't want to turn back. If you're so concerned about the weather, why do you have that poor boy out there on a ladder?"

Doyle groaned and pushed past the ubiquitous Elise to the door. "Fenton!" he shouted, and the rest of his words were cut off by the front door closing behind him. Alison smiled at Elise, who regarded her dispassionately. She was an excellent statue. Doyle returned, Alison's cloak in one hand and the collar of the boy's shirt in the other.

"Downstairs," Doyle said to the boy, "change those clothes, and use some common sense next time I tell you to do something, right?" He gave the boy a gentle shove that propelled him toward the employees' door, then seemed to realize he still held Alison's cloak and held it up to watch it drip onto the carpet. "Sorry," he said.

"We can hang it up over the heater Device in your office. I have some things to talk to you about," Alison said, though she didn't think any Device had the power to dry something so thoroughly soaked.

With Elise standing guard outside the office, Doyle slumped into his chair and rummaged around in his drawer for the bottle of whiskey. "Sit down, Allie, and have a drop. If this isn't a day that calls for a fire in the belly, I don't know what would."

"Doyle, no, I...all right, just a little."

They drank, and Doyle put his feet up on his desk, cursed a little at the water that came off his shoes, and went back to sitting straight in his chair. "Please tell me you've got good news about the licensing requirements."

"I do. The regulations are complicated, but it seems relieving theaters of them is as simple as redefining the classes of business they govern. It will still take some time, mostly because Commerce isn't thrilled about losing chunks of itself, but in maybe a month the actor licensing requirements will be gone, and I can start drafting new regulations that make more sense for theaters. Particularly ones governing the physical facilities, which should make it easy for Anthony to go ahead with his plans."

Doyle frowned. "Assuming he still wants to."

"Well...yes. But I didn't think he'd given up entirely, just because of a few roadblocks."

"A few roadblocks? Allie, this is more like a ten-foot-tall stone wall covered in pig fat and set on fire. Or do you know something I don't?"

"I feel as if we're having two different conversations, Doyle. What are you talking about?"

Doyle leaned forward. "You haven't heard."

"I think it's clear by now I haven't."

"I—Alison," Doyle began, then pulled out the bottle again and poured another splash into her cup. "You may need that."

"Doyle!"

He set the bottle aside, carefully squaring it with the corner of his desk. "The Crown Prince has an illegitimate child," he said.

She sucked in a deep, horrified breath. Mechanically, she picked up her cup and gulped the whiskey down. The burn of the alcohol down her throat worked like a slap to the face to restore her ability to speak. "That can't be true," she said, faintly.

"Like I said, do you know something I don't?"

Alison shook her head. "Who's saying that he...that it's true?"

"The little girl's mother has accused him," Doyle said. "Says he refused to take responsibility when the girl was born and he paid her off to keep quiet."

Alison clenched her hands so hard her nails dug painfully into her palms. It couldn't be true. Surely he wouldn't have...but she knew, better than anyone, that he was inclined to protect himself, his reputation, at the cost of doing the right thing. It was possible. Even probable. *But commit a crime like that? Leave a child, his own child, without a family bond?*

"No," she said. "It's not true. Anthony's done a lot of reprehensible things, but he's never committed a crime. He might be the father of the child, but I can't believe he refused to take responsibility for her or tried to pay off the mother."

"I'm surprised to hear you take his side," Doyle said. He poured himself another slug of whiskey and tossed it back.

"I'm not. I mean, yes, I am, but it's because I know I'm right, not because I care—not because I have any stake in wanting him to be innocent. I just don't believe it."

Doyle shrugged. "I hope you're right. Though I don't know as it matters what you believe. There's no way to prove he's not the father short of someone else stepping in to claim responsibility."

"I'll wager Zara will find a way." Zara had to find a way. She could not allow her heir to be tainted by this accusation. And suppose she couldn't? Would Anthony have to claim the child as his heir? Would he have to marry...? She ruthlessly chased the thought away. *It's nothing to you. Zara won't let it happen.*

"I hope you're right," Doyle repeated, but he sounded skeptical. Alison took her cloak, which was still dripping, and rolled it into a bundle. "Sorry about that," Doyle added. "Let me get you another one from Props."

"That's all right, I'm just going from the door to the carriage and from the carriage to the palace," Alison said. "Doyle—"

"I know. He's innocent. I'll take your word for it, Allie. Heaven knows I want to believe you."

"I'll be back in four days. The vote will be over by then, so who knows what might happen next?"

"I know you won't give up. Hang in there, Allie." He gave her a hug, cursed again when the cloak bundled between their bodies left a wet mark along his midsection, and waved her out the door.

Traffic was picking up outside the theater, the clatter of wheels muted by the splashes of water those wheels kicked up. Their carriage was coming along the street toward them. "No, stay here," Elise said, pushing Alison back into the shelter of the doorway and trotting out into the rain. Alison tried to hold her wet cloak away from her body without dropping it and jigged from one foot to the other, trying to stay warm. She watched Elise dodge puddles and the floating garbage that always appeared during a heavy rain. The air smelled of excrement, which Alison found strange because the rain ought to wash away such smells, not make them worse. She breathed shallowly through her mouth. She would go back to the palace and talk to Zara. The idea of facing Anthony was…it felt awkward, embarrassing, as if they still meant something to each other and she had a right to confront him about his possible crime. They weren't even really friends now. The empty ache returned and she quashed it again, more ruthlessly this time. It didn't matter, because it wasn't true.

Over the sound of the traffic, she heard a faint *pop*, like the sound of a firework going off, and she looked up before remembering it was unlikely anyone would be setting off fireworks at this time of year, let alone in this downpour. A bird swept by silently and landed in the eaves of the theater roof, shaking its wings to rid itself of the rainwater.

Elise was nearly to the carriage now, which started to pull in toward the theater. She was probably soaked to the bone. Alison heard the *pop* again, and Elise jerked, slid a little on the wet cobblestones, then fell to the ground, not trying to catch herself. Instinctively, Alison ran to help her. "That looked painful," she began as she reached her bodyguard's side. Elise didn't move. Alison tugged at the woman's shoulders, thinking, *I didn't realize she was wearing a cap*, then looked more closely and realized that the redness spreading across Elise's short hair was blood, that there was a ragged-edged hole in her forehead, that her eyes were open and staring sightlessly up at her. Alison screamed. The coachman, who'd been huddled under his heavy coat, looked up in surprise, then began climbing down only to fall heavily at Alison's feet as another shot echoed in the air. Blood began spreading across the back of his coat. Alison screamed again and ducked behind the carriage. Someone was shooting at them. No one seemed to notice anything was wrong.

"*Somebody help me!*" she screamed, and one corner of the carriage's roof exploded into shards of wood and fabric. The horses, spooked, reared up in their traces and tried to bolt, rocking the carriage and dragging it forward. Alison scrambled to stay behind it, falling to her hands and knees and sliding on the cobbles as Elise had. *Now* people were noticing, and carriages were stopping, and several people tried to control the horses, and someone was exclaiming over Elise and the coachman and another person tried to help Alison stand. She pulled away from those helping hands, afraid to move away from the carriage. "No, someone's shooting at me," she said. "You have to find them. You have to stop them."

"Inside," the man said, and hurried her back into the theater. "Why would someone shoot at you?"

Alison shook her head, in her shock and fear unable to explain the chain of events that had led to Elise lying in the street with a rifle ball in her head and the coachman bleeding heavily on the cobblestones. "I just need to get to the palace," she said.

The helpful man gave her a strange look, no doubt wondering

why such a scruffy woman—she'd not bothered to dress up just to see Doyle—thought she could just casually walk into the palace, but he nodded and said, "Wait here, and I'll see if someone can take a message. You're certain they were shooting at you?"

Alison nodded, and the man gave her another strange look, but went outside. Alison stood and looked out the glass doors, then a jolt of panic went through her—if she could see out, the assassin could see in—and she retreated all the way to Doyle's office, which was empty. She sat and settled her wet cloak across her knees. Gowan had nearly succeeded that time. The thought set her shaking hard, though the office was warm enough to feel muggy. The shooter had killed Elise and the coachman and had nearly killed her. She was never going to be safe. Gowan would keep trying until she was dead.

"Allie? What are you doing back here? Allie. Look at me. Sweet heaven, you're in shock. What happened?" Doyle took the cloak from her and rubbed her hands between his.

"Gowan's man shot at me," she said. Her voice sounded as if it were coming from very far away. "He killed Elise and he's going to kill me too."

"No, you're safe, Alison, listen to me, you're safe here," Doyle said. He brought out the bottle and made her take a drink. The alcohol cleared her head briefly, then settled over her like a warm whiskey-scented blanket. "You're trying to get me drunk, aren't you?" she said with a smile.

"Not likely. You're probably a mean drunk. You need me to get word to anyone at the palace?"

"I asked someone to take a message there."

"Good." Doyle sat in his chair, then pounded the desk once with his fist. "Damn it, Alison, this is too much! Why doesn't the Queen just have the bastard assassinated?"

"I think even queens have to operate within the law."

"And we've seen how successfully the law's protected you so far."

331

Alison realized tears were running down her cheeks. She wiped them away. She didn't feel sad, or angry; she felt frozen. "He'll slip up, and then Zara will have him."

"You've got more faith in her than I have, and I say that realizing I'm talking about my sovereign monarch here."

"I don't see what else I can do. Doyle? Can I take you up on that costuming offer? I'm so cold."

Wrapped in a fur-lined white cloak from the *Wintersmeet Ball* costumes, she waited in Doyle's office, numb and unthinking, until after a few eternities someone came to tell her a coach had arrived to take her to the palace. The coach was larger than hers and was filled with guards; more guards sat on the coachman's seat and others rode on the perch at the back. It seemed unlikely the horses would be able to pull all of them, but once Alison was settled between two women in green and brown Tremontanan uniforms, they stepped out without any trouble and trotted smoothly through the streets of Aurilien to deliver her to the front door of the palace.

Chapter Twenty-Seven

The guards flanked her on all sides as they ascended the stairs, which must have looked ridiculous to any observer, one small woman surrounded by tall, looming soldiers. Most of the guards peeled off once she was safely inside the palace doors, but two remained to escort her through the halls of the palace to the north wing. The messenger, whoever he or she was, had been very effective. They took her all the way to the Queen's office door, bypassing the secretary at the marble desk, and opened the door for her without knocking.

Inside, Zara sat at her desk, pen in her unmoving hand. She glanced up when Alison entered and laid the pen down. "Have a seat," she said. Alison sat. Zara regarded her with that blue-eyed gaze that at the moment could have cut diamond.

"I'm told the coachman will live," she said. "I am sorry about Elise Garan. She was careless, and she paid for it with her life. No, Alison," she said, cutting off Alison's angry protest, "if she were alive, she would be the first to admit to her mistake. Protecting you from unexpected threats is precisely the job she was trained for. But that's not relevant. It's sheer luck you weren't killed."

Sheer luck. How long before that well runs dry? Something inside Alison snapped, and her terror and fury and confusion propelled her out of her chair to shout, "When will this end? Do I lock myself inside the palace for the rest of my life? Am I going to live in fear, wondering every day if this is the day Gowan finally succeeds? Tell me you can fix this, Zara!"

"I have no answers for you," Zara said. "I cannot act against Gowan without proof, and he has been very clever about hiding his involvement. This time, however, we may have him. I've had someone watching you covertly every time you've left the palace in the last two weeks, and if that person saw the assassin...even so, that's a slender hope to hang your fate on. Alison, I am sorry. I suppose it will all be irrelevant in a few days' time. If the vote doesn't go our way, I'm sending you home on the condition that the Scholia appoints someone other than Arnold Gowan as your replacement."

Once again Alison couldn't breathe. "You can't do that."

Zara went to the window and looked out at the rain. "My power may be diminished by the results of this vote," she said, "but I believe I still have the right to appoint the Royal Librarian. Your safety is far more important than the keeping of the Library. Don't argue this point with me, Alison Quinn."

Alison closed her eyes briefly. "Yes, your Majesty," she said, sinking back into her chair.

"I don't have to tell you to stay inside the palace," Zara said. "Gowan will likely not try the same tactic twice, but it will be easier to keep you safe here than out on the streets."

Alison nodded. "Is Anthony the father of that woman's child?"

Zara put her hand flat against the cold glass of the window. She didn't react to the abruptness of the question. "He says he is not."

"Do you believe him?"

"I believe he believes he is not. The woman was his lover, and the child is of the right age. He could be mistaken."

"What will he...what will you do?"

Zara turned away from the window to face Alison. "Endure," she said. "She will have to produce more evidence if she wants Anthony to agree to an entailed adoption, to provide support for her and the child in perpetuity. Even more evidence if she wants Anthony to declare the little girl his heir. It's possible she wants Anthony to marry her, I suppose, though I think not."

Alison realized her hands had contracted into fists and forced them open. "So much happening all at once," she said, trying for a light note. "The vote, Gowan's attacks, this woman, it's almost absurd."

"Yes," Zara said, her voice flat.

Alison drew in a shocked breath. "You think the Scholia's behind it," she said. "That they found this woman and put her up to it—but why?"

"One more distraction," Zara said grimly. "One more thing to occupy my attention when I should be focusing my efforts on this vote. I have people investigating this woman, Lydia Brown. Anthony says she is the sort of person who would not have waited four years to claim her right to his support if he truly were the father, which adds weight to my belief that she has been encouraged in this action by the Magistrix. But I doubt I will be able to prove Miss Brown's allegations false in time to prevent them from affecting this vote."

"I don't understand why it matters. Surely Anthony's…it's not as if the Scholia endowment has anything to do with what he's accused of doing."

Zara went back to looking out the window. "Anthony is accused of knowing he had a child and refusing to provide support and a family bond for it, which is a crime, and guilty or not, that is an accusation that reflects poorly on the Council," she said. "Roger Lestrange has already called for an emergency meeting tomorrow in which he will ask for a vote of no confidence in Anthony, removing him from his Council position."

"That's insane!" Alison said, this time rising so quickly that she shoved her chair back several inches. "He hasn't been convicted of anything! Can't you stop it?"

"Any member of the Council can call for such a measure at any time," Zara said, "and no, I cannot stop it without making it appear that I believe Anthony to be guilty and, incidentally, making myself seem a tyrant, which would encourage my councilors to vote against me in the matter of the endowment."

Alison turned away and pulled her chair back into its original position. Its legs had left divots in the thick carpet, which she used to align it perfectly, minutely shifting it until she felt capable of speaking normally. "What can *I* do?" she said.

"Stay indoors. Don't give up. Keep the Library running." Zara went to sit at her desk, which Alison took to mean that their meeting was over. She had her hand on the doorknob when Zara added, "Do *you* believe Anthony is telling the truth?"

Alison squeezed the cold metal hard, as if she could mold it like clay. "Does it matter?"

There was a long silence. Then Zara said, "It might matter to him. He has discovered, in the last two days, that everything he has done to reclaim his good name counts for nothing with some people. He could use your friendship, if you're able to offer it to him."

The empty ache returned, extending from her chest throughout the rest of her body. "I believe him," she said. "I'll vote to retain him on the Council. I don't think I can do more than that." She felt a pang of guilt she couldn't quite dispel. She didn't hate him, she believed him innocent, but the idea of approaching him, of giving him sympathy, was too intimate, too much a reminder of things she would prefer to forget. "But you can tell him I believe him, if you think it would help."

"I see," said Zara. Her voice was cold, disappointed, and Alison felt even guiltier. "Thank you, Countess. I will send word if there is any news about the shooter."

Alison felt red blotches spreading across her skin. She left the office without saying anything else, then closed the door behind her and waited for the blotches to fade. She wasn't ready to be Anthony's friend. Zara had no right to expect it of her. Someday, possibly, but not now.

Alison sat at the Council table and ran her fingers over its smooth surface. She looked at Belladry Chadwick, Countess of Harroden, who sat directly across the table from her, and tried to smile. Belladry nodded once in acknowledgement and turned her attention elsewhere. This was not a time for pleasantries. Everyone knew why they were there.

The door opened, admitting several other councilors, including Roger Lestrange, who took his seat next to Belladry and tugged at the front of his coat to smooth it. He wasn't smiling either, but there was a look of satisfaction in his eyes that infuriated Alison, a look that said he knew he'd already won this vote and anticipated winning the next as well. He glanced at Alison, and then he did smile, an expression of appreciation that was all too familiar to her. Rather than making her freeze up, it filled her with anger. How dare he look at her as if she belonged to him? She coolly raised an eyebrow at him, gave him a look that said *You will never have a chance with me,* and watched the smile turn into humiliation and then into anger. Alison saw no point in pretending their relationship was cordial. She was already doomed to lose the Library; his antagonism could not hurt her.

Now all the councilors were present except for Zara, Anthony, and the Baron of Highton, who was always late. Alison tapped her fingers on the smooth wood, stilled them, and put her hands in her lap. If the Council voted to remove Anthony, it would leave them with an even number of votes for the endowment issue; what would happen in the event of a tie? Whatever it was would almost certainly benefit the Magistrix's faction, for Lestrange to push so hard to remove him. She clasped her hands together to keep them from shaking. All she could do was cast her vote and pray for the others to see sense.

The door opened again. Zara entered, followed by Anthony, who took his seat next to Alison without saying a word. She fixed her attention on the table before her, counting the rings. What was he thinking now, what did he see when he looked at them all? Guilt rose up in her again, and she pushed it away. She would support him. That would have to be enough.

"Councilors," Zara began, still standing, and the door banged open and the Baron of Highton practically fell through it in his hurry. "Sorry, sorry," he said, and flung himself into his seat. "Please continue, your Majesty. So sorry."

Zara regarded him dispassionately for a long moment, during which he squirmed and tried not to look at her, then sat in her throne-chair and said, "Roger Lestrange has requested an emergency meeting of this Council to address a serious issue that has arisen in the last few days. Mister Lestrange, you may speak."

Lestrange stood and bowed to the Queen rather perfunctorily. "Thank you, your Majesty. You must all be aware now of the accusations made against his Highness, Anthony North. Failing to acknowledge a child born outside a family bond and to provide for an entailed adoption is a serious crime, and for a member of this Council to have committed such a crime reflects badly on all of us. It implies that we condone such behavior, that we are willing to look the other way if the person involved is of high enough rank. I therefore ask Anthony North to voluntarily surrender his seat on this Council to protect its reputation." He sat, his round face still unsmiling, to all appearances a concerned and upright citizen trying to protect the laws of the kingdom, but Alison could see his eyes, and there was a light in them that said he was thoroughly enjoying his humiliation of the royal family.

Zara inclined her head to him. "Thank you for your concerns, Mister Lestrange. You are correct that the people of Tremontane hold the behavior of my councilors to a very high standard. If his Highness is convicted of the accusations made against him, I will not allow him to continue serving in his department. But I would like to point out to all of you that an accusation is not a conviction, and I hope you will remember that." She took a moment to catch the gaze of each of her councilors. When she came to Alison, there was a look in her eye that made Alison blush painfully, a look of reproach that left her feeling guilty and angry at the same time. "Prince Anthony, you may now address this Council," Zara said when she was finished impaling her councilors with the blue-eyed stare.

Anthony pushed his seat back and got to his feet, rather heavily, Alison thought. For a moment, he was silent. Alison didn't dare look up at him. "I know what my reputation is," he said. "I know the idea that I might have paid Lydia to conceal the child's birth seems plausible. I'm not denying I could be Sophy's father. I *am* denying that I knew anything about her existence before three days ago. Whatever else I may have done, I would never have done such a monstrous thing as to leave my own child unsupported. I intend to make the situation right and adopt her now, and I ask this Council to believe I am only guilty of youthful indiscretion and stupidity. I will not surrender my Council seat." He sat down. Out of the corner of her eye Alison saw him lace his fingers together and rest them on the table. She thought they might be trembling.

"Thank you, your Highness," Zara said.

"Your Majesty," Lestrange said, half-rising from his chair before she could continue, "since his Highness chooses not to resign, I must call for a vote of no confidence. The Council must protect its reputation."

Zara raised an eyebrow at him. "Very well, Mister Lestrange, your request is noted. Voting will proceed immediately." She didn't even bother pretending she had not known this would happen. "Since some of you have never participated in a Council vote before, I will explain the procedure. Each of you will be given two balls, one red and one white. You will place one of these into the vase at the back of the room to cast your vote and place the other into the box beside it. When all the votes have been cast, my assistants will break the vase and count the votes twice. A red ball is a vote to relieve Anthony North of his position on this Council; a white ball is a vote to retain him. Anthony will of course not be voting on this matter, and as the one who appointed Anthony to his position, I now recuse myself from this vote. *My brother* and I will now leave you to deliberate and will return when the votes have been cast." She pushed back her chair, and she and

Anthony left the room so quickly Alison felt lost.

"I think the situation is clear, don't you all?" Lestrange said as attendants liveried in North colors began passing out painted wooden balls the size of large marbles. Alison took hers and clutched them in one hand, feeling them warm almost immediately from the heat of her skin. There was no tactile difference between them, but Alison imagined one was hotter than the other, its red surface glowing with malice.

"It's not clear at all, Roger," Belladry said. "We shouldn't take such a drastic step before the Prince has even been convicted."

"It's a formality," said Fern Harcourt, Countess of Cullinan. "Everyone knows what he's like."

"He's not that man anymore," Clara Unwin protested.

"It's not about who he is now, it's about who he was," Lestrange countered. "Anthony North has been a scandal and a blot on the North name for years. Trying to make up for that by belatedly giving his illegitimate child a family bond is ludicrous."

"Foolish and careless, yes," Unwin said. "But so lost to all decency as to conceal his child's birth? Not a chance."

"You'd stand by him in any case," Harcourt said with a mean smile. "Groomed him to be your successor, didn't you?"

"Groomed him to be the next king," Unwin shot back, "something I think all of you are forgetting in your haste to condemn him. He has her Majesty's support, and I don't think anyone is quite ready to suggest that our Queen cares so little for the law that she would help him circumvent it, brother or no."

"Zara doesn't have a say in this," Lestrange said.

"Well, I do, and I say this vote is a farce. Anthony's innocent and that's the end of it."

"You don't know that," said Bernard Forsyte, head of Agriculture and, from what Anthony had told Alison, a hardcore reactionary. "It's shameful how young people these days think they can flout our moral code with impunity. This is our chance to send a message to Tremontane: no one is above the law."

"And the law says no one is guilty simply on someone else's say-so," said Belladry.

"That say-so combined with the boy's reputation is enough for me."

The gnawing, empty ache had begun in Alison's chest again. Their tainted history didn't matter; she had to speak what she knew was truth. "He's innocent," she said in a clear voice that cut across whatever Belladry had begun to say in response. "He didn't know about the child until just days ago. He hasn't broken any laws."

They all looked at her in varying degrees of amazement, all except for Lestrange, who regarded her with a calculating expression. "I suppose you might be expected to take his side," he said.

Alison looked back at him for a long moment. For once his round face, distorted at the moment by a nasty sneer, looked like that of an adult, if a calculating, mean-spirited one. She wasn't sure what he saw in her face, but whatever it was made his expression go uncertain. Then she pushed her chair back and stood leaning forward a little, one hand clutching the marbles and the other flat on the smooth surface of the calcified wood. "Might I?" she said. "I think none of you can be unaware of what the Prince was to me. You know better than I do what rumors surrounded him, and me, at the beginning of the year. Mister Lestrange, I am the *last* person in this room to blindly protest Anthony North's innocence. So I think you should all consider what it means that I believe him to be innocent of these charges. Anthony may be many things, but he has never been a criminal. He is already being crucified in the court of public opinion. He doesn't deserve to be betrayed by his peers on the Council too. I intend to vote to retain his Highness on this Council. And I'm ready to cast that vote now."

She sat down, held the red marble in her left fist, and raised the white marble in her fingers so everyone could clearly see its color. "I don't know what the order of precedence is, in voting," she said. "But I'm not interested in waiting long for my turn. So if you have anything else to say, now would be a good time for it."

Silence. Lestrange looked as if he wanted to explode, but couldn't find the right words. Belladry smiled at Alison in approval. "I don't think anyone else would like to speak," she said, "and I believe I'm ready to cast my vote as well. Countess, the vote proceeds by seniority," she told Alison.

"You have no right—" Lestrange began.

"No right?" said Monica Delarue, who'd never spoken in any of the times Alison had been present for a Council meeting. "On what grounds, Roger? That she disagrees with you? Matthew, cast your vote already and let's see how they fall."

Matthew Godwinson, head of Internal Affairs, stood and shoved his chair back with more force than was necessary. He didn't reveal the color of the ball he dropped into the vase and returned to his seat in silence. One by one, the councilors went to cast their votes, until finally Alison dropped her white ball into the vase and tossed the red one into the box so hard it rattled inside. She hadn't yet taken her seat when an attendant left the room and returned with Zara and Anthony in her wake. Zara returned to her throne-chair; Anthony stood behind her rather than resuming his seat.

"Please count the votes," Zara said, and shortly there was the ringing crack of shattered pottery, and the clicking of wood against wood. Alison glanced in the direction of the vase and couldn't see the balls. The clicking stopped, then resumed.

"Your Majesty, everyone has voted," the attendant said. "In the matter of retaining Anthony North as head of Communications and member of this Council, the vote is seven in favor, four against."

Alison turned to look at Anthony just in time to see a look of utter surprise be replaced by his now-familiar stony visage. *He didn't think he'd win*, she thought, *he didn't think anyone believed him*, and guilt struck

342

her so hard she couldn't breathe. *I can't,* she thought, and the rest of that thought was lost in confusion.

"Councilors, thank you for your service. Anthony, you may take your seat," Zara said. How she managed not to sound smug astonished Alison. "I assure you all that the Crown's investigation into the allegations made against his Highness are underway, and I have confidence they will reveal the truth. I am pleased that you are all so concerned about the reputation of this Council and I hope we will provide a *united* front in this matter." She looked directly at Lestrange as she said this. Lestrange went red.

"I am certain we will all cooperate in clearing the Prince's good name," he said, trying not to sound as if he were choking on the words.

"Thank you, Roger. Now, in two days the Magistrix will present her formal proposal to the Council, after which we will vote on her request. I suggest you continue to discuss privately so you will come to that meeting prepared to deliberate and make the best decision for this country. Thank you again for your service." She stood. The meeting was over.

Alison followed Anthony out of the room, pausing once to look back at Zara, who was deep in conversation with Belladry Chadwick. She looked at his back, at those broad shoulders that at the moment were slumped a little, and guilt filled her once again. She was being spiteful. They were both committed to the theater, they were on the Council together, *he* had behaved so well to her since her return to Aurilien; she could never forgive him for what he'd done to her, but it didn't mean she couldn't be his friend. "Anthony, wait," she said.

He stopped, hesitated a moment, then turned to look at her, his face expressionless. The Baron of Highton brushed past them both with a muttered apology, and then the hall was clear except for the two of them. "I just...I wanted to tell you I believe you," she said. "I know you wouldn't do such a thing."

"Thank you," he said, and turned away. It was so definite a

rejection that she felt stunned, then angry with herself. Never mind what he'd told her in his office the day Henry had betrayed her; he clearly wasn't interested in being her friend. Well, she didn't want to be his friend either. It was only guilt that had made her think so. But she had no reason to feel guilty, because *he* was the one who'd wronged *her*. She watched him walk away and ignored the empty ache inside her that wished he'd chosen otherwise.

Chapter Twenty-Eight

Despite Zara's instructions for her councilors to discuss the upcoming vote privately, Alison didn't see any of them during the next two days. She guessed that, as she was the most junior member of the Council, none of them thought her opinion was worth having. She didn't care. Having already made up her mind as to which way she was voting, she had no interest in discussions about it. She threw herself back into Library business, stayed indoors, and managed to forget for minutes at a time that Gowan had tried to have her killed and would likely try again.

She couldn't eat, the morning of the vote, though she forced herself to choke down a soft-boiled egg and her usual two cups of heavily sugared coffee laced with cream. She dressed with greater than usual care, forgoing trousers and shirt in favor of a dark blue morning gown and allowing Belle to pile her curls atop her head with a few dangling loose around her face. If she were going to lose the Library today, she would at least look good when it happened.

She was almost last to the audience chamber, which adjoined the Council chamber, with only the perennially late Baron of Highton missing when she arrived. The audience chamber's white vaulted ceiling, thirty or more feet high, looked impressive at first glance, but a closer inspection showed Alison that it needed a fresh coat of paint. The room felt in general as if it needed renovation. The biting smell of mildew came from somewhere nearby, possibly from the cracks in the plastered walls. Wall to wall carpet covered the floor in a thick gold pile that swallowed footsteps and kept them from echoing off the walls and ceiling. Double doors of six-inch-thick oak rose fifteen feet high to a rounded top, and at the far end of the room facing them stood a round dais reached by three steps upon which stood the throne of Tremontane, a plain chair carved not from wood but from a single block of green and black marble. It bore no cushions and looked terribly uncomfortable. Zara sat in it with no evidence of discomfort. The rest of the councilors were ranged on either side of the throne, facing the doors.

Alison joined the rest of the councilors, who turned to look at her, and immediately felt herself go blotchy. She had forgotten the North colors were dark blue and silver—and Anthony was dressed in a North blue frock coat that matched her gown as perfectly as if they'd planned it. Pretending nothing was wrong, she held her head high and took her place next to Anthony, who had his hand over his mouth to conceal a smile. Alison swallowed hard, then smiled brightly at everyone and pretended she was wearing pink.

Zara gave no indication that she was aware of the tension among her councilors. "I see it is time to begin," she said.

"Morton isn't here yet," Lestrange said. He was definitely more tense than everyone else, his eyes skimming across the assembled councilors as if trying to change their votes by some inherent magic affecting thoughts. If the Baron of Highton, Lestrange's toady, didn't arrive soon, he might lose his vote, and while Alison didn't know exactly how the votes lay at the moment, she felt certain Lestrange's support wasn't so great that he could afford to give up any advantage.

"The Baron knows the time and place of our meetings," Zara said. "If he—"

"Sorry, sorry," the Baron of Highton said, darting into the room and tripping over the carpet before stumbling into his place. He was out of breath and his forehead was a little sweaty. "I hope I didn't keep everyone waiting."

"Not at all, Morton," Zara said. She beckoned to an attendant. "Please ask the Magistrix and her party to enter."

The attendant went to the double doors and, with the help of another blue-and-silver liveried attendant, pulled them open with some effort. Immediately beyond, the Magistrix and her two Magisters, again in full blue and black regalia, stood posed in a loose triangle with the Magistrix at the nearest point. Beyond them was a double column of red-robed Masters, far more than had been in the Magistrix's party. Alison, looking closely, didn't see Gowan among them, but recognized two of the Masters from the north wing offices. The Magistrix was attempting to intimidate Zara in her own palace. No, she was trying to intimidate Zara's councilors, a ploy that, infuriatingly, might actually work.

The procession came forward slowly, the Magisters matching their pace to that of the cane-assisted Magistrix. Despite the cane, the Magistrix walked with confidence, her warm brown eyes never leaving Zara's icy blue ones. When she was within five feet of the dais, she stopped and bowed, equal to equal. It was an insult Zara should not ignore, but the Queen said only, "Magistrix. Welcome. You come before us with a proposal. Speak, and you shall be heard."

"Thank you, your Majesty," the Magistrix said. "I come before you as voice of the united will of the Masters and Magisters of the Scholia. Our reputation as the premier educational institution in Tremontane has guaranteed that those serving as Royal Librarians are far more skilled than any other possible candidates. In fact, the Scholia provides an unparalleled education to anyone in Tremontane regardless of rank. In turn, those Masters provide exceptional service to the entire country. We fear the Crown's usurpation of the Scholia's longstanding association with the Royal Library may be seen as a vote of no confidence in the Scholia itself. We request the Crown remedy this imbalance by creating an endowment that will allow the Scholia to continue its work without fear of its reputation being damaged."

Zara concentrated her attention on the Magistrix. "If I understand your argument," she said, "you are asking for an endowment so the Scholia's reputation may remain intact now that the Royal Library is no longer under your purview."

"We are willing to stipulate the Crown's authority over the

Library as a sign of good faith," said the Magistrix.

"We get the Library, you get your endowment," said Zara.

"I would not put it in those terms. We would receive the endowment as a sign of respect for our valuable work."

"And what of your responsibility to the Crown? We provide security, and you provide...?"

"Scholia-educated Masters to serve in every area of government, naturally. The security of knowing the quality of those serving you."

"I was speaking more of accountability," said Zara. "Your request seems not only for money, but for autonomy as well. Would that not be a great amount of power for a single institution?"

"Do you suggest we would not be honorable in exercising that power?"

"I suggest that as a recipient of government funds, the Scholia ought also to be under government oversight."

The Magistrix sat up, looking shocked. "An educational institution must have a free and open exchange of ideas! The oversight of any outside entity must surely degenerate into suppression. Our reputation would be sullied."

"And what of financial oversight? Is the Crown to have no say in Scholia matters?"

"I fail to see why the Crown would want a say in Scholia matters. Much of what we do is impenetrable to outsiders, who do not understand our peculiar needs."

"Then, to clarify: you want the Crown to provide you with an endowment that will leave you free to pursue educational goals."

"That is precisely correct, your Majesty."

Zara nodded, slowly. "And how will this endowment offset our, as you put it, usurpation of the Royal Library? Since you have been so assiduous in attempting to reclaim it?"

"We are convinced the Royal Library is too valuable to remain in inexperienced hands. We have done everything in our power to convince the Countess of Waxwold of the justice of this. Since she remains obdurate, and since your Majesty will not remove her from office, we conclude that the Crown disagrees with our position and must therefore bow to your wishes. This capitulation makes us seem weak, which lessens the public trust in us. We simply ask that you balance the scales."

"By giving you money."

"By allowing us to act without the need for constant fundraising. By allowing us our freedom."

Zara nodded again. "I invite my councilors to ask the Magistrix any questions they might wish to clarify their understanding of the situation."

Alison wanted to ask the Magistrix what she thought of Gowan's attacks, but there was no point. She still didn't know what to do about him. Maybe she wasn't devious enough.

Clara Unwin was speaking. "—to the Crown if we comply with your wishes? Who is to determine how much the endowment would have to be for the Scholia to support itself on its interest?"

"Our bursars have calculated that amount and are willing to work with the Crown to decide on the final disposition of funds."

"And if we disagree?"

"I think it won't come to that, if we are reasonable individuals."

Alison could almost hear Unwin thinking that wasn't very likely, but the councilor kept her tongue.

Roger Lestrange stepped forward. "Magistrix, perhaps you could explain the uses to which the endowment would be put."

"Of course. It would pay for instructor salaries, maintaining the physical facilities to keep them up to date, creating educational materials, and a few other things necessary to continue the Scholia's mission of excellence in education. It would also allow us to fund scholarships for deserving students, something we have not been able to do to date."

"Thank you." Lestrange resumed his place. Alison's stomach sank. Now everyone had a picture of the Scholia as some benevolent institution that even tried to give poor people an education. How could Zara allow Lestrange to exercise such influence over the Council?

Zara rose, inviting everyone to do the same, and said, "Thank you for your time, Magistrix. We will deliberate now and return with an answer for you within the hour. You may wait here."

Alison had to stop herself from smiling. There were no chairs in the audience chamber aside from the throne. She ought to feel sorry for the Magistrix, leaning on her cane, but she remembered Trevers, and her terror while she crouched behind that carriage, and felt no compassion at all.

Alison followed Anthony and the other councilors into the Council chamber, feeling Zara's presence at her back like a cold pressure down her spine. The councilors took their seats, Alison feeling terribly conspicuous sitting next to Anthony in their matching attire. Zara remained standing. She said, "If anyone has any final remarks before we vote, now is the time to share them."

Clara Unwin stood immediately and said, "I wish to remind you all once more of the precarious financial position this endowment would put the country in. We have no resources to afford such an expenditure. The Scholia's goals may be laudable, but we are in no position to further them. Please consider this when you cast your vote."

She sat down, and Lestrange was standing almost before Unwin's bottom touched her seat. "The Scholia has served Tremontane for over a century. Its Masters are well respected and serve in all areas of government and business. It aims to educate everyone who chooses to attend and will use this endowment to provide scholarships for those who cannot afford tuition. This endowment not only helps the Scholia in its goals, but serves as a gesture of thanks for everything it has done for us over the years."

He sat down. No one else seemed inclined to stand. Zara gestured to her aide, who went around the room, handing each councilor the red and white wooden marbles. "The white balls are a 'yes' vote in favor of funding the endowment, the red balls 'no' in opposition. Voting will proceed by seniority. I will cast the final vote," Zara said.

Matthew Godwinson got heavily to his feet and went to the vase. The ball hit the bottom of the vase and bounced a few times, making a series of wooden tapping noises. As soon as Godwinson sat down, Lestrange rose and repeated the process. One by one, the councilors stood to cast their votes, until it was Alison's turn. She suddenly had the irrational fear that she would accidentally put the wrong ball into the vase, and had to peek at it before dropping it in. Zara was up before Alison had even seated herself. She must have thrown the ball rather than dropping it, because the sound it made was louder than the others and seemed to echo.

Zara returned to her seat and lowered herself into it gracefully. "Has anyone not cast a vote?" No one moved. "Please break the vase and count the votes."

Alison unclenched her fists, which were sweating. She didn't know if she was more nervous about her own fate or that of the kingdom. The aides struck the vase, which broke with a dull musical tone. She was afraid to watch, afraid to look at anyone else for fear of somehow influencing the results. She heard the sound of wood clicking against wood, which stopped, then repeated itself. Her heart was pounding.

"Your Majesty, we have a resolution. In the matter of funding an endowment for the Scholia, the vote is seven in favor, six in opposition."

Alison held her breath. The alternative was making the same incredulous noise Clara Unwin was on the other side of the table. Alison looked to Clara's left and saw Albert Fisher's face go blank. It couldn't be. Zara couldn't have lost. Alison knew she was blotchy and didn't care. *Say farewell to the Library, foolish girl.*

"Thank you for your service," Zara said, sounding very far away thanks to the roaring in Alison's ears. "Ladies and gentlemen of the council, we have a decision. If you will join me in the hall, we will present our resolution to the Magistrix immediately."

Chapter Twenty-Nine

The Magistrix and her entourage stood in the same positions they had been when the Council left them. The Magistrix might have been leaning a little more heavily on her cane, but with her legs concealed by her robe it was impossible to tell. What was obvious to Alison as she took her place on the dais was the subtle change in the woman's features that said she knew the vote had gone in her favor. Probably Lestrange had given her some indication. The Queen had lost, the Magistrix would get her endowment, and Lestrange's power in the Council would increase, forcing Zara to work even harder to maintain control. Alison felt herself beyond crying. This was too great a disaster for tears. It was the kind of disaster that demanded shouting and hitting things and raging defiance at the world. Alison would have to settle for showing the Magistrix a cool, unafraid visage. She had already lost the Library; she would not lose her composure as well.

"Magistrix, the Council has reached a decision," Zara said, her voice as cool as Alison hoped her face was. "We will fund an endowment for the Scholia as you have requested."

The Magistrix didn't even try to conceal her triumph. "Thank you, your Majesty, and my thanks to the Council as well," she said. "I assure you the Scholia will use this endowment to serve Tremontane."

"As you are the voice of the will of the Scholia, that assurance carries extra weight," Zara said. "I hope — Who is opening that door? Major Casson, why have you intruded on these proceedings?"

The double doors at the back of the room had opened silently, and Major Casson stood in the opening, his bearing erect and proper. There was a swishing sound as the members of the Magistrix's party turned to look at him. "I beg your pardon, your Majesty," he said, "but there has been a development I believed should be brought to your immediate attention."

353

"I fail to see what is so important that you felt the need to interrupt this meeting," Zara said, but there was a note in her voice that told Alison with utter certainty that Zara knew exactly what Major Casson was doing there. Her pulse raced. Something important was about to happen, and Alison felt unexpected hope rise up inside her.

Major Casson stepped fully into the room and pulled the door open a little wider. Two soldiers entered, followed by three men whose hands were bound to a rope linking them together. Alison didn't recognize any of them at first, as they all had the look of men who'd spent some time in a cell, but a second glance revealed, to her shock, that the third man was Arnold Gowan. The three men were followed by another soldier and a tall, lovely woman who was not bound in any way. Alison heard Anthony, standing beside her, take a single horrified breath.

"Your Majesty instructed me to investigate the attacks on the Library and the Royal Librarian," Major Casson said. "We were finally able to track down the man who killed Lieutenant Elise Garan and attempted to murder the Countess of Waxwold." His voice was strained; there was fury there just under the surface. "He led us to his co-conspirator, who admitted to having orchestrated the attack that left apprentice Trevers Stofford nearly dead. Both men named Arnold Gowan as the one who hired them to commit these crimes."

The Magistrix drew in a gasp. "Your Majesty, I am *shocked* to learn of Master Gowan's treachery! I assure you I had no knowledge—"

"No knowledge, Magistrix?" Gowan said. "Your Majesty, I would like to testify in court that Margaret Bindle instructed me to do whatever it took to hound the Countess of Waxwold out of the Royal Library."

"That is a serious allegation. Magistrix, how do you respond?" Zara said.

"I—I repeat, I'm shocked Master Gowan could believe I would want—"

"Then you deny you earlier said you have done everything in your power to convince the Countess that she should resign her position?"

"No, but of course I spoke of logic, reason, not vicious attacks! Master Gowan must have misunderstood me."

"There was no misunderstanding, your Majesty," Gowan said. "She specifically told me to make the Countess suffer and that it did not matter in what condition she left the Library."

His matter of fact recounting of the Magistrix's instructions left Alison feeling a little faint. She breathed deeply and focused all her attention on Gowan, glaring at him as if she could burn a hole through his chest. He didn't look at her; he was looking at the Queen, whose expression Alison couldn't see.

"I categorically deny these accusations," the Magistrix said. "Master Gowan has clearly been coerced; his physical condition is testimony of that. Such a testimony will not stand at trial."

"My physical condition, as you call it, has nothing to do with my testimony," Gowan said. "I wasn't your only stooge, Margaret, and I don't intend for you to drag me down with you when you're convicted. And you," he added, addressing the assembled Masters, "I suggest you decide which side you're on before it's decided for you."

The Masters began muttering among themselves, glancing around as if hoping to gauge where their support lay. Major Casson said, "Your Majesty, on that other matter you asked me to investigate, well...." He turned to the woman who was still standing in the doorway, shifting her weight from side to side, her eyes darting in all directions. She startled, took half a step forward, then clasped her hands in front of herself and bowed her head. "You should speak now," Major Casson said, his voice barely reaching Alison's ears.

The woman raised her head and looked directly at the Queen. "Your Majesty," she began, too quietly, cleared her throat and in a louder voice said, "Your Majesty, that woman—" she pointed at the

Magistrix—"she came to me and said she would pay me to claim Tony—his Highness was my Sophy's father, and that he'd abandoned her when she was a baby. I didn't know she was the Magistrix. I just...Tony, I'm so sorry, when they started talking about how awful you were I knew I'd done wrong but I didn't know how to stop it. It was just...it would have meant a better life for me and Sophy. I'm sorry."

Alison glanced at Anthony, whose jaw was rigid and whose fists were clenched tight. "You could have come to me if you needed help, Lydia," he said. "You didn't need to lie to get it."

Tears rolled down Lydia's cheeks. "I'm sorry," she repeated.

"Your Majesty cannot possibly listen to these baseless accusations!" the Magistrix said.

"You *lied* to me!" Lydia shouted. "You said it would make things better for my little girl. This isn't what I wanted!"

"Magistrix, I find it increasingly difficult to believe these accusations are baseless," Zara said. "I believe this warrants further investigation. Major Casson, please take Margaret Bindle into custody. Nathaniel," she said to her aide, "please take the names of these Masters and Magisters. We will need to investigate them as well."

"You *dare*!" the Magistrix said as Major Casson beckoned to two of his guards to take hold of her. "You think the Masters of this kingdom will endure this insult! One word from me, your Majesty, one word and every Master in any position of power will walk away from his or her post. You think your government will survive it? You will bring Tremontane to its knees!"

Zara leaned forward a little. "Nathaniel, take a note," she said. "Margaret Bindle is to be tried for treason as well."

The Magistrix's mouth dropped open. "You—"

"*Do not try my patience further,*" Zara said, her voice as cold as her eyes must surely be. "You have attempted to manipulate my government through violence and blackmail and now you have threatened *me*. My response is this: any Master who leaves his or her position *for any reason* in the next six months will be tried for treason by your side. As you have explicitly represented yourself as the united voice of the Scholia, I must conclude that the Scholia as a whole stands behind your actions. You will therefore stand trial on behalf of the Scholia, and if you are convicted, my sentence as representative of the Crown will be to divest the Scholia of *all* monies it receives from the government of Tremontane." Zara leaned back on her throne. "Major Casson, please find the Magistrix a comfortable cell. Take these men and this woman into custody as well pending trial."

Lydia gasped and struggled as a soldier took her arm. "Zara, don't," Anthony said.

Zara turned on her throne to look at him. "Falsely accusing someone of failing to provide a family bond is a serious crime," she said. "She knew what she was doing when she accepted Miss Bindle's offer."

Anthony stepped down from the dais and stood facing Zara. "She made a stupid mistake," he said, "and it's about to cost her her future. She regrets that more than she can say."

"She nearly cost you *your* future, Anthony." Zara's voice was quiet, intimate, as if she and Anthony were the only people in the room.

"Then I'm the one who can forgive her," he said. "Please, Zara. Just let her go home."

Zara was silent for a long moment. "Release her," she finally said. "Miss Brown, go home to your child."

Lydia, her face streaked with tears, curtsied to the Queen. She looked once at Anthony, who continued to face Zara, then turned and left without saying anything.

"The rest of you," Zara said, raising her voice and standing to address the Masters, who were still standing around muttering to each other, "once Nathaniel has your names, you are free to go. I suggest you consider whether it would be more beneficial to your continued well-being to give the Crown whatever information you might have voluntarily, or under questioning. You're dismissed."

The Masters left, trailed finally by the blue-robed Magisters, who looked as if they couldn't believe they weren't being escorted out in chains. Zara turned to look at her councilors. "The vote was, of course, anonymous," she said. "And I am certain those of you who voted in favor of the endowment had no idea of Margaret Bindle's perfidy." She locked eyes with Lestrange and added, "However, from this point forward I shall look very closely at anyone who continues to support the Scholia, in light of what we have learned today. I would hate to think anyone on this Council could possibly approve of an institution that would allow such underhanded dealings to continue."

Lestrange opened his mouth, and Zara's eyes narrowed. He shut it again. "Thank you for your service," Zara said. "Alison Quinn, a moment of your time, please."

That was the signal for everyone else to disperse. Zara waited for the door to the Council chamber to close behind them, then leaned against the back of the throne and rubbed her eyes with the heels of her palms. "You were worried, weren't you?"

"I—what?"

"It's all right. I was worried and I orchestrated the whole thing. I think the hardest part was when I cast my vote for the other side."

"You did *what?*"

Zara removed her hands and smiled. "I knew how the vote stood. I also knew I had no chance to rein Roger in without letting him think he'd won. The timing was the least predictable part—I never like counting on other people's roles in my plans, though Major Casson is reliable and devoted to me. Still, it all worked out perfectly, didn't it? And the Magistrix got the independence she wanted, though not in the manner she'd anticipated. I did feel guilty about confining that young woman while my men hunted out the assassin, but not terribly guilty.

She did try to destroy my brother, after all."

Alison continued to gape at the Queen. "It's over, Alison," Zara said. "The Library is yours."

"You cast your vote for the other side."

"You really *were* overwhelmed, weren't you? You're not usually this slow to understand."

"But how did you find them all? And the woman — how did you — "

"I have excellent resources, Alison. And Miss Brown came to me. She is not terribly intelligent and never considered the repercussions of her attempted blackmail."

"What do you mean, blackmail?"

Zara looked into the distance, out one of the tall, narrow windows through which spring sunlight poured. "She went to Anthony and threatened to expose him if he didn't pay her off."

Alison gaped again. "But...he had to have known what the consequences of her speaking out would be, and he said he wanted to help her. Why didn't he just pay her?"

Zara turned her gaze on Alison, her expression unreadable. "Because he has *learned his lesson*," she said, articulating her words just slowly enough that each one felt like an arrow piercing Alison's chest. "And I wonder very much why you have not."

"I — " Alison's words ran up against the iron wall that was Zara's gaze. Zara said nothing more. Alison turned and left the audience chamber at a near-run.

She passed through the Council chamber and fled through the halls, unseeing, trusting her familiarity with the palace to take her to safety, which turned out to be her own apartment. She shut and locked the door behind her against...it felt as if something were pursuing her, something she dared not face. She leaned back against the door and closed her eyes.

I'm not going to forgive him. I can't forgive him.

I won't I won't I won't.

She put her hands over her ears, once again trying to shut out the treacherous voice that came from within her own head, and realized it had been the thing pursuing her, and she couldn't lock it out.

It told her, *You love him.*

It said, *You're so afraid of being hurt that you're hurting yourself.*

It said, *It's not about what he deserves. It's about what he needs. What you need.*

She had a flash of a memory, of Anthony saying of Lydia, *She made a stupid mistake, and she regrets that more than she can say.* He did, didn't he? She remembered how he'd looked on the tower roof, his plea for her forgiveness, for her understanding—

"I can't," she wailed aloud. "He didn't care that he was hurting me. He'll just go on doing it."

It was her father's voice this time, coming to her out of memory: *I loved your mother very much. Sometimes I hurt her, and sometimes she hurt me. But I have never regretted giving her the chance to do so, because it gave her the chance to love me.*

She flung herself onto her sofa and lay curled up, not caring how she was crushing her dress. All the memories she had been suppressing rose up behind her eyelids, riding in the Park, laughing and crying at the theater, every kiss and every touch and every single time he had looked at her and saw *her*, not her body or her title but her, as no one ever had. Possibly as no one else ever would. Her memories tore at her, filled her chest with that empty ache she recognized now as her need for him, because she loved him and he meant everything to her, and she was the one who was wrong. He needed her forgiveness, and she needed his. A faint echo drifted back to her from the recesses of her mind: *I can't*...and then it was gone. *I can,* she thought.

She was out the door and halfway down the hall before something occurred to her: it might be too late. He might not care anymore. Part of her, a tiny, ignoble part, rejoiced at this thought, because it meant she didn't have to face him and tell him how wrong she'd been. She stomped that part of herself into a distant corner of her mind. It wasn't about how he felt. It was about finally being able to do what was right.

She stopped at the Library door, struck by inspiration. Maybe it was foolish, maybe he'd be disdainful of her offering, but it felt as if it should be part of her apology. She ran through the scriptorium and into the Library and pulled Flanagan's book of plays off the shelf. She hadn't had it catalogued yet. Maybe part of her had always believed it would eventually go to its rightful owner. She stroked its smooth binding once, then left the Library and hurried along the hall, trying not to run.

She was so used to finding Anthony in his office that she was momentarily thwarted when it turned out he wasn't. No one in the north wing seemed to know where he'd gone. The ignoble part of her tried to climb back into the light and she had to crush it again. She tried Zara's office; she was gone too. Alison sat in a chair in the waiting room, balancing the large book on her knees, more to give herself time to think than because she expected Anthony to return. He wouldn't have left the palace, probably; he lived here now. She hopped out of her chair and headed for the east wing.

The guards at the east wing door hadn't changed, or, rather, they probably had changed but since they all looked the same and had the same stern demeanor, it was impossible to tell. They raised their weapons as she approached, which amused her; she was barely five-foot-two and, though not slender, certainly not someone anyone would consider a physical threat. Possibly they thought the book concealed some kind of exotic weapon. North guards were suspicious and paranoid and therefore perfect for guarding the royal family. "Hello," she said, halting far enough away that they wouldn't feel even more threatened. "Is Prince Anthony here?"

They stared at her, silently. "I'm here to see Prince Anthony," she said. Silence. Alison began to feel paranoia was overrated. "I'd like to speak to him," she continued. More silence. "Oh, for heaven's sake," she said. "Couldn't you at least take him a message?"

"Take who a message?" Anthony said from behind her, making her heart leap and the rest of her turn around fast with a squeak.

"I wanted to talk to you," she said. His proximity was making her heart beat faster.

He looked at her with a curious expression, eyed the book under her arm, then nodded at the guards, who opened the door for them, and led her into the east wing.

"I just came back to change into something a little less formal," he said. "I'm going for a ride in the Park. I feel...I know it will take some time for the truth about Lydia's story to get around, but right now I feel like a free man."

"I can imagine. I'm so glad she decided to tell the truth."

"So am I. I'm arranging to do what I can for her and the child."

"You're not afraid that will look bad?"

"I don't really care what it looks like. I cared about Lydia, once, and I hate to think of her struggling."

They came to the great central drawing room. Anthony sat on one of the overstuffed lemon-yellow sofas and gestured for Alison to take a seat anywhere. She perched on a chair adjacent to his. She couldn't think how to begin. She probably should have come up with something before seeking him out. Alison knew she was becoming blotchy and her awareness of it made the situation worse. The silence stretched, until, grasping at anything, she said, "Anthony, I—"

"You wanted to—" Anthony said at the same time, then said, "I'm sorry. You wanted to talk to me about something?"

"Yes." She still didn't know how to begin. "I...actually, I don't...Anthony."

"Alison, you're making me very nervous." He didn't sound nervous. He sounded amused and completely composed, and it made her a little angry that he could be so calm when her insides were being ripped apart. She took a deep breath. One more memory, this one of the Dowager embracing her and saying *I've never regretted being the first to apologize.* She hoped it was true.

She held the book out to Anthony and said, "This belongs to you."

He took it from her, puzzled, flipped the cover open, and said, "Jerald's book. I don't remember owning a copy."

"I know," she said. "It was supposed to be your Wintersmeet gift. Obviously I couldn't give it to you, but...." This was going all wrong. She'd sounded so bitter just then. Anthony's look of confusion deepened. "I just thought you should have it," she said abruptly.

"Oh. Thank you," he said. He ran his hand over the cover just as she'd done minutes before. Her heart sank. That had sounded like the kind of thanks you give just before you show someone the door. Why couldn't she just say something simple? *I'm sorry,* or *Please forgive me,* or even *I love you?*

She opened her mouth, hoping some part of her mind, or heart, would come up with something, and was horrified to hear herself say, in a voice that echoed with pain, "You hurt me."

All the confusion left Anthony's face as if someone had pulled a plug and let it drain away, leaving him completely expressionless. *Why that? Why an accusation?* But it seemed as if those words had unleashed a torrent, and she had no choice but to let them carry her along.

"I trusted you," she went on. "I never trusted anyone the way I did you, and you betrayed me after you said you wouldn't. You don't know what that did to me. I wanted to die. I did die, a little, I think, curled in on myself and froze so it couldn't happen again. I couldn't forgive you and I didn't want to forgive you. I wanted you to suffer. And I was so wrong about all of that."

Anthony had turned to stone again, the occasional blink the only indication that he was still alive. She couldn't look at that face and keep her composure. She looked down at the impossibly white carpet and said, "I loved you, and the first time you did something that hurt me, I turned on you. I never gave you a single chance to redeem yourself. I loved you, and I hurt and betrayed you as surely as you did me. We both know what you did was wrong, but you're the only one of us who learned from it. I just let it turn me to ice. Anthony, I'm sorry. I should have forgiven you long ago. I hope you can forgive me."

Silence. She didn't dare look at him. She wondered if she could possibly stand and leave the room without having to meet his eyes, run back to the Library and let her embarrassment and pain soak out of her into the stones that were far more forgiving than she was. She heard him shift his position, saw his feet move as he stood, then he was kneeling before her and his hand was on her shoulder. "Alison," he said, his voice husky, and then he took her in his arms and held her, his body trembling. She put her own arms around his neck and laid her head on his shoulder and felt the aching emptiness inside her begin to fill with the comfort of his familiar touch, his body against hers, his arms enveloping her as if she were infinitely precious to him.

"I love you," she whispered. "I hope it's not too late for me to say that."

"It could never be too late," he said. "I never stopped loving you."

"I'm sorry it took me so long to realize the truth. I've been so stupid."

"Don't cry, love. I'm a better man because you walked away from me that night."

"I wish I could say I'm a better woman now, but I think a better woman would have forgiven more easily."

"I've always thought you're the most wonderful woman I know, so you would be truly amazing if you improved."

Alison laughed, a little damply through her tears, and Anthony lifted his head and drew back just far enough to look at her. "You told me once that sometimes creating something new meant destroying the old," he said. "I think we've accomplished that."

Alison smiled. "It was a rather complete destruction. And it will never happen again."

"I don't think I could survive it." He laid his hand along the curve of her cheek. "Alison Quinn, will you marry me?"

She leaned into his touch. "With pleasure, your Highness."

He made a face, but his eyes were full of laughter. "I know what I am. I would prefer it if you'd call me Anthony."

Alison cast her eyes down demurely and said, "I don't believe we know each other well enough to make free of our given names."

"We don't?"

"It's only been seven months, your Highness."

"Really?" Anthony ran his hand over the back of her head and tugged her hair free of Belle's careful arrangement, making it fall in wriggly blond cascades around her face. "Then we certainly don't know each other well enough for this," he said, and then his lips were on hers and she responded with a passion that had been banked for far too long. He guided her off the chair until they were both sitting on the floor, holding each other close, touching and kissing and touching again until Alison was sure she was going to die if he didn't tear her clothes off right there in the middle of the east wing drawing room. She reached down to unbutton his coat, and Anthony made an amused sound and withdrew to arm's length. He looked as mussed as she felt. "I think we should do this the right way, as long as we're starting something new," he said.

"I hate the right way," Alison said. "I know you have a bedroom around here somewhere."

"I do, but we'll have our own apartment once we're married," Anthony said, laughing, "and you, Countess, used to be the voice of reason in this relationship."

"It's a new relationship. You can have a turn being reasonable." By this time they were both laughing, and Alison tied her hair back at the nape of her neck and stood, brushing off her dress. Anthony reached out and took her hand. "Change your clothes, and come riding with me," he said. "Then have dinner with me. I want to do everything with you, no secrets, no hiding what we are to each other. I want the world to know I love you, Alison Quinn."

"I want to tell everyone I love you, Anthony North." She put her arms around him and felt the last shreds of resentment and pride slip away from her. "And I'm never leaving you again."

Chapter Thirty

Two months later

It had taken weeks to find it, but now Alison had a copy of *Starfall*, acquired from Mistress Inkpen at hideous expense. Finally, the sequel to *Hearthsfire*, and maybe she'd overpaid for it, but what was the point of being Royal Librarian if you couldn't indulge once in a while? She sat cross-legged on her bed and turned another page. She glanced again at her watch Device. Just after ten-thirty. Plenty of time. Enough to read just one more chapter.

Someone knocked at the door and entered without waiting for an invitation. "Oh, my dear, I thought Anthony was right when he said you might need me, but I cannot believe I've found you in this state!" The Dowager came into the bedroom, followed by Belle and three of the Dowager's own maids. "Get up, dear, and Lucille will draw you a bath. I really am astonished. I almost think you've forgotten, but that's too absurd for me to believe it."

Alison stood and beat her thighs to restore feeling to them. "Forgotten what?"

The Dowager's mouth dropped open. "You did forget. By heaven, Alison, if I hadn't come along you would have missed your own wedding!"

It was Alison's turn to let her mouth drop open. "That's hours from now," she said, snatching up her watch. She looked at it more closely. Her heart plummeted as she realized the hands weren't moving. An image of Anthony standing in the antechamber to the coronation hall, waiting for a bride who didn't show up, flashed in horrifying clarity across her mind. "Oh, Milady, I—what time is it? It's not too late, is it?"

"It's just after noon, and you have about five hours, which I judge is barely enough time to get you ready. My goodness, dear, where are all your clothes? Did you leave your wedding gown in your new apartment? Belle, fetch your mistress's gown at once; I assume you know the way. Alison, put that ancient book away, surely nothing is so important that you can't set it aside for now."

Alison began to understand where Zara's personality came from. The Dowager directed her into the bath, directed her out of the bath and into a dressing gown, supervised her manicure and pedicure, neither of which Alison had ever had in her life, and personally rubbed creams into Alison's already smooth skin until she glowed, pink-cheeked and radiant "as a bride should look," the Dowager said. "Your skin is perfect, dear, but even perfection can stand a little enhancement. Now, about your cosmetics...."

"I don't need cosmetics. They make me look like a clown. I want to look like myself."

"Trust me, dear, you won't look like a clown when Eleanora finishes with you. This is so you won't look washed out from a distance, which is how most of your guests will see you. From a distance, that is, not washed out. Just hold still and I promise you won't regret it."

Alison had to admit the finished product still looked like her, only more so. She turned her head to see herself from both sides. "I look good," she said.

"You look *magnificent,* dear. Oh, I am so pleased to have you for a daughter! Just between the two of us, Anthony is lucky you were willing to give him a second chance. I really am so pleased, my dear."

"No, I'm the lucky one," Alison said, and had a flash of a memory of that moment when she'd walked away from him on that tower, and pushed it to the back of her mind. They were neither of them the same person they'd been that night. She was marrying him in a few hours. The rush of joy she felt at the thought outshone the pleasure her book gave her the way the sun outshone a candle.

"Now for your hair. Oh, my dear, it *is* lovely, but I imagine it's a trial to you. So much frizz if you don't care for it properly. Justine, if you wouldn't mind — thank you — Justine is an expert and she will tame that mass of locks for you in no time."

Justine was, in fact, an expert, and Alison started plotting how to get her away from the Dowager when she saw how her skinny, long, frizzy ringlets became smooth under the woman's hands. The Dowager's short hair certainly didn't require much maintenance. Who knew her curls could look like this? Justine arranged it high on her head and allowed the trailing ends to fall over one shoulder. Alison turned her head and felt the arrangement move not at all. She ran her fingers through the cascade and was stopped by the Dowager's sharp rap on her knuckles. "Don't touch, dear, you don't want to damage the look before the wedding."

They laced her into her corset. Eleanora turned out to have remarkably strong hands, and Alison wondered if she might faint from being unable to breathe. The skirt and bodice, pale green and embroidered all over with seed pearls, provoked exclamations of admiration from everyone, including Alison when she saw herself in the mirror. Anthony would love it. They would make a beautiful couple, walking down the center of the coronation hall.

"Oh, my dear," the Dowager sighed, "you look every inch a princess. Turn around and let me look at you. Lucille, adjust that petticoat, the one hanging down just the tiniest bit too low. That's better."

"Am I?" Alison asked. "A princess?"

"Not by title, though the rulers of Veribold and Eskandel will treat you as such. Unless Anthony becomes king, you will simply be Lady Alison North. I was Lady Rowenna North for years before Sylvester took the Crown."

"I think the title of Royal Librarian is more to my taste, anyway." It had never occurred to Alison that the Dowager had once stood in her place. More hesitantly, she asked, "Should I call you Rowenna, now?"

The Dowager's eyes filled with tears. "If you like…that is, I would dearly love it if you would call me Mother…but I know your own dear mother will always—"

Alison took her hands. "I would love to call you Mother," she said.

Now the Dowager really was crying and smiling at the same time. "Oh, my dear—oh no, we should be going. I'll escort you to the antechamber. I realize you know the way, but you should have at least one attendant."

Alison did know how to get to the coronation chamber—just the week before she'd stood in the antechamber to renounce her claim to the title of County Waxwold in preparation for this day—but with her growing nervousness she was grateful for the Dowager's company. The Dowager hustled her along, saying things like, "I don't know how the time got away from us" and "Don't worry, dear, they won't start without you" which combined to make Alison far more nervous than if they'd gone in silence. The Dowager finally stopped at a double door twenty feet tall and air-kissed her on both cheeks. "I'll see you soon, dear. The guards will open the inner doors when it's time." Alison watched her leave, then turned her attention to the doors. She was so nervous she was shaking. Was she making a mistake? Was it too soon? Before she could work herself up into a panic, she put her hand on the door and pushed it open.

The slight breeze from the doors smelled faintly like roses and furniture polish. The room beyond looked like the Dowager's apartment, all white and gilt and mirrors, but what in the Dowager's small apartment looked gaudy, in this vast room with its high ceilings looked grand. Her feet left prints on the soft carpet as she walked through the door. Across the room, Anthony turned around. "You're here," he said, his voice and face neutral. He didn't approach her.

"Did you think I wouldn't come?" she asked.

"I had just about convinced myself of that, yes." He looked elegant in a fitted coat of gold satin with a waistcoat a few shades darker than her dress, white knee breeches and tawny shoes.

"I'm sorry I'm late. I didn't realize how much effort it took to produce a bride."

His smile was strained. "It was worth the effort. You are beautiful."

"So are you," she said. "I mean, not beautiful. Handsome."

They silently gazed at one another, unsmiling, until Alison's nerves gave way and she said, "You haven't changed your mind, have you?"

That provoked a reaction. Anthony said, "Of course not," astonished, then added, "Have you?"

"No. Why are you behaving so strangely?"

"Why are *you*?"

"I'm not behaving strangely. You're the one who won't stop staring at me like I'm a stranger."

"Well, you're the one who nearly forgot her own wedding."

"I—what? I didn't forget."

"Only because Mother rousted you from whatever you were reading. I can't believe I came second to a book."

"That's unfair. And how do you know that, anyway?"

"It was an informed guess." Anthony turned away and muttered something under his breath. "What was that?" Alison demanded.

"I said I keep expecting you to walk away from me again."

Alison crossed the room to him and took his hand, blinking back tears of anger. "I'm five minutes late—"

"Twelve."

"—Twelve minutes late and you assume I've run off?" She raised their clasped hands and shook them in his face. "Anthony North, in a few minutes I'm going to cross that hall with your hand in mine, and I am going to put this ring on your finger, and then I'm going to take your hand again and it will take seven burly men with crowbars to part me from you, and even that might not be enough. Do you think, after everything we've been through to get to this day, I'm going to abandon you so easily?"

He looked at her again and this time he smiled and shook his head. "You don't have a single worry about all this, do you?"

"Of course I do. I worry we haven't known each other very long and we'll find out things about each other that we hate. I worry I'll get lost in a book and you'll get caught up in work, and we'll forget to say we love each other, and I worry I don't know how to make a marriage work and I'll get everything wrong. But mostly, I worry I've waited all this time for my wedding night just to find out I hate sex."

He burst out laughing, leaned against the wall with his head on his arms and roared until Alison started to get angry. "Oh, sweetheart, I don't know what I was thinking," he said. "I would take you in my arms and kiss you until you forgot all your worries, but I'm afraid my mother would kill me for mussing you."

"She would kill me first. She thinks I have all the self-control in this relationship."

"I'd say she was right, except that I've spent the last seven days thinking about what you look like naked and *not* trying to convince you to give me another look."

"Just a few more hours and I won't need convincing."

"I wonder why they haven't opened the doors yet." Anthony suddenly looked horrified. "You don't suppose everyone heard our argument, and they've been waiting for us to wrap it up?"

Alison grinned. "Then I guess we gave them an earful." She took his hand and they gazed at one another again, this time smiling, until a few minutes later they heard the doors open.

"Are you ready, Countess?"

"I am, your Highness."

Alison was glad to have a hand to hold because despite Zara's comments about the scope of the ceremony, she hadn't really understood how many people "a few hundred" were. Men and women dressed in the finery of three nations crowded in on either side of an invisible aisle, silently observing Alison and Anthony, and it made Alison so nervous that she kept speeding up, anxious to cross the vast chamber that was surely five miles wide. She smiled a frozen smile, reminded herself *This is about you and Anthony, not about them* and managed not to break into a run, towing Anthony behind her. It took nearly forever, but finally they climbed the three steps of the dais to stand before Zara, with Martin Quinn and the Dowager behind her.

"We are here today," Zara said in a clear, carrying voice, "to witness the joining of Alison Quinn to the house of North by adoption, and to witness the joining of Anthony North and Alison North by oath of marriage. If anyone disputes the right of these people to make oath to one another, speak now." She waited only a token few seconds before saying, "Alison Quinn, come forward."

Alison released Anthony's hand and stepped forward to clasp Zara around her right wrist as Zara took her right wrist in return. "Alison Quinn, do you of your own free will relinquish all claim to the Quinn name, to take the name of North to yourself and your children?"

"I do," Alison said, and felt the power of the new family bond rush through her like a cool stream. Zara released her. "Anthony North, step forward."

Anthony stood next to Alison. "Join left hands, please," said Zara, and Anthony took Alison's hand and squeezed it just a little. "Anthony North, do you take Alison North as your wife, mother of your children and strong left hand for all your days?"

"Yes," said Anthony, his smile wide and brilliant. Alison knew she should look at Zara at this point in the ceremony, but she couldn't bear to look away from him. She knew her smile was just as broad.

"Alison North, do you take Anthony North as your husband, father of your children and strong left hand for all your days?"

Alison let out a deep breath. "Yes," she said.

"Then make your heart's oaths to one another."

373

Anthony released Alison's hand just long enough to produce a slender gold band. "Alison, always my love, I will be strength to your weakness all the days of my life."

Alison slipped her wider gold ring onto the center finger of Anthony's left hand. "I swear to be yours forever, Anthony, strength to your weakness until the end of my days." She took his hand in hers again.

Zara said, "Do you gathered here today bear witness?"

The roar of assent nearly deafened Alison. "Then as matriarch of the house of North," Zara shouted over the din, "I declare this marriage sworn and sealed!"

Fire swept over her, filling her to the point that she could barely breathe. It was like nothing she'd felt before or even imagined feeling, like joy made tangible, and her knees trembled with the effort of holding her up. "Alison. Alison, what's wrong?" Anthony said in her ear, and she realized she was leaning a little too heavily on him.

It was impossible to explain—but then, he'd have felt the same, wouldn't he? "I was just a little overwhelmed," she said. She stepped just far away enough to continue to hold her husband's hand and looked around the room at cheering, expectant faces. "What are they waiting for?" she asked.

"This," said Anthony, and slid his hand along her cheek and kissed her. Then he kissed her again, and she joined in enthusiastically. When they parted, he said, "I think if we do that again, some of those people might scream so loudly they'll pass out."

"Let's do it anyway," Alison said, and they did.

It took only minutes for Zara to sweep the family, Martin Quinn included, across the coronation room and out into the antechamber. Alison didn't mind. She still felt a little shaky and welcomed Zara's decisiveness. Her sister. She'd never had a sister before. To her surprise, Zara unbent long enough to embrace both her and the groom, though there was a look in her eye that said they shouldn't expect it again anytime soon. Then Martin Quinn held Alison close and whispered, "You know I'll always be your father, whatever family you join."

Tears in her eyes, Alison responded, "I wouldn't want any other father but you."

The Dowager was radiant with happiness, embracing her son, then her new daughter, and Alison laughed and said, "Aren't you afraid of mussing me?"

"The important part is over, dear. And it's not as if I'm running my fingers through your hair. I'll leave that to Anthony." She winked and smiled, and Alison, who'd never imagined the Dowager could say anything even the least bit suggestive, blushed.

"Now," Zara said, "let's go over the rest of the evening. A wedding supper will be served in the dining hall in about twenty minutes, after which there will be a reception with dancing in the ballroom. The newlyweds should stay at least four hours. Anthony, try not to look at your watch too obviously or too often."

"Why are you talking at me?"

"Because I know how you dislike these events and I suspect you would leave immediately if I did not give you explicit instructions. Alison, you and Anthony will lead off the dancing, but I would prefer you not dance too often. We have many visiting dignitaries and I think it would be a good idea for you to greet them, give them a chance to meet the heir's bride."

"Of course, Zara." More strangers to stare at her. Alison gripped Anthony's hand a little tighter.

"Martin, you'll sit at Alison's left hand. Mother, you'll sit at my right. Any questions?"

"Are you going to tell me which fork to use?"

"Any *non-frivolous* questions? Good."

Supper was delicious, though Alison was distracted by Anthony's occasionally running his fingers up and down her thigh under the high table, making that part of her body heat up in a way that was incompatible with carrying on a conversation. She swatted him discreetly, once or twice, but he only gave her an innocent look and kept right on doing it.

They had the floor to themselves for the first dance, and Alison thought, as she had once before, how good they must look together, him dark, her fair. "Do you remember our first dance?" she said. "Heaven knows I wouldn't have guessed then you would be within hours of seeing me without my clothes on today."

"I'm ashamed to say I was drunk enough only to remember that you slapped me."

"Well, you deserved it, in case you don't remember that either."

"I'm sure I did." He looked serious. "You don't hold that against me, right? It's not something you're going to bring up again someday when we're fighting about something else?"

He sounded uncertain, and it made her heart fill with love for him. "I swear I never will," she assured him. "I promise only to bring up the good memories from that time. Like your first play."

"And when we raced in the Park."

"And when you tried to get me into the Library."

"And when I kissed you for the first time."

"That's one of my favorite memories."

"Give me time, and I promise we'll make more of them."

They made the circuit of the hall twice, then separated to visit with their guests individually. Anthony was starting to look a little tense around the eyes, as if his patience was wearing out, and Alison judged he'd be able to bear the last hour and a half better if she wasn't around. Alison herself was starting to feel weary of meeting new people and keeping track of who should receive a curtsey and who a nod. It was disconcerting to be addressed as "your Highness" by foreign dignitaries and leered at by people who'd just seen her make her marriage oath. Only knowing that Anthony was nearby in the crowd kept her from freezing up.

She was in the middle of an interesting conversation with a visiting Eskandelic princeling's harem when someone tugged on her skirt and Anthony said, in her ear, "I'm leaving. Follow when you can." Then he was gone. Alison suddenly found it difficult to stay focused on the conversation. She extricated herself as soon as was gracefully possible and made her way through the crowd, deflecting courtesies and conversational gambits. More people thronged the hallway outside the ballroom; she made noises about needing to use the facilities and fled.

She hurried along the halls, her dress swaying around her ankles, until she came to the east wing. Two guards stood sentinel even though everyone was at the ball. Well. Everyone but two people. They passed her through without comment, though she was sure the female guard winked at her.

Their new apartment was on the far side of the wing from Zara's, something Anthony swore had not been part of his calculations when he chose it. "You can redecorate it any way you like," he'd told her, but she liked the bright colors of the sitting room and the shades of blue in the bedroom. Her heart pounded a little faster. She opened the apartment door and went inside.

He'd left one light burning so she wouldn't have to stumble through the darkness of the sitting room. The bedroom door was partially ajar. She pushed it open to find the lamp Devices glowing softly, dimly lighting the room, and no Anthony visible anywhere. "Hello?" she said quietly, feeling awkward despite this being her room as well as his. Or maybe that was why she felt awkward, sharing a bedroom with someone else for the first time in her entire life.

"Just a minute," Anthony said from his dressing room, and soon he emerged wearing nothing but a loose pair of cotton trousers, his hair a little ruffled as if he'd just pulled his shirt off over his head. The smile he gave her was wicked.

"I think I need some help taking this off," she said, plucking at her bodice.

"Not the skirt?"

She reached inside the waist and pulled at the drawstrings, undid the hooks. The skirt and her petticoats fell to the floor. "No, that I can do myself," she said, smiling demurely.

Anthony put his hands around her waist and held her up, turning in a slow circle. "Don't think that smile fools me, Alison North," he said, and she laughed to hear her new name on his lips. He set her down gently and drew her close for a long, wonderful kiss. "Let me help you with that," he whispered, and in no time the bodice and the detested corset lay on the floor, and she stood before him clad only in her chemise and drawers.

She leaned up against him, their bodies touching the whole length of them, and laid her cheek against his bare chest. "Say it," she said.

"Say what?"

She put his hand on her waist and took his other hand in hers, and danced him around the room. "I know you remember, however you claim otherwise," she said. "I want to hear you say it."

"Oh," he said, and laughed, then bent his dark head to hers. "You are beautiful," he whispered in her ear. "But I'll wager you're even more beautiful with your clothes off."

She moved her hand to the waistband of his trousers. "I'll wager you are too," she said. "Let's find out."

Read on for a bonus short

story —

"Long Live the Queen"

Long Live the Queen

She'd had a lifetime to learn how to school her face to reveal only the emotions she chose. Now Zara North wished she had learned how *not* to control herself, how to run screaming and laughing and sobbing through the corridors of the palace without fear of how it might affect the hundreds of thousands of Tremontanan citizens under her care. If her face showed no emotion today, it was because she was numb from the revelation Dr. Trevellian had quietly, inexorably handed her the way one might offer an unwelcome legacy from a long-dead relative.

It had to be a relative, didn't it? These things, these…the doctor had called it a gift, and maybe it was to him, but to Zara it was nothing but a curse, deadly to everyone except herself. But they had to come from *somewhere*, didn't they? Which of the faces in the long gallery two flights above had secretly harbored this, this *infection*, handed it off to child after child until it had sprung into full poisonous flower in her?

There was no one she could tell. Dr. Trevellian was a good man, but he wasn't a confidant except in medical matters, and this had gone so far beyond a simple medical matter that Zara went even more numb just thinking about it. She wished she could tell herself that she didn't know what to do, but Zara prided herself on her cold, analytical nature, and the solution to her problem was all too clear. Clear, but impossible for her to manage alone. She had to tell someone. The right someone.

She reversed her course and made her way down two flights of stairs to the Library. Alison had been right to insist on its being moved. In only five years the collection had grown to match the dimensions of the new room that rose three stories high, with wide balconies at each new story holding shelf after shelf of books. Unfortunately for Zara, Alison wasn't there. A stammering apprentice directed her back to the east wing.

Alison reclined on a sofa in the great drawing room with her arm over her eyes, her two children chasing each other around it, shouting words Zara couldn't make out. They broke off their game when they saw Zara and threw themselves at her, Sylvester jumping up and down for her attention, Jeffrey flinging his arms around her knees. "Auntie Zara, we're playing horses!" Sylvester shouted. Jeffrey made a sound very much like a horse whinnying. "I always win 'cause I'm the biggest!"

"Want to win!" Jeffrey demanded. "Auntie make me win!"

"Children, leave Aunt Zara alone," Alison said without moving. "Come here now." Both boys detached themselves from Zara and ran back to their mother, and Zara felt a pang deep inside at their smooth faces, their agile limbs. *I will never have this. I never wanted children and now I would give anything to have my own baby screaming defiance at me.*

"I thought it would be nice to spend the afternoon with them," Alison said, not moving her arm, "but I didn't count on this awful headache. Children, why don't you play horses in the dining room. Sylvester, if I hear your brother complaining about how you never let him win, you and I will have a race, and the loser will go to bed early for a week."

"Not fair! You're bigger!"

"That's the point. Off you go, now, before Ellen comes for you."

The boys racketed off down the hall, neighing and whinnying. Alison let her arm flop to one side and stared at the ceiling. "I love my boys, but sometimes I think I was not cut out to be a mother."

"You are a *wonderful* mother," Zara said, more intensely than she'd meant. Alison sat up and stared at her, concerned.

"It's mid-afternoon. I've never known you to leave your offices before six o'clock. What's wrong?"

Zara turned and walked toward the empty fireplace, turned again and came back to stand behind a chair near Alison's sofa. She closed her hands on its back until her knuckles went white and the tendons stood out on the backs of her hands. Head bowed, she said, "There is so much wrong that it would be faster to tell you what is right. If there is such a thing."

"Zara, you're frightening me. Did something happen to Anthony?"

She shook her head. "He is well. I am well. I've never been more perfectly healthy in my life."

"I see Dr. Trevellian finally healed your leg. Did he say why it took so long? Granted that two days is better than however long it takes a broken leg to heal on its own, but I've never known his healing to be so slow."

Zara raised her head and regarded her sister-in-law. "What I am about to tell you cannot go further than the two of us, do you understand?" she said fiercely.

"What do you mean? Zara, you don't expect me to keep whatever this is secret from Anthony, do you? I can't do that!"

"I don't mean Anthony. This touches him as much as anyone. But *no one else*, understand?"

"Zara—" Alison whispered.

"Swear it, Alison!"

"I swear. I—sweet ungoverned heaven, you're crying. You never cry."

Zara reached up and felt the damp trail streaking her cheek. She shook her head as if denying it would make the tears vanish. "Dr. Trevellian didn't heal me. I healed myself."

Alison's mouth made an O of astonishment. "But...you can't possibly...Zara, you can't have inherent magic."

"Apparently I can."

Alison looked quickly around the room as if afraid someone had come in without them noticing. "But...healing...surely no one could object to that? Even if you are the Queen."

She felt her head shaking from side to side in negation, had to clasp her hands hard together to keep them from shaking too. "Not like Dr. Trevellian. Alison, I have never been sick a day in my life. I never bruise, I never have headaches. My body heals itself with no direction from me."

"Zara, to me that sounds like a good magical ability for a ruler to have."

Her eyes ached with tears she was afraid to shed, afraid if once she started crying she wouldn't stop. "Do you know what the doctor told me this morning? He said that aging is like hundreds of tiny injuries that happen every day, deep in the blood and bone where we can't see them. We're born dying, Alison, everyone except me, because my body heals itself over and over again, all those tiny wounds we don't even—" She covered her face with her hands and choked on a sob. Crying hurt. That was why she never did it. The unknown ancestor who'd bequeathed this dubious gift to her had taken her dignity along with the rest of her life.

She felt Alison tentatively put her arms around her. How closed off was she, that the people she cared most about were afraid even to touch her? She clung to Alison and shuddered with dry, tearless sobs.

"I understand," Alison murmured in her ear. "You'd live forever. Be Queen forever. It would be a nightmare."

And that was why she could tell Alison; she was quick to see the ramifications of any problem. The eternal reign of an undying Queen— what a disaster for Tremontane. She gently removed Alison's arms from around her shoulders and wiped her eyes. "The doctor doesn't think I'll live forever. My ability isn't perfect. It took two days for my healing to do what Dr. Trevellian's could have put right in a few hours. At any rate, I will still age, but far too slowly." She didn't tell Alison the other thing the doctor had told her, the cruel reality that her body would see any child she might conceive as an infection, and destroy it. That humiliation was too great for her to share with anyone. "But it would mean the end of the North family sooner than that, as soon as it became clear that I wasn't aging. Once the citizens of Tremontane knew their royal family was tainted by inherent magic…it might not mean our deaths, but it would certainly mean a demand for me to step down as Queen, let the Crown pass to another family. I think you can see the problem there."

"Civil war," Alison said. "None of the provincial rulers has a good claim to rule. Belladry Chadwick and Fern Harcourt would certainly be at each other's throats. You're right, no one can know about this." There were tears in her eyes as well. "So what are you going to do?"

"What I have to," Zara said. "I will have to die."

"It's going to be complicated," Alison said, "and require perfect timing, and we have to control every detail. That's why we came to you."

Davis Doyle sat behind his desk, regarding them both with wide, unblinking eyes. He lifted the bottle of whiskey as if to pour a measure into his cup, looked at it as if he didn't know what it was or why it was in his hand, and set it down again. "I," he began, then shook his head. "You want—Alison, this is insane. It can't possibly work."

"It will work, Mister Doyle," Zara said. "Alison and Anthony will make it happen. The doctor will make it look real. You need only provide the setting, something I expect you are good at given your occupation."

"We've given this a lot of thought," Anthony said, "and this really is the only way, Doyle."

Doyle looked around at his office in the Waxwold Theater. "The building is no problem," he said, "so long as the excuse for the new construction holds. There are just so many things that could go wrong…are you sure about this, your Majesty?"

"The alternative is that my death is real," Zara said. "I cannot quite bring myself to do that. An assassination, on the other hand, will be very convincing."

Doyle sighed. "We'll construct the trap door in box 3," he said, "try to keep it quiet, but if anyone starts nosing around we can give out that the royal family wants a private way in and out. You sure you don't want the assassin captured? He'd be guilty of attempted murder even if you did hire him to do the job."

Alison and Anthony exchanged glances. "We're sure," Alison said. "Just have it come out near the back door, just past the facilities."

"I'll do what I can. The Waxwold has a lot of extra space under the boxes because of the way we had to put in the stairs, but it will be crowded—sweet heaven, I can't believe I just said that. As if crowding were the issue."

"Thank you, Mister Doyle," Zara said, extending her hand. After a moment's hesitation, he took it. "I wish there were some way to repay you for this. I know I'm asking a lot of you."

"I don't think I want repaying for engineering my sovereign monarch's murder," Doyle said. "Allie, Tony, I'll let you know when the construction's complete, and you can show your assassin how it works." He sighed. "I don't want to know where you're going to find anyone who's willing to go along with this."

"No, you don't," Alison said.

"You can't possibly be as calm as you seem," Anthony said to Alison, who was standing at the front of box 3, waving at people she knew.

"I'm not," she replied. "I'm trying not to think about what comes next. And being happy that I'm not wearing a corset. Those things are horrible."

"I ought to be the one, Alison—"

"We already determined you're not fast enough, and everyone will be looking for you when it happens. It has to be me, Anthony." Her voice sounded strong, but Zara could see her sister's lips tremble, and the sick, anguished feeling she'd been carrying around all evening grew stronger. How coldblooded was she, that she could ask such a thing of Alison?

"But you shouldn't *have* to." Anthony took her hand and drew her close to his side.

"None of us should *have* to do any of this," Zara said. She sat behind them, afraid if she stood the tremor in her arms and legs would be visible. She had thought three weeks would be enough time for her to become accustomed to her fate, but instead it had been like slow death. There were so many last times: her last Council meeting, her last visit with her mother—that had nearly broken her, and she had gone to the privacy of her bedroom and howled into her pillow until she was hoarse. The obliviousness of everyone around her maddened and relieved her by turns. She found herself more aware of Anthony now, of how confidently he moved and spoke, of the tenderness in his look and his voice when he addressed his wife and the joy in his eyes when he tossed Sylvester or Jeffrey into the air, both of them laughing. Was he ready for this new responsibility? Had she trained him well enough? *Yes,* she thought at supper—the last one—*he's ready,* and it eased her burden somewhat.

Now she looked at him standing with Alison near the front of the box. His hand curled around hers casually; five years of marriage and they still acted like newlyweds. Well, they'd earned that. It eased her burden more to know she wasn't leaving behind a Consort to mourn her. What a heartbreak that would be. She thought, briefly, *Suppose that waits in my future,* and quashed the thought. Time enough for planning for the future when this was all over. Dr. Trevellian had warned her that it was possible this could actually kill her; it was a chance she was willing to take for the sake of her country, but she hoped she would survive it. And then she could think about what came next.

The curtain rose and the lights went down, Alison and Anthony took their seats, and Zara made herself concentrate on the play. It was a tragedy, which was fortunate; she would have had trouble pretending to laugh in all the right places for a comedy. As it was, she barely heard the words because she was running through the plan in her head. Alison had been correct—it would require perfect timing, and they hadn't been able to practice all the steps as they'd wanted. She clasped her hands in her lap to still their shaking and prayed to ungoverned heaven that all would be well.

Too soon, the lights came up on the intermission. Anthony stood. "It's not too late to change the plan," he said. "We can find a way to fake your death."

"We've discussed this thoroughly," Zara said. "I must remain convincingly dead long enough for independent witnesses to affirm my demise. Drowning is far too complicated. An accident isn't complicated enough and could involve innocents. We tried to imitate a fatal illness, but no poison was capable of doing more than inconveniencing me. This is the only way."

"You know an assassination could destabilize the country. What if we succeed at this only to throw the country into the very turmoil we're trying to avoid?"

Zara took a deep breath. "I have faith in you both," she said. "We've planned how to organize the search. The 'assassin' will be found dead at his own hand rather than face trial—you have all the evidence to prove his guilt. No one else need die over this."

Anthony gripped the back of his chair hard. "Zara, if this kills you...."

"Then I will go to heaven, or hell, knowing that I have caused the two people I love most immeasurable pain," Zara said. "But if we do nothing, this family will suffer as much as the kingdom. That is the sacrifice we're all making tonight. Please."

Alison and Anthony exchanged glances. "There's really no other way," Alison said.

Anthony closed his eyes briefly. Then he took his sister's hands and raised her to her feet so he could embrace her. "I hope it works," he said. "Goodbye, sister." He let her go, then offered Alison his arm. "Shall we?" he said. Then, more loudly, he said, "I think I'm in need of the facilities," and opened the door.

"Take one of the guards," Zara said.

"Zara, I don't think that's necessary," Anthony said.

"We've had too many threats I have been unable to eliminate," Zara said. "Humor me."

"All right, sister dear." Zara heard him say, "Lieutenant, the Queen asks that you—"to one of the pair of guards standing sentinel outside the door before it closed on his words. She began to count. They'd timed this part, Alison pacing from the box to the facilities while Zara waited and counted as well. Now, when Zara reached a count of fifty, she stood and opened the door. "Please fetch my fan from the carriage. It's rather warm in here," she said.

"Your Majesty, I can't leave you unattended," the woman said.

Zara's throat tightened. Who knew what might happen to this guard for leaving her post tonight if Anthony couldn't engineer a pardon for her? "It will only take a few minutes, and I will be perfectly safe," she said. "Go now."

The guard hesitated, but in the face of the blue-eyed North stare she had to back down. Zara shut the door, then knelt by the trap door and opened it. Seconds later Alison emerged, climbing easily through. "I couldn't have done that in a corset," she said quietly. She was wrapped in a dark cloak she'd left wadded up in a corner of the props room. It completely covered her blue silk gown.

"I'm ready," Zara said. She took her seat and crossed her hands in her lap. How strange that they were still now that she was facing death.

She heard Alison take a deep breath, then felt the muzzle of a black powder pistol pressed against the back of her head. "I love you, Zara," Alison said. "Goodbye."

Then there was noise, and pain, and then nothing.

She woke, confused at her surroundings; her bed was too hard, it was darker than it should be for 6:30 in the morning, and instead of the refreshing smell of hot coffee, there was only the dry, musty smell of a room long disused. She sat up and discovered that she was in some kind of shed, lying on a thin mattress in a wagon that creaked as she moved. Piles of hay lay haphazardly against the rear walls, and cracks between the gray, unfinished boards let in faint slivers of light. Why was she—?

Memory returned like a whirlwind, threatening to carry her away. She put her hands to her head to stop the world spinning and discovered that her black hair had been cut short, its ends now brushing her cheeks. She felt around the back of her head and found nothing amiss except a round, ridged circle of scar tissue, almost imperceptible through her hair. She breathed out slowly. Dr. Trevellian had been correct; even being shot through the head was not enough to kill her. She felt along her face and her forehead, pinched the bridge of her nose, and finally found more scarring along the outside of her right eye socket where the ball had exited. *That must have been very convincing*, she thought, then imagined Anthony's face when he saw the wreck her face would have been, and had to squeeze her eyes shut to keep from crying. There was no way he could have been prepared for that, no matter how well he knew what would happen. How could she have done that to him? To them? *It's not over yet. Time for tears later. Or never.*

She climbed down from the wagon and looked it over. It was old, but still in good shape, and would be sufficient for her journey. There were sacks and barrels and crates, not many, stowed near the seat of the wagon, which was unpadded and probably would not be comfortable over the days to come, but it was more important that she not draw attention to herself by looking unusually prosperous.

She went around the front of the wagon to unlatch the shed doors and push them open. The yard was mostly shadow in the pre-dawn light, and nothing moved except the horses drowsing in their stalls opposite the shed. Zara walked over to them and went down the line until she found the one she'd chosen the week before, a chestnut gelding with a white blaze on its nose that looked a little like her own profile stretched out, which had amused her. She stroked the blaze and the horse whickered at her companionably. "You and I'll get along right fine," she said, trying out the accent she'd been practicing in private since she and Alison and Anthony had made their plan. It still sounded wrong in her ears, like a bad actress in a play, reciting lines she'd learned by rote, but it was the best she could do. It would have to be enough.

She went back to the wagon and dug around until she found something to eat. The bread was a day old—well, Dr. Trevellian had had no idea how long it would take her to heal. She would have to find out what day it was. At least he'd managed to smuggle her out of the palace, hopefully without involving anyone else. Had Anthony been able to draw attention away from Alison so she could escape? Whom would they blame for the assassination? What had happened to the guard? She tore off more bread and wished she had coffee. Past time she weaned herself of the habit.

When the sun rose, she found someone to help her hitch the horse to the wagon, then drove out of the yard and down the road away from the city. Ravensholm. Dr. Trevellian had been able to transport her farther than she'd thought. She prayed that his part in the ruse had not been discovered either. She snapped the reins over the horse's head and he picked up the pace. Driving a wagon wasn't much different from driving her own carriage through the Park, fortunately. There were so many things she would have to learn, so many things she would get wrong, but at least she was certain that no one would recognize her outside Aurilien. That was the thing no one ever realized;

the Queen was well-known, but few people saw her closely enough, and regularly enough, to be able to identify her in a crowd. Most Tremontanans saw her face only on coins, and that portrait was so idealized Zara hardly recognized herself in it. The farther east she went, the less likely it was that anyone would know the short-haired, travel-worn woman was Zara North.

She reached Savantry by nightfall, which meant she hadn't made very good time. At this rate it would be another two or three days before she arrived in Kingsport. She found an inn where she could stable her horse and wagon and went into the taproom and sat at the bar, too weary to think.

"What'll it be?" a voice said. She looked up at the barman, who was tall and wide and had a cheerful face with an enormous mustache.

"Beer," she said. She'd never had beer before, but it seemed the sort of thing a countrywoman might drink. A large ceramic mug appeared in front of her, foaming over, and she picked it up and took a healthy swig, afraid to look foolish by sipping at it. It went down smoothly and had a strange taste, but her stomach approved.

"You from the capital?" the barman said. She shook her head. "Too bad. Was hopin' for more news about the Queen. Seems everyone's got a story to tell and they ain't all true."

"What...are they saying?" Zara said.

The barman shrugged. "Says they caught the bastard what did it," he said, "some kid at the theater with a grudge against royalty. That's true for sure. He'll hang in a few days."

Zara buried her face in her mug again. That was wrong. They should have found the "assassin's" body after a short chase; no one should have been blamed for her death. Had Anthony been unable to take command of that search? "Makes sense," she said, "her being killed in the theater, that it was someone who knew the place well."

"The royal family's in mourning, o' course. Heard they shot a bunch of guards what let the killer get past. Damn if they don't deserve it, too."

That was definitely wrong. It had all gone wrong. She had to get out of there. "Sounds right," she said, and laid down a coin on the counter. "I don't suppose—I mean, maybe you've got a room I can rent?"

He showed her to the room, which was little more than a bed and a cupboard, and she sat on the bed and shook. That rumor had to be false. Anthony would definitely have spared the guards. If he could. *It has to look real*, she thought, *and what are a few lives against the welfare of the kingdom?* She stared blindly at the unpainted wooden wall. That she'd sacrificed her own life for that cause was not comforting.

In the morning she went out and bought a newspaper. Seven days since her death. *Could* she die, ever? Dr. Trevellian's assurances aside, it was a question she couldn't bear to entertain. She settled for reading the headlines. The supposed assassin's name was Fenton; she'd never met him, but there was no doubt Alison and Anthony, owners of the Waxwold Theater, knew him well. She had no idea why he'd been accused of the crime and the newspaper was not forthcoming with the details. The guards who had been on duty that night hadn't been shot; they were in prison, and their sentence had not yet been handed down. *Anthony will save them. I know he'll find a way.* New measures were being taken to protect the royal family, who had not emerged from the palace since the assassination. Zara folded the paper and threw it away, then went to hitch up her wagon. There was no more she could do, except let Zara North go.

She let her mind wander as the horse plodded eastward. She would need an occupation. That would be difficult; the only thing she was good at was running a kingdom, and it was unlikely anyone would ask her to do that. She thought briefly of joining an Eskandelic harem, running a principality behind the scenes, but the idea of having to share power with four or five other women wearied her, and besides, she didn't want to marry for duty. She never had, which was why she had no Consort to leave behind. She could learn a trade. She was good at needlework, thanks to her mother's training, but she'd never really liked it...though she no longer had the freedom to do only what she liked, did she? *Tailoring. Embroidery. Tatting lace.* If she had the ability to sense source, she could be a Deviser, but that was unfortunately out of the question. *Weaving?* That had potential. It looked so soothing, working the loom and watching the fabric grow by inches along the threads. She was old to be an apprentice, was too old even by her apparent age, but if she could manage a recalcitrant Council into voting her way she could certainly manage someone into taking her on.

Suddenly the wagon lurched and sagged, jolting her nearly off the seat and into the road. She scrambled to rein the horse in and hopped down to examine the problem. A wheel had slipped off the rear axle and now lay in the dirt a few feet away, thankfully undamaged; the axle too was intact, though the way the wagon's weight pressed down on it couldn't be doing it any good. She went to lift the wheel, got it upright with only a little effort, but the wagon was canted so sharply that she would need another four hands to raise it to where she could slide the wheel back on. She dropped the wheel and stepped away, wiping her hands on her trousers. Damn. She'd wanted a convincingly aged wagon, but not one that was actually falling apart. Now what was she going to do?

She looked along the road in both directions, not expecting to find help—the road had been mostly empty all day—so she was surprised to see someone on horseback approaching from the west. She stepped to one side and waited for the rider to draw closer. It was a man, she eventually saw, wearing a hat pulled far down over his eyes and a coat grimed with road dust. He came to a stop several feet from her and said, "You know, that wagon won't go 'less it's got all four wheels on."

Zara's eyes narrowed, and she was about to unleash a torrent of sharp-edged sarcasm at him when she realized he was grinning in a friendly way. She laughed a little self-consciously and said, "That's what I hear."

He dismounted and walked toward her. "Happen I can give you a hand," he said. He was a big man, broad in the chest and shoulders, and looked as if he might be able to lift the wagon with one hand and the wheel with the other. He took off his coat and folded it, laid it by the side of the road, and added, "Might want to shift that load though. Makes it easier to move the wagon."

Zara nodded and began handing out bundles and boxes that he set on the ground in a neat pile next to his coat. When the wagon was empty, he said, "You lift the wheel, and we'll see if we can't get it back on."

She felt flattered that he assumed she could manage the wheel by herself. She got it upright again and rolled it toward the wagon. The man crouched, got his hands under the frame, and with a grunt heaved it up until Zara could manhandle the wheel back onto the axle. He let the weight of the wagon settle back onto the wheel with another grunt. "Will it stay on?" she said.

"Hmm." The man looked around. "You need that crate?"

"I...no." She had no idea what was in it, other than something intended to help her set herself up in her new home, wherever that would be. She opened it and found dishes packed in straw. "I think I can wrap these in the quilt, if you need the box."

The man took hold of the empty crate and broke it apart as if it were made of matchsticks. "This should work," he said, showing her a length of wood that had been one edge of the crate. He wedged it into the hole where the pin holding the wheel in place had been. "Should hold long enough for you to get to Maraston, about two miles down the road," he said. "Someone ought be able to fix it right, there. But I'll travel with you that far, make sure you don't break down again."

"Thank you, Mister..."

He grinned again and held out his hand for her to shake. "Hank

Hobson."

Zara realized she had never given any thought to a new name. She groped about and fell on the first thing that came to mind. "Agatha," she said. "Agatha...Weaver."

"Good to know you, Mistress Weaver," Hobson said.

"Miss," Zara said.

He smiled again, and this time there was an unfamiliar light in his eye. "Then it's *very* good to meet you, Miss Weaver," he said, removing his hat and bowing to her, just a little. His face was rugged, not exactly handsome, but there was something about him that made Zara blush for the first time in her entire life. "Where are you headed? After Maraston, I mean."

"What makes you think I'm not staying there?" Zara asked.

"Maraston's not a big place," Hobson said. "You look like someone who's got her sights on bigger things."

Zara blushed again, this time with frustration. Was it still so obvious, what she'd been? "I'm looking for a change, not rightly sure what," she said. "Where are *you* headed?"

"Sterris. It's a handful of miles south of Kingsport. Also not a big place, but I like it." He put his hat back on and tugged on the brim to settle it. "Not a bad place for a fresh start. If someone were looking for something like that."

"I reckon that's true," Zara said. "Of course, it would help to know someone there." She turned away, just a little, feeling awkward about meeting his eyes.

"You know me," Hobson pointed out.

"I've only just met you, Mister Hobson." She flicked a sidelong glance at him. "Of course, you always get to know people better when you share a road with them."

"That's true," Hobson said, keeping a straight face. "And as long as two people are going the same way, well, they ought at least talk to each other."

"It's the friendly thing to do," Zara said. *Sweet heaven, I'm flirting with a total stranger.* She felt like a stranger to herself, free of responsibilities to anyone, without the need to watch her words and her demeanor constantly. It was exhilarating.

"Miss Weaver," Hobson said, "that was my thought exactly."

Zara began gathering her things and stowing them in the wagon. "Then I think we should be moving on, Mister Hobson," she said. "We've got a long road ahead of us." *And I have a new life to begin.*

About the Author

Melissa McShane is the author of EMISSARY and THE SMOKE-SCENTED GIRL as well as the novels of Tremontane. She lives in Utah with her husband, four children, and three very needy cats. She wrote reviews and critical essays for many years before turning to fiction, which is much more fun than anyone ought to be allowed to have. She is currently working on the sequel to this book, RIDER OF THE CROWN.

You can visit her at her website **www.melissamcshanewrites.com** for more information on other books and upcoming releases.

To receive special offers, advance notice of new releases, and other fun stuff, sign up for my newsletter here.

CPSIA information can be obtained at www.ICGtesting.com
Printed in the USA
LVOW10s2156120716

496080LV00014B/160/P